Custer's Luck

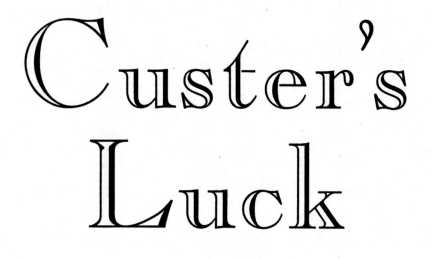

Custer's Luck

* * *

ROBERT SKIMIN

with William E. Moody

HERODIAS
New York London

© 2000 Robert Skimin and William E. Moody

Published by HERODIAS, INC. 346 First Avenue, New York, NY 10009
HERODIAS, LTD. 24 Lacy Road, London, SW15 1NL
www.herodias.com

Manufactured in the United States of America

Design by Charles B. Hames
Map by Vicki Trego Hill

LIBRARY OF CONGRESS CATALOGING-IN-PUBLICATION DATA

[TK]

BRITISH LIBRARY CATALOGUING IN PUBLICATION DATA

[TK]

ISBN 1–928746–14–4

1 3 5 7 9 8 6 4 2

First edition 2000

Acknowledgements

This is an alternative history, a very possible "might have been." Some events and dates have been changed to fit the story. Such is fiction. It was a delight to work with Judge Bill Moody, who not only did much of the research, particularly the political part, but also contributed many story ideas. In addition to my deep appreciation to him, I wish to thank the many librarians who helped, and to those who had the foresight to archive the newspapers of the era. The entire process was a most intriguing and stimulating experience.

—ROBERT SKIMIN
El Paso, Texas, 2000

The river lay placid in the searing afternoon sun, unsuspecting, never dreaming that it would swirl a vivid crimson within the hour. For days its meandering current had quenched the thirst of thousands of people and ponies, and had also provided the cooking and washing water for the women as they tended to the needs of their families.

It was the largest campsite in the history of the American Indian.. It was both accidental and fateful that so many had come together to partake of the great leader's prophecy during these days in the month of the Juneberries. But at this lazy hour, with so many drowsing in their tipis along the quiet sharply meandering stream, no one had thought of a battle . . . until the first shouts of warning at the edge of the Hunkpapa village. That was where the assault burst, and the mad scramble to move the huge encampment began. No one knew just who—other than some Long Knives—was attacking them, nor did they have an idea of who or what was looking for them from the backside of the hills above. . . .

There, George Armstrong Custer suddenly drew in his mount from a brisk trot and threw his right arm up to signal a halt. His adjutant, Lieutenant Cooke, quickly caught up with him, as did Captain Tom Custer. "Hold the command here!" Custer barked.

As Cooke touched his hat brim in acknowledgment, Custer urged his horse into a fast trot toward the embankment off to the west. Tom shouted, "What's up, Autie?"

Custer hollered back, "I just got one of those hunches of mine! *C'mon!*"

Together, with dust from the dry Montana grassland throwing up a soft brown cloud behind them, the two brothers galloped side by side to the high peak on the escarpment above the river. Two minutes later they reined in, barely stopping in time to avoid the steep drop. As Custer pulled out his binoculars, Tom stared down at the lush heavily treed valley. The water, flowing innocently within its narrow confines, sauntered fully unaware that it would soon become one of the most famous rivers in the world. The cloudless sky smoked mercilessly with heat and the sun beat down with the glare of molten brightness. The only sounds were the breathing of the heaving horses and the squawk of a solitary hawk overhead.

"By God, there are a lot of them in there!" Custer said softly, his blue eyes narrowing.

"You see 'em?"

"I can *taste* them."

"How many?"

Custer swung his glasses to the benchland across the river and downstream about a mile. "I don't know, but I see enough ponies grazing over there to mount an army!" He handed the glasses to Tom.

The younger Custer peered at what looked like a huge pony herd and then swept his gaze down river another mile. "There's a hell of a lot of smoke coming out of those trees, considering how hot it is, Autie!"

"Must be quite a few cooking fires."

"Yup. What do you think?"

"I think there are a lot more hostiles down there than we figured."

Tom nodded his head.

"And I think Reno's going to be in an awful of a lot of trouble. *C'mon, we're going back!*"

With Tom racing along behind him, Custer galloped all out back to where the guidon lazily marked the location of the regimental headquarters detachment. Cooke hurried out to meet him, his long black whiskers flying. As they converged, Custer shouted, "We're going to join Reno in the valley, *pronto!* Give the orders!"

Quickly, with trumpet orders jarring the humid June air, the five companies of the Seventh Cavalry swung around to follow their flamboyant commander towards the shortest route to the river.

While Custer rode at a canter, he thought about Benteen and wished he hadn't sent the hard-fighting captain off to the south on that reconnaissance with those three companies. He'd surely be able to use them shortly.

★ ★ ★

Captain Frederick Benteen stuck his straw hat back on his squarish white head and stared off to the northwest over the rough dry draws. The late afternoon sunlight seemed hotter than usual. He wiped the sweat off the back of his neck with his soiled yellow bandanna as his trumpeter's horse whinnied softly. Leather creaked behind him as troopers climbed down from their mounts to stretch and ease the stiffness from the last hour in the saddle. Benteen shook his head. "There aren't going to be any goddamn Indians in there!" he said to Captain Tom Weir, the commander of D Company, who was sitting on his horse beside him.

"Doesn't look like it," Weir replied, sipping some whiskey from his flask. He handed it to the battalion commander, who took a swig.

"This was a wild goose chase to begin with."

"Appears so."

"To hell with Custer's orders," Benteen said suddenly. "We're going back to the Little Bighorn. That's where the goddamn fight's gonna be!" He swung his horse around. "I just hope Reno hasn't gotten his ass kicked already!"

"You think the scouts know what they're doing?"

"I don't think *Custer* knows what he's doing!"

Weir shrugged. "You never do."

"He's an asshole."

★ ★ ★

To say that Major Marcus Reno and his three companies of troopers had their hands full was a gross understatement. Custer had devised the plan well back up the valley less than an hour earlier. In it, Reno would crash into the upper end of the village and start the rout of the Sioux. Then the commander would come galloping in behind with the main body of the regiment to support him. But for some reason, Custer and those five companies had last been seen heading off somewhere on the upper ridge to the north.

But the Sioux hadn't run.

There are a hell of a lot of them! Reno thought as his thin line of skirmishers fell back a few more yards. His flying formation had never even

[*3*]

reached the village. Not only that, so many warriors had burst out of the edge of the tipis that he'd had to order his troopers to dismount and fight as skirmishers just to survive.

Rifles and revolvers cracked, their flashes lashing out like short-lived yellow snakes in the eerie brown smoke and dust cloud that was enveloping the position. A wounded horse screamed, another whinnied fearfully. Sioux battle cries split the smothering air; a wounded trooper, hit in the chest, let out a strangled screech for help. A sergeant cursed and tears of fright ran down a young cavalryman's cheeks.

Thank God for that timber on the right! Reno thought. His rightmost troopers were already in it and he'd get the rest in there as soon as possible. *Where in the hell is Custer?* The damned hostiles were all over the place, brazenly riding right into their position. Why had Custer left? Reno fired his revolver, knocking one painted warrior from his saddle a few yards away. The din was incredible! He'd have to do something drastic soon—

Faintly, he heard the rousing sound of a bugle off behind him. It was calling out the thrilling tune of the "Charge."

He turned and caught the bright reflection of sun on metal above galloping horses roaring down the valley toward their position. In the forefront, the red-and-blue guidon—Custer's personal flag—stood out, flapping like a guardian angel above the lead riders.

Reno could sense an instant shift in the mood of the hostiles. They seemed to stop, reign in their ponies, and turn toward the onrushing trumpet call. A sudden moment of silence fell over the fire fight. The warriors lowered their rifles and after just a moment began to trot back toward the village. A trooper jammed his carbine in the air and let out a cavalry yell.

★ ★ ★

Riding at the head of the charge, George Armstrong Custer knew he had just made an eventful decision. He'd modified his plan as Reno had begun his three-mile march to the village, deciding to ride around and block the other end of the village so the hostiles couldn't escape—sound theory in Indian fighting. That's what they always did, they ran out the other end and escaped to fight another day. But today something had stopped him, had told him to look over that escarpment And it had been fateful . . . This was surely the largest hostile village ever assembled anywhere, anytime.

The realization had been sudden—he was about to face a *very* large number of fighting Sioux and their allies. *And they weren't going to run!* How and why, he didn't know. But Custer's luck had caught him just in time—there was no time for a divided force!

Now if he could just find Benteen and get him back, the mighty Seventh Cavalry would be intact and ready to do battle. He felt the old thrill. Everything he'd hoped for was about to happen—he could *taste* the victory he needed to put everything in his life back together. Grant be damned! Not even the president of the United States could deny glory to the leader of a great victory such as the one ahead of him.

At that moment, his brother Tom rode in close and pointed off to the left. There, rapidly descending a ravine a half mile away, guidon flying, was another cavalry command—Benteen.

A brief grin creased his face as he nodded to Tom. Then he held up his arm to stop the column and wheeled his horse towards Reno's flag.

★ ★ ★

Red Elk had led his warriors in the first thrust to meet the threat from Major Reno's attacking force at the edge of the Hunkpapa village. As the youngest and most ambitious Hunkpapa war leader, the tall seventeen-year-old had welcomed the attack. He had brought fame on himself in the glorious victory over Three Stars eight days earlier, and now he knew the People were invincible. Besides, there was Sitting Bull's great vision of the blue-clad Long Knives falling out of the sky. Now they had come, in answer to his prayers. He hoped it was Long Hair.

His warriors had done well repulsing the initial attack, chasing the Long Knives back to the woods. He personally killed two of them and maybe a third, and made two first coups. Now, according to Sitting Bull's defense plan, he had to pull back to the edge of the slope leading to the pony herd. He didn't like it. Now that many more Long Knives had joined the first party, he knew they'd come charging headlong into the huge camp and he wanted to meet them directly, crash into them, battle axes swinging. *The medicine was there! The People were invincible!*

[5]

But Sitting Bull was right, the women and children and the old ones had to be saved. Surely his beautiful Late Star, pregnant with their child, must be kept safe as possible. But he wanted more Long Knife blood.

The river was called the Little Bighorn by the whites to distinguish it from the other stream known as the Bighorn. Both were named for the nearby Bighorn Mountains from which their waters emanated. Now, in late June, these waters were still cold, filling the river beds with runoff from the hills. The valley of the meandering Little Bighorn was plush and green, bordered by grassy hills and populated by stalwart thickets of shady cottonwood trees as the stream flowed generally from the southeast to the northwest. On its east side, several abrupt bluffs, broken by rough arroyos, rose sharply as high as three hundred feet. On the opposite side, the ridges were irregular and generally not as steep.

The Indians called the stream the Greasy Grass.

In it on this June 25, nearly one thousand lodges of Sioux, Cheyennes, and the other tribes who had cast their lot with the famous Sitting Bull, filled the valley. The summer roamers had ridden in constantly after the great Hunkpapa had moved his already large village to the Greasy Grass the day after the battle with Three Stars. Word of Sitting Bull's visions, and the story of the remarkable fight with the Long Knives on the Rosebud a week earlier had spread like wildfire, and it seemed that every lodge of reservation Sioux that could move had headed for the huge encampment. Great medicine was to be found there!

Crazy Horse of the Oglala had spoken with Sitting Bull earlier on this warm early summer day and they had agreed that close to seven thousand of their people were assembled in the valley. It was without a doubt the largest gathering of Indians since the Grand Teton council in 1857.

The newcomers had joined quite a celebration. From the moment the tipi poles were in place after the arrival of Sitting Bull's people on the Greasy Grass, the festivities had been on. Everyone had danced and stuffed himself on good food night and day, and many of the reveling warriors from the Rosebud battle had been at it for *six* days. Only the hunters and the cooks who prepared the game had to interrupt their fun to keep the celebration going. Now the village was recovering like a mammoth bear that had gorged himself, danced for a week, and was trying to shake off the effects of a hangover.

The huge encampment was anchored by the Hunkpapa circle, on the upper, or southeast, end. As it was a custom to retain tribal integrity, other circles stretched up the valley—the Miniconjous, the Oglalas, Sans Arcs, Blackfeet Lakota, Brules, and Two Kettles. One hundred twenty Cheyenne lodges constituted the rest of the main body. A small number of Santee Sioux, Yanktonais, and a few Arapahoe lodges completed the enormous body of tipis.

The village stretched along the rapidly flowing Greasy Grass for over two miles from the first Hunkpapa lodge pole. The pony herd on a mesa above the western side of the valley was also mammoth—more than twenty thousand head. In fact, the grazing needs of this huge number of horses, combined with human need for food and firewood, dictated that Sitting Bull must move on very soon. Only the report of nearby game had kept him there this long. And still that morning, the newcomers continued to arrive.

The Little Bighorn River varied in size and depth and was mostly fordable—in places it was as wide as eighty feet; at others it narrowed to some forty feet. In the area where the village was located, the stream ran generally southeast, with several sharp hooks and bends.

Word of the intruders had flashed through the huge camp when they were first sighted. In the Oglala village, between the Cheyenne and the Sans Arcs, Crazy Horse had hurried through his pre-battle ritual, applying the lightning blaze to his left cheek and dabbing the white hail spots on his torso. His first coup feather was in its customary place, standing straight up behind his head. He stuck the small stones behind his ears and fastened them, then removed his sack of fighting dust from his war bag. Sprinkling it over his head, he had quickly tethered his war pony and sprinkled more dust over its neck. But by the time the great war leader had assembled his fighting party, many scrambling fearful people separated him from the Long Knives.

Sitting Bull stood outside his tipi and briefly reflected on the situation. On another day, at an earlier time, he too would have dabbed paint on his face and rushed off to lead his warriors into battle. After all, he was the greatest living war chief of the Lakotas—probably the greatest in their history. But now it was different; the people looked to him for his spiritual leadership. He was their father. The women and children were his responsibility more than any glory in battle. It was the prophecy, he knew it. The vision. The soldiers falling from the sky. And he knew who had come. It was foretold.

His nephew One Bull trotted up with three horses, including the big black stallion that was his uncle's favorite. Hastily they helped their women onto the other two horses. Down through the miles of the huge camp and throughout the circles of the other tribes, the escape plan for the women , children, and elderly went into effect. The shouts of people rushing about and of dogs barking their concern filled the air as the warriors rushed to defend them.

★ ★ ★

"Gentlemen—" Custer paused for effect as he knelt in the grass and glanced at the eyes of his gathered company commanders. "Obviously all chance for surprise is gone, so we must act swiftly. Near as I can guess, there are several thousand Indians in this village, possibly including a couple of thousand warriors. Something tells me we don't have to worry about them running. So here's what we're going to do . . . we're gonna crash right into them and smash 'em up. We'll swing around this hook in the river, and charge full out. The village appears to be about a half-mile wide. I'll lead the assault with Companies C, I, and L . Companies E and F under Captain Yates will drive in on my left flank three minutes behind."

The one-time "boy general" looked around again, the excitement glowing in his eyes. "Five minutes behind him, Captain Benteen will support in whichever direction the battle may be flowing. My guess is it'll be up against that hill to the left. Major Reno, reorganize your command. Companies A, G, and M, will act as reserve." Once more Custer paused. This time his gaze rested briefly on Benteen's cool look. "Any questions?"

As though their visual encounter had triggered it, Benteen spoke up. "Yeah, Colonel, how do you plan on defeating them if the odds are three to one?"

Custer's eyes narrowed. "The women and children. We capture enough of them, the hostiles'll cave in."

Benteen's responded with a begrudging shrug.

"All right," Custer barked. "We'll attack in five minutes. Form up!"

★ ★ ★

As Custer quickly checked his saddle and his weapons, his mind drifted back to all the troubles he'd had just getting here—mainly his falling-out with President Grant, and having to beg General Terry to intercede to get command of the Seventh Cavalry back for him. He *had* to have it! A major victory over the hostiles was his only way out of the mess he'd gotten himself into—and to perhaps get his stars back.

The edict to the hostiles back in January had set up this whole thing—Sitting Bull and his recalcitrants had been ordered onto reservations by presidential decree. They had blithely and arrogantly ignored the order, which had brought on this campaign. Now, by golly, he'd have his victory. He could *taste* it!

Mounting Vic, his handsome sorrel, he looked around. The three lead companies were forming up and the headquarters staff were already mounted. His brother Tom, acting as aide, was a few yards away. Cooke, his bewhiskered adjutant, was waiting for his signal. Sergeant-major Sharrow finished shoving in a fresh chaw of tobacco. The chief trumpeter had his bugle at the ready. Leather creaked. A nearby horse whinnied. Vic nickered in a kind of equine response. The color sergeant, holding the special red and blue guidon that Libbie had sewn for him so long ago, watched him closely. Custer glanced back at Captain Keogh, twenty yards back. The troopers were ready. Vic shook his head and, for a moment, it was utterly silent.

Custer's eyes narrowed. The old thrill coursed through him. He raised his arm and jammed his heels into his horse's flanks as the notes of the "Charge" filled the air!

Riding at a full gallop, it took just under two minutes for Custer to hit the edge of the Hunkpapa village. His troopers were bunched behind him, covering no more than a sixty yard front. Pandemonium set in at once. Well over a hundred mounted warriors in war paint met them as they reached the first tipis. Nearly all of the hostiles were armed with rifles, a few with pistols. Arrows from other braves, whistled from their kneeling positions on the ground. Rifle fire, black smoke, and rapidly accumulating dust quickly turned the air an eerie dark brown. Lakota war cries added to the bedlam. Here and there a wounded horse cried out as Sioux battle axes came into play in the close contact. Sergeant-major Sharrow was one of the first to die—an arrow through the throat killed him almost instantly. Other cavalrymen were hit, including some of Keogh's front line of troopers. The Irish captain himself suffered a grazing bullet wound as he waded into the Sioux, revolver flashing, but he didn't seem to notice it. Tom Custer, the junior captain, let out his own war cry. He loved battle every bit as much as his older brother and had two Medals of Honor from the Civil War to show for it. In another three minutes, at least forty Sioux were down, dying, or out of the fight. Custer slashed forward, firing his Wembley revolver and waving his Remington sporting rifle . . . strangely unhit in the vanguard. As usual, he never expected to get hit. It was Custer's luck.

The battle raged savagely as many more warriors poured in; but just then Captain George Yates with his two companies, E and F, galloped in on Custer's left. The fresh troopers filled the air with cavalry shouts, firing effectively and scattering numerous Sioux.

On the bluff eight hundred yards to the west, Sitting Bull sat on his black horse watching the battle unfold. His small entourage of relatives waited quietly behind the great man as he turned to the new trumpet call to his right. There, streaming in behind the Long Knives fighting in what was left of his own smoking Hunkpapa village and in the Blackfoot tipis, was yet another large number of troopers. He looked up the valley, wondering where Crazy Horse was. And then he saw him! Coursing down from the ridge line to the northeast of the Oglala and Cheyenne Circles to a ravine the White Eyes would later call Medicine Tail Coulee, the great war leader was executing his favorite tactic—the flanking assault. Sitting Bull nodded in agreement. Crazy Horse would knife through the edge of the Miniconjou circle with his hard fighting Oglalas and Cheyennes. But would he be in time?

Below him, Red Elk watched in horror as his beautiful young wife, Late Star, went down with a scream. He kicked his pony in the flanks, but it was impossible to ride through the horde of fleeing women, children and old people. He jumped down and pushed his way to where his wife lay under hurrying moccasins, crying out, blood gushing from a terrible stomach wound. Reaching her, he tried to pick her up, but she cried out in pain, her eyes wild, showing no recognition. He pulled her face to his bare chest, trying to comfort her, but suddenly she was still. *No!* He swooped her pregnant body up in his arms and tried to force life back into her, but her breathing had stopped. Barely able to see, he joined the exodus of noncombatants as they tried to reach the bluffs.

In the midst of the battle, Custer ordered Yates to move left toward the bluffs and cut off the escape route. A moment later, Tom Custer, shouted, *"More Injuns coming in a thousand yards to the right!"*

Custer reared Vic and saw the mounted warriors hurrying out of the coulee. At the same moment, he caught a flash of Benteen at the head of his command closing with warriors a hundred and fifty yards off to his right by the tree line along the river. Pushing his horse toward the white-haired captain, he felt a sting on his right thigh but disregarded it. Knifing through to Benteen, he pointed to Crazy Horse. Benteen sized up the problem at once and gave an order to his trumpeter. In moments, Companies H, D, and K, crashed into the lead elements of the Olglalas. Custer joined them and got a glimpse of a light-haired warrior with white spots on his torso. He'd heard from his scouts about Crazy Horse in battle. He spurred forward, rifle waving. But before he could reach the famed Sioux leader, he saw the spotted torso go down. At that moment, Tom hollered at him, "You want to seal off these noncombatants?"

Custer threw another glance at where he'd seen the spotted war chief, but he was nowhere in sight. Following Tom, he quickly reached elements of Jimmi Calhoun's Company L. He directed the commander to move left, then led the troopers through an opening in the Miniconjou circle. As near as he could guess, there had to be several hundred noncombatants who hadn't reached the bluff. They'd be ransom enough, he guessed.

As Red Elk lowered his wife's body to the ground on the side of the bluff, he wondered if there was a way to save the unborn child. He looked around frantically for a midwife, but saw none. Besides, Late Star was only five months along—not long enough. It was then that Captain Yates's first troopers managed to cut between the fleeing Sioux civilians and the bluffs. Red Elk's anger flooded over him, but he took a moment to kiss Late Star's cheeks. Standing, he vowed, "I will avenge your death, my wife. I *swear* it!"

He turned, burning with anger and pain, frantically firing his repeating rifle, and ran toward the blue-clad soldiers. Reaching his pony in the middle of the pandemonium, he quickly mounted and began to look around wildly. A trooper raised his revolver from three feet away, but Red Elk swung his heavy battle ax into the soldier's face before he could fire. The Long Knife slid out of his saddle his eyes already glazing. But another first coup was the least of Red Elk's concerns at the moment. He wanted the Long Knife leader. Picking his way through the screaming Sioux women and children, he rode toward the river. Smoke and dust were everywhere, the noise deafening. Suddenly he saw the man he had seen ride at the head of the main charge. He was in light tan buckskins, wearing a wide-brimmed light hat . . . riding on a fine horse. Red Elk urged his pony ahead, readying the battle ax. It was the only way—close and touching, the Lakota warrior way. . . . He let out a war cry from ten feet away. *His enemy had to see him, had to know!*

Custer turned, saw the raised battle ax coming straight at him, whipped his pistol around and fired. The bullet ripped across Red Elk's right cheek and as his charge carried him past the Long Knife leader, another round in the shoulder from Tom Custer's revolver knocked the warrior from his pony.

Major Reno had reorganized as ordered and Custer brought him in with what was left of Companies A, G and M. His command formed the blocking force on the east side of the battle, closing that part of Custer's noose on the Indian civilians. Smoke from burning tipis now added to the limited visibility. The sound of firing was still intense, mingling with shouts and screams. Ahead, the assault companies under Keogh had fought through the Hunkpapa and Blackfoot circles, and swung around, joining Yates, who was blocking the approach to the bluffs. Benteen's command by the river had valiantly thrown back Crazy Horse's large force of horsemen and many of the warriors had ridden back up Medicine Tail Coulee. Benteen edged his troopers back into the tipis, completing the encirclement. Custer had been everywhere, with his hard-fighting brother not far away. As usual the ex-general had an amazing grip on the battle. It was just like when he was a twenty-three year old brigadier in the War Between the States. He seemed to have remarkable intuitive powers as a battle developed and somehow his famous luck stayed with him. He found Mitch Bouyer, the half-Santee Sioux scout and translator who spoke excellent English, and motioned for him to approach. "Is Sitting Bull the big chief here?" he asked.

Bouyer, called by the Sioux, "the man with the calfskin vest," nodded his head vigorously, replying, "I think he's up there." He pointed toward the southern bluffs.

At that moment, a woman's voice pierced the din, "*Custer!* "

He whirled at the voice he hadn't heard in years, and saw a beautiful Cheyenne woman at his stirrup. "Monasetah?"

She took his boot in her hand. "Don't kill my people, Custer!" she implored. Instantly Custer found a use for the Indian woman who had once been so close to him. "Monasetah," he shouted, "I want to stop this battle. No more killing. Go with Bouyer here and help him convince Sitting Bull to stop!"

She's still beautiful when she smiles, Custer thought as her white teeth flashed and she replied, "I will do it Custer, yes, I will do it." She reached up for Bouyer's hand and he pulled her up behind his saddle.

Custer said, "Find the chief and tell him we have six hundred of his squaws, old people and children. If he wants to save them, he must surrender!"

The scout nodded and wheeled his pony around toward the bluffs.

Mark Kellogg, the correspondent from the Bismarck *Tribune,* finished jotting a note in his pad and asked, "Think they'll quit, General?"

Custer's eyes hardened. "They'd better. But you know what, Mark, I almost wish they wouldn't." With that the buckskin-clad commander whirled his horse and was off to make sure Crazy Horse hadn't pulled one of his tricks to deceive Benteen.

★ ★ ★

Even as Mitch Bouyer and Monasetah picked their way through the smoldering, wrecked village, Sitting Bull had made his decision. He could not justify any more bloodshed among his innocents. The Long Knives had hit too hard with too much concentrated strength. Without the innocent ones to worry about, there was no doubt in his mind that the large number of skilled warriors under his superb war leaders would have won out in any kind of prolonged fight. But the sacrifice wasn't worth it. As the spiritual leader, it was his responsibility to safeguard his people. He ordered the signal to break off the fight, hoping it would be seen through the haze and smoke. His nephews mounted up and hurried down the embankment to spread the word.

A few minutes later, Bouyer and Monasetah were brought to him bearing a white flag. He listened as the man who had once shared his campfire offered Custer's ultimatum. Monasetah added in Lakota, "Long Hair will be fair, Great Chief."

Nodding his head, Sitting Bull, said, "Tell Long Hair I will talk with him."

★ ★ ★

It was the end of the battle. Slowly the firing died out and the sullen warriors put down their weapons. Custer, accompanied by his adjutant, Cooke, and his brother Tom, approached the solemn Lakota leader as he sat quietly on his elegant black pony. Bouyer reined in at the commander's right elbow. Behind them, Custer's guidon flapped in a light breeze as the hot June sun hung over the low hills to the west. He looked into the famous chief's grim eyes and knew if they had met on another day the result might have been different. Custer, the ultimate warrior, knew another of his cloth when he met him. He turned to Bouyer. "Tell Sitting Bull my terms. His warriors are to lay down their arms and all of his people are to go to the appropriate reservation as soon as directed. When General Terry arrives, escort companies will be assigned to each contingent, and we will provide partial provisions. My doctors will see to their wounded if they desire."

The interpreter nodded, relaying the colonel's orders as two of the major Sioux war leaders rode in—Gall and Crazy Horse. The latter had some blood on his right shoulder, but otherwise appeared to be unharmed. Hearing the part about surrendering their arms, both Lakota war leaders vehemently protested to Sitting Bull. Bouyer turned to Custer. "They say they need their arms to hunt and feed their people."

Custer's eyes narrowed as he regarded the three Sioux leaders. Finally he replied, "All of their firearms are to be turned in. On the journey to their respective reservations, they can use their bows and arrows to hunt game, and our soldiers will assist them. If General Terry desires, their guns can be returned later."

Sitting Bull sat on his horse quietly throughout the meeting. His dignity was unruffled. He, too, knew a strong leader when he encountered one, and he had heard much of Long Hair. He looked down to the Greasy Grass where so many of his people awaited their fate. Finally, he nodded his head. "It will be as Long Hair says."

The brave do never shun the light.
—NICHOLAS ROWE

Brigadier General Alfred Terry looked up from his camp chair as the detachment of cavalrymen galloped into his command post, located some twelve miles north of the Greasy Grass. Twilight and it's long shadows were reaching into darkness, and the murmuring of soldiers preparing for their precious hours of rest could be heard through the one-night bivouac. The rest of the general's command, of which the Seventh Cavalry was a part, was spending the night here before moving down to the valley of the Little Bighorn in the morning. The plan was to have the two wings attack

Sitting Bull—if they found him. Placing his coffee cup on the ground, the dark haired General Terry got to his feet and looked curiously at Colonel John Gibbon. "What's this?" he asked, as a rider approached.

Gibbon, the commander of the Seventh Infantry Regiment, who was known as being truthfully "steel-cold," shook his head. "Appears to be someone from the Seventh Cavalry."

Moments later, George Armstrong Custer wheeled in his horse, jumped off, and with a grin drove a Sioux battle lance, complete with streamers, into the ground at Terry's feet. Saluting briskly, he said, "Sir, compliments of Sitting Bull!"

Terry looked at the lance and back to Custer's grin. "Would you mind telling me what this is about, Armstrong?"

Custer shrugged and grinned again. "As I said, General, I bring this directly from Sitting Bull who, along with some eighteen hundred warriors and another five to six thousand Sioux and Cheyennes, are presently dead or my captives on the Little Bighorn River."

Terry studied Custer's blue eyes for a moment, glanced up at the smile on Tom Custer's face where he sat on his horse. Turning back to Tom's older brother, the general's voice was a bit wondrous as he asked, "You found them and defeated them already?"

"To the bone, general. I have their firearms and they await escort to whichever reservations you want to send them to. The fighting was all over at five-twenty-five this afternoon."

It was Terry's turn to grin. With a glance at Gibbon, he shook Custer's hand. "By damn, Armstrong, that's remarkable! Congratulations—*well done!*"

Gibbon shook Custer's hand as well. As the infantry commander found a smile and said, "I knew you'd get greedy, Custer."

Tom Custer and the rest of the escort dismounted as Custer said, "I want to take the wounded back to Fort Lincoln right away, General. May I use the *Far West?*"

Terry nodded. The *Far West* was the shallow draft river steamer that was the expedition's support boat. It was anchored a few miles north at the confluence of the Little Bighorn and the Bighorn rivers. The general replied, "I don't know why not. How many casualties do you have?"

Custer frowned. "About twenty-seven dead, and seventy-one wounded. It was a pretty sharp fight. The dead will be buried at the battle site." He paused. "One of the wounded is my old friend, Captain George Yates. He got a nasty arrow wound in the leg."

"I'm sorry to hear that. Do you trust Sitting Bull?"

"Yes, I do. He strikes me as a man of honor."

"And you say he had about eighteen hundred warriors? My God, where'd they all come from? I never heard of that many warriors in one place!"

Gibbon, ever the infantry officer, broke in. "You sure that isn't cavalry reporting—divide by two and then cut it in half?"

Custer grinned again. "Tell you what, John, I'll let *you* count 'em!"

★ ★ ★

An hour later, after his orderly, Pvt. Burkman, had put up his tent and found some supper for him and Tom, Custer lay wide awake in his bedroll. His boundless energy finally seemed sapped, but he couldn't sleep. He was far too full of himself. Everything had worked out beyond even *his* expectations! The fight had been vicious, but it had reaped a remarkable reward—*seven thousand* hostiles. It was by far the greatest victory over belligerent Indians in history. The country would go crazy. He couldn't wait to tell Libbie and wished he could see the faces back East when they read the first telegram! He could picture Sheridan now, the little banty Irishman, and Sherman, the voluble, excitable redhead. But mostly, he wished he could see Grant's expression. Darn his soul! Now he'd be glad he relented.

At thirty-six, George Armstrong Custer was still nearly as lean and strong as he'd been in his early twenties. Power emanated from his erect physique. He could ride all day and go on all night if necessary. At five-feet-eleven inches, he was about four inches taller than his average trooper, and since he never wore a uniform that wasn't unique, he was always distinguishable. His famous yellow hair had darkened and receded somewhat and he now wore it much shorter than when he'd been the flamboyant "boy general," but his penetrating blue eyes could still wither a recalcitrant or slipshod subordinate. They could also turn merry in an instant, as when he participated in horseplay with his brothers or joked with his beloved Libbie. His prominent cheekbones accented an almost gaunt face that many women found exciting. A thick reddish mustache drooped over his mouth.

He'd had his ups and downs in the eleven years since the Civil War—even been court-martialed and relieved from duty for a year. There had also been financial failures. The recent trouble, when in a run of poor judgment he'd appeased the Democrats, appearing before a senate committee and giving hearsay evidence against Grant's younger brother, had brought the wrath of the quiet president down on him like an avalanche in snow country. But now it was all behind him, *well* behind him.

He swung his legs out of the bedroll and got to his feet. Touching the makeshift bandage he'd applied to the shallow bullet wound on his right thigh, he was pleased there was little pain. Just a scratch, he told himself, but he hadn't told anyone about it. He *never* got hit.

He wished some of his hounds were with him so he could take them for a walk. Going outside to stretch, he saw a red ash marking a cigar. "Evenin', General," Mark Kellogg said.

"What are you doing up?" Custer asked.

"I've been working on my story of the battle," the journalist replied. "Can't sleep. It's going to make me famous, you know—what with your connection with the *Herald* and all." He was referring to the New York *Herald*, whose publisher, the famous James Gordon Bennett, Jr., had put Kellogg, a reporter for the Bismarck *Tribune*, on a special retainer to accompany the Seventh Cavalry on its campaign.

Kellogg grinned in the dark. "But not as famous as you, General. As much as the press loves you, you're going to be the most celebrated man in the world!"

★ ★ ★

"The *Far West* is a river queen, pure royalty plying the western waters of our country's wilderness like a churning behemoth from another world. She is a special character in this great saga of America that unfolds with each passing adventure," Mark Kellogg scribbled on his ever-present writing pad as he sat by the stern of the speeding steamer. "Constructed in

1870 in Pittsburgh, the *Far West* has two decks, is 190 feet long and measures thirty-three feet at her beam. She can carry 400 tons and still draw only four and a half feet of water. Empty, this queen needs just twenty inches of water to clear a sand bar. One comment on the river is that her brilliant skipper, Captain Grant Marsh, can navigate her on a heavy dew or if her bottom is wet. The venerable, gray-haired captain also knows the Yellowstone country's streams as well as old friends or wary enemies. . . .

"Now his fine steamer bears a mixed cargo of jubilation and sadness. In her cabins and lying about on her decks are the forty-six most severely wounded from the Seventh Cavalry—victims, but survivors of General Custer's great victory over Sitting Bull and his nearly 2,000 hard fighting warriors at the Little Bighorn.

"The disturbed river bubbles in white wonder in our wake as we speed on toward the Missouri River and Fort Lincoln where these brave men will be returned to the hero's care they so richly deserve. Above them and the churning noises of the *Far West's* toiling two engines, the strains of military airs from the regiment's band play for all to hear. The Seventh's bouncy, jubilant song, "GarryOwen," is joyfully rendered over and over as we press on with the world's most famous cavalry general to announce the greatest victory ever wrought in America's struggle with its recalcitrant natives."

Kellogg paused to reread what he'd written. It would all be voraciously consumed by thousands of readers when the *Herald* hit the streets. In fact, it would be even more readers, because he'd be quoted in newspapers all over the world—a heady thought for a small town reporter.

Such was Custer's fame, but many of those readers wouldn't know much about his origins. Kellogg began again to write:

"George Armstrong Custer was born in the village of New Rumley, Ohio, on December 5, 1839, the son of blacksmith and Justice of the Peace Emanuel Custer and his second wife Maria. The yellow-haired boy was full of life, impulsive, bright and mischievous. Always an instigator of pranks, Autie, as young Custer was called, seldom studied but always "had his lessons" and invariably was the leader among his schoolmates.

"When he was ten years old, he went to live with his older, half-sister Lydia Ann, in Monroe, Michigan. Located thirty-five miles south of

Detroit on the western bank of Lake Erie, Monroe was one of Michigan's early settlements and in 1852 had nearly 5,000 residents. Although Monroe would play a major role in young Custer's life, he returned to Ohio while in his mid-teens and eventually began teaching school there.

"In 1857, young Custer finagled an appointment to West Point and his dream of being a soldier began. That June, he reported into the U.S. Military Academy to begin the five-year program. Ever fun-loving and disruptive, Custer didn't bend well to the iron discipline required. Demerits or 'skins' were awarded for every imaginable infraction of the many rules, with two hundred per year as the maximum. Every year, he flirted with the limit, and he scraped by academically. By the time he graduated in 1861, he stood last in his class."

"But the American Civil War had started two months earlier and class standings would mean nothing in the next four years. Sporting a new uniform and a borrowed horse, Second-lieutenant G. A. Custer got right into the thick of it at the Battle of Bull Run. Following several brave and reckless exploits that brought him some fame and citations over the next year, Autie came to the attention of Major General George McClellan, the commander of the ponderous Army of the Potomac. "Little Mac" made Custer his aide-de-camp, and Autie's exploits continued. He admired McClellan fiercely, though he chafed at the general's sometimes cautious planning. Following a long leave in Monroe, during which Lincoln relieved the troublesome Little Mac, Custer returned to a cavalry assignment. He was now a captain.

"At the end of June—it was now 1863—in a daring experiment to inject vigor into the Union cavalry corps, three young captains were vaulted directly to brigadier general and given command of brigades. Custer was one of them. Since a general could prescribe his own uniform, the dashing Custer immediately outfitted himself in a black velvet ensemble that set off his long blond curls. His brigade was made up of, appropriately, Michiganders—'Wolverines' . . ."

★ ★ ★

Custer leaned over the bunk where Captain George Yates fought the pain from his infected wound. "You awake, George?"

The wounded officer's voice was weak, "Hurt too much to sleep, Autie."

Yates and Custer had met when they were on leave together in Monroe in early '63 before Custer got the stocky blond lieutenant appointed to General Pleasanton's cavalry staff. Yates had seen action in several major battles and had been promoted to captain, then brevetted major and lieutenant-colonel for conspicuous gallantry. After the war he found himself in the Seventh and was given command of the Band Box Troop, the show company. His wife, Annie, was one of Libbie Custer's closest friends.

Custer put his hand gently on the captain's shoulder. "It'll get better. You know, you did quite a job back there at the river."

Yates found a smile. "Good troopers, Autie."

"More than that, George. You led them very well. We wouldn't have had that victory without what you did."

Yates eyes widened. "You mean that?"

Custer nodded. "I'm recommending you for promotion, and I'm sure you'll get it."

The smile stayed on the captain's handsome face as he closed his eyes. Custer turned to go. "I have to see some of the other wounded, George."

"Good night, general."

A couple of minutes later, Custer ran into Doctor Henry Porter, the senior surgeon who was accompanying the wounded home. Porter had been practicing medicine in Bismarck, the town outside of Fort Lincoln, until just before the campaign, when he signed a three month contract for service. The twenty-eight-year-old doctor was hardly new to the army, having served against the Tonto Apaches in the Department of Arizona, where he had been cited for gallantry by General Crook. Custer liked him.

"How're the lads holding up, Doc?" Custer asked quietly.

The physician's eyes were tired in the swaying lantern light. "Good as can be expected, General. We may lose a couple of them, but most are doing well."

"How about Captain Yates?"

Porter shook his head. "I don't like the way that damned arrow wound is acting. It may have some kind of poison. Or it could be just the usual infection."

Custer scowled. "Is he going to be all right?"

"Can't say. Those kind of wounds can do funny things."

"You won't have to amputate or anything, will you?"

"I hope not. I'm keeping a close eye on him."

"He's one of my best friends."

Doctor Porter nodded his head. "I'll do the best I can."

"I want to see the rest of the wounded."

"Very well, sir. I'll come with you."

Custer, carrying a lantern, moved about in the dim night light of the main boiler deck where many of the wounded lay. Some of the men were asleep, most unable to drift off for long due to the pain they were suffering. "Water!" a dry voice croaked.

Custer knelt, recognizing the face of First-sergeant Edwin Bobo. Turning back to Dr. Porter, he murmured, "Water okay?"

The surgeon nodded. "Yes, he has a shoulder wound."

Custer uncapped his canteen and held it to Bobo's lips. The first sergeant of C Company drank thirstily, then dropped back to his hard bed. "How do you feel, First-sergeant?" Custer asked.

"Hurts like hell, General."

"Well, we'll be home in the morning and you'll be mended in no time."

"I hope so."

"I heard you did quite a job in the battle. The regiment will need a new sergeant major. When you're well, we'll talk about it."

Getting back to his feet, Custer sighed. He wasn't good at this part. He could lead them into hell and give them victory, but he was never comfortable around the wounded. Bobo was the sixth patient he'd spoken to, and he needed to get outside for some fresh air.

A few minutes later, Custer walked into the wheelhouse, where the low light outlined Captain Grant Marsh's features. "I thought you didn't take the helm," Custer said.

"Only when we're moving at night, General."

"Played in any good poker games lately?"

"Not since that night."

"Uh huh, that was quite a game." It had taken place on board the *Far West* the night before the regiment pulled out for the Little Bighorn. It was the biggest game Custer had ever sat in. He'd been lucky and had only lost about eighty dollars before getting out. Counting chits, and that meant most of the money, he'd heard there was eventually some six thousand dollars in the game. A ransom! He could pay off his stock debt with that kind of money. Losing even eighty was bad. Gambling was the only thing on which he'd backslided with Libbie. He'd quit drinking way back in the early part of the war after getting drunk while on leave in Monroe and almost losing all chance of winning her hand. Hadn't had a drink since, and he almost never cursed. As of other women, well, he never actually *promised* her anything about that because she'd never cornered him on it.

But he had promised her he would quit gambling. Now that was hard—there was something about gambling that was akin to battle, a certain thrill that was raw excitement to him. "How much do you think that captain from the Sixth Infantry won?" Custer asked.

"Several thousand. I know he got about eight hundred of mine," Marsh replied. "How much he'll collect on those chits nobody knows."

Custer was silent a moment, watching the river from between the two tall smokestacks. Finally he asked, "What time do you think we'll hit Bismarck in the morning?"

"I'd say long about seven-forty-five or so."

"We'll stop to send dispatches, then go right on down river to the fort."

The captain nodded. "Yes, sir."

3

Red Elk watched grimly from the crag above the river as the Hunkpapa portion of the huge village slowly filed by five hundred yards below him. At its head, with his wives and nephews riding a few paces behind him,

Sitting Bull rode tall on his fine black pony. Not even in defeat, Red Elk thought, would the great man lose any of his strong power or bearing. The column of Lakotas, Cheyennes, and their allies stretched for miles, trudging toward imprisonment on various reservations.

At least it *meant* imprisonment to Red Elk and the other followers of Sitting Bull. Any restriction on where a proud Lakota warrior and his family could live, hunt, and make war was imprisonment.

The great sadness struck at him again. He had no family. A Long Knife bullet had cut down his beautiful Late Star and the child she was carrying in an instant, and that same bullet had also cut out his heart, leaving a bloody hole in his chest that could be closed only when his revenge was complete.

Long Hair had departed for somewhere, and Gibbon had become chief of the Long Knives at the Place of Death—which is how he would always remember the Greasy Grass. Gibbon had permitted them to bury their dead in the honored Lakota way, high from the ground with their possessions. There had been many, including those who had died from wounds. Over one hundred, he'd heard. But the only death that truly mattered was that of his beautiful Late Star. Soon he would return to her spirit. For now, he had to remain free from capture.

Tall and spindly for a Sioux, Red Elk was exceptionally strong and so fleet of foot that no one had beaten him in a race in many moons. His nose was hooked, as his father's had been, and he was considered handsome. He wore his erect first coup feather proudly. He'd been a *blotahunka*—war leader—for more than six moons, earning that honor when sixteen. No other Hunkpapa had held, in recent times, such a prestigious fighting position at such an early age.

But he had done many things at a young age—killed a lion with an arrow when he was eleven, been accepted into the Kit Fox society at fourteen, made his first coup just over a year later. He had won the love of the exquisite Late Star and had married her at sixteen. Now he was alone—his mother dead, his father, Bald Wolf, killed three years earlier in a Shoshone raid. Late Star . . .

He ground his teeth together, trying to shut out the pain. Why had Long Hair gone? It would have been easy to get to him in the Long Knife camp at night. He had been cheated. He looked down again at the column. He would have to curb his impatience, plan carefully, make no mistakes, keep the fire burning . . . if it took his whole life, he would take the yellow hair of the Long Knife chief.

With it's foghorn blaring like a huge, excited frog, the *Far West* eased into the wharf at Bismarck at 7:42 A.M. on the Fourth of July. Only a handful of people awaited, one of whom was the publisher of the Bismarck *Tribune*, former colonel Clement Lounsberry. The moment the steamer came to a halt, Custer bounded across the gangplank, a grin creasing his face. Spotting the newspaperman, he shouted, "Is your telegraph key open?"

"Sure is, General!" Lounsberry responded. "Have you got some big news?"

"Big as it comes!" Custer said, thumping him on the shoulder. "I've won the biggest victory in the history of Indian warfare!"

Custer filled him in as Tom Custer and Boston Custer, along with Mark Kellogg, traipsed along behind the striding commander and the editor. They soon reached the railroad telegraph office, where Custer handed Lounsberry the message he had labored over for the past hour, the message he had prepared in his mind a hundred times before landing, the message he had been dreaming of sending for years. He knew very well that its words would ring around the world, would see the front page of some of the greatest newspapers, would long be repeated by school children and immortalized in history books.

It read:

> "*To Ulysses S. Grant, President of the United States of America, and to my superiors in the Army, but most particularly to the Citizens of our proud country on this, its Centennial:*
>
> *'On June 25th inst. I led the proud Seventh United States Cavalry into battle against a mighty force of Sioux and Cheyenne Indians and roundly defeated them. Although outnumbered three or four-to-one by diehard warriors, my brave boys followed me resolutely to a complete victory over Sitting Bull and his hard fighting chiefs. Never before has one gallant regiment met such a huge enemy force in the field. I am distinctly proud of every member of my command. When I asked them to follow me into the jaws of death, they responded bravely to the man! Happy 100th birthday, America!'*
>
> —*George Armstrong Custer*
> *Bvt. Major-general, USA*"

Lounsberry looked up, his eyes wide. "Is it true?"

"We whipped 'em cold!" Tom said.

"I have several dispatches written as well, boss!" the beaming Mark Kellogg added.

The editor shook his head as he handed Custer's message to the telegrapher, a little spectacled man named Carnahan. "Get this off right away. I think you are going to be quite busy for a while."

Custer turned to Kellogg. "Will you get that dispatch off to the New York *Herald* post haste?"

"Sure will, General, but we want to get the scoop right here on the *Tribune*. Right, Mr. Lounsberry?"

"If you have it ready, Kellogg, I'll start the type to flying in a few minutes!"

Custer grinned. It didn't make any difference to him who got the scoop.

★ ★ ★

Once the *Far West* was back out in midstream and heading down the broad Missouri, Captain Marsh ordered the deep throated fog horn be sounded every two minutes until they reached the Fort Lincoln landing six miles south. Smoke belched from the steamer's tall stacks as she quickly reached a top speed of well over twenty knots.

Custer stood at the rail in the bow, his signature red kerchief streaming out over his shoulder, his thoughts speeding like the bubbling white wake of the steamer. Throughout his many proud moments in life, he had never been fuller of himself. Soon his beloved Libbie would fly into his arms, and he would tell her about his great victory. The post would rejoice with them—the golden couple. What incredible timing! The Centennial! The gods were truly shining down upon him. His little Standby, one of his nicknames for Libbie, would be absolutely delighted.

He couldn't quell the excitement. He didn't know what was next—he'd have to wait on the response from Washington—actually Philadelphia— whereever his superiors might be. Surely he'd get his promotion, and there had to be more, much more. The band, assembled on the foredeck behind him, struck up a lively version of "Yankee Doodle." He turned and nodded to the band leader, then turned his attention back downstream to where Fort Lincoln would soon come into sight on the west bank of the river.

Fort Lincoln, Dakota Territory, was one of the army's finest new posts in Indian country. Begun in 1872 as a small infantry fort behind a log palisade, the post had been enlarged considerably a year later to accommodate the Seventh Cavalry. The original group of buildings on the north hill still housed the garrison's infantry unit. The foot soldiers primary mission was to protect the post from marauding Indian bands while the cavalry was away on whatever campaigns the commanding general might prescribe for it. Slightly more than a mile separated the center Infantry Post from that of Cavalry Post, which was wide open with no protective wall. The main buildings of Cavalry Post formed a rectangle with the officers' quarters on the west side.

It was Custer's fort, the center of his fiefdom, and in the middle of Officers' Row, the three-storied commander's house stood like a baronial castle. Allegedly one of the finest houses on the frontier, it had a billiard room, a reception room, and a double parlor thirty-two feet long sporting a large bay window. A huge verandah set off the grand house, which was the center of social life and also served as an unofficial chapel for the officers and their families on most Sundays. It was also large enough to accommodate the theatrical presentations that were often part of the Custer household entertainment.

As Custer continued to stand at the bow, he thought of how comfortable life had been in that fine house, how at one time he had thought having command of the Seventh Cavalry on such a fine post really was a pleasurable way to live. *His* regiment, *his* fort, *his* domain. He had once berated himself for wanting more. But he did—much more.

He expected to be called *General* because he *was* one. He didn't care that it was a brevet rank, a temporary one from the war. Above all else, he wanted the stars back that he had won in his early twenties. The *stars*. And now they couldn't deny him. He had just won the biggest Indian battle in history, defeated the mighty Sioux and their allies on their home ground. Even Grant would have to forget his ire and reward him. . . .

★ ★ ★

Elizabeth Bacon Custer was, at thirty-three, an extremely attractive woman. With dark brown hair and deep-set gray eyes that caused more than one man to take a second look, the slender but shapely native of Monroe, Michigan had been the object of men's desires and affections since entering her teens. At that age, she'd been forced to slap a doctor's face when he kissed her. Her mother died when she was twelve and she was placed in several girl's schools while her father, Judge Daniel Bacon, conquered his grief and looked for a new wife. "Full of life," one friend from Monroe had described her at the time. Certainly she was vivacious and adventurous as she reached her later teens. Suitors came calling by the dozens, but the young Libbie Bacon was mostly bored until the Civil War began. Then a rather wild and romantic young West Pointer with long red-blond curls began to pursue her while he was on leave in Monroe. At first she wasn't particularly attracted to him, but his attention to her girlhood rival, Fanny Fifield, was the spur that gave her newfound interest in him. When he came back again on leave as a captain, she found him even more appealing. He wrote poetry to her and, in spite of her father's objection to him, showed remarkable persistence in his suit for her affection. However, it was when he returned as a twenty-three-year-old brigadier general commanding all of the Michigan cavalry regiments that she finally, totally, fell for him. Newspaper phrases such as "Boy General" and "Fearless National Hero" captured her romantic imagination and when her father came around, she finally agreed to marry the dashing young officer.

That had been over thirteen years earlier.

Libbie Custer was still very much in love with her "Nomad," as she often called him. She had vastly enjoyed her adventurous life as his wife, from back when they rendezvoused during the war, throughout her years as the first lady of the Seventh Cavalry.

She was outside in the back yard tossing kernels of corn to her flock of chickens when she heard the faint sound of a boat's foghorn from up toward Bismarck. She didn't pay attention to it for a couple of minutes until she noticed its incessant, demanding bleat. And then she heard the faint sound of music . . . it seemed to be playing "GarryOwen," the Seventh's famous theme song that Autie had given it. What—?

She tossed the last of the corn high in the air, dashed up on the verandah and ran around to the front of the house to get a better view of the river. The music got louder. It *was* "GarryOwen!" Other wives and their children were coming out of their quarters. A couple of soldiers tumbled out of the barracks across the way, a dog barked, and a horse over in the stables whinnied as if an old flame were returning. That set off two of Custer's hounds with their deep bays of alarm. "Hush!" admonished Libbie as she stared past the barracks across the quadrangle and upriver to where the sounds were emanating.

There was the *Far West* ploughing toward her, with black smoke billowing from its tall stacks, creating a dark blanket in its wake. Her heart skipped a beat. "Oh, dear Lord," she pleaded, "let it be good news. Oh dear Lord, bring him safely to me."

As she headed toward the wharf on the far eastern side of the quadrangle, other families began streaming out of their quarters. Maggie Calhoun, her young sister-in-law, caught up with her; Annie Yates hurried up on the other side. Her eyes were shining. "It *must* be them, Lib," she said excitedly, "or at least some good news! *Listen!*" The strains of music from the regimental band were now louder as it switched to "Home Sweet Home."

As the three women reached the wharf, it seemed that everyone at Cavalry Post was heading toward the landing—children, laundresses, the soldiers who'd been left behind for post housekeeping. Anticipation marked everyone's expression, some with glee, others with trepidation, as the big riverboat began to slow and turn ashore from midstream. And then Libbie saw him, standing tall on the front of the low main deck, unmistakable in his tan buckskin jacket. She let out a huge sigh and gave silent thanks to the Lord, as the band struck up "The Girl I Left Behind."

★ ★ ★

On board the riverboat, as it glided into the landing, Custer was full of the moment. He was savoring every ounce of his returning hero role, anticipating the pleasure of arrival. The moment the *Far West* nudged up against the dock, he sprang off the deck and bounded to Libbie. She flew into his arms, kissing his mouth, his cheeks, murmuring, "Darling, darling, I've been so afraid."

He kissed her soundly on the lips, lifted her and swung her fully around. "I did it, my little Standby! I did it!"

Libbie pulled her face back. "A big victory?"

He grinned. "Big as they come!"

Maggie Calhoun caught his arm and kissed his cheek. "Where's my husband, big brother?"

"Back with the main body. He's fine," Custer replied.

It was Annie Yates' turn. "How about George?"

Custer sobered. "He took an arrow, Annie. He's on the boat."

A shadow crossed her face as she turned anxiously and moved toward the gangplank that had just been put in place.

It seemed that everyone at Cavalry Post was pouring onto the landing. The band switched to another rousing rendition of "GarryOwen" as Custer held up his hands and announced the battle results, finishing with, "The Seventh Cavalry will soon be the most famous regiment in any army in the world!"

A spontaneous cheer went up, followed by a soldier shouting, "*Three cheers for General Custer!* "

PHILADELPHIA, PENNSYLVANIA *July 4, 1876*

The United States of America was having a grand birthday party—its Centennial. Nowhere else was the celebration greater than in its shrine of liberty, the city where the republic was formally born, the City of Brotherly Love. The festivities had begun officially the night before with a torch light parade that lasted into the small hours, keeping a major part of the city awake. In fact, due to the continuing exuberance, several thousand of the celebrants hadn't gone to bed at all.

Other citizens awoke at dawn and jumped into the red-white-and blue celebration. The proud colors were everywhere. Flags flew in the light breeze on every street, bunting hung wherever there was a ledge or a place to tack it, and even clothing followed the same theme, with red prominent. Beribboned boaters jauntily adorned the heads of nattily dressed men, while the women twirled fancy silk parasols above their elegant, brightly trimmed gowns.

The active, zestful, irreverent American attitude permeated the downtown part of the city as visitors and locals merged like drops of rain in the Schuylkill River. On this grand holiday, perhaps the grandest ever in the young country, there was no evidence of social rank. Children in knickerbockers ran with pickaninnies in rags, the shop girl joked with the fine lady, the mechanic and the factory owner pounded each other on the back, and the dogs barked at everyone. Since dawn, farm wagons gaily accoutered with colorful bouquets and flowing over with hearty lads and bouncing lassies with pretty roses stuck in their shiny hair—all of them dressed to the hilt in their Sunday-go-to-meeting clothes—had jammed into the tumult.

The blaring music from marching bands accented everything with all-American songs. Shiny tubas and French horns reflected the light of a cooperative sun in every direction. Sleepy-eyed musicians marched smartly, interspersed with military units that had formed for the parade along Chestnut Street at half-past seven.

Now, with the huge throng crowding every vantage point, the parade marched east to Fourth Street, past Independence Hall. At the head rode Governor Hartranft and his aides, presenting a gallant show of feathers and lace. They were followed by the Philadelphia City Troop, also in the saddle. Next came the mounted cornet band, blowing "The Battle Hymn of the Republic." The first burst of applause was elicited by the Black Huzzars, whose long black plumes swept from their helmets over their shoulders. They were followed by the corps of West Point cadets, precise in their dress-parade uniforms. A sea of multi-colored uniforms marched behind them as the warm sun rose higher in the clear July sky.

Independence Hall stood on Chestnut, the only building on the square bordered by Chestnut, Walnut, Fifth, and Sixth Streets. A grandstand built to accommodate 5,000 had been erected on the north side of the square. Festooned with the national colors, the stand also held a rostrum for the speakers and top dignitaries. It was there, at twenty-two minutes past ten, as a chorus of over six hundred finished singing the special Centennial hymn composed by Oliver Wendell Holmes, that an aide hurried up to the center seating section's front row and handed a message to Lieutenant-general Philip Sheridan. The little Irishman read hurriedly, then let out a whoop.

"Well, I'll be goddamned!" Sheridan snorted, breaking into a wide grin. "Look a *this*, Cump!" he said, handing the message to General William Tecumseh Sherman to his right.

Sherman read the telegram hurriedly, shook his head, and also broke into a grin. Leaning over to his right, he handed the message to the short, bearded president of the United States. "Look at this, Ulyss."

Ulysses S. Grant was quiet and nonexcitable, even enigmatic. He rose from obscurity to command all Union forces in the Civil War before becoming president, and had been described as the quintessential common man. Never garrulous, he spoke and acted directly. Custer had embarrassed him a few months earlier by going before Congress without permission from his seniors and testifying on hearsay that Grant's younger brother, Orvil, had been involved in questionable practices with army post traderships. In a rare stroke of what many thought was spite, but was more in the way of chastisement, the president had summarily relieved Custer of command of the Seventh Cavalry. A few days later in St. Paul, when Custer actually got on his knees and begged General Alfred Terry to intervene and get him back at the helm of the Seventh, the department commander wrote a strong, carefully worded recommendation that elicited from Grant a private summation: "I'm between the proverbial rock and a hard place. If the campaign flounders without him, I'll be blamed. If he wins out there, I'll be criticized more for relieving him in the first place." But ever the general, Grant went along with Terry's request. Now, as he quickly scanned Custer's telegram from Bismarck, he sighed, then turned to Sherman. "There won't be any living with him now."

Sherman shook his head. "No, but we have to hand it to him—he did it."

"Yes," Grant replied. "And apparently very well. Let's get a message of congratulations off to him from me, with your and Phil's added remarks."

Sherman nodded in agreement. "Yes, sir."

"And Sherman—"

"Yes sir?"

"Who's the next speaker?"

"Mayor Stokely. He's going to read the Declaration of Independence."

Grant nodded his head. "I want you to go on ahead of him and tell the audience about Custer's victory. Read his telegram, then tell them how proud I am of the Seventh Cavalry."

Minutes later, when the commanding general of the Army finished with his announcement, a giant roar went up from the crowd. Shouts of *Custer! Custer!* filled the large square as the news reached the assembled multitudes outside and more cheers began. It was indeed a superb birthday present for the country. The timing couldn't have been better.

★ ★ ★

Standing a couple of rows back from the president and his entourage was a well-dressed man who was smiling quietly in the midst of the cheering. His name was James Gordon Bennett, Jr., owner and publisher of the New

York *Herald*, the country's most successful newspaper. He had every reason to grin—his typesetters at this very moment would be madly composing the big Custer story. Even though he had just heard the news, he knew it would have already arrived in his newspaper offices because he had set up a special telegraph line in Bismarck and the reporter, Mark Kellogg, was on his payroll.

What a scoop it would be! But more than that, what pleased Bennett most was the remarkable fame this would bring Custer. And he would see to it. A newspaper was a powerful instrument in the hands of a man who understood its uses and if ever a man knew how to use that power it was James Gordon Bennett, Jr.. Another smile touched his lips as he pulled out a cigar.

What price glory? someone
Wrote. A shell-pocked hill, a
Sinking boat? An urn of blood, perhaps
A soul? The bugle blows its
Saddest note.

                    —Robert Elwayne

Annie Yates sat quietly beside the bed, holding her husband's hand. The large number of wounded unloaded from the *Far West* far exceeded the capacity of the post hospital, so a temporary ward had been set up in a warehouse.

Annie had insisted that George be brought home where he would have her constant care. Doctor Porter, a friend, had agreed. "It's a strange infection," he'd said. "I'm almost sure the arrow was poisoned."

How she loved her blond Michigander. He was such a gallant man. She'd been twenty-one when he started courting her in 1870 at Fort Hays while she was visiting her uncle, Colonel George Gibson. What a handsome suitor he'd been—so attentive and romantic—and brave, breveted Lieutenant-colonel in the past war. She found out later that he'd paid Libbie Custer's maid's young son to alert him when she was coming to visit so he could meet the arriving transport, flowers in hand, to help her alight. She met the Custers at the Seventh Cavalry's little tent city on Big Creek. Armstrong and Libbie, the youthful general and his storybook bride, had been so attractive, so romantic. One scene involving them was imbedded in her mind. It was a nice summer day and Libbie was languishing in a hammock while Armstrong leisurely rocked her. Now and then he would lean down and whisper something in her ear that seemed to please her. Once it pleased her so much that she blushed. It was then that she knew for a fact they were not just romantic, but had a special erotic side to their love. She had hoped then that her love for her handsome young captain would hold the same excitement, if indeed it would become love And it certainly had!

Usually, she scared off eligible suitors because she could outride and outshoot many of them. She wasn't actually pretty, rather on the lean side, and not afraid to speak up. Growing up the daughter of a noted railroad engineer who had built the track from Rio de Janeiro to the middle of Brazil's jungles, had given her a grasp of South America few young Carlisle, Pennsylvania, girls had a chance to acquire. Familiarity with foreign countries also fueled her gift for languages. With her high cheekbones and a ready wit to go with her sharps hooting, she was known as Buffalo Annie by the hunting crowd. But she didn't scare off the blond captain. Her father had objected to George's suit. "I'll not have you marrying a divorced man!" he had insisted. George's other marriage had been a short misconceived affair and finally his wife's family gave them permission to divorce. Although her George had never reached the level of raciness she suspected Armstrong Custer had in his marriage, there had been enough spice to keep their marriage bed lively. The thought excited her a bit, even in this moment of stress.

"*Annie!* " George cried out suddenly, jerking up in bed and sobbing.

She took him in her arms. "I'm right here, darling," she said soothingly.

"*Annie!* " he cried out again, his eyes blank, staring.

Then he relaxed and she lowered him back onto the pillow. She kissed his fever-hardened lips and began to dab his sweating brow with a cool washcloth.

Suddenly, George's chest seemed to stop moving! She leaned her head down and pressed her ear against it. It was still. "*No!* " she screamed! "*Burkman!*"

Custer had loaned his orderly to her as a runner in case she needed help. He stuck his head through the door from where he'd been dozing outside the bedroom. "Yes'm?"

"*Get Doctor Porter at once! Immediately, do you hear?*"

"Yes, ma'am," Burkman replied, and hurried outside.

Annie turned back to her husband and again laid her ear on his chest. "*No!*" she shouted again, as she began to push on it, finally pounding as hard as she could, with tears streaming down her cheeks.

★ ★ ★

Custer stood quietly near the foot of the bed as Libbie tried to console Annie Yates. But Annie was inconsolable. Sobs racked her lithe body. Maggie, Custer's sister, also offered soothing words. Custer turned to Porter. "Is there *anything* more we could have done, Doc?"

"No, General. Whatever it was gave him a blood infection his body just couldn't cope with."

"He was truly a heroic officer," Custer said softly. "We'd been friends since early in the war."

"Do you want to bury him in the post cemetery?"

Suddenly an idea struck Custer. It was perfect. Just as George Yates had honored the Seventh Cavalry in battle, he could now honor it by personification in death. He nodded to himself, pleased with the inspiration. He moved to Annie and put his hand on her arm. "Annie, I want to do something special for George."

She looked up through the tears. "What do you mean?"

"He's a great hero. I want to have him buried at Arlington Cemetery near Washington so people from all over the world can visit his grave."

Annie blinked. "Can you do that?" she asked in a tiny voice.

"I'll wire General Sheridan right away." More of the plan was developing in his mind. What an opportunity for him to go to Washington and be feted! And it truly would be an honor for George. "I'll ask permission to accompany George's remains myself."

Annie found a brief smile. "Oh, Autie, that would be so wonderful."

He took her in his arms and held her for a few moments, saying, "It's the least I can do. I couldn't have won the battle without him."

TRIUMPHANT CUSTER BRINGS HERO'S BODY TO ARLINGTON! *Washington. July 11th.* Brevet Major-general George Armstrong Custer, America's premiere Indian fighter, will arrive in the nation's capital today escorting the remains of Captain George W. Yates, the heroic commanding officer of the famous Band Box Troop of the valiant Seventh Cavalry. . . .

The front-page story in the Washington *Daily Patriot* went on to elaborate on the battle, centering on Custer, his Civil War achievements, and his exploits on the Plains. The other newspapers in the city, both daily and weekly, devoted front-page spreads to the story, but the *Patriot* had the most complete information. This was due to the fact that James Gordon Bennett, Jr. had a specific interest in the relatively new newspaper that had opened in 1871. He didn't own it, but the popular daily was conservatively Democratic in its political bent, and the content of the New York *Herald*'s front-page feature on the same story had been wired ahead.

The train bearing George Yates's flag-draped casket arrived at Washington's Baltimore and Ohio depot at twelve minutes past two. Wearing a standard semidress blue uniform with the silver leaves of a lieutenant colonel, his active duty rank, Custer looked out the window as the train slowed to a stop. His brother Tom, Mark Kellogg, and six troopers from the band were the only other members of the party.

Custer suppressed a smile as he saw the huge crowd assembled at the station. Several American flags were waving and a band was playing "GarryOwen." Many hand-held signs were in evidence, one reading in bold letters, "Hail Custer!" He liked that.

"Just like Caesar," Tom said with a quick smile.

Custer nodded as moved to the door. Yes, he liked it.

Stepping out of the special car onto the platform that connected it to the adjacent car, he was met by a roar of greeting. There had to be several hundred people there. He took off his broad-brimmed hat and raised it in greeting as the crowd shouted "*Custer! Custer!*"

Finally, he held up his hands for silence. Once the noise subsided, he spoke loudly, "Thank you for coming, my friends. Captain Yates deserves your homage and appreciation. He was not only a valiant officer, but a great hero. I could not possibly have won such an important victory at the Little Bighorn without his courage and leadership! Thanks to his fearlessness and that of all the other members of the Seventh Cavalry, the Sioux menace to the northern plains has now been brought to heel."

Another roar of approval burst forth from the crowd. When it was quiet, Custer went on, "Captain Yates, whom I shall recommend for posthumous promotion to brevet colonel, will rest in peace over in the national cemetery at Arlington. I was unable to bring his grieving widow along, so I would like to ask this—" He paused as the crowd grew utterly still. "Are there women here who will decorate this brave hero's grave from time to time to keep his memory fresh?"

"*Yes!*" "*Yes, I will!*" several women shouted back.

"Good." Custer said. "Thank you. His proud widow will thank you as well, knowing he is being cared for."

"Now again, thank you for meeting us and paying your respects to this brave leader."

Custer gave one final, long look at the casket. A pang of sadness struck him, as he said to himself, "George, I'm truly sorry. I shall miss you very much. I promise you that Annie and your kids will never want . . . I promise on my honor." He felt the moistness in his eyes and unconsciously blotted them with his yellow-gloved hand.

★ ★ ★

Custer had written articles for the New York *Herald* and was entertained by Bennett earlier in the year when he and Libbie visited Manhattan. He also knew that Kellogg was on Bennett's payroll, and further that the active role the New York newspaper played in continuing coverage of his victory at the Little Bighorn was a strong boost to his prospects for promotion. And he was the first to admit that George Armstrong Custer had never been adverse to fame.

In fact, if a man ever courted it, he did. From his first self-designed general's uniform of black velvet, to his horse "rearing out of control" during the Grand Army victory parade after the war, he had created exceptional "press" for himself. During the war he was the flamboyant darling of newspapermen and they hadn't lost their affection for him. Now, with this great new victory, he was back at his height of publicity—and the *Herald* was his spearhead.

James Gordon Bennett, Jr. had instigated the parade type of escort for the burial that was scheduled for the next day, or at least his minions in Washington had arranged it in cooperation with the War Department. And Bennett had reserved a posh suite for the Custer party at the luxurious Arlington Hotel. The hotel's name alone was appropriate for the occasion. It had been built by William Wilson Corcoran, the richest man in Washington and the founder of the Corcoran Art Gallery. Named after the estate of Corcoran's good friend, Robert E. Lee, it was considered the finest hostelry in Washington. The new hotel, which faced the White House on the choicest location in the city, had opened in 1869 with lavish celebrations and fanfare. The Arlington had three hundred and twenty-five rooms, an elevator, and its food and service was unparalleled.

The suite Bennett had reserved consisted of two bedrooms, a sumptuous bath and a parlor. Tom Custer and Mark Kellogg took the beds in the smaller bedroom, while Custer settled into the larger one. Tom arranged for the regimental bandsmen to be billeted in barracks across the river at Fort Whipple shortly after their arrival.

To say that Custer was the talk of the town would have been an understatement. Everywhere he showed his face, people stopped to congratulate him. Every newspaper in the city ran stories about the battle and about him. His picture graced their front pages, and the stories ran the gamut from rehashes of his Civil War victories to excerpts from his book, *My Life on the Plains*. Just an hour before, a messenger had arrived with a note from Matthew Brady. The photographer was in town and wanted to take a new portrait of him.

The burial ceremony was big news. Actually, a congressman from New York, who was also on Bennett's payroll, pushed ahead the idea that Captain Yates be accorded the highest possible honors, and he and a Michigan senator rushed the special promotion for the dead officer through the War Department. Now, as he perused a copy of the weekend paper, Donn Piatt's lively *The Capital*, Custer read that the celebrated American prima donna, Clara Louise Kellog, was to sing in *Mignon* and was also to be presented at a joint session of Congress. An idea struck him and he looked up, an animated energy in his expression. "Tom," he said to his brother, who was dozing in one of the parlor's easy chairs, "Why don't you go over and see General Sheridan, and tell him I'm thinking about addressing a joint session of Congress. See if he will give me permission."

Tom got to his feet and stretched, "Okay, Autie. Anything else, as long as I'm going out?"

"Uh huh, pick up my dress uniform downstairs at the presser's."

Tom grinned and gave his brother a gnarled finger forelock salute. "Yes, *sir*, noble general!" He gave the title the French pronunciation of general.

Custer guffawed. "Naw, I was just kidding." Jokes were a frequent pastime between the brothers. "Although it isn't a bad idea."

He read another item in *The Capital*: "Mrs. Kate Sprague, Washington's most beautiful wartime hostess and daughter of deceased Secretary of the Treasury and Supreme Court Chief Justice Salmon Chase, has come out of seclusion at her estate, Edgewood to attend a charity affair." He remembered her. They'd met briefly back during the war. Exceptional woman.

He picked up *The National Republican*, the somewhat middle of the road daily he'd bought earlier. On page two, there was a rather large article about Colonel John Gibbon arriving at the Red Cloud reservation in Dakota Territory with the huge contingent of captured Sioux and their allies from the Little Bighorn victory. He read it eagerly. A preliminary head count indicated that there were over seven thousand Indian men, women and children. He figured that at least fifty warriors must have slipped away during the march to the reservation. Still, it was the largest number of Indians ever gathered together in the West. The article went on, "This makes George Armstrong Custer's victory all the more remarkable. It means that his regiment of some 600 men faced over 2,000 or more savage warriors at the Little Bighorn. General Custer is staying in the city in preparation for the burial ceremonies of one of his bravest officers, Captain George Yates, who died from wounds received while leading his command at the battle."

A telegram had come to him earlier through the War Department from his adjutant, First-lieutenant William Cooke. It stated that the regimental command had split the day before, allowing the companies from the outlying posts to head for home, and the companies stationed at Fort Abraham Lincoln to ride triumphantly into their heroes' welcome. One wounded trooper had died en route, and one more who had come back on the *Far West* had passed away. He enclosed the comment, "And Mrs. C. misses you."

He thought about all of those Indians at the Red Cloud reservation. Many would soon return to their own reservations, but the chiefs would be closely supervised—particularly Sitting Bull and Crazy Horse. Yet he believed Sitting Bull would keep his word and not break out for some time. There was something special about him, an aura of honor that even in defeat was palpable.

On fame's eternal camping ground
Their silent tents are spread,
And glory guards with solemn round
The bivouac of the dead.
                    —*Theodore O'Hara*

It was another hot clear day in the capital. Though thunderheads would form and grow that afternoon, at quarter past eleven in the morning, it wasn't yet too muggy. Several thousand Washingtonians and quite a few

Virginians had turned out to attend the funeral. Many of them lined the route that led from Fort Whipple to the grave site in Arlington National Cemetery. At the head of the procession, two of the bandsmen in their Seventh Cavalry uniforms rode abreast on horses Tom Custer had arranged with the commanding officer at Fort Whipple, a colonel by the name of Spurrier. In fact, Colonel Spurrier had been extremely helpful with all of the details, having been ordered to assist by General Sherman himself.

Behind the bandsmen rode the color guard bearing the national flag and the regimental flag with its battle streamers. Next, Custer rode on one of Spurrier's best horses, a shiny black stallion. He was erect in the saddle, handsome in his dress uniform. Behind him, led by another bandsman, was the riderless horse, with an officer's boots customarily positioned backward in the stirrups. Next came the caisson, drawn by two teams of well-groomed horses. On it the flag-draped casket bearing the body of George Yates rolled slowly along. A snare drum played by one of the bandsmen quietly ticked off a cadence in lieu of an actual dirge. Immediately behind, elements of a guards regiment from Maryland marched to the beat of the drum.

At the entrance to the cemetery, the procession turned down a lane that led to the grave site. A canopy had been erected near the freshly dug grave to protect the attendees in the event of rain. Among the many notable persons there were General Sherman, Lieutenant-General Phil Sheridan, four congressman from Michigan, both senators from Michigan, the Secretary of War, a number of wives, two newspaper publishers, W.W. Corcoran, and several lower ranking officers. Tom Custer and Mark Kellogg stood off to the side.

As the casket was unloaded from the caisson and placed over the open grave, the honor guardsmen from Fort Whipple marched into place with their rifles. A chaplain stepped forward to read the eulogy, praising Brevet Colonel Yates for his years of valiant service, his heroism in the big war, and his bravery at the Little Bighorn. The congressman from the district that included Yates's and Custer's hometown of Monroe had to get in a few words, praising the dead officer. Finally, Custer stepped forward. "Ladies and gentlemen," he said gravely, stuttering only once, "One of the finest officers in the army lies in repose before us. He was a great credit to the uniform he wore so proudly. As you have all heard, the Seventh Cavalry's great victory at the Little Bighorn bears his noted mark. I am most proud to have been his commanding officer and his friend. I shall miss him greatly." He started to say more, but obviously moved, he was unable to speak. His gloved hand moved up to wipe away a tear. He stepped back and saluted.

The flag was removed from the casket and folded. Then the honor guard raised its rifles and shattered the air with twelve volleys. The ceremony was over.

Quietly, Mark Kellogg, standing off to the side scribbling on his ever present pad, made note of Custer's tears.

★ ★ ★

"Armstrong, you did a hell of a job." Phil Sheridan turned back from where he was looking out of the window in the transit general's quarters at Fort Whipple. A view of the unfinished stump of the Washington monument could be seen in the distance. "But I knew you would. I just couldn't go against the president when he relieved you. And goddamnit, you deserved it—spouting off in Congress like you did, when you didn't even know what the hell you were talking about!"

"But I heard—"

"I don't even want to hear it." Little Phil was the dark Irishman who had not only been Custer's commander and benefactor in the latter part of the Civil War, but had been almost a father to him in the intervening years. Stumpy, combative, and outspoken, Sheridan was tight in the clique of U. S. Grant and William Tecumseh "Cump" Sherman, the head of the army. Their friendship went back to the war, and their mutual respect had never waned. They were a strange trio: the taciturn Grant, the staccato-voiced Sherman, and the contentious Sheridan. The forty-five-year-old Sheridan, who commanded the Division of the Missouri headquartered in Chicago, was the second ranking officer in the army. "I was so damned angry with you, I could have relieved you myself."

"But you supported me when I appealed to him."

Sheridan sat on the arm of an overstuffed chair. "Because you're the best damned field commander I've got. Okay, now here's what's going to happen. Originally, we were going to send you to Paris as liaison to the French Army, but you deserve a reward. You will be the new boss of the Department of California."

"That's a star command," Custer said.

Sheridan frowned, "Dammit, I know it is."

"So . . ."

"The honorable members of Congress from Michigan have banded together, regardless of party, and are going to get you promoted to brigadier general. That's right, skip you right over full colonel, like they did Crook."

Custer grinned, wanting to pound Little Phil on the back and shout to the heavens. *It was happening!* Keeping himself under control, he asked, "When?"

"You should be promoted at the end of the month. We'll send you out to California right afterward."

Custer grinned again. This time decorum be damned! He jumped straight up and clicked his heels. Sheridan just smiled and shook his head. Once, back in the war, this zestful subordinate of his had whirled him around dancing a jig.

There's something in the parting hour
Will chill the warmest heart—
Yet kindred, comrades, lovers, friends,
Are fated all to part.
　　　　—Elizabeth Bacon Custer, 1868

FORT ABRAHAM LINCOLN *July 27, 1876*

Custer looked around at the faces of his officers and saw anticipation in all of them except Benteen's. Captain Frederick Benteen seemed to be forever against him. Yet he bore the man no malice. He didn't hold grudges. In fact, he'd recommended to Sheridan that Benteen be given field command of the Seventh Cavalry after his departure. The officer was collected and brave under fire, he'd been a colonel during the war, and he was mature. His part of the action at the Little Bighorn had been exemplary. Holding to a standstill Crazy Horse and Gall, with their huge numbers of fierce warriors, he had truly been the key that had made the threat to the women and children possible. He didn't have to like Benteen for it, but neither could he withhold rewarding the man.

Custer recommended other officers for promotions or brevets for their conduct in the battle: his brother Tom, Myles Keogh, Captain Myles Moylan, Captain Tom French, Captain Tom Weir, First-lieutenant Algernon Smith, his brother-in-law—First-lieutenant Jimmi Calhoun, First-lieutenant Edward Godfrey, and his adjutant, First-lieutenant William Cooke. Second-lieutenant Varnum's promotion was already approved.

Now, as he looked at their faces, he realized it would be the last time everyone would be gathered at a formation like this. There had been many others in the preceding years, and he felt a short pang of nostalgia. He cleared his throat. "Gentlemen, I'll make this short and sweet. This is our last officers' call. As you can see, I'm wearing the new shoulder boards of a brigadier general. It was effective today. I have recommended many of you for promotion as well, and I think all of those will go through. As most of you know, I will be leaving in two days to assume command of the Department of California at the Presidio.

"You have all read my note of appreciation, I'm sure, so you know the depth of my gratitude for the noble way you conducted yourselves at the Little Bighorn. Once more, I thank you. I hope our paths cross again." He smiled, raised his fist, then barked, "GarryOwen!"

The officers jumped to their feet responding, "GarryOwen!" as they came to the position of attention. Custer strode briskly out of the room with Adjutant Cooke following.

★ ★ ★

Naturally the regiment held a farewell parade for its famous commander and his lady. All decked out in their fanciest, it's horses groomed to their shiniest, the parade was joined by the post infantrymen and reviewed not only by its departing general and his wife, but by General Alfred Terry, who had come over from St. Paul. The mayor of Bismarck was there and Clement Lounsberry, the newspaperman. Even a dozen "ladies" from the "hog ranches," the whorehouses across the river, had donned their finest, broken out their parasols to protect their tender skin against the summer sun, and were ignoring the hostile stares of the post wives. After all, they'd seen at least parts of many of the men in the regiment.

From the reviewing stand, the lovely Libbie, wearing a dress she had designed and made that resembled a uniform at the bodice, said quietly, "Autie, don't you think it's pretty brazen of *those* women to be here."

Custer chuckled, "I suppose they're a part of the regiment too."

Libbie sighed, "Guess you're right. I noticed the sergeant's wives glaring at them though."

Custer shrugged, smiled again. "I guess they're no threat to any laundress when they're standing up."

Libbie pinched his arm, "You're naughty!"

At that moment the troops began to pass in review to the lively music of the regimental band and Custer stepped forward on the stand, just ahead of General Terry in a position of honor. In spite of his joyful mood, a sudden feeling of sadness enveloped him. It reminded him of the parade when he'd departed his beloved Third Cavalry Division after the war. But that had been different, the Seventh Cavalry, for better or worse, had been his own for a decade, and Fort Abraham Lincoln had been the first permanent home he'd known since he was a boy. It was *his*.

As if to match his thoughts, the band switched to its most spirited rendition of "GarryOwen." Custer pushed back the threatening tears and stood even taller. Could there be any greater tribute?

9

"Oh, darling, it's gorgeous!" Libbie exclaimed. "Now put me down; I'm not a young bride any more."

Custer continued to hold her up in his arms as they moved into the parlor. He nuzzled her neck and said, "Tonight you'll be a bride, my love. I'll make love to you until dawn!"

"Shhhh!" she admonished with a giggle, looking back over his shoulder to where Tom Custer and William Cooke were coming in from the porch. "They'll hear."

Custer nuzzled her neck again. "I imagine they saw that house at Fort Lincoln rock more than once."

Libbie wiggled down, shaking her head in mock dismay. "You are *terrible*, Autie Custer."

The cook, Mary, and Sergeant John Burkman, the orderly, stood smiling in the dining room. They had been sent out a week earlier to get the house ready for its illustrious new occupants. There were no adequate quarters for a brigadier general on post at the Presidio, so the division quartermaster had rented this three-story wood frame house on Lombard Street. It wasn't quite the residence they'd had at Fort Lincoln, but it would certainly do, Libbie thought as she hugged Mary and looked around.

Custer nodded his head in satisfaction as he greeted the servants and walked into the study. He was already picturing where he'd put his trophies on the walls.

The captain who served as the department quartermaster, a bespectacled, white-haired man named Szarzynski, had met them at the train. He said, "Your single officers, General, will be billeted in the Corral, or Bachelors' Hall, on post."

Custer had brought his brother Tom along, as well as William W. Cooke, the Canadian with the magnificent whiskers who had been his regimental adjutant for so many years. Because of the enormous fame of the victory at the Little Bighorn, he wangled all of those promotions for his officers. Several of them had to be jumped over many officers who outranked them—regardless of regimental vacancies—but General Sherman had bowed to the will of the congressman's request and Sheridan's endorsement. It had been some time since the Army had been so popular with the public, and Sherman was astute enough to take advantage of it. Cooke, who held a brevet lieutenant colonelcy from the war, had been promoted to captain. Since Tom had just been promoted to captain a few months before the battle, he remained in that active duty rank. Fred Benteen—in spite of having been Custer's outspoken adversary for years—was promoted to major and given temporary field command of the regiment because of Major Reno's extended leave of absence. The Irishman Myles Keogh had also been promoted to major and remained as a battalion commander.

Various other regimental officers had been awarded brevet promotions of a lower rank and sere "mentioned in dispatches," as the saying for written commendations was described. Numerous Medals of Honor had been awarded for valor, most notably to Benteen, Captain Tom Weir, Lieutenants Godfrey, McIntosh, Varnum, Algernon Smith, and Doctor Porter. Custer had also seen to it that his brother-in-law, Jimmi Calhoun got one. George Yates was awarded the medal posthumously.

Six sergeants, three corporals, and seven privates were also awarded a Medal of Honor. And one part-Sioux scout, Bloody Knife, was given the rank of sergeant. John Burkman had been promoted to sergeant by Custer the day he pinned his star on.

Another member of the "royal family" whom Custer had brought along was his youngest brother, Boston. The twenty-eight-year-old Boston had at one time aspired to attend the Naval Academy, but instead opted to serve as a civilian forage master for the Seventh Cavalry's regimental quartermaster. He was hired on as a guide for the Little Bighorn campaign and had been with the pack train as the battle developed. But in its midst, he had pitched in as a trooper and bravely accounted for himself with Reno, who had commended him for gallantry. Boston was more religious than his two older brothers, but also full of fun, and often participated in their practical jokes.

As the Custer trunks were brought into the house by orderlies, an open carriage pulled up outside, and an aide hurriedly opened the back seat door to permit its occupant to step down. He was Major-general Irvin McDowell, the fifty-eight-year-old commanding general of the Division of the Pacific and Custer's new boss. Having lost the first Battle of Bull Run, and later exercising poor command at other battles, McDowell had been shipped out to California in the middle of the war. He had recently returned to command the division that governed the West Coast and some adjoining territories. He was described as squarely and powerfully built with a frank, but quite agreeable manner.

With his aide in tow, General McDowell hurried up the porch steps and through the front door. Cooke saw him, brought his heels together, and shouted, "*Attention!*"

McDowell waved a hand at him. "At ease. Where's General Custer?"

"Right here, General!" Custer said, coming into the parlor and tossing off a salute.

McDowell stuck out his hand. "Welcome to San Francisco, General," he said warmly. "I want to congratulate you on the Little Bighorn and on your promotion."

At that moment Libbie came into the room smiling, and curtsied. McDowell took her hand and kissed it as he murmured, "I've heard of your bounteous charm and beauty, Mrs. Custer. I bid you welcome."

A few minutes later, General McDowell drew Custer into a bedroom and closed the door. "I'm leaving early this evening for Vancouver, Custer, so I won't be in the office for a couple of weeks. Consider this your briefing. Your headquarters is downtown with mine in the Phelan Building. You'll have plenty of time to get settled, but I want you to know about a major change that's taking place. General Sherman has agreed to transfer the Territory of Arizona to your Department of California. The Apaches are acting up down there again, and since you are our most famous Indian fighter, we feel you're the man to get it settled."

Custer nodded, feeling a tinge of excitement. This wasn't going to be just a quiet, boring assignment after all. "When do you want me to leave, sir?" he asked.

"Take a little while to get acquainted with the rest of your command, then prepare to go on down to Tucson."

★ ★ ★

Libbie took off her wide-brimmed hat and let the cool breeze blow her brown hair back from her face as she looked far out to sea and thought of all the ships that had sailed toward where she now stood. She loved the Presidio and enjoyed going on post for any reason. She liked the large, low Spanish-style building that was the oldest on the fort, and she enjoyed looking at the quarters on Officers Row, as well as the views of the bay. She came out as often as possible, doing some of her shopping at the post trader's store, and of course, seeing the post surgeon for any medical problem. She also went to see Autie's two horses that were stabled at the post, sometimes to exercise the dogs. Since their rental house didn't have a very large garden, they had brought only the five most favored of Autie's hounds.

A hundred years earlier, as the Declaration of Independence was being signed in Philadelphia, a small group of Spanish colonists had raised their nation's flag over this beautiful promontory overlooking the Golden Gate. The flagpole was in the center of the tiny adobe fort they built, which they named the Presidio of San Francisco. In 1822, with the independence of Mexico, the Mexican flag was raised over the post. It would fly in the often strong onshore winds until 1846, when California became part of the United States as a result of the Mexican War. Now, thirty years later, Libbie could sit on this bench at an old gun emplacement overlooking the water and ponder the richness of history she had joined. It gave her such a warm feeling!

She had developed a strong respect and a *feel* for history in the years during her marriage to one of America's most flamboyant officers. After all, he had helped make some of it. Certainly she'd been treated well by some of its leaders such as Sheridan, who'd welcomed her to his Fort Leavenworth quarters when Autie was court-martialed, and had even given her one of the tables Grant and Lee had used for the surrender at Appomattox.

She had just finished attending a tea in her honor at the post commander's house. All of the officers' wives had attended. They had all been most gracious, she thought as she watched a big four-master sailing ship work its way past Alacatraz Island. *Isla de los Alcatraces* (Isle of the Pelicans) the Spanish had called it. She liked to watch the silvery beams of its lighthouse at night. She had decided to write about it in the story she was beginning to piece together about the Presidio. It was something to fill her time. Being here was different from Fort Lincoln—there she had responsibilities, while here she was the *second* ranking officer's wife, even though Autie had his star back. She sighed. Perhaps a charity for the enlisted children would be a worthy cause. She looked back to where Sergeant Burkman sat with the surrey. Yes, she'd go home and start planning it now. Too bad Annie Yates wasn't here to help her.

Red Elk squatted beside Crazy Horse as he placed feathers in the shaft of a hickory arrow. "I want to learn the *Wasicus* language," he said abruptly.

Crazy Horse didn't look up. The famous war leader was a man of few words and fewer expressions. The latter was partially due to the revolver wound that had shattered his jaw several years earlier—the result of his adulterous affair with the beautiful Black Buffalo Woman, a niece of the great Sioux chief, Red Cloud.

Although he was Oglala Sioux and Red Elk was Hunkpapa, the young warrior had served as a strong war leader under him during the recent battle against Three Stars, General Crook, at the Rosebud. "Why?" he asked.

Red Elk had told no one about his vow to kill Long Hair, had in fact spoken to no one at all since his wife's funeral, except to ask for directions on the reservation. He had just now ridden into the Oglala camp, but he knew he could confide in the great Crazy Horse with total trust. "I will kill Long Hair," he replied.

Crazy Horse looked up with sudden interest. "How?"

"I don't know. But I will—sometime."

"I heard he is gone from our country."

"I'll find him."

"When?"

"By the end of my life."

Crazy Horse nodded his head, a touch of his hair's light color highlighted in the rays of the early September sun. "Perhaps the *Wasicus* agent can help. Or I heard Standing Bear has come back to mend his problems with Sitting Bull. He is a *Wasicus*. Talk to the chief."

★ ★ ★

The huge collection of Sioux from the Little Bighorn had been brought to two reservations in the northeast corner of Nebraska—that of Red Cloud and of Spotted Tail—the powerful Sioux leaders who had made treaties with the government. At this stage of reservation life on the Plains, it meant the different branches of the tribe such as the Teton Sioux—or Lakota Sioux, as they were often called—would have their own villages over a wide designated area.

The biggest problem with the reservation system was that it put borders on a tribal unit's hunting domain. Then there was the problem of food supplies that had been promised, which were always inadequate, whether because of crooked agents and other forms of graft, or because the supply system itself was inadequate. In fact, Secretary of War Belknap's near impeachment for kickbacks had proven how bad the system was being managed. Ruthless men who saw the Indian as a savage standing in the way of progress and wealth, downright Indian haters, or simple settlers making a new way of life, clashed with an impractical, philosophical faction. The proponents of a liberal Indian approach, including some vociferous activists who liked to castigate the white man, had no idea of the truth of the situation. A basic fact was that the stronger tribes subjugated the weaker ones. The strong Sioux warrior nation had been at war on the Plains for the century it had been there—taking lands as they saw fit from their weaker predecessors.

Within the tribal units, power struggles were nothing new. The current situation at Red Cloud's reservation was an example. Red Cloud was a powerful leader who wasn't actually a chief. He was a "shirt wearer" or senior councilman, who had assumed firm control of his people. And now, thrust into his fief was the powerful chief and spiritual head of the tribal elements who had for years refused the *Wasicus'* offers—the stubborn Sitting Bull.

There were two kinds of Indians according to Sitting Bull—agency Indians and free Indians. His earlier taunt, "You are fools to make yourselves slaves to a piece of fat bacon, some hard-tack, and a little sugar and coffee," had made the proud Red Cloud angry. It was said that there wasn't room on the same agency for the two Lakota leaders.

Sitting Bull and his Hunkpapas were encamped some four miles away from Crazy Horse's Oglala's. It was Red Elk's home village, but both of his parents were dead, and with Late Star gone, he felt that he no longer had a home. He'd given the beautiful tipi she had made to one of her friends, and the rest of her belongings to those women who had lost everything in the battle. He could sleep in a robe or a blanket next to his one remaining pony anytime, for his home was on the path of Long Hair.

Sitting Bull was sitting in front of his tipi talking to the barrel-chested Gall when Red Elk walked up. After a minute, the chief told him to join them and he squatted next to Gall. "Great chief," he said, "I've come for your advice."

Sitting Bull nodded for him to continue.

"I have made a vow of vengeance to kill Long Hair," Red Elk continued, "and I think I can best carry it out if I speak the *Wasicus'* language."

Gall listened intently as Sitting Bull nodded again, apparently unfazed by the young war leader's announcement. Red Elk went on, "I have been told that the traitor, Standing Bear, has been forgiven by you and has returned to our people."

"It is so," the chief replied. "The war against the Long Knives will end only when they leave us. Standing Bear knows their ways and is valuable to us."

"Will you, honored chief, permit me to learn the words from him?"

Sitting Bull looked at the young war leader for a couple of moments, then slowly nodded his head in agreement.

★ ★ ★

Red Elk found Standing Bear grooming his spotted pony at the corral. Known among the Sioux as "The Grabber," Standing Bear's American name was Frank Grouard. He was born on a South Pacific island in 1850, the son of a Mormon missionary and the daughter of a high chief. From his mother, he inherited the dark complexion that later made the Sioux believe he was Indian. He was raised in California and Utah, striking out on his own as a teamster and mail courier in his mid-teens. Captured by the Sioux and kept prisoner, he was adopted into Sitting Bull's family after several years with the Lakota. He had a falling out with Crazy Horse in 1875, and had left his Sioux life to become a scout for General Crook. Strangely, he was acting as such when Crazy Horse attacked and fought Crook to a standstill at the Rosebud shortly before the Battle of the Little Bighorn.

Grouard was a very big man with a large head and neck, thick black hair, and large, expressive dark eyes. When Red Elk, who had known him for years, explained what he wanted, Grouard signed back, "I speak with my hands mostly. How can I teach you English?"

"You know the white man's words. Sitting Bull says you can help me."

Grouard thought for a moment. His return to the Sioux was tenuous, to say the least. Sitting Bull was a great spiritual leader, but he was also one who could be affronted—and having left an intimate position in his family to fight for the Long Knives had been a major affront. The fact that the chief had accepted him back at all was because the leader had some plan working, some forthcoming action against the *Wasicus* that was known to no one. It would be wise to accept any wish Sitting Bull might voice.

"All right," the Grabber said in Sioux, "I will teach you English verbally—aloud. But you must work hard. I will try to get a primer from the agent."

Red Elk nodded, pleased. "Primer?"

Grouard made a gesture indicating a book. "Words on paper."

The young war leader had just made his first step into the world of the white man.

Far to the southwest, in the center of Arizona territory, another family of Indians had been forced into reservation life in an area that made the Dakota and Nebraska agencies look like Utopia. They were the Apaches, a named derived from the Zuni word for "enemy," and they were among the most formidable warriors the North American continent had ever seen. For centuries they had been at war with the northern Mexicans, sometimes, it was said, observing a peace to allow those who owned *rancheros* and *haciendas* time to restock them as a farmer might allow his land and herds to grow healthy again, but the bitterness never ended. Too many Apache scalps had been paid for by the Sonora and Chihuahua governments for the *N'de*, as they called themselves, to ever forget.

The San Carlos Apache reservation as worse than bleak. The Indians referred to it as absolutely the worst place ever stolen from them. No one had ever lived there with any permanence. It seemed to be Ussen's—their God the Father—abomination. Catholics might call it a purgatory, hell. The only vegetation was some cactus, and the insects were ghastly, hatching by the millions in the pools alongside the channel of the sluggish river that provided brackish, nearly unpotable water. Clouds of mosquitoes came from the same water except in the cold weather. Gila monsters, centipedes, tarantulas, and the hated rattlesnakes abounded on the reservation. In the summer the temperature could reach 120 degrees, and in the winter the place could get as cold as a high mountain peak in a blizzard.

San Carlos was where a disdainful Indian Bureau had determined all the clans of Apaches would reside. And clans they were, much the same as the Sioux. Some tribes might be classified as Indian nations, but not the Apaches. A great chief named Mangas Coloradas came the closest to unifying them. He married off his daughters to chiefs such as Cochise and Cuchillo Negro to effect a degree of unification.

With the coming of the white man to Apacheria, roughly the area encompassing much of the territories of New Mexico and Arizona, the encroachment resulted in a change of enmity. So-called depredations by the Apaches were met with force by blue-coated soldiers. In 1863, Mangas Coloradas was treacherously murdered and rumored beheaded by soldiers under a General Joseph West. Cochise, a powerful and wise leader of the Chiracahuas who saw the wisdom of peace with the white man, died in 1874. This left leaders such as the crafty Eskiminzin, the less-than-honorable Geronimo, the fighting Victorio, Juh, Loco, and lesser types to continue the struggle in justifiable reaction to government perfidy or at their whim.

With such a stubborn warrior culture, it was only natural that elements of different clans under strong war leaders would break out of reservation control and go back to their pillaging ways. General George Crook had brought sensibility and control to the situation in the early seventies, but now a strong hand was again needed

★ ★ ★

Enter Brigadier-General George Armstrong Custer.

The major who was attached to the San Carlos reservation was named Leslie. He was tall and thin, an infantry officer. He spoke quietly as he briefed Custer and his brother Tom, who was now his big brother's aide-de-camp. "General, the biggest problem is Geronimo. He's a bad one. Years ago, the Mexicans treacherously killed his family. You can't blame him for hating them, but he hates whites as well, and he supposedly has some of that Indian power you hear about. His word means nothing. He'll promise one thing, and take twenty or thirty warriors on a breakout the next day."

"Is he a chief?" Custer asked.

"No, some kind of a medicine man."

"How come you don't put him in irons?" Tom asked.

"It's Clum's call."

Custer had read about John Clum in Crook's report. The Indian agent had taken over San Carlos two years earlier at the tender age of twenty-three, and had immediately taken on a strong role. He was short in stature, but agile and strong, presumptuous, belligerent and cocky. Custer knew all about that sort of thing. What he didn't like in the report was the statement that Clum was contemptuous of the military in general and officers in particular.

"John Clum is a little Napoleon, General. He insists that he's in command here, and goes out of his way to demonstrate it."

"General Crook stated that he's totally honest and utterly fearless." Custer said.

"Yes, I think he's dedicated," Major Leslie said. "He's just inclined to be, well, an *arsehole*."

★ ★ ★

That evening Custer met with Clum at the agent's house. Clum was cool, as expected. "I really don't know why you are here, General," he said. "I have everything under control."

"Arizona has been placed under my command," Custer replied casually, "I'm here to see what needs to be done."

"Nothing more by the military. My Indian police can handle things quite readily."

"I understand Geronimo and Victorio are outside, raiding and stirring up trouble. Is that handling things quite readily, Mr. Clum?"

The twenty-five-year-old agent's eyes narrowed. "I will tend to them without any military interference, General. This isn't Sioux country."

Custer smiled. In a way, he liked Clum's arrogance. "Nor are any of these Apaches a Sitting Bull. But I don't want a struggle with you, Clum.

I hear you are, in spite of your being difficult, an honest man with the best interests of the Indians primary in your agenda. Now tell me something about this Victorio."

Clum frowned and walked to a small bookcase, getting control of himself before he turned. "Victorio is chief of the Warm Springs. Their homelands are generally on the west side of the Rio Grande in southern New Mexico. A place called Ojo Caliente is what you might call his home—thus the name. There are rumors that he was a captured Mexican child, but I don't believe them. He's stubborn and a brave war chief."

"How many followers does he have with him?"

"About seventy warriors and perhaps twenty women and children."

"And Geronimo?

"Possibly twenty-five followers and maybe fifteen women and children."

Custer thought about all of those Sioux at the Little Bighorn. "Doesn't sound very formidable."

The agent snorted. "You don't know the Apaches. A half-dozen of them on the warpath can create hysteria."

"What about Al Sieber, the scout?. I've heard he's quite good."

"Mr. Sieber is most dependable."

Custer nodded his head. "What do you plan on doing about these renegades?"

Clum frowned. "General, if you'll keep your soldiers out of the way, I'll bring them back in my own manner."

Custer smiled. "Young man, my soldiers are my business."

★ ★ ★

Custer rode north over the Salt River with his small escort. He had acquired the services of the highly regarded Al Seiber as his guide and chief scout. Mark Kellogg had also joined him, having come down from Bismarck at the general's invitation. Custer planned on making short shrift of this Apache problem and he didn't want any of its success to be missed by the public. Besides, he knew who was still picking up the tab for Kellogg's expenses—Bennett of the New York *Herald*. The officer in charge at Fort Apache, Major Tom Waugh, was no friend of John Clum.

That reservation—the White Mountain Apache—had also been designated as part of Clum's agency, and the major had once arrested the agent's San Carlos policemen who came up to establish authority.

Custer spent three days at Fort Apache, interviewed two Apache chiefs, and rode back down to Fort Lowell near Tucson. There he spoke with the commander of the three troops of the Sixth cavalry that were stationed there. "Captain Cavaretta," he said at length, "I'm going to make my temporary headquarters here, although I'll stay in Tucson." I plan on taking to the field quite soon and will need a good horse, a Sibley tent, a few mules for a pack train, and an escort of twelve of your most experienced troopers."

★ ★ ★

Tucson was the territorial capital, but it was still a dusty little adobe town trying to stretch its muscles and be another Santa Fe. The trouble was, it hadn't been around long enough, nor was it big enough. It was sun-baked and had more than a few men who not only hated Apaches, but were quick to make a fast a buck from them. Some of the broken faith as well as downright murder and treachery that plagued the Arizona Apaches was purportedly organized by what was referred to as the "Tucson Ring" or the "Indian Ring."

One writer referred to them as "border bums . . . a shifty population of gamblers, road agents, cattle rustlers and loafers who hung around town like a cloud of dirty insects." A more sinister element were the shadowy vultures who made their money on unscrupulous Army contracts and supplies for the reservation. It was rumored that these predators kept some of the Apaches stirred up so the Army would keep more soldiers stationed in the area who, along with their horses, had to be fed.

There were, of course, staunch and honest citizens in Tucson as well, but they couldn't counteract the bad elements. When Custer was interviewed by the editor of the Tucson *Star*, he stated, "I'm going to look closely at all of the contracts, and if I find malfeasance or any element of criminal conduct on the part of anyone regarding the Army or the Indians, I'll take swift action."

Mark Kellogg took notes to send off to the *Herald*.

The only hotel in town that suggested quality was the Orndorf. Standing on the northeast corner of West Pennington and North Main, the two-story adobe structure had a rather imposing upper verandah. Its dining room was considered the best in town and its saloon was where the governor, mayor, and other influential citizens conducted much of their business. Custer took over a two-room suite for himself and another room for his brother Tom. Mark Kellogg slept down the hall.

When he was in town, Custer spent every evening working on a lecture series he was preparing. Several months earlier, he had been approached by the Lyceum Circuit people to go on a highly paid lecture tour. This would have defrayed most of that big debt he'd incurred, the one he'd had to welsh on to this point. When this Apache business was settled, which brought him more fame, he planned on taking an extended leave of absence to cash in on the offer.

It seemed as if he always needed money.

October 17th Inst.

My Dearest Standby,
I hope you are warm and comfortable without me in San Francisco.

I have been out in these hills now for over three weeks. I've met with Old Nana (he must be 75! and hard as iron) and with Cochise's son, Taza, who is out with about fifty Chiracahuas.

He agreed to take them back to San Carlos. I also found Victorio and about a hundred of his Warm Springs up in the mountains near Silver City, NM Territory. It's out of my departmental area, but General Hatch, who's in command over there, doesn't care. All of those Apaches are supposed to be in San Carlos anyway.

Victorio is a proud and ornery sort. He wouldn't promise me anything, so I told him the story of the Little Bighorn, and stated that my horse soldiers would come and take his women and children, even if it meant harm to some of them, as it did with Sitting Bull. I think he'll come around. Geronimo is the one I want. He's a liar and malcontent, and belongs in irons. It's the only way he can be trusted.

And now my beautiful and passionate bride, I hate to think of yet another night without you, without your smooth hot skin against me,

The election is a standoff!" Mark Kellogg exclaimed, looking at the telegram a boy had just delivered to Custer's suite at the Orndorf Hotel in Tucson.

Custer looked up from his writing. He'd been keenly interested in the presidential election for several reasons. He wanted the Democrats to win, but he had known the Republican candidate, Rutherford Hayes, during the war. Hayes had been heroic on a number of occasions and had a horse shot from under him at Cedar Creek, where Custer had also had his moments of glory. Hayes had also been brevetted Major-general about the same time as Custer. One other factor connected them: both were Ohioans.

"Tilden has won the popular vote, but is one electoral vote short of victory," Kellogg added.

"How many states to go?" Custer asked. Samuel J. Tilden, the sixty-two year old New York Democrat, was a reformer and the man who became famous for bringing down the notorious Tweed Ring during his governorship.

"Florida, Louisiana and South Carolina, plus one challenged vote in Oregon."

"Aren't they Republican carpetbag states, the Southern ones?"

"Yes, sir."

Custer shook his head. "Politics is unbelievable. Most Americans want one candidate, but they can't elect him outright. The politicians do it."

Kellogg grinned. "Sure doesn't sound like democracy, does it, General?"

"When will they know?"

"Don't know. An electoral commission may have to rule on it."

Custer shook his head again. "A man would have to be crazy to get involved in politics."

Al Sieber was thirty-two years old. Born in Germany, he came to the United States as a boy and later fought in the Civil War. Soon after, he began his career as a scout for the army. He was a natural outdoorsman, a good tracker, and spoke Apache well. His special knack for managing Apache scouts made him extremely valuable for any army commander wishing to find and reach renegades. Geronimo was the most defiant of the renegades.

When he was a young man, Geronimo had taken his family along to a feast sponsored by the Mexican army at a town named Janos several miles into Old Mexico. A treacherous commander had gotten the Apache men drunk, and then attacked the camp where their families were sleeping. Geronimo's mother, his wife, and his three children were all killed. With burning vengeance, the warrior had killed many Mexicans over the years. Though he didn't hate the white men who had come to Apacheria with the same passion, he had no qualms about stealing from them or killing one once in awhile. He was also a noted medicine man among his people.

When evading the American army, he led his followers into the wilds of various Mexican mountain ranges, which he knew quite well. Sieber's scouts found him two weeks earlier and he agreed to meet with Custer. Now, as the general rode into the appointed place in a pass surrounded by tall, quiet mountains, his escort of thirty troopers looked around uneasily. Tom rode on his left, Sieber on his right. Mark Kellogg followed. Reaching the center of the pass, Sieber led the small column to a spot where boulders dotted the side of a grassy hillside. He dismounted, saying, "This is where we'll wait, General."

Custer frowned. He didn't like being the one to wait, but he nodded his head and got off his horse. He was wearing his trademark light tan buckskins and a broad-brimmed black cavalry campaign hat. He took it off and wiped the sweat from his neck and brow. It was a warm day for mid-November. He looked around at the surrounding peaks. It was a good place for an ambush. As if he sensed Custer's concern, Tom said, "I'll deploy the men among these rocks so we'll be okay."

★ ★ ★

After an hour, Custer's patience was wearing thin. "They must know we're here. I'm sure they observed us for the past two or three miles."

"Time means nothing to Indians," Sieber responded. "He's just asserting himself."

"Well, by God, I'll *assert* him!" Custer snapped. He pulled out his pocket watch. "I'll give him fifteen more minutes."

Five minutes later, some of the renegade Apaches began to appear almost mystically. Their clothing was quite ragged and each warrior carried a rifle as they edged in closer to Custer's force. Suddenly a stocky man with a broad face wearing a multi-colored bandanna strode from a small group of nearby rocks. There was no mistaking his air of authority.

Sieber moved out to meet him and greeted him in Apache, then introduced Custer. Some dried beef was offered as Custer sat on a rock and Geronimo squatted slightly above him. Custer was very good with the universal sign language of the Plains, and his hands flew through his opening comments. "I have come to meet the great medicine man and warrior."

Geronimo watched him coolly. As Custer continued signing, he turned to the chief scout. "Tell Long Hair I do not speak with him in the language of the cowards to the north."

Sieber translated. Custer remained impassive as he said, "We can speak through you, but I did not come all the way here to be insulted. Tell him I wish to know why he left the reservation."

Geronimo's aloofness continued as he replied, "I do as I wish."

"But what about your promises?"

"They are but words to please Clum."

Custer frowned. "When you break them, you lie. I am told the great Cochise and Mangas Coloradas do not lie. Why should you?"

Geronimo shrugged. "I am not Cochise."

Custer got to his feet, looked away, then drew one of his bone-handled pistols and aimed it away from the Apache leader. "It will soon be cold. I offer you new clothes for your people, and a fine horse for you, if you will accompany my escort back to San Carlos."

Geronimo remained impassive as Sieber translated.

Custer went on, aiming the pistol again and *clicking* it on an empty chamber. "If you do not agree, I will bring many soldiers and hunt you until I kill you and everyone with you. I will hunt you forever." He looked coldly into the renegade's eyes. "I will kill you, cut off your head, and leave it hanging from the tallest tree."

Geronimo's eyes narrowed, showing anger. Finally he said, "For our women and children, I will think on Long Hair's words."

"I will wait just one day for your decision," Custer said, holstering his pistol. "If you do not come, my soldiers will begin the hunt at the first moon."

★ ★ ★

The following day at mid-afternoon, the small column of Apaches, led by their stocky leader, slowly filed into the pass. Al Sieber again hurried out from the encampment to meet them. Mark Kellogg scribbled, "Looking bedraggled, as only families who have lived in the wilderness, staying constantly on the move, can look, the clan of Geronimo came trudging into the bivouac of General George Armstrong Custer. The hero of the Little Bighorn had once again conquered a powerful Indian opponent, but this time with diplomacy and the power of his iron will. The warriors looked sullen, the women downcast—"

★ ★ ★

When Custer returned to Fort Lowell, a telegram awaited him. Its news was stimulating.

> BRIGADIER-GENERAL GEORGE ARMSTRONG CUSTER:
> Due to the promotion and reassignment of Major-general Alfred H. Terry, you are directed to report to Headquarters, Department of Dakota in St. Paul, Minnesota, no later than January 30, 1877 to assume command of that department. Travel and administrative orders to follow.
>
> W. T. SHERMAN
> CMDG. GEN., US ARMY

Custer stared at the telegram. He had never been particularly close to Terry, even though he had served under the man for over three years. Terry *had* made a strong appeal to Grant to return command of the Seventh Cavalry to him prior to the Little Bighorn, so he was glad to hear of his promotion. Terry had a reputation of being a bright and a nice man, and he was the only non-West Pointer to keep stars on his shoulders after the war. But enough of Terry, the orders excited him. He'd be working for Sheridan again, and the Seventh Cavalry would be under him again as he supervised the reservations of the Sioux whose defeat had made his return to power possible.

And now he could go home to Libbie.

The climate of the northern Plains could be most pleasant or it could be vicious in its extremes. The summer sun could parch the prairie grass, cause the streams to dry up, and beat down with unrelenting heat for weeks at a time. Or it could turn arriving Pacific moisture into towering thunderheads that often burst with darkly driving downpours, transforming complacent valleys into sudden ponds and drowning everything that didn't escape. In the winter, similar storms might dump heavy snow that could be whipped into deep drifts by icy gales, plunging temperatures to levels that rapidly froze nearly anything that breathed. In their violent tossing of moisture to freezing levels, these storms could produce hail projectiles that endangered everything in their path. The northern Plains was certainly not a place for the timid. Yet it yielded rich game of a wide variety, including the prized buffalo from which the Sioux garnered not only the red meat that comprised so much of their diet, but the many other products its carcass produced.

The Lakotas always followed the buffalo herds. And the buffalo herds knew no boundaries. The Lakotas were hunters and warriors, and any other life was totally alien to them. It was particularly alien to Sitting Bull, who simply could not accept his role as a prisoner. No words could change that opinion; he was a *prisoner* of the United States. A week after Red Elk came to the village, the chief went to the army commander overseeing the reservation and told him his Hunkpapas and their friends the Blackfeet Sioux could not remain with the troublesome Red Cloud. It would mean war, he insisted, asking that they be moved north to the Standing Rock agency. The move was approved quickly, and the long trip north began.

It was all part of Sitting Bull's plan. And now the second phase of the plan had been completed. Red Elk and a strong force of young warriors who had served under him at the Rosebud raided north to steal horses and some rifles from the despised Rees. Leaving the thirty-two head of stolen ponies in a secure canyon with two of his warriors, he led the rest of the party back into Yellowstone country and in a series of fast midnight raids, made off with nearly one hundred ponies from the hated Crow. Splitting his force, he headed back to Dakota country where the Ree horses were hidden. The angry Crows came after the herd, but Red Elk ambushed them twice, and dissuaded them from further pursuit.

In a large canyon twenty miles northwest of the Hunkpapa/Blackfeet camp on the west side of the Standing Rock agency, the young war leader left his stolen mounts and rode in to inform the great chief that his mission was a success. Now phase three of the plan had been executed. On the night after rations were issued by the government, meaning there would be at least a short period when they wouldn't be missed, Sitting Bull led one hundred and fifty-one lodges—over a thousand Hunkpapas—away from the White Father's minions. Departing at the fall of dark, the column quickly split into three prongs, heading for the waiting horses.

Since none of the agent's people missed the fleeing Lakotas for three days, no pursuit was mounted until the rapidly moving columns had a good head start. Sitting Bull crossed the Little Missouri River, skirting Fort Buford to the south and veering above Fort Peck to the north, then headed directly to Grandmother country. Pushing his people, now guarded by warriors with more stolen guns on the appropriated ponies, he managed to avoid contact with US Army pursuers, and reached Wood Mountain in Canada without a major conflict or encountering a winter storm.

There, he settled his people into new surroundings. The same warriors who had guarded the column now found a large herd of buffalo and killed enough to provide food until Sitting Bull could convince the redcoats of the Grandmother to help.

He was again free from the Long Knives and their hated reservations.

* * *

Custer received word of Sitting Bull's breakout shortly after arriving back at the Presidio, and before departing for his new assignment. He stared at the telegram from Sheridan that Captain Cooke brought into his office. Glancing up at his adjutant, he said, "Looks as if we aren't finished with the old boy yet."

"No, sir. He's a strong one."

"I wonder what those officers were doing to let him slip through like that. Surely all of those Sioux must have passed close to Fort Lincoln. Benteen must have been asleep. He's still in temporary command of the Seventh Cavalry, isn't he?"

"Yes, General, he is."

Custer frowned. "Well, we'll just have to see about him, won't we? By the way, do you remember how the government structure works up there in Canada, William?"

Cooke, who came from a wealthy family in Ontario, stroked his whiskers and replied, "No, but I'll write to pater and find out."

Custer nodded his head. "Good. Now see to the orders getting you and Tom transferred to St. Paul." As his adjutant departed, Custer looked out the window and thought about Sitting Bull. In a way, he respected the powerful chief for breaking free.

It was something George Armstrong Custer could understand, but that didn't alter the fact that he'd soon have the responsibility of getting all of those Sioux back where they belonged. And without a doubt, that would mean defeating Sitting Bull in some way again.

Was that noble chief's star really aligned with his own?

* * *

Major Frederick Benteen, interim commander of the Seventh Cavalry Regiment, wasn't a happy man. Yes, he'd been promoted after the Little Bighorn, and he'd been given the plum field command of the regiment (actual command rested with Colonel Samuel Sturgis, who remained away on extended administrative duty). But something was missing. Maybe, he'd told himself, it was not having Custer around to hate. Life just wasn't interesting enough. Actually, the Virginian was suffering from back pain that he feared was spinal meningitis—a logical assumption since three of his four children had died of the dreaded inflammation. Whatever it was, the white-haired cavalry officer who had distinguished himself through-out the Civil War and at the Little Bighorn was thinking about doing something else with his life before getting to the rocking chair stage.

He had a well-to-do cousin in Syracuse, New York, who had written him about running for Congress from that city's district. The cousin was also the county chairman of the local Republican party. New York State had peculiar requirements regarding residency for those who wanted to hold office and he would be eligible to run soon after establishing a home there. "Your heroics in the battle," his cousin had written, "as described in the New York City newspapers, have brought you forcibly before the public. I can safely say the patriotic voters here will be easily enough led, should you decide to run for office.

"The incumbent has recently undergone some adverse publicity regarding his part in the war. It seems he was on detached duty in the capital during the Battle of Fredericksburg, rather than performing heroic duty in its midst, as he had previously stated. A bloody shirt can easily defeat him." Fred Benteen knew what a bloody shirt was—a nickname for a man who was active in battle, a hero.

"When you get out of the army," the letter went on, "I have a livery stable that I can give you to manage, and pay you quite handsomely to do so. That will get you by until the election in '78. Let me know." It was signed, "Your admiring cousin, Charles Abernathy."

Benteen went into the dining room of the big Custer house that he was now occupying and found his wife, Catherine, seated at the table reading a book. "I think I'm going to do it, Cate," he announced.

She looked up. "Do what?"

"Get out and do as Cousin Charlie suggests—become a politician."

"Aren't you a bit outspoken for that?"

"Perhaps, but I think sometimes the public likes to hear it direct."

She sighed, "Oh, Fred, I love this house so, and being the commander's wife is so invigorating for me."

Benteen relit his pipe. "Being a congressman's wife will have its perks too."

"But are you sure you can win?"

"Cousin Charlie seems to think I can."

"Well, I'll go along with whatever you decide, darling."

Benteen nodded his head. "I'll write my letter of resignation tomorrow, requesting an effective date of February 28. That should give the War Office enough time to get a replacement here. Maybe they'll call Reno back from his extended leave."

Cate Benteen wasn't the only army wife making a change that didn't suit her. Libbie Custer really didn't like the idea of leaving San Francisco. In the few months she had lived there, she had become quite attached to both the city and the Presidio. She'd made some casual new friends, and her charities were challenging. But, as Autie often told her, she was "a good little trooper" and "would answer to the call to duty, wherever it might be."

Now, as she served the chocolate cake she had baked herself, she looked at the small clan of Custers sitting around the dinner table and announced, "This was personally constructed by Standby Custer, the last of the little tag-alongs, for her three frolicsome boys. May they continue to conquer the world and always share their talents."

Tom and Boston raised their wine glasses, as Custer held up his coffee cup. They all said in unison, "Hear, hear!"

Tom patted her on the fanny and said, "And may they always have their lovely mommy around to give them a wonderful piece of cake."

"Speaking of that," Boston said, looking at Custer, "I've made a decision, big brother."

"And what's that?" Custer replied.

"I've decided not to give the girls of St. Paul my sparkling company."

"Oh?"

"No, I've found one right here I like. My new job is going to start paying well as the market continues to boom, and lastly, I *like* California. I think it has a great future. So I'm staying here."

Custer shrugged. "Well, it's your life." Boston had been selling real estate since his arrival in the city.

Tom's light eyes twinkled, "Autie'll be glad he doesn't have to feed you anymore. You eat more than all of his hounds."

"Ha! And what about you? You're always hanging around at mealtime."

Tom raised an eyebrow in mock affront. "I, sir, am here to spread my wit and great charm amongst the family, and to make sure that such remarkable chocolate cake does not go to waste."

Custer chuckled, then asked, "Who's the girl?"

Tom laughed again. "He found her in a sporting house down on the waterfront."

"*Tom!* " Libbie scolded as Boston threw him a look of mock anger

"Not true," Boston replied. "She's the daughter of my mortgage banker, Sharon Rose Conroy. She's beautiful, smarter than any of those sporting types Tom fools around with, and I think I'm going to marry her."

"Oh, Boston," Libbie exclaimed, "I'm so pleased!"

Everyone raised a drink in a toast. "When is all of this going to come about?" Custer asked.

"Probably in the spring. I've already found a room in a boarding house on Sutter. I'm moving in on Sunday."

Custer nodded his head. "We'll all miss you, but if that's what you want—"

"I'm twenty-eight, Autie. It's time for me to quit drifting."

"I understand." Custer thought back to when he was twenty-eight. He'd been a general for five years.

Libbie beamed. She'd been trying to get the two younger Custers married for years. "You'll have to bring her to St. Paul for your honeymoon." She kissed Boston's cheek. "Congratulations, my dear."

★ ★ ★

CHICAGO, ILLINOIS *January 24, 1877*

"I told Sherman, I *wanted* you, Custer. That's why you got transferred back here so fast."

Lieutenant-general Philip Henry Sheridan was the number two man in the army, outranked only by General of the Army W. T. Sherman. His military career had a stormy start—his got suspended and spent five years getting through West Point because of fighting. Then he'd spent seven years as a bold second lieutenant fighting Indians before the Civil War. Fighting was one thing "Little Phil" knew how to do. Never known as a strategic genius, he was aggressive, and endeared to his troops because of his bluntness and fearlessness. Now forty-five, and expanding a bit at the waistline, the stocky Sheridan was the commander of the Division of the Missouri and still one of President Grant's inner circle.

"What do you want me to do, General?" Custer replied, accepting the cup of coffee Little Phil's sergeant major handed him.

"I don't think we're ever going to get this goddamned Indian thing settled until we get Sitting Bull back on the reservation where we can control him."

"Isn't he out of our hair up in Canada?"

"No, the son-of-a-bitch has become the biggest folk hero in the history of the country. The press plays him up to high heaven." Sheridan sat scowling on the edge of his huge walnut desk. "You'd think he was Jesus Christ wearing a feather! As long as he can trot around, crossing and recrossing the border and thumbing his nose at the United States Army, we'll have trouble with *all* of the tribes. He's a goddamned idol for them, and particularly for all those Sioux and their traveling companions."

"What about the Canadians?" Custer asked. "Won't they kick him out if we ask them?"

"They can't. His being up there has created a very touchy political situation. They want him out but they want *us* to get him out. That means you, Custer. *That's* why you're the new boss up in St. Paul, and I don't have to tell you the president expects you to fix this problem."

Custer frowned. "I was kind of hoping I could take a leave of absence for a couple of months, General. I'm a little short of funds and the Lyceum people have offered me a substantial sum to do some speaking for them."

Sheridan sat down behind his desk. "You get that Sitting Bull problem straightened out and I'll give you whatever time you want."

Custer got to his feet and tossed off a casual salute. "Yes, *sir*."

★ ★ ★

St. Paul, Minnesota *January 28, 1877*

The Department of Dakota headquarters occupied the second and third floors of the large three-story building on the corner of Wabashaw and Fourth Streets. Tom and Captain William Cooke, as well as Sergeant Burkman and Mary, accompanied Libbie and Custer on the long train ride through Chicago to the Minnesota city. Before leaving the Presidio, he had orders cut transferring Myles Keogh to St. Paul to serve on extended detached service with him. He'd have a strong Custer team in the new job.

The St. Paul area had been inhabited by the Sioux before the coming of the white man, which occurred when Zebulon Pike first arrived in 1805. The Lakota branches had begun their migration to the western plains just before that. Fort Snelling, a now dilapidated army post, was built in 1817 at the confluence of the Minnesota and Mississippi rivers when white faces consisted only of soldiers and a few trappers. However, the city was founded by its first settler, Pierre "Pig's Eye" Parrant, a French Canadian trader. From him, the name of the settlement derived: *Pig's Eye*, which lasted until 1841, when it was changed to match a local chapel dedicated to St. Paul. It became the territorial capital and later the state capital when

Minnesota entered the Union in 1858. It was now becoming a major rail hub, shipping much livestock.

When the Custer entourage arrived, the city was covered by a deep snow and the temperature was hovering just below zero. Major Myles Keogh, who had arrived a week earlier, met them along with Captain William Ludlow, the senior engineer who had been a classmate of Custer's at West Point. Keogh had arranged for a brass quartet that vigorously played "GarryOwen," as Custer stepped down from the steaming train and lifted Libbie from the step. The general returned the salutes, shook hands with both officers, and waved to the musicians. "They're going to get their lips stuck to those horns," he said.

Keogh grinned. "Sure, General, but you had to be met by your own song."

Custer laughed. "Thanks, Myles. Now you can let them go and get warm somewhere."

"Your carriage awaits, sire." Keogh pointed to two large sleighs standing nearby. "We'll have your baggage brought along."

The two-story mansion the army rented for General Terry was located on Summit Avenue, overlooking the ice-covered Mississippi River. Since its lease was a long one, it had been retained for the new department commander. Now it's lamps were lit and a cheery warmth seemed to exude from its many windows. As Ludlow pointed it out, Libbie exclaimed, "Oh, Autie, it looks like a painting!"

"There's another nice house closer to the headquarters near the end of Fourth Street where you bachelors will stay with me," Keogh said. "Got a good housekeeper who can cook anything." He winked at Tom. "And now and then a pretty St. Paul girl gets lost and winds up there."

"You fellows never change, do you?" Libbie said with a shake of her head.

Soon they were inside and Libbie was off on a tour with the resident housekeeper.

Ludlow went on to the other house with Tom and Cooke, while Keogh stood in front of the fire in the large comfortable room that had been Terry's study. "Well, General, what in the world are you gonna use this Irish lad for? I'm a fighting man, not a headquarters dandy."

"You're my rock, Myles. I want you here running this place while I'm off gallivanting around."

The handsome Irishman who had fought so bravely in the big war and at the Horn nodded his head. "I figured as much."

"That'll be vital to me with whatever's down the line."

Keogh raised an eyebrow. "Sitting Bull?"

"That's one thing."

"And?"

The general winked at him. "Who knows? This is Custer country now."

★ ★ ★

At a little before five o'clock the next morning, Custer slipped out of bed and into a bathrobe. He stirred the nearly dead coals in the small fireplace before going to the window facing the river. He sighed as he looked out into the silvery cold and drew in its beauty. The bright light of the nearly full moon made the snowlit landscape look as if it were bathed in mock daylight. It was utterly still. One could hear trees cracking in the brittle air.

The river, covered by ice and snow as well, was wide and silvery white. The Mississippi, he thought, the great river that meant so much to America. On its lower, strategically vital stretch, Grant had finally taken Vicksburg during the war, essentially winning the River for the Union. Together with the victory at Gettysburg—which had been his first real battle as a general—it had sounded the death knell of the Confederacy. He could still see his Michigan Wolverines tearing into Jeb Stuart's vaunted rebel cavalry. That was the first time the world heard about a young general named Custer. He was twenty-three years old then, taking his first steps toward becoming the third most famous Union general in the war, after Grant and Sherman.

What was ahead for him now? Surely more glory was within reach. Was there some way to get his second star back? It would take something spectacular like another Little Bighorn for him to vault over all those other brigadiers who ranked him—but it was possible. He had to get the second star to position himself for the third. Sherman wouldn't head the army too much longer—he despised the politicians too much. Sheridan was still quite young, but who really knew about mortality?

But there had to be war, had to be battles for him to win, for him to jump over those others. Maybe he could stir up something with Canada. He laughed to himself.

What great campaigns such a war could bring. Victoria would send her British legions, and he, Custer, would defeat them. Surely he would get a field command of at least a corps. Maybe, knowing he always won, they would give him the invading army command. And why not? Wasn't he the "ultimate warrior?"

He chuckled. He had a great idea—why not align the mighty Sioux to help him fight the Canadians? The French had used Indian allies in earlier wars—what a great concept—using Sitting Bull and his paint-streaked warriors on his flanks! A brigade of well-equipped Ogalala Sioux under Crazy Horse on his left, and a division of other Sioux under Sitting Bull himself on his right!

He smiled again. *That* would be using the Little Bighorn to the maximum advantage. What more could there be? He laughed aloud.

This *was* Custer country now. . . .

We're marching off for Sitting Bull
And this is the way we go—
Forty miles a day, on beans and hay,
With the Regular Army, O!
                    —Old Army song

As it crossed the Canadian border, Frenchman's Creek became White Mud River. It then meandered crookedly northwest through rolling grasslands that were the beginning of Canada's vast plains. The Land of the Grandmother in that area was bordered to the west by the thickly wooded Cypress Hills and to the east by the mist-shrouded Wood Mountain.

In the frigid days of February, 1877, Sitting Bull's beleaguered people were hunkered down against the biting cold along a valley of the White Mud some sixty miles above the border near Pinto Horse Butte, a craggy arm of Wood Mountain that rambled out to the frozen river. Nearly one thousand of the hungry and uncertain refugees crowded the great chief's battered lodges, worried that the Grandmother would not protect them if a *Wasicus* chief such as Long Hair were to somehow follow their trail and swoop down on them in the dead of night or in another afternoon's red sun.

Sitting Bull tried to assure them that it couldn't happen, that his wolves—his scouts—were ever alert. Besides, the Grandmother's redcoats would further protect them. They weren't many, but the North-West Mounted Police carried the powerful badge of the Queen. Three hundred strong, the "mounties" had ridden west to impose the law of the Dominion on its subjects as well as its visitors, and that was what Sitting Bull's Sioux were. Not only did they not belong to Canada, they were a potential problem to Canada's own tribes in the area. There were just so many buffalo, and old enmities remained.

Major James Walsh commanded the small mountie outpost in the area. Named

appropriately Fort Walsh, it was located in the Cypress Hills. The major was a man of honor and of steel, and Sitting Bull had quickly grown to trust him. Walsh pulled no punches in firmly stating that the Grandmother would tolerate no returning to the United States to steal or kill. Any of Sitting Bull's tribesman doing so would be banished, and if it occurred on any large scale, the Grandmother would force all of his people to return to Montana.

As the days passed and February turned into March, Sitting Bull met three times with Walsh. At each meeting he asked the policeman for food for his people and the Grandmother's representative approved the purchase of grains from a friendly trader.

Red Elk kept busy hunting and studying English with the Grabber, who had stayed with Sitting Bull during the long exodus. The primer he used was rudimentary, employing drawings of hand signs with the English words. They consisted of only the basics, but they were enough for the young war leader to learn a fair vocabulary. Grabber drilled him in phrases, emphasizing verbs and their tenses. Red Elk was an apt pupil with a knack for languages, so he learned quickly. There was a Black Robe visiting at the East End mountie post, and he soon became acquainted with him, adding to his proficiency. When the priest departed, he rode over to Fort Walsh and offered to bring in game in exchange for English conversation with the Canadian cook.

On March 16th, while Red Elk was at the main village, one of the wolves who had gone into Fort Peck for information, returned with word that Long Hair had made a short visit to the army post. The wolf had seen him with several other officers as they went out on horseback to hunt.

Red Elk's pulse quickened at the news. *Long Hair!*

"Is he still there?" he asked the scout.

"No, he left next day."

"For where?"

The scout shrugged.

★ ★ ★

St. Paul, Minnesota *March 30, 1877*

The inspection trip included Fort Lincoln, Fort Buford, Fort Berthold, and Fort Peck. At Fort Abraham Lincoln, Custer was greeted warmly by the remaining officers of the Seventh Cavalry. A spirited parade was held for him, and he had a pleasant reunion with his sister, Maggie. Marcus Reno had returned as a new lieutenant-colonel to assume field command of the regiment, replacing Major Fred Benteen, who had gone on leave prior to discharge.

At Forts Berthold and Buford, the visits were short, designed mostly to impress the troops stationed there that George Armstrong Custer cared enough about them to visit during the cold of early spring. This was part of his plan to make a reputation as a commanding general who got well away from his desk and lived in the field. Grant had done it in the last part of the war, when he was general-in-chief, keeping his headquarters away from Washington and close to the front lines with the Army of the Potomac. Why shouldn't Custer? After all, he *was* going to be head of the army someday.

The visit to Fort Peck had another meaning. That post, at the juncture of the Milk and Missouri Rivers was the closest army installation to Frenchman's Creek and the Valley of the Mud where Sitting Bull was residing with his growing band of Sioux. It was here at Peck that he would learn more of the Lakota chief's present existence. His favorite former scout, Bloody Knife, was living there, working for the post commander. The part Hunkpapa, part Ree, had been discriminated against as a mixed breed while being raised in the Hunkpapa tribe and he held an undying grudge against Sitting Bull's people, particularly Gall. They spoke shortly after Custer's arrival, fingers flying in the universal language of the northern plains.

"Have you spoken with his wolves?" Custer asked.

"Yes," Bloody Knife replied. "Sitting Bull says he will stay in the Land of the Grandmother all his life."

"How many warriors does he have?"

Bloody Knife shrugged. "Maybe four hundred. If Crazy Horse joins him, maybe eight."

"Do the Canadians feed them?"

"Some. They still hunt the *pte*." The *pte* was the buffalo.

"South of the line"

Bloody Knife shrugged again. "Sure. The *pte* knows no line."

Custer stroked his chin. If only there were some way to catch him south of the border. But surely Sitting Bull didn't hunt, and if he did, he definitely wouldn't hunt any place where soldiers could get near him. No, it was a matter of waiting until the doggone diplomatic clearance came through.

Custer went out with the hunting party that had been arranged for his benefit for three days—brought down a large elk. Then he headed back to St. Paul.

★ ★ ★

"What did your father say?" Custer asked.

Captain Cooke stood before Custer's large desk just after the general's return.

"It's a bit ticklish, General. As you know, the Dominion is just eleven years old, and the powers in Ottawa don't like to give the impression that their big friend to the south can wag their tail."

"No, the Queen wags their tail."

"But they don't look at it that way."

"Don't they want to get rid of the American Indians?"

"Yes, sir, but in their own fashion."

"Hogwash!" Custer said. "Have you read anything about what our new president thinks about the Indian situation regarding the Sioux?"

Cooke shrugged. "No, sir. The mess of his getting confirmed as president has overshadowed policy."

Rutherford B. Hayes had finally been made president of the United States by a 15-man electoral commission of five senators, five congressmen, and five Supreme Court justices. They had voted strictly along party lines, 8-7 Republican, to award all disputed states and their electoral votes to Hayes. He won by one vote, but he mollified the angry Southern Democrats by promising to end the military occupation of the South and to bring about meaningful reconstruction. The whole affair became known as "The Great Fraud." When he first heard of the electoral commission's decision, Custer had laughed and told Libbie, "And some people think the *military* is ludicrous at times—the politicians make us look positively brilliant. Sherman, in his disdain for them, may be the smartest man in America."

"How can I get to Sitting Bull?" Custer asked.

"I've prepared a letter to General Sherman, through General Sheridan, requesting that the State Department ask for permission for you to enter Canada for the purpose of a conference with Sitting Bull and other Sioux leaders in the Cypress Hills district."

Custer nodded his head. "Good. But that'll probably take weeks. I need to get in touch with the officer in command out there now to see if he can talk that hard-headed old Indian into seeing me." He turned to Mark Kellogg, who had been quietly listening from a nearby sofa. "Can you leak this to the *Herald* in some form that won't endanger the process or upset my bosses up the line?"

The journalist nodded his head. "I think we can go with the line of my asking you what you think is the wisest path regarding Sitting Bull. The old boy is getting so much attention in the national press that such a question would be logical."

"Okay, do it. And Cooke, what's the name of that mountie chief up there?"

"The one at Cypress Hills is Walsh, Major Walsh."

"Let's send him a letter."

★   ★   ★

It took five weeks for permission to come from the Canadian government for Custer to go to White Mud country to meet with the Sioux leaders. But it took more than two months for Major Walsh, who now had Sitting Bull's trust, to talk the chief into meeting Custer. It was finally arranged for the general, accompanied by only a small cavalry escort and his brother, Tom, to go to Fort Walsh for the historic meeting early in July. The party crossed the border on the 8th and arrived at Fort Walsh on the 11th.

Major Walsh, who had been described as having Custer's self-confidence as well as his ambition, was a courageous, muscular man of medium height and dark hair who wore a carefully trimmed imperial. Walsh greeted the general effusively, presenting him with the seal of the mounties. Custer in return handed the major a custom minted "Custer" coin. It was the size of a half-dollar and was embossed on one side with the crossed sabers cavalry insignia topped by a "7". The words, "General George Armstrong Custer, Victor at the Little Bighorn" adorned the other side.

Sitting Bull and his chiefs had arrived the day before and were camped just outside the mountie post. They had been there two days.

Custer liked Walsh the moment they met. Later, at dinner in the commandant's cabin, he asked about Canada's approach to the American Sioux. "We really can't provide for them," the major replied, "and there are old hostilities with our own Indians that could flare up at any time."

"Then Ottawa will be happy if I can talk that old devil into going home, right?"

"Unofficially, yes. But how do you plan on getting him to leave?"

Custer smiled. "I'll just have to outsmart him."

★ ★ ★

The following morning, the headquarters conference room was arranged for the meeting. At one end of the room two tables were set up—one for Custer, Tom and Mark Kellogg, the other for Walsh, a stenographer, and two other journalists, one Canadian, the other from the Chicago *Times*. Frank Grouard, the Grabber, had been accepted as the interpreter; he stood along the wall. At the other end of the room, buffalo robes had been spread out for Sitting Bull and seven of his chiefs. Gall was among them. They sat cross-legged as the traditional smoking pipe was passed. When Custer finished the pipe and it was handed back to Sitting Bull, the general began his entreaty. He spoke for only ten minutes, mostly lauding the bravery of the Sioux fighting men and the wise judgment of Sitting Bull. Then he went directly to the point, "If the great chief will take his people back to his homeland, I will change the White Father's order."

Custer nodded to Tom, who pulled a beautiful engraved Sharps .50 rifle from under the table. He solemnly walked to Sitting Bull and handed it to him amid sounds of approval from the other Sioux. Gall's eyes shone. Grabber translated Custer's words, "This fine rifle is a gift from Long Hair to the great chief to celebrate the new policy. If Sitting Bull's people will return to their hunting grounds . . . they will be permitted to keep their arms and their ponies."

As Tom returned to the table, Custer went on, "It will be the same as if you were here, except that the White Father will give you food when you need it. In the cold season and when the *pte* are scarce, your people will not want."

Sitting Bull's expression had been unreadable throughout, even when Tom handed him the Sharps. Now his eyes narrowed as he stared into Custer's direct look.

After several moments, he asked, "Where? Which reservation?"

Custer replied, "Standing Rock."

Sitting Bull shook his head.

"At Standing Rock, you will be treated well. I will personally supervise the agent there to make sure."

Sitting Bull shook his large head again.

Custer frowned. He had already stuck his neck out, changing the order that required the surrender of all arms and horses, and he didn't want this to turn into a harangue, so he made a quick decision and played his trump card. "If the great chief will take his people home, I will let him have his own reservation that will be called the 'Sitting Bull Agency.' It will be exclusively for his tribe and any others with whom he wishes to share his hunting grounds."

As Sitting Bull remained impassive, weighing this exceptional offer from Long Hair, his chiefs spoke among themselves, shaking their heads in animated approval. When they quieted, Custer added, "As long as your warriors do not raid your enemies or commit other crimes against the White Father's laws, you may be virtually independent."

Gall spoke briefly to Sitting Bull, then turned to Grabber. "Tell Long Hair he will have his answer soon."

★ ★ ★

Outside the stockade, Red Elk brushed his fine painted pony. He had to do something! When he first heard the news that Long Hair was coming, he was gripped with excitement. At last he would kill his enemy as vowed, and his beautiful Late Star would smile in the Happy Place. He had begun to make a plan—he could shoot him at any of several ambush places en route, or he could surprise him at the house of Long Lance, the Sioux nickname for Walsh. But before he could make a decision, Gall came to him. "Sitting Bull has said you must wait on your vengeance for Long Hair. He is coming in peace and the chief has agreed to council with him. If harm comes to him, the great chief's honor will be stained."

The disappointment had been bitter, but he couldn't go against Sitting Bull's order. He had, however, been permitted to be part of the chiefs' entourage to Fort Walsh. At least he would be able to see his enemy and refresh his memory about his looks. And now, with the sun at its zenith, he put away the brush, patted his tethered pony, and walked inside the compound. He had only a short wait before the council broke up. He watched from where he squatted by a cottonwood tree as first Sitting Bull and his party came out of the building, and then the white men. And *there!* he recognized the dark blond hair and confident gait of the man he so hated. Long Hair. He was headed right toward the cottonwood.

Custer was pleased with the way the meeting had gone. It was agreed that the reply would be given in council at midday on the morrow. He grinned at Tom as he slapped his brother on the back. "By George, I think we did it! It all started with that Sharps. What a bully idea that was."

Kellogg, traipsing along behind, agreed. "I don't think they can refuse, General. You gave them everything."

"Everything but full freedom," Tom said, "and I think that's a big stumbling block with Sitting Bull."

"He's also a wise man, and we know from the battle how important his people are to him. I think he'll come around."

At that moment, they passed under the cottonwood tree. Custer looked up into a pair of the coldest black eyes he'd ever seen. They belonged to a tall, slender young Sioux who stared at him with unmistakable hate. As they passed by, he turned back and saw that the brave's eyes was still following him with the same intensity.

★ ★ ★

All of the players were assembled in the same places in the conference room the next day shortly after twelve o'clock. Sitting Bull, known for his speech-making reticence, had Gall speak for him. The barrel-chested fighting chief got to his feet and began to talk about the heroic deeds of Sioux warriors as the Grabber translated. He described the defeat of Three Stars—Crook—at the Battle of the Rosebud. Finally, looking solemnly around for effect, he went into an apology for the Little Bighorn. "If there had not been so many of our women, children, and respected elders there—had they been out of danger . . ." Gall's eyes flashed as he raised his fist. "Our mighty warriors, inspired by the visions of Sitting Bull, would have *crushed* Long Hair and his soldiers!"

As Custer waited quietly, Grouard finished the translation. It was totally quiet in the big room. Then the general spoke, "But we are not here to talk of the Greasy Grass. That is finished. We are here today to speak of our future—that of the proud Sioux and also the White Father's people, who, more and more, will come to break the ground and build sturdy houses. If the great chief will let me give him a new reservation, in his name, this future can be accomplished with good for all. Your people will never be hungry again."

When the translation was finished, Sitting Bull, wearing a long headdress of eagle feathers, instead of his usual first coup feather, got to his feet. Looking directly at Custer, he said in his low voice. "In the past, the words of the White Father have been false, but I accept those of Long Hair. By the Moon of the Hairless Calves, I will lead my people to the place that will be known by my name. There, I will remain by the White Father's laws. But, if the whites do not always act as Long Hair promises, my warriors will sharpen their lances and kill them as never before!"

After a long pause, he nodded to Gall, who walked to Custer with a long object wrapped in soft yellow doeskin. Handing it to the general, he said, "The great chief offers this in return for his fine rifle, and to seal the treaty."

Custer smiled as he opened the doeskin parcel and found a beautifully carved bow and one arrow, also engraved with tiny, colorful markings. It's message was clear: not only was this a return gift, it was *significant*. Custer would have just this one shot to make the agreement work.

CUSTER BRINGS IN SITTING BULL!
CUSTER CORRALS THE CHIEF AGAIN!
LITTLE BIGHORN REVISITED!
CUSTER DOES IT AGAIN!
Custer Lassoes Sitting Bull!

Headlines across the country blazed the story of Custer's latest victory, mostly lauding his ingenuity. The New York *Herald* and the Chicago

Times shared the scoop, although, naturally the *Herald* had more details. The Washington *Daily Patriot* stressed his diplomacy: "Custer is well known as the Boy General with dozens of Civil War victories under his belt. His image in buckskins as a great Indian fighter is still vivid. But who among us would have guessed that the flamboyant general also possessed the diplomatic skill to bring the vaunted and truculent Sitting Bull back to American without a shot being fired? Can our new president sitting in the White House, whose victory was stolen by the Republicans, claim such dexterity in statesmanship? Sitting Bull, the most famous Indian in the world, bowed to Custer's will and finesse, and. . . ."

★ ★ ★

Custer arrived back in St. Paul six days after his Canadian council. Though it was the capital of Minnesota, the city was still rather small and it's reasons to celebrate were few. Custer was asked to preside over a parade in his honor three days after his return. He accepted the invitation with relish. He had a week from that date to take care of command matters and get ready to depart for New York, where he would begin his lucrative tour with the Lyceum Agency.

Libbie, who would accompany him throughout, had been packing her trunk for some time. It would be a grand leave—a week in her hometown of Monroe, Michigan, a month in New York City, and an opportunity to meet new and interesting people while she basked in the limelight of her wonderful husband in the other cities on his schedule. She loved being Mrs. George Armstrong Custer!

★ ★ ★

The leave was most pleasant for both of the Custers. The well attended lectures brought heavy newspaper coverage in each city, and Custer was lauded wherever he went. On September 7, while in Philadelphia, he received a telegram from St. Paul that disconcerted him. "Sir: On Sept 5 Inst. Crazy Horse was killed in a scuffle with a soldier who was supposedly guarding him. The facts are hazy, but apparently Crazy Horse received a bad bayonet wound and died soon after. His Oglalas are quite disturbed. What do you recommend? Signed, Keogh, Major."

Custer felt a pang of sadness. From what he knew about Crazy Horse, the famous Sioux leader was perhaps one of the best natural generals the country had ever known. His slashing attacks with warriors who tended to act without discipline in battle bore the stamp of great leadership and brilliance. He had commanded the Sioux force that attacked Crook at the Rosebud and fought an American command of some 1,200 soldiers to a draw with an equal number of warriors. Never had an army command of that size been attacked. Indians simply didn't have the means to get replacements, so it wasn't their way. But Crazy Horse had done it. Apparently, the fiery war leader had led a charmed life in battle—just like himself. And now, for him to suffer such a needless, humiliating death seemed a sacrilege.

He wrote back,

"Have an announcement made at all Sioux reservations—both in English and in Sioux—that I am personally sorry about Crazy Horse's tragic death. Then send orders to the agent servicing the Oglala to speak to their chiefs and again express my sympathy, then move them to Sitting Bull's reservation. I will send a telegram to that agent, asking Sitting Bull to be the great father to the Oglalas and heal their wounds.

-Custer, Brig. Gen., Cmdg."

Sitting Bull did as Custer requested, taking Crazy Horse's angry and grieving people under his wing. It would be the only major problem Custer would face for the next two years of his command.

15

"Armstrong, I didn't come all the way to St. Paul, just to avail myself of your fine hospitality."

Custer watched James Gordon Bennett, Jr. hold the match flame to his cigar and take several big puffs to make sure it was well lit. They were in Custer's study after a fine dinner with Libbie and Mark Kellogg. The reporter stood quietly off to the side, sipping from a glass of cognac as his boss spoke. The slender, heavily mustached newspaper magnate looked Custer squarely in the eye, then went on, "I have a proposition for you."

"Which is?"

"This will possibly be the most momentous proposal of your life." Bennett paused again, then said softly, "After long consideration and careful planning, I'm offering you the Democratic nomination . . . for the presidency of the United States."

Custer stared at the New Yorker. He'd heard it suggested ever since the Little Bighorn, but it had always been in off hand comments. Bennett was anything but offhanded. *My God!* He drew in a deep breath, blew it out. He stuttered slightly when he finally responded, "How can you make such a stupendous offer, Mr. Bennett?"

"As I said, I've been working with my powerful friends in the party for a number of years now. I've known all along that you were our man, but I had to wait and see how the positioning of other candidates might develop. It's a matter of logic. Primarily, we need a *bloody shirt*, a hero. That's how the Republicans have won ever since the war. First there was Grant, then Hayes. My guess is, they'll run another one this time."

"But what about the other politicians who want to run?"

Bennett nodded his head. "There are some. Samuel Tilden graciously conceded to Hayes when the Republicans rigged that election, and he's the sentimental favorite. But he's palsied and arthritic—elderly looking—and he has had his own share of bad press lately. Furthermore, he's had a rift with Honest John Kelly, who is now the boss of Tammany Hall. Tammany Hall rules New York, and no candidate can win without the huge number of electoral votes in New York."

Bennett went on, "Blaine from Maine is still the 'magnetic man,' Senator John Sherman, the general's brother, also wants it. Senator Bayard from Delaware might throw his hat into the ring. And, as you know, we control the House, so Speaker Sam Randall is a possibility. Additionally, there has been a small ground swell for another bloody shirt, General Hancock."

Custer was still taken aback. This wasn't conjecture. Bennett was one of the most powerful of the world's publishers and his newspaper carried huge influence. He turned to Kellogg, but the reporter's face was a mask. Now, he knew why the man had been assigned to him for so long. "Hancock has a brilliant war record," he said. "I served under him after the war."

Bennett smiled. "I've had a poll taken, Armstrong. After General Grant and General Lee, you are the most famous Civil War general. Hands down! The public is still well aware of your huge victory at the Little Bighorn, and your success with the Apaches. And now you are headline news following your Canadian adventure with Sitting Bull. You are the nation's preeminent Indian fighter, and you have *charisma*!"

Kellogg added, "Mr. Bennett's newspaper and other publishing connections have kept your name constantly before the public. General, you are possibly the most famous man in the world."

Custer tried to control the rush of excitement. *This couldn't be real!* Becoming the commanding general of the army someday was logical. That's what he did—he commanded. That was his world. He was a soldier—a West Pointer, a military leader—not a politician. "What makes you think I could win the election I'm got nominated?" he asked.

"As you know," Bennett went on, "the South is solidly Democratic now. With New York and a few other key states, you can be our new man in the White House. We have already made a carefully orchestrated plan to get those states. Your immense popularity will do the rest. By the time election day arrives, every voter in America will know your name as well as his own!"

Custer studied Bennett's enthusiastic expression for a moment before replying, "If I'm elected, what makes you think I can *be* president?"

"Don't worry, you'll grow into it. And we'll be right there to help you."

★ ★ ★

Custer could hardly contain himself as he washed his face prior to retiring. The excitement of the publisher's word continued to flood over him like an impossible dream, a fantasy. *President of the United States! President of the United States!* He toweled and then turned from the white porcelain bowl to his wife. Libbie was in bed reading. "Well, how did your talk with Mr. Bennett go?" she asked as he sat down beside her.

"You won't believe what he offered me."

"The moon?"

"Practically. Guess again."

She laid her book aside and took his hand. "Let's see . . . hmm . . . I know, he wants you to write a regular column for his newspaper."

"Nope. Much bigger."

She laughed. "Mayor of New York City?"

"Much bigger."

Libbie's gray eyes widened. "Not—"

Custer grinned. "How would you like to live in a big mansion on Pennsylvania Avenue in Washington, D. C.?"

It took her a moment to find her voice as she jumped to her feet and faced him. "Tell me about it!"

"He's been planning it for three years. Says I can't miss." He told her about the discussion.

When he finished, she shook her head in wonder. In a tiny voice, she said, "Do you think I could actually be the First Lady?"

He pulled her into his arms. "Does kind of seem impossible, doesn't it?"

She looked up at him. "I wonder what kind of a bed we'd have?"

"A busy one."

★ ★ ★

Custer sat on the edge of his desk the next morning and looked around at the expectant faces of his Seventh Cavalry intimates. Tom Custer, Cooke, and Keogh were still his "palace guard," having served him well in his two plus years as the department commander. "Gentlemen," he said, "I have something to tell you that is quite startling. In fact, it's so much so that you will want to run out and tell everyone you know, but you can't. You must swear to absolute secrecy!"

He looked each of them in the eye again. "Is that understood?"

As each nodded his head, Custer said quietly, "Mr. Bennett has offered me the Democratic Party's nomination for president of the United States, and I have decided to run."

Tom whistled and grabbed his hand, Keogh slapped him on the back, and Cooke let out a war whoop. Congratulations filled the office as Tom and Keogh linked arms and danced a do-si-do. Finally Tom asked, "Has he got it all sewed up? I mean, he couldn't have come out here with such an offer without having his bully boys in tow."

Custer smiled. "Uh, huh. He and his friends are confident I can win."

Cooke asked, "You say it's secret—for how long, General?"

"Until something comes out in the *Herald*. His connections with other newspapers in the country will follow his lead. Probably not too long after the first of the year."

"What about Sheridan?" Tom asked, "And Sherman, for that matter. What are *those* old war-horses going to say. Hell, you're gonna be their boss!"

Custer shrugged. "I'll cross that bridge when I get there."

Each of the staff officers shook their heads in disbelief. Keogh asked, "Where will we fit in? I mean, we *are* regular officers. So are you, for that matter, General."

Custer nodded his head. "I've thought of that. Until this thing becomes a reality, I'm the only one who will be involved. We'll worry about detached duty or indefinite leaves of absence later. In the meantime," he grinned, "ain't we gonna have fun!"

★ ★ ★

Two weeks later some *unexpected* fun occurred. Preceded only by a telegram that arrived one hour before his train, Lieutenant-general Philip Henry Sheridan descended on the country capital of St. Paul with a grim visage and his even grimmer Black-Irish dander up. He was armed with a copy of the New York *Herald* that had come out two days earlier, the one that contained a half-page editorial from James Gordon Bennett, Jr., announcing the candidacy of George Armstrong Custer for the presidency.

Little Phil had never been one to mince words. Slamming the copy of the newspaper into his palm as he descended from the train, he snapped, "What's *this* shit, Armstrong?"

Custer, with Tom in tow, tossed off a salute from where he waited a few feet away. In genuine surprise, he asked, "What are you talking about, sir?"

"This *presidency* shit is what I'm talking about!" Sheridan barked as he held out the newspaper. "Is this true?"

It was snowing lightly in front of the small St. Paul depot, but the flakes were large. "Uh, sir," Custer replied, "I have a carriage waiting. Why don't I explain on the way to the house?"

Sheridan glowered at him. "A little snow never hurt anybody. *Is it true?*"

"Yes," Custer replied quietly. "Bennett has talked me into running."

"Goddamnit! I've known you were daft for some time, but I didn't think you were *this* daft! You don't know the first damned thing about politics. Every time you open your mouth, you put your whole damned leg in it!"

Custer smiled as he followed his boss inside the closed carriage. "I've changed, General. Now I put only my toes in it."

Sheridan was still scowling. "You know what I mean. You're one of the best fighting men this country's ever seen. Like me, you've got an *instinct* for it. What's going on?"

"Bennett told me something Lincoln once said, and I'll be darned if it isn't true. Old Abe, in his whimsical way, said, 'You know, there's a funny thing about being president. Once a man starts getting it in his head, the strangest things start happening. His mouth keeps on denying that he ever wants any part of it, but that head of his starts getting more and more familiar with Pennsylvania Avenue.'"

Sheridan pondered him a moment under lidded eyes. "That's where Bennett's got you, huh? He's fed you all that bullshit and you bought it like a stable hand with nothing to do."

"He gave me a lot of logic. He's sure I can win."

"What if Grant comes back in for a third term? There's a lot of talk about that."

Custer shrugged. "If he gets the Republican nomination, I'd just have to run against him."

"Could you keep dirty politics out of it, or would you go after his jugular? I must tell you right now, Armstrong, neither Sherman nor I would condone your slandering him."

Custer replied softly, "I can keep it clean."

"But what about your bully boys like Bennett? They'll go after him like vultures."

"I'll contain them, sir. Don't worry about it."

Sheridan's eyes narrowed. "I'll be watching closely, and I promise you this—if you don't keep your word, I'll personally shoot you! Regardless of what happened in his administration, Grant is the most honest, heroic man in this whole damned country."

Custer nodded his head as the carriage pulled up in front of the mansion on Summit Street. "I'll keep that in mind, sir."

Sheridan caught his arm as he started to rise. "I've got a couple more things to say. What if I told you a second star might be on its way for you?"

Briefly Custer thought of a promotion's allure, and how much it would have meant to him a few months earlier, but the presidential carrot had been dangled and its allure was too strong. He shook his head. "I've committed myself, sir."

"Okay, what does the lovely Libbie have to say about all this nonsense?"

Custer chuckled. "She's already redoing the curtains in the White House."

Sheridan just shook his head and blew out a deep breath.

16

James Gordon Bennett, Jr. was eighteen months younger than Custer. In his youth he had been everything they said about rich kids. He was born with more than a silver spoon in his mouth, it was diamond encrusted. Not only was he "to the manor born," he was "to a *manner* born." His father, James Gordon Bennett, brilliant, arrogant at times, autocratic, and utterly independent, built the New York *Herald* into the richest and most powerful newspaper in the world. The old man had been dead for seven years , but "Young Jim," the satrap, had been running the robust newspaper empire for nearly twelve years. He had learned the manner well—inheriting from his father boldness, brisk decision making, and enterprise—and had multiplied all three.

Young Jim originally had been raised by his mother in Europe. He got as much education from private tutors as he could stomach, and by his mid-teens, his arrogance and profligate ways had manifested themselves—he was sent to live with his father. Life in New York with father was tasty. Ladies of the stage intrigued him, notably a British blonde who had been described as having "the voice of velvet and the lost arms of the Venus de Milo." He spent a lot of time in the aristocratic Union Club at Fifth Avenue and Twentieth Street, and later put its other wealthy members on an unofficial "sacred cow" list that precluded their being mentioned in the *Herald* in any derogatory manner. Other favorite haunts were Delmonico's restaurant and the Jockey Club. Among the talented and well-paid newspapermen who surrounded him at the *Herald* he was referred to as the "Commodore" due to his command of the New York Yacht Club squadron.

It was said that next to William Astor and Commodore Vanderbilt, Young Jim had the largest assured income in America. But one thing was missing.

As he approached his thirty-ninth birthday, he was about to achieve a goal that had eluded even his father. The English novelist, Anthony Trollope, writing in 1862 of a visit to America, observed that "No newspaper in America is really powerful; and yet they are tyrannical and overbearing. The New York *Herald* has the largest sale of any daily newspaper—but it is absolutely without political power. . . ."

When he read Trollope's comments, Young Jim was twenty-one, and it had never ceased to rankle him. The years passed, he came to know how Tammany Hall and the New York political system worked, but no means of political power presented itself. When Custer returned to glory with his victory on the Washita, followed by his celebrity for his book *My Life on the Plains*, a light began to flicker for Bennett. He courted the charismatic Custer, took him to lunch at Delmonico's during his visit to the city in 1876, ran his articles in the *Herald*. And then it happened—*The Little Bighorn*. Suddenly, it was all in his hands; with some superb maneuvering, James Gordon Bennett, Jr. could control the White House. Was that enough political power? What would that goddamned Englishman say to that? He had long been a bit partial to the Democratic party, though in no way publicly. . . . This was the way in because the Democrats had no dominant candidate. And there was no expense he couldn't meet. It was a challenge for him, but it was more—it was incredible—the biggest, most exciting game of his life. Now he was ready for his next step.

★ ★ ★

Custer's one year leave of absence from the army commenced February 21, 1880. Numerous things had to be accomplished, according to Bennett, and several of them had to do with New York. The Custers arrived there on the 27th, and where they checked into a suite in the St. Nicholas Hotel on Broadway between Broome and Spring Streets. The hotel, a stately Italianate structure, had been built nearly three decades earlier to supplant the famous Astor House as the most elegant hostelry in New York. It's interior was still dazzling, though a bit polished. Its satin damask curtains, gleaming gaslit chandeliers, and black walnut wainscoting still bespoke grandeur. Only the Fifth Avenue Hotel, constructed in 1859 on the corner of Fifth Avenue and 23rd Street, opposite Madison Square, was larger and more opulent. It's passenger elevator, called a "vertical railroad," had been the first such contrivance in any hotel in the country.

But the St. Nicholas still quietly exuded quality, and the Custer's suite was, next to its famous bridal suite, the finest in the hotel. That was one thing about Bennett—he didn't spare the horses when it came to taking care of the man who was going to fulfill his dream.

Shortly after the general's arrival, Bennett set up a luncheon in a private dining room at Delmonico's. "I want you to meet some of the most powerful men in America," the publisher told Custer.

"Such as who?" Custer asked.

"Commodore Vanderbilt, Andrew Carnegie, and perhaps one or two others."

"But aren't they Republicans?"

"To the core."

"I don't understand," Custer said, shaking his head.

"My dear General," Bennett said with a smile. "You are so unknowing. They *are* Republicans, but they want to meet you. Later, after you are nominated, I want them to contribute to your political treasure chest."

"Why would they do that if they are Republicans?"

Bennett smiled again. "Because they don't ever want to be completely on the losing side. If you become the president for eight years, they certainly don't want to be left out in the cold altogether."

Custer shook his head. "I guess I've got a lot to learn."

"And Armstrong—"

"Yes?"

"We'll need to do something about your stutter. It's infrequent, but it harms your image as a persuasive orator and statesman who will lead this country to great power."

"What do you recommend, James?"

"Your friend, Lawrence Barrett, a master of elocution, might be a marvelous tutor for you."

★ ★ ★

It seemed that Lawrence Barrett had always been Custer's good friend. Actually, Autie had met the successful actor, who was just two years older than himself, in 1866 in St. Louis when Custer was on his way to the Plains to assume the lieutenant colonecy of the Seventh Cavalry. Barrett was starring in the play *Rosedale*. Custer went backstage to meet the thespian, who in turn was excited to meet the famous cavalry leader. It was the beginning of an exceptional friendship, for it filled a gaping void in Custer's life—the theater. Autie had been in love with the theater for as long as he could remember; it was his most cherished entertainment. It seemed inconceivable that a powerful leader of men, a general who relished combat and was utterly unafraid in battle, could giggle watching comedies and sob without shame in the middle of a tragedy or melodrama, but it happened.

It also seemed that Lawrence Barrett had been put on earth to fill that void. Their friendship was so stimulating that they could spend hour after hour together, lost in lively conversations. They soon came to love each other as close brothers sometimes do. When they were apart, they wrote long letters to each other; when they were together, they often walked arm-in-arm down the street. Once Libbie laughed and scolded, "Autie Custer, what will people *think?*"

Custer was fascinated by Barrett's skill and passion on the stage, for the actor's range was very wide, as gifted in Shakespearean dramas as he was in comedies. He was also a talented director. Barrett, a Michigander, had been a captain during the Civil War and hadn't lost his sense of military adventure. He marveled at Custer's romantic role as a flamboyant army officer and vicariously lived out his desire for adventure through his friend. He was an intimate of Edwin Booth, probably the greatest actor in the country—*and* the older brother of John Wilkes Booth, Abraham Lincoln's assassin—and other notables of the American stage. He was currently playing in his most famous role as Cassius in *Julius Caesar* in Booth's Theater, which he also managed full-time.

His wife, Mary was also Libbie's friend, and often took her sightseeing when the Custers visited New York. They were off on a jaunt to some bookstores one afternoon when Custer took Barrett to the Jockey Club to meet Bennett for a late lunch. Custer had a sarsaparilla while the other two men sipped an apÈritif and exchanged small talk. Shortly after the salads arrived, Custer looked at Barrett and asked, "What do you know about Demosthenes?"

"He was a famous Greek orator," the actor replied. "Why?"

"Didn't he have a speech impediment?" Bennett asked.

"Yes, and he often spoke with pebbles in his mouth to cure it."

"Do you suppose you can find the pebbles," Bennett said, nodding toward Custer, "to help our friend here get rid of his little stutter?"

"It's not very pronounced or frequent," Barrett replied.

Bennett's gaze was steady. "If the general is going to win this election, he should speak without any hesitation or impediment. Can you help him?"

Barrett glanced at Custer. "Do you want to work on this, Armstrong?"

"Yes, if you think I can get better."

"There's more to it," Bennett said, "As you know, candidates don't go to the public. But the general has so much appeal, I've arranged with the Lyceum people to send him on another tour. He will go to nine major cities that are democratic bastions and give lectures. If he can do so forcefully without a stutter, it'll be one more brick mortared in."

Barrett shrugged as the waiter brought the roast duck. "I'll do my best."

★ ★ ★

"Annie!" Libbie exclaimed as she hugged her old friend. "I'm so glad to see you!"

Annie Yates had spent some time in Monroe with her in-laws after her husband George's death, then had gone to visit her parents in Carlisle, Pennsylvania, for a few months before moving to New York. She had finally settled in a small rental house in Yonkers, not far from the stable where she gave riding lessons to budding young equestrians. Her eyes were moist and smiling as she returned Libbie's embrace. "I can't remember wanting to see anyone more than you, Libbie Custer!"

Libbie pushed her back to arm's length, startled. "My goodness, Annie, is that white hair peeking out from under your hat?"

"Yes," Annie replied. "It started turning gray right after the battle, and soon went all the way."

"I can't believe it! You can't be more than thirty."

"Every day of it. But forget my hair, what's this crazy story about Autie running for president?"

Libbie smiled. "It does sound pretty crazy, doesn't it?"

Annie's eyes were wide. "What'll you do if he wins? I mean, the *White House?* First *Lady?*"

Libbie threw her head back and laughed. "That's the craziest part of the whole thing."

"I hear that big old mansion's a pretty dreary place. It never recovered from Mrs. Lincoln, they say."

Libbie laughed again. "Well, I guarantee you, Annie Yates, I'll fix that!"

Annie looked around the hotel suite. "Pretty nice. Who's footing the bill for all this?"

"Bennett, I guess."

"And what about income, now that Autie's not on the Army payroll?"

Libbie shrugged. "Also Bennett, I guess. I just know there's more money than we ever had before, even when Autie was on that Lyceum tour. Now he's going on another one."

A hotel maid poured tea for them at a sideboard and they sat down to catch up. After some twenty minutes, Libbie said, "Do you think you might be able to break away from your kids for awhile, Annie?"

"What do you mean?"

Libbie took her hand. "I mean get on this crazy bandwagon with me, dear. Once we start electioneering, it's going to get pretty hectic. I'm going to need some help. You'd be my secretary, so to speak. And if Autie manages to win, you'd go right on with me to Washington."

Annie stared at her for a moment, then asked, "What makes you think I'm the person for all of that?"

"Your father was chief engineer for a railroad, wasn't he? You grew up in style, traveling, living abroad, learning foreign languages. You know protocol, you know how to write, and—" Libbie smiled. "you are one of the smartest women I've ever met. Will you do it, Annie? Please say yes. I'll need you so!"

A smile spread slowly over Annie's face. "Sounds like fun to me."

Superintendent Richard Pratt regarded the tall, slender Sioux standing before him in his office for a couple of moments before speaking. Finally, he said, "Welcome to Carlisle Indian Industrial School, Red Elk. I see that you speak English."

Red Elk shifted his weight uneasily. "Yes, a little."

Major Pratt glanced down at the young man's folder. "You were accepted for this school on that basis, as well as on your record of leadership in the Hunkpapa tribe. The agent on your reservation gave you an excellent report."

Red Elk said nothing. He had curried favor with the agent, restraining that part of himself that had made him a powerful war leader by the time he was sixteen. It hadn't been easy, making the decision to come to this white man's school and be a lowly student with all of these children, but he'd decided it was the best way to learn better English, as well as the ways of the *Wasicus*. Red Elk had not yet counted twenty-one summers, and there were others older than he at the school. But none of them was a war leader, none had earned his first coup feather at fifteen summers; that was the difficult part—lowering himself to being just another, as they called the People—*Indian*.

Major Pratt, who, after fifteen years of army service, had sold the government on the idea of opening the Indian School at Carlisle Barracks, an old army post not far from Harrisburg, Pennsylvania, was a zealous proponent of teaching the youth of various western tribes as a way of promoting cultural assimilation. He had developed his theories on education and vocational training while assigned to Fort Marion, Florida, where a large number of Indian prisoners were incarcerated. The school at Carlisle had enrolled its first students the previous year. "I see," Pratt continued, "that you are an artist, that you draw very well. Perhaps, when you have become familiar with the mandatory courses, you can concentrate on art."

Red Elk nodded. He wanted to say that he wished most of all to learn to read and write English, but he remained silent. The *Wasicus* chief could do the talking.

"We have students from the Kiowa, Arapaho, Cheyenne, Comanche and Sioux reservations here, Red Elk. So far there have been no problems in regard to differences among the tribes. You will be assigned to a company much the same as in the army. There you will learn discipline and order. The students in each company elect officers to represent and lead them. Daily drills, formations, inspections, and marches are held. Student officers are held accountable for the appearance and behavior of the members of their companies.

"A student court, composed of student officers will rule on infractions of the rules, in much the same manner as your headman councils back in the tribe. With your background and your ability to speak a certain amount of English, I hope you will soon become a company officer." The superintendent continued the briefing for two more minutes, then shook Red Elk's hand and dismissed him.

Red Elk was assigned to D Company. He was issued two uniforms, one tan and one dark blue that buttoned to the neck, and other elements of clothing and toilet articles. Everything felt strange to him, mostly the shoes, since he'd never worn anything on his feet but moccasins. The next stop was the barber shop, where his long hair was cut short. Among his private belongings, he kept a sharp knife with an eight-inch blade. That, a small tin of war paint and his first coup feather were his only touch with his warrior past.

His roommate was a an eighteen-year-old Kiowa named Little Bear from a reservation in the Oklahoma territory. The Kiowas were a warrior nation much similar to the Sioux, and had been subdued in 1875 when their horses and armaments had been confiscated and their chiefs sent off to prison in Florida. In fact, some of the very prisoners Superintendent Pratt had taught at Fort Marion had been the war leaders of the Kiowa. But Little Bear had been too young to participate in the Kiowa wars. Instead he was a bit of an anomaly; he was intrigued by his studies and already spoke good English. "You see," he explained to Red Elk during their first night together, "our proud Kiowa nation has had a written language since before the rocks were hard. Not with words, exactly, but we've always painted pictures, or signs, on animal hides to use as calendars and to record our history. I want to go back when I graduate from this school and be both a teacher and a historian." He grinned, "What about you . . . what are your plans?"

Red Elk didn't intend to tell anyone his true intentions regarding Carlisle, let alone a young Kiowa. "I don't know. Learn good English, read, write."

Little Bear was a cheerful sort. "Oh, I'll help with that."

Red Elk nodded as he hung up his new uniforms.

He was another step closer.

★ ★ ★

James Gordon Bennett, Jr. had made a major project of finding a campaign manager for Custer. There were several men in both New York and Washington with excellent tools for the job, but Bennett wanted more; he wanted someone who would do almost anything short of murder to get Custer elected. That man was Major Edward "Ned" Burke from New Orleans. Burke was a notorious charlatan. He seldom told the same story about his background, which included some shady deals in Texas before he popped up broke in New Orleans in 1870. Within a couple of years, Burke had risen from day laborer to executive with a small railroad, as well as being the political agent for the influential Louisiana Lottery and a growing force in the Democratic party. He became publisher and editor of what would become a powerful voice in the South, the New Orleans *Times-Democrat*. His next step was Washington, where he made his influence peddling keenly felt. With no one disputing his bogus rank of major, he, like the famous fox in the hen house, had been elected Louisiana state treasurer in 1878. Now he ruled the Democratic party in that state, and had influence with the Democratic leaders in other southern states.

Bennett knew his man. In addition to what Burke might be stealing from the state treasury, he needed money to keep up his grand lifestyle that included the upkeep of a mansions in the Bahamas and New York. Bennett also knew that Burke had an insatiable hunger to be near power. He offered the "major" $50,000 to run Custer's campaign, plus a $25,000 bonus if he won . . . an astronomical amount of money in 1880. Now, as Burke joined himself, Kellogg and Custer for lunch at the Jockey Club, Bennett was pleased with himself. Astute planning combined with the money and power of a great newspaper could accomplish almost anything. The conversation proceeded along introductory lines for about a half hour through the first two courses of the meal—a delicious oyster stew spiced by fried scallions, and the special Jockey Club salad, a creation of lettuce greens flavored by an English walnut and garlic vinaigrette. Custer mostly listened as Bennett and the newcomer traded comments about politics in the South. He noticed that Burke's speech seemed more Northern than one would expect in a man from Kentucky.

"I was stationed in Kentucky," he said at length. "Where was your home?"

"Uh, Covington," Burke replied quickly, "Across the river from Cincinnati."

Custer nodded. That could explain the lack of accent. He knew the man was some kind of a crook, but his origins didn't matter, only what he could deliver. And Bennett always seemed to know what he was doing.

"Mr. Bennett tells me that you have a solid grip on Southern politics and that you can deliver the South to me intact."

Burke, an owlish, slightly rotund man in his mid-forties, replied, "Yes, General, I can. First of all, your conduct in the South after the war was acceptable. You did nothing to alienate important people and you mixed in most agreeably. And you are a horseman. Secondly, I have made inroads. As you may know, I went to Washington in the spring of 1877 and became the Svengali that led the famous Wormley's Hotel bargain that brought Florida, South Carolina and Louisiana back into the hands of the white Democrats. Let's say I have more than a little influence."

Bennett smiled. "He's also close to General Nicholls, the governor of Louisiana."

Custer nodded his head. "West Point, Class of '55. Lost his foot at Chancelorsville. I know about him. A true Southern aristocrat."

"I can promise his support for you," Burke said.

"Do you have influence with other Southern newspapers?" Kellogg asked. The journalist was taking on a stronger role in Custer's campaign, becoming less of an observer, and more of a planner.

"Yes," Burke replied. "Once it becomes known that I'm connected with the general, most of the Southern newspapers will follow my lead in order to get inside information about him and the progress of the campaign."

They talked on for the rest of the excellent meal. Burke was the first to leave, and as he departed, Bennett looked at Custer and asked, "Well, what do you think?"

Custer smiled. "He's just conniving enough to make a politician out of me yet."

★ ★ ★

Congressman Frederick Benteen scowled as he read in the Washington *Evening Star* that General G. A. Custer was to go on another Lyceum tour to speak about how the Indian situation in the West had changed in recent years. The white-haired former army officer growled, "If I hadn't saved his ass by stopping Crazy Horse, he'd be dead or sitting in some administrative assignment doomed to remain a lieutenant-colonel all his life."

"Sir?" his secretary, former captain Tom Weir asked.

Benteen tossed the newspaper down on his desk. "I said if I, actually *we*, hadn't stopped Crazy Horse's wild counterattack on the right at the Little Bighorn, that goddam Custer wouldn't be running for dog catcher, let alone president."

Tom Weir had commanded D Company in Benteen's battalion in the Seventh Cavalry at the battle and had received the Medal of Honor for his heroic part in stopping Crazy Horse. He also had a brevet for lieutenant-colonel for heroism in the Civil War, so it wasn't his first act of valor. Unfortunately, after Benteen turned over command of the regiment to Lieutenant-colonel Reno in the late spring of '77, Weir had gone back to his heavy drinking, and had finally been court-martialed for being drunk on duty, attempted kidnapping, and desertion. After being missing for sixteen days, he staggered out of a Bismarck whorehouse, gone out to Fort Abraham Lincoln, and for some unknown reason had tried to abduct

Reno. In spite of his military honors, the resulting court-martial board had been forced to dismiss him from the army. It's leniency had, however, kept Weir out of prison.

Benteen, out of loyalty to his former subordinate, gave him a job the moment the captain hung up his uniform. Now, with his drinking under control, the bright Weir was ably assisting the junior congressman. Weir bore no resentment toward Custer. In fact, he had been secretly in love with Libbie for over a decade, but that didn't affected his admiration for the general. It was another example of Custer's contradictory nature and his paradoxical effect on people. Weir's true allegiance lay with the man who had brought him back to a position of respectability after the debacle that ended his military career. "I don't see how he got sold on this presidency thing," he said, handing Benteen a steaming cup of coffee.

The congressman snorted. "Huh! With his arrogance, someone could tell him he's God, and he'd agree. I tell you, Tom, it'll be a sad state of affairs if he gets to the President's House."

"Might be good for the army, though."

"Only if there's something in it for him. His own interest will always come first, you can rest assured."

Weir shrugged. "Sometimes, Fred, I think your dislike of him overpowers your judgment."

Benteen shrugged. "You may be right, but I'll do everything in my power to thwart any of his schemes that might be harmful to the country!"

INDIANAPOLIS, INDIANA *May 28, 1880*

In Mark Kellogg's forty-seven years, he had known many disappointments. He was twice defeated for public office, expelled from his Masonic lodge, his feed and grain store burned to the ground, and even the baseball team on which he played lost its biggest game. Before he turned full-time to the pen for a livelihood, he was a telegrapher and a freelance writer using the noms de plume of "Jentleman Jerks" and "Frontier." His columns appeared in various small Midwestern newspapers before he connected with the mighty *Herald*. He'd been described variously as humorous, honest, cheery, neighborly, and having high personal standards. From the upper Midwest, he was a small, slender man with dark hair and mutton chop sideburns who didn't seem to have a care in the world. The ample salary Bennett had paid him since the Battle in '76 made him financially stable for the first time in his life.

But it was more than the money. He loved the merry-go-round of being a Custer insider, and he admitted to being an unabashed political enthusiast. While his personal integrity made him balk at some of the blatant self-promotion Custer enjoyed, as well as some of the manipulations in which he took part, he was amused by and enjoyed the more audacious side of some of the machinations that Bennett assigned to him. A current example was his hiring shills to cheer Custer during the Lyceum tour speeches. For three dollars, he could get a lot of applause and huzzahs.

"*Hear! Hear!*" the man named Mason shouted as Custer finished telling about sticking his neck out to give Sitting Bull his own reservation. It sparked applause and more verbal approval.

Custer went on, "Except for some rather minor troubles with the West Coast Indians, and some ongoing problems with a few of the Apaches in the Southwest, the settling of sitting Bull on his reservation ended the Indian wars."

"*For now!*" a man in the second row shouted.

"Yes," Custer replied, "For now. But there will never be a major resurrection again. The Indians are scattered, being cared for, and their capacity to conduct war is limited."

"*But not their capacity for hatred,*" the man insisted.

"That will subside with time and education." Custer went into a short description of activities at the Carlisle School. "We are expecting a certain amount of assimilation, and for those who attend this type of school to go back to their tribes and teach there."

Custer went on, pleased with the progress he'd made on his diction. He'd stuttered momentarily just a couple of times. He had a small entourage that included Kellogg, Barrett, Burke and Keogh with him here at the Bates House on the northwest corner of Washington and Illinois streets. With the reputation of being the finest hotel in the Midwest, the Bates House, with its luxurious Victorian rooms, had provided lodging for three presidents when they visited the city. Keogh was in charge of security and had hired a handful of off-duty policemen to keep an eye on the large crowd. Bennett had selected Indianapolis for one of Custer's speeches because he knew that Indiana might be a crucial state in the election. Other speeches, except in the South, were scheduled for New Jersey, New York and California—primarily for the same reason.

Custer was about to go on when he saw Bennett and his party come down the aisle to their reserved seats in the second row. Two women and a man were with the publisher. One of the women was tall and spectacularly beautiful. She was wearing a black dress cut to fit her remarkable figure like a glove. A large brimmed hat, embellished with green ostrich feathers, sat on titian-colored hair caught at the nape of her neck. He couldn't tell the color of her eyes, but they regarded him coolly. Strange, he thought, Bennett hadn't told him about bringing guests.

He was brought back to his task at hand when another loud-voiced man near the front hollered, "*What makes you think you can be president?*"

Custer smiled. He'd been coached on that very question. "First of all, sir, it wasn't my idea. I'm quite content being a general. And besides, I haven't even been nominated."

"*The newspapers are full of it!*"

Custer grinned. "You know the newspapers, they're full of a *lot*."

That brought the house down for a full minute. When the laughter and applause ended, Custer quietly said, "If, by chance, I am nominated and fortunate enough to be elected, I believe I can do a good job as president. How many of you are veterans?"

Many arms shot up.

"How many of you were wounded, maybe lost an arm or a leg?"

A few arms shot up.

"I would do my darndest to get legislation passed to get you a pension."

Some cheers and whistles followed. "I'd also do some things for today's soldiers and sailors—raise their pay for one thing."

Kellogg's man, Mason, shouted, "*Three cheers for President Custer!*"

★ ★ ★

Following the speech, a reception was held in the luxurious hotel lobby. Members of the Indiana Democratic party, the press, and several other influential citizens were in attendance, as were many of their wives. "Major" Ned Burke was moving about, speaking with a banker here, a publisher there. His own credentials as a publisher gave him access to everyone. Bennett had been wise to hire him as campaign manager, Custer thought fleetingly, as he was introduced to the editor of the *Indiana State Sentinel*, the city's staunch Democratic newspaper. A couple of minutes later, Burke interrupted to introduce a black-bearded, balding man. "General Custer this is the illustrious William English."

Burke had briefed Custer about English prior to coming to Indianapolis. The fifty-seven-year-old Indiana native had served as a member of Congress from 1853 to 1861. He had organized and been president of the First National Bank of Indianapolis until recently and was not only prominent in that city's business community, but was also a factor in the state's Democratic party. He was currently building the most pretentious building in the city—the English Hotel and Opera House. He had not served in the war. As they chatted, Custer noticed the collection of men around Bennett and his guests. It appeared they all wanted to get near the tall, chestnut-haired beauty with the publisher. As if she felt his attention, she gave him a fleeting glance, then went back to her admirers. A few minutes later, Bennett steered his charges away from the throng and over to the general.

"First of all, General Custer, let me introduce Lady Sebright."

Olivia Sebright made up in sagaciousness and wit what she lacked in looks. A rail-thin brunette with large brown eyes, she was known for gambling wildly on the stock market and for being a good amateur actress and a leading London dilettante. She had, in effect, introduced her female companion to London society a few years earlier. Now she was accompanying the famous beauty on her first trip to America. Custer kissed her gloved hand, murmuring, "My pleasure, Madame."

"And this is James Whistler," Bennett continued, "the artist who has deserted us for London for the last few years. Actually, he's been in Venice until two months ago."

"In exile," the diminutive Whistler said with a smile. "Financial exile."

Custer remembered having read in the *Herald* that the artist had sued the British art critic, John Ruskin, for demeaning his Japanese works, and had gone bankrupt in the process. Custer grinned. Whistler was one of the most famous cadets *not* to have graduated from West Point. "A pleasure, sir. I understand you attended my alma mater."

"Ah, yes, pater forced me to go there. I escaped as soon as I could."

"Well," Custer said ruefully, "I *almost* didn't graduate." He was referring to having finished last in his class of June '61 and having beaten a court-martial for fighting on top of it.

"And this lovely woman, General, is the celebrated British beauty, Lillie Langtry," Bennett said.

The tall woman, born on the isle of Jersey in the Channel Islands and a member of British high society, was now twenty-seven years old and in the prime of her pulchritude. She was known as the Jersey Lily to the admiring public. She curtsied slightly as Custer stuck out his hand and looked into her cool eyes. They were *violet*. Lillie Langtry, the famous Jersey Lily who was Crown Prince Albert's exotic mistress. "I guess men and women don't shake hands in England," he said, continuing to hold her gaze, but we do things a little differently at times."

Her voice was steady, a trifle deep, as she shook his hand, "My pleasure, General Custer. When in Rome, don't we humor the Romans?"

Custer smiled. "And what brings the British Empire's most famous beauty to the colonies?"

"I'm on my way to visit a friend's ranch in Wyoming. And since Jimmy—Mr. Whistler—is part of my escort and has known Mr. Bennett for some time, we were invited to stop off here and meet the famous General Custer."

"The pleasure is mine, I assure you, my lady. And who might your friend be?"

"Moreton Frewen, a very dear boy who gave me his favorite riding horse, Redskin, when he departed for your cowboy country. He has been begging me to come for some time."

Bennett broke in, "I enjoyed your speech, Armstrong. I think the local veterans will give you strong support." He turned to the auburn-haired woman. "As you know, Mrs. Langtry, you are speaking with the next president of the United States. Now you know *two* men who will be world leaders."

She opened her eyes a bit as she smiled at Custer. "I hope there will be an opportunity for me to get better acquainted with the next president."

Custer felt a surge of excitement, but replied quietly, "Who knows what the future holds?"

If asked what state he hails from,
Our sole reply shall be:
He comes from old Ohio,
And his name is General G.
　　　　　—Slogan for Garfield

CHICAGO, ILLINOIS *June 3, 1880*

"One of the most splendid barns ever constructed." That was the way one journalist described Chicago's Exposition Building, the egg-shaped amphitheater where the Republican National Convention had opened on June 2. Richly colored banners and bright streamers added to the life-sized portraits of Republican heroes that hung from the walls. The famous photograph by Matthew Brady of then General U. S. Grant, leaning against a tree, held the prime location. Other noted Republican generals joined him, including the current president, Rutherford ("Rutherfraud") B. Hayes, Senator John Logan, who had been a corps commander under Grant, and James Garfield, who had only recently been sworn in as a U.S. senator from Ohio.

For the first time in party history, 756 delegates from every nook and cranny of every state in the Union were in attendance. Excitement and exuberance flooded the air like static electricity. More than ten thousand gallery spectators added to the hubbub. It was a grand celebration of democratic politics at their most robust. Garfield wrote to his wife, "It's like sections of Paris in the ecstasy of the Revolution!"

But all was not jubilation. Crafty politicians were working their machinations both behind the scenes and up front. Since there was no serious division over issues, the infighting was over credentials, organization, and voting methods. The party was generally split into two factions. The "Stalwarts" were the conservative element that essentially wanted no part of civil service reform or any drastic change of the status quo that gave the longtime party faithful their power. Their opponents were called the "Half-Breeds." They were more liberal and less in favor of patronage and less opposed to civil service reform. Senator Roscoe Conkling from New York led the Stalwarts, while Senator James G. Blaine of Maine was the head of the Half-Breeds.

Following the near debacle of the previous election, President Hayes had announced that he would serve only one term, and he was sticking to that promise. Therefore, Conkling and Blaine, who controlled some eighty-five per cent of the delegate votes, each had to find a winner.

For the Stalwarts, General U. S. Grant fit the bill. The former president had been out of the country on a grand world tour for two years, returning the previous September. The Stalwart leaders had ensured that the many honors awarded Grant during his journeys received wide publicity, a well-planned program to help voters forget the scandals that had marred his two terms in office. Upon the general's return, he was greeted with wild enthusiasm by the public, but Republicans in general didn't want him back in office. Nevertheless, he was the front-runner when the convention opened.

Mark Kellogg arrived with James Gordon Bennett, Jr. to represent the *Herald* at the convention. "I know from inside information," the publisher told his reporter as they drank a beer in their hotel bar, "that Conkling and company are going to push for unit rule, in which delegate votes will be lumped in favor of the majority for each state. This will favor Grant, leaving him just thirteen votes short of a first-ballot nomination."

Kellogg, who had never before been to a convention, asked, "If they impose that rule, what will happen?"

Bennett shrugged, "Thirteen votes are nothing. Grant could pick those up in five minutes."

"What do you think is going to happen?"

"James Garfield from Ohio is the dark horse, and he's chairman of the Rules Committee. He's also against Grant serving a third term. I think he'll defeat Conkling's unit rule move and give each delegate the right to vote individually. That should release a bunch of Grant votes and leave the whole shooting match up for grabs."

"Does Garfield want it?" Kellogg asked.

"I'm sure he does, and he's smart. We'll see. In the meantime, Blaine is Grant's strongest competitor, and he's immensely popular."

★ ★ ★

Shortly after he arrived at the Exposition Building, Kellogg heard someone call out his name. Turning, he saw the white-haired Fred Benteen striding toward him. He didn't know the former captain very well, since the cavalry officer had been stationed thirty miles down river from Bismarck at Fort Rice. He knew, of course, about the bad blood between Benteen and Custer, and that the congressman had belittled Custer in a newspaper article regarding the general's ability to be president.

"I thought you were Custer's hip pocket journalist, Kellogg. What're you doing here—spying?"

Kellogg grinned. "As a matter of fact, I am. No, Congressman, I'm just covering the convention for my newspaper."

Benteen's owlish pale eyes rolled. "And *I'm* just here out of curiosity."

Kellogg knew that Benteen wanted some sort of political chestnut in return for his support of Garfield. "May I ask, sir, if you would have a place in a Garfield cabinet."

Benteen's expression was cold as he replied, "I seek nothing personal. But in the event that Custer manages to get the Democratic nomination, I want us to have a man to beat him."

★ ★ ★

Bennett couldn't have been more correct. The unit rule was defeated. When other organizational matters were settled, the nominations began. Conkling was first in nominating Grant with a strong and stirring bid for the general. A fine orator, he opened with a paragraph from a Miles O'Reilly poem:

If asked what state he hails from
Our sole reply shall be
He hails from Appomattox
And its famous apple tree!

His moving tribute brought the rafters down in a thundering ovation. Then it was Garfield's turn to quietly but eloquently nominate Treasury Secretary and fellow Ohioan, John Sherman, the former U. S. senator and brother of General William Tecumseh Sherman, the head of the army.

Blaine's nominator did a lukewarm job of recommending the popular senator from Maine, and the other nominations were unimportant. The balloting began. At first, Grant led Blaine 304–284 votes, while Sherman garnered only ninety-three. For the next thirty-three ballots, the voting varied minimally, but then on the thirty-fourth ballot a dramatic change took place. Garfield's hat was thrown into the ring by the Indiana delegation. Now three Ohioans were in contention. Congressman Fred Benteen spoke from the podium on his behalf, "Gentlemen, this great American who was born in a log cabin and left fatherless at the age of two, worked his way up from poverty to serve proudly as a general officer in the past War of Emancipation." He went on, continuing his praise for another ten minutes before relinquishing the podium to a Grant supporter.

Kellogg, sitting in the front row of the gallery with Bennett, scribbled furiously on his notepad. Turning to his boss, he said, "Have you got a crystal ball?"

Bennett beamed as he puffed on his cigar. "I'd say it was a lucky guess, but I knew he was planning this all along. I have a friend in the Indiana delegation."

Both newspapermen turned back to the convention floor as the thirty-fifth ballot began. When it was over, Grant had 313 votes and Garfield had fifty. The next ballot began a short time later, marked by a powerful "stop Grant" reversal. Grant received 306 votes, Blaine got forty-two, but incredibly, Garfield received 399—*twenty more than the required majority.*

Roscoe Conkling rushed to the podium and shouted, "Fellow Republicans, I move that the nomination be made unanimous!"

A roar of approval followed.

★ ★ ★

A messenger brought the telegram from Kellogg to Custer in his hotel room two hours later. Handing the young man a dime tip, the general tore open the message and read it quickly.

"*It's Garfield!*" he announced to Libbie, who was reading in a corner chair.

"But I thought you said it would be Grant."

"I know. Politics is crazy."

"What does that mean for you?"

Custer scratched his head. "I don't know. One thing's sure, I won't have to worry about sullying the general's name. That ought to keep Sheridan and Sherman happy."

"But I'm sure they wanted him back in office. They're his close friends."

"Doesn't make any difference now."

★ ★ ★

Later Custer read the notes Major Ned Burke had just handed him about the man he would be facing if he, indeed, received the Democratic nomination—not yet a foregone conclusion.

Senator elect James Abram Garfield: Born Nov. 19, 1831.

6' tall, robust, handsome, light brown hair, blue eyes, prominent forehead (balding), bearded. Graduated Williams College 1856 with honors. Religion: Disciples of Christ. Former Ohio educator, lawyer, state senator. US congressman 1863-1880. A Union hawk, he rose from lieutenant-colonel to major general during the war. Cited for daring heroism at Chicamauga as chief of staff to Rosecrans. Served on the electoral commission that gave Hayes the disputed election in 1876. Accused of involvement in the Crédit Mobilier scandal in 1873. Extramarital affair with a New York woman in 1862. Otherwise clean. He has wisely chosen Chester A. Arthur from New York as his vice-presidential running mate.

As Custer reread the biographical summary, Burke said, "He was cleared on the Crédit Mobilier accusation sufficiently to get reelected back in Ohio six years ago, but we could still air it."

Custer pursed his lips. He had never stolen anything, never accepted any graft, so he was totally clean of monetary malfeasance. Of course, there was the matter of his court-martial, but that was easily explained. He said, "Unless there's proof of thievery, why pursue it?"

A smile creased Burke's round face. "You just don't understand politics, General. It's the *taint* that's important. *T'ain't* necessarily true, but it smells bad."

Custer shrugged as Burke went on, "As far as the woman in New York goes, it's the same thing. He admitted his infidelity years ago, but a lot of sanctimonious voters might vote against him because of it." He paused a moment. "How many indiscretions have you had, General?"

Custer thought back to some flirtations several years earlier, but that's all they had been. There was the Monasetah thing, his relationship with the Cheyenne chief's daughter, but he had staunchly denied anything had ever happened, and it had been considered just camp gossip. "No real ones. Women are drawn to me, but I just joke around with them." Lillie Langtry flashed through his mind. But he didn't even know her. He grinned. "I guess it happens with all great warriors."

"Well," Burke said, "We don't want any bad surprises."

James Gordon Bennett, Jr. knew a lot about Tammany Hall. No newspaperman in New York, let alone the publisher of the world's most powerful daily, was blind to it's remarkable arrogance and background in New York politics that included outright thievery. Nevertheless, he went to the *Herald*'s morgue and pulled out the huge file that held Tammany clippings. Lighting a cigar, he told the librarian to get on with his business and leave him alone as he began to sift through the compiled history. . . .

The Tammany Society was founded in 1789 as a benevolent and patriotic fellowship opposed to the autocratic principles of the Federalist Party. It was named for the powerful seventeenth-century chief of the Delaware Indians who gave William Penn the land that would become the great city of Philadelphia. Organized along Indian lines, each of the thirteen states had a "tribe" led by a "sachem." Its head chief was called the grand sachem, and its motto was "Freedom Our Rock." Aaron Burr gained control of the society in 1798 and organized it as a New York political machine that helped elect Thomas Jefferson president and himself vice-president in 1800. Between 1817 and 1840, New York became the largest city in North America and also its financial center. It was during this period that Tammany Hall, as the society later became known, learned that courting the steady flow of immigrants streaming into the city was an unlimited source of power that could be manipulated. In 1836, its grand sachem, MartinVan Buren, was elected president.

In 1852, a new force slipped into Tammany's power structure when thirty-year-old William M. Tweed, a former fireman, was elected city alderman. A bright, charming fellow, he quickly got himself elected to Congress. But those hallowed halls weren't as much to his liking as Tammany, so he returned to New York with some brilliant ideas about making money—*lots* of money. By 1868, Tweed had put together a group of henchmen so brazen in their larceny of public funds that they were known as the Tweed Ring. Tammany Hall came to symbolize the ultimate in predatory machine politics. Pictured as a fat and corrupt, monumental rogue, Boss Tweed—as he became known—glowered malevolently out of 1870s *Harper's Weekly* cartoons by Thomas Nast.

The amount of money the Ring purportedly stole ranged upwards to $75 million, although some believed it as high as $200 million—unbelievable figures in nineteenth-century dollars. Tweed, at six feet and almost three hundred pounds, was unfailingly courteous and witty, never losing his temper and never double-crossing anyone. If ever the term "honor among thieves" pertained, it certainly did to Boss Tweed. His chief advisor was Peter "Brains" Sweeney, a lawyer and district attorney. Another Irishman became Tweed's money man: Richard "Slippery Dick" Connolly, the county clerk. Well-born Yale graduate George Barnard provided the legal arm to Tweed's machine, becoming his easily corrupted judge. The bright and witty Barnard made great theater; he usually wore a white top hat while on the bench, sitting with his feet propped up in front of him while he whittled pine sticks and sipped brandy. Young lawyers loved his lewd repartee and humor, as well as his keen knowledge of the law. Tweed eventually got him appointed to the New York State Supreme Court. A mayor who was part of the Ring was the flamboyant Oakley "Elegant" Hall.

Politically, Tweed's grasp on the city was ironclad. In every ward in New York, he had his own totally subservient representative as ward leader, and everyone was on the take. Again, part of the key was the constant stream of immigrants. Once they stepped off the boat, a Tammany contact got them a place to live and a job So what was a vote when it came time to be cast? Or several votes? One fireman supposedly voted seventeen times in one day!

Tweed owned a paving company and a printing company that cornered the city's business in both areas—at exorbitant pricing. But perhaps the most unbelievable farce was the construction of the new county courthouse. Originally budgeted at $250,000, the final cost was believed to be *$13 million*—more than Alaska had cost!

But even such a powerful machine had an Achilles heel: the press. Bennett wasn't too proud of the fact that *The New York Times* had spearheaded Tweed's exposure. Of course, the *Times* was the only fully Republican newspaper in the city, so a blasé public took its attacks on Democratic Tammany in stride. The game was up, though, when the guy who cooked the city's books died, and a man who hated Tammany brought copies of the payouts to the *Times* publisher. But before it happened, Slippery Dick Connolly offered the publisher, George Jones, a bribe of $5 million to let up. When the comptroller told Jones that he could go to Europe and live like a prince, the newspaperman replied, "True, sir, but I should know that I was a rascal." The *Times* plunged on.

It was reported that Thomas Nast could have been the richest cartoonist in the world. He was offered $500,000 to cease and desist, but turned it down. In short, Boss Tweed was finished. He was convicted, sent to prison, and escaped to Europe, where he was caught and returned. He died in prison at age fifty-five. The major thorn in his side during the latter part of his reign was Samuel Tilden, who was sitting on the fence about running in the forthcoming presidential election.

The scandal almost did in Tammany, but a savior was at hand. Honest John Kelly, a quiet, devout Catholic took over the society once the Tweed

Ring was crushed. He brought the distinct Irish Catholic complexion to Tammany as he cleaned it up and remade its political power base. Heavyset, stolid, wearing a short beard and sometimes referred to as a U.S. Grant look-a-like, Kelly was an intelligent, exceptional organizer. But he was vain, susceptible to flattery, and vengeful. Originally a friend of Tilden's, he was now his avowed enemy.

Bennett relit his cigar stump and wrote: *vain, susceptible to flattery, Irish Catholic* on his note pad. He had an idea.

★ ★ ★

That evening Bennett called a council of war in Custer's hotel suite. Present were Ned Burke, Tom Custer, Kellogg and Myles Keogh. The publisher related his findings about Tammany to the others, then stated, "I want to remind you that we *must* carry New York at the convention to win. To do so, we must carry Tammany, and that's Honest John Kelly's private fiefdom. Kelly rules." He looked around at the expectant faces. "Okay, I've got a plan. Kelly sees everything in Irish green and hasn't missed mass in years. He's also got a price—patronage. Therefore . . ."

Custer broke in, "I don't understand patronage."

Bennett raised an eyebrow. "You will. It's the power to appoint jobs and positions on a political basis. To you, it will mean giving Tammany, and thus Kelly, the right to select federal appointees in New York."

"Is that honest?" Custer asked.

"It's a way of political life."

Custer shrugged. "Go on."

"Okay," Bennett said, looking directly at Keogh. "We have in our midst, a native Irishman who served in a Catholic war and has two papal medals to prove it. He also owns some kind of an estate in Ireland, and is close to Custer. I think Colonel Keogh, decked out in the Pope's medals, should go to see Honest John Kelly to elicit his sworn support."

Burke let out a loud laugh. "*Capital, James, capital!*"

Everyone grinned as Keogh shook his head. "What do I have to promise him?"

"Nothing you're not forced into," Bennett replied. "Let him make the demands."

Keogh looked at Custer. "What do you think, General?"

Custer shrugged. "Do it." He smiled. "I'd sure like to hear the blarney fly at *that* meeting!"

The Kelly plan was born.

★ ★ ★

Brevet Lieutenant-colonel Myles Walter Keogh at forty, was three months younger than Custer. With thick, slightly curly dark hair and blue eyes, he was strikingly handsome. A full mustache and a small goatee under his lower lip framed his infectious smile. Born in Ireland, he entered manhood as a soldier of fortune, serving briefly in the French Foreign Legion before going to Italy in 1860 to join the Papal Army that was fighting against Napoleon III. He was decorated with the *Orine di San Gregorio* and the coveted *Pro Petri Sede* for gallantry in action before sailing for America to join the Union Army in 1862. He served as aide to several generals and was heroic in a number of battles, finally being brevetted lieutenant-colonel by the time the war ended. He obtained a regular commission as a captain when he joined the Seventh Cavalry at the time the regiment was organized in 1866. He was one of Custer's favorite officers, supposedly giving the general the regimental song, "GarryOwen." He enjoyed the women, and like many an Irishman, never met a drink he didn't like.

His appointment with Honest John Kelly was at two o'clock on the Friday after the Custer party returned from Indianapolis. Tammany had been housed in a number of edifices, but its most famous wigwam was the building on Fourteenth Street, completed in 1868. A high three-story brick building with tall arched windows, it was crowned by a statue of the Society's patron Saint Tammany. Its Long Room was big enough to have housed the Democratic National Convention the year it opened.

The portly Kelly met Keogh with a big smile and a hearty handshake as the colonel entered his office exactly on time. Keogh was in uniform, wearing his papal medals. They sat at a small conference table where a secretary served tea. The conversation was light as Kelly asked questions about Keogh's early life in County Carlow in Ireland. "Do you intend to go back?" Honest John asked.

"Maybe some day," Keogh replied, affecting a bit more brogue. "I have inherited a Georgian mansion in Connemara known as Clifden Castle. Perhaps some day when I've won the American medal of honor and have hung up my saber, I'll go back there in the summers."

Kelly's eyes were bright. "What a pleasant thought. Now tell me about the Papal War. I heard you were decorated by the pope himself."

"Just the *Pro Petrie Sede*," Keogh replied, pointing to that medal.

"Wasn't it exciting meeting His Holiness like that?"

Keogh smiled. "I just stood at attention as he pinned it on my tunic." In actuality, a general had presented the medal to Lieutenant Keogh, but this was politics.

They talked on about Rome for a few minutes before Kelly switched to the present. "So, Colonel, what brings you here today?"

Keogh was direct. "The election, sir. We feel strongly that General Custer will not only be nominated by the Democratic Party, but will definitely win the national election. We would like for you and your proud Tammany friends to be our friends."

The boss nodded his head enthusiastically. "We want to be your friends, sir. It has been quite awhile since a president has visited our great Wigwam."

"I guarantee the general will come. Perhaps as often as you might wish."

"And if his Tammany friends are supportive enough, say at the convention, and in the national election, how, uh, friendly will he be from Washington?"

Keogh shrugged. "How friendly would you want him to be?"

Kelly smiled. "I would imagine giving us the run of patronage in both the city and the state would certainly be acceptable."

Keogh smiled back. "I think General Custer would be most amenable to your suggestions, sir. But who could promise a full run? I think we could give you the city, but don't forget we have to get along with your old enemy, Samuel Tilden. He will want a piece of the pie for his people, that Irving Hall bunch."

"Seems to me, Colonel, you army boys have got to decide who you want to get in bed with."

Keogh leaned forward. "Actually, Mr. Kelly, we'd like to be in bed with both of you, but you've got to remember that I'm just a novice at this political stuff."

Kelly let out a roar of laughter. "Novice, my ass. You're going to make a hell of a good politician, Keogh!"

They shook hands and the colonel tossed off a salute as they parted.

Bennett had been right again.

Unless a candidate were a delegate, such as Garfield had been in Chicago, he normally didn't attend the convention. Grant had never attended a convention. In fact, candidates didn't even campaign, which is why Bennett had come up with the Lyceum gambit. But there were other ways to skin a cat, as the saying goes. It was a good time for Custer to leave New York for a spell and go back to his roots. With his brother Tom accompanying him, he stopped for a day in New Rumley, Ohio, where they visited Autie's birthplace, a two-story house that had been a rather rowdy tavern well before his birth. The next day they caught the train that connected to Monroe, the small Michigan city south of Detroit that Custer had adopted as his home and where Libbie grew up. There, amidst quite a bit of fanfare, along with Myles Keogh who had joined them, they settled down to await the news of the Democratic convention as it poured off the wire from Kellogg.

★ ★ ★

CINCINNATI, OHIO *June 22, 1880*

The city's modernized Gothic Music Hall was quite an elaborate showplace. Tile and stone mixed with colored brick ornamentation to contrast with the tastefully and attractively paneled walls and ceilings. Its hard-wood floors glistened with polished wax, and colorful bunting was draped throughout. The Hall was Cincinnati's pride and joy and the city fathers wanted the country's Democratic delegates to know it. Red, white, and blue flags hung everywhere, and on the podium the national coat of arms announced the business at hand. The entrance to the auditorium was decked out with a huge white and blue sign that read, "Ohio Greets the Nation." Both Custer's and General Winfield Scott Hancock's likenesses were prominent.

But there, the vigor that had marked the Republican convention seemed to end. There were several factions but only one problem added any zest to the proceedings—whether Honest John Kelly and his Tammany bunch be given any seats. In a fight with Sam Tilden over con-trol at the earlier New York convention, Kelly and the Tammany Hall group had bolted and selected their own delegates. When the convention opened, Kelly got a slap on the wrist when he was told that his delegates might not get seated.

Boston Custer was present, having come in by train from California. He married the banker's daughter, Sharon Rose, had done well in real estate very quickly, and became established in Democratic party circles in San Francisco. Although it was stretching protocol somewhat, Libbie and Annie Yates were also in attendance as observers. Bennett had decided the matter, knowing that Libbie's charming presence could only add to Custer's allure.

One of the most interesting points of the convention for Libbie was the appearance of Susan B. Anthony on the schedule. Both she and Annie waited quite excitedly until, at shortly after four o'clock on the 23rd, the famous champion of women's suffrage walked to the speaker's stand.

Susan Brownell Anthony was born in Adams, Massachusetts, in 1820, the daughter of a Quaker abolitionist. An anti-slavery crusader from an early age, in the 1840s she also founded the first women's temperance asso-ciation, The Daughters of Temperance. In 1869, along with Elizabeth Cady Stanton, Anthony organized the National Woman Suffrage Association. With her hair severely parted in the middle, her long black dress simply trimmed with a single ivory broach, Miss Anthony looked about her for a moment then launched into her plea, "Gentlemen, the Fifteenth Amendment to the Constitution of the United States gave the vote to the Negroes of this country, but *only to the men!* That has been the backward and narrow thinking in this country since it was born. 'All men are created equal,' but not women. In 1878 Senator Sargent introduced the Women's Suffrage Amendment, but it has languished for two years. It's time that half the population of this proud country, the half that bears the children, have the right to . . ."

Libbie listened, enthralled, as Anthony continued with her forceful plea. Noting a certain lack of attention by many of the delegates, she frowned and nudged Annie. "They don't even care," she whispered.

"What are you going to do about it?" Annie asked, a slight smile lurking in her eyes.

"I don't know, but I'll do *something*"

★ ★ ★

Mark Kellogg, who was constantly sending telegrams to Custer in Monroe, was also writing the running commentary for the *Herald*. He wrote: "Since Kelly worked out his problems with Tilden and finally got his delegates seated, the pervasive opinion on the floor is not to alienate Kelly and his Tammany brood too much. A candidate must be selected who will satisfy the New Yorkers, and who will not be objectionable to the Solid South. Tilden, who is still on the outs with Kelly and who is also quite sick, will not do. Pennsylvanian Samuel Randall, the Speaker of the House, Senator Thomas Bayard of Delaware, and General Winfield Scott Hancock are the only serious candidates who oppose General Custer. No one knows for sure what is in the mind of Honest John Kelly, but he seems to be favoring Bayard. That, however, could be a ploy to keep Tilden out of the race for good. It's possible that Kelly will switch if there is a trend toward Custer and throw full support his way.

"The Democrats last held true power in 1861. They control the House, but not the Senate and the presidency—where the true power lies. They want it now. The Republicans are running two bloody shirts. Which one of the Democratic bloody shirts will the Democrats pick, if either? A name from the past has appeared from New Jersey to nominate

Custer—the former commanding general of the mighty Army of the Potomac, who had, himself, run for the presidency against Abraham Lincoln in 1864—Governor George B. McClellan."

★ ★ ★

As expected, Randall, Bayard and Hancock were nominated. Tilden scrapped a last minute effort to have his name put forth, and the last name to be presented was Custer's. When George McClellan took the podium, he stood still for several moments until silence prevailed over the large hall. At that moment a huge poster of Custer in his buckskin suit and cavalry hat was unrolled to hang behind the speaker. A loud roar went up from the delegates, forcing McClellan to again wait until the noise subsided. Finally, the former general spoke, "Gentlemen, I had the privilege of knowing George Armstrong Custer as a heroic young lieutenant, when he came to my staff in 1862 as my aide-de-camp. He went on to command a brigade as a general at the age of twenty-three, and was immediately successful against Jeb Stuart at Gettysburg. His amazing leadership skills as a cavalry commander continued to bring huge success to Union forces throughout the remainder of the war. At the age of twenty-five, he was promoted to major general. . . ."

Little Mac paused for more effect in the quiet hall, then proceeded, "In all modesty, gentlemen, the four names that were most famous in the Union press during the war were Grant, McClellan, Sherman and Custer. After the war, Custer went on to become the country's greatest Indian fighter. His brilliant victory at the Little Bighorn marked the end of major Indian hostilities and his brilliant diplomatic skills brought the recalcitrant Sitting Bull into the American way of life. During his service in the South, he proved his admiration for the people of that great part of the United States, a friendship so strong that I almost didn't get to nominate him. A southern general named Rosser wanted to do it, but I wouldn't let him."

When the laughter subsided, McClellan went on, "Now, we are gathered here to select a leader who will return the presidency to the Democratic party, a man whose great popularity among the electorate will sweep him into office, a man who can give us the sweet taste of victory that we so strongly desire. *Gentlemen, I nominate George Armstrong Custer for the presidency of the United States of America.*"

Instantly, led by Bennett's hand-picked and well-coached delegates, the shouting began. Within moments it swelled to a roar. The band blared, "Yankee Doodle," "Dixie," and "Hail to the Chief," then switched to "GarryOwen" and played it over and over as the chairman pounded his gavel in a vain attempt to regain order. With a smile, Kellogg put down his pencil and went to find Libbie.

Once it quieted down, the second ballot was taken. The magic number of the majority required for nomination was 492. The results were:

> Custer 269
> Hancock 162
> Randall 96
> Bayard 87
> All Others 112

That evening, as the jockeying behind the scenes grew more intense, Bennett and Burke moved from delegation to delegation. Boston Custer, having secured California's votes, brought a box of cigars to the already smoky rooms of the Wisconsin delegation. There, over, a stein of good Milwaukee beer, he made his case for Autie. At the hotel where they were staying, Libbie and Annie drank a cup of coffee with Susan B. Anthony and listened attentively as the women's suffrage advocate enthusiastically enlisted their support. Finally, at midnight, Kellogg sent the last telegram of the 24th to Custer:

GENERAL:
A profitable evening. New votes have been secured and it looks good for tomorrow. It's possible that you might get the majority on the fifth or sixth ballot. Maybe earlier. Wouldn't it be interesting if we could make a charge, like at the Little Bighorn? It will be June 25th!

SIGNED, KELLOGG

The fourth anniversary of the battle was a hot and humid day in the Queen City on the Ohio River. It was sweltering inside the Music Hall as the third ballot was about to be taken, but no one seemed to care. There was a special electricity in the air that had been missing the first day, an almost palpable stir that forecast something special. Again, bright colors were rampant and music permeated everything. More than one breath was scented with alcohol, but there was no animosity; anticipation ruled. On cue, a barbershop quartet, dressed in cavalry uniforms, burst into "GarryOwen!"

The voting commenced, with Custer getting his share. Then, suddenly, Wisconsin switched completely to Custer. A ripple of enthusiasm ran through the crowded hall and all at once delegation chairmen were heading for the podium to change their votes. A frenzy swept over the seven thousand yelling delegates as they waved at the chairman for a chance to caste their votes for Custer. It seemed that no one could wait to jump on the Custer bandwagon as the whooping and hollering made a bedlam of the hall. Poor Hancock and the others never had a chance! Soon it was unanimous and this time the band played "Dixie" first before switching to the "Star Spangled Banner." The leaders of the party, including Honest John Kelly, joined hands and grinned from the podium as cheer after cheer rang from the rafters. The Democrats had selected a candidate.

★ ★ ★

The Custers, friends, and relatives were gathered at the Monroe telegraph office trying to appear calm, but quite eagerly awaiting the news. Food and drink were in ample supply, as were reporters from many of the country's major newspapers. Custer was outside, basking in both the warm sunshine and the well-wishes of gathering Monroeites. As he mopped some perspiration from the back of his neck with a handkerchief, Tom burst out the door, waving a telegram and shouting, "*You got it, Autie! You've been nominated!*"

Custer grabbed the message. The words stared out at him:

> Victory is ours! The charge routed the enemy. Cincinnati is your newest Little Bighorn. You are officially the 1880 Democratic

Party candidate for president of the United States. The war is half won!

Signed,

James Gordon Bennett, Jr.

Tom let out a whoop and jumped up and clicked his heels in midair as the rest of the party came tumbling out of the telegraph office. Keogh popped the cork from a bottle of champagne and took a swig from its frothing top before handing it to a reporter from the Chicago *Tribune*. More shouts broke the air as Custer reread the telegram.

It had happened. He still couldn't believe it, but it had happened. His eyes filled momentarily and he had to wipe them with his sleeve. It had happened.

★ ★ ★

As Custer knew, the brain trust of Bennett and Burke had long before divined that Indiana would be the key state in the national election. It's fifteen electoral votes could be pivotal, and the best way to get them would be to have a vice-president from that proud state. Of course, all of that was in the mill when Custer delivered his Lyceum speech in Indianapolis, and met the man they thought could best deliver the state. He was the distinguished banker and former member of Congress, William H. English. In addition to his banking and congressional background the handsome English brought his interest in history to the election table. Custer was looking forward to their friendship.

The party readily accepted the man from Indiana as the vice-presidential candidate, then moved into platform discussions and decisions. The following day, just after a delegate from Kentucky finished reading an innocuous point about tariffs being for revenue only, a murmur in the crowd quickly swelled to an ovation as Custer, with Libbie on his arm, strode into the hall.

With his right hand raised to the roars of acclaim and the band's rendition of "GarryOwen," the general mounted the podium and held up his arms to quiet the deafening cheers. After another two minutes, he spoke loudly and clearly, "Gentlemen—and what ladies there are in the gallery—you have honored me greatly by making me your candidate. I intend to fully return that honor as resolutely as I ever entered into a military campaign. I will give the great Democratic Party of the United States the presidency of this marvelous country! We shall occupy the White House for eight years to come and bring America the leadership you want!

Once more, the large hall rocked with cheers. The race with Garfield and Co. was on!

It was a night for major celebration in Democratic circles throughout America, but in the large hotel suite Bennett had rented, it was one of joy. Party dignitaries were patting themselves on the back, William English and his Indiana friends were particularly boisterous, and the Custer party was its inimitable zestful self. Custer, true to his pledge of abstinence, shook off several glasses of champagne from well-wishers, but Libbie, who liked her glass of wine, was enjoying the bubbly. Annie Yates, her hair a couple of shades closer to white since accepting her position with Libbie, also lifted a couple of glasses. To Tom Custer and Myles Keogh, who had shared many a bottle back in the Fort Lincoln days and since, it was just another occasion to have a party. The champagne was only an appetizer for what they had planned. James Gordon Bennett, Jr. was in his glory. All of the strings he had pulled so far were tightly wound and ready for the next big step. Even Boss Kelly was present, with a glass of the best Kentucky bourbon in his fat hand.

Custer was, as usual, full of himself. To him, it was part of the ongoing saga of the ultimate warrior—his due. This was a step, a big one, but still just one of the steps leading to his ultimate glory. He had recently spent much time thinking about the warrior presidents of the United States: Washington, Jackson, Taylor, Grant—wartime generals all. Washington had personally led in battle, but had he ever raised his saber and led a charge into a hail of bullets? The same was mostly true of Old Hickory Jackson and Zach Taylor. They'd directed armies, but as far as he knew, they'd never led just a few companies into small scale, up close battle. The stories of Grant as a young officer in the Mexican War bespoke reckless, personal heroism, but none of them had, over and over, led regiments and brigades into withering fire like George Armstrong Custer had. No one had.

He had visions of himself, in a resplendent uniform he himself would design, taking a vast American army crashing into battle. He'd be the first to do so at the head, leading, where a commander ought to be. The first *president* to ever do so! An American Napoleon. He liked the idea. . . .

Custer spent long hours thinking about enlarging the country's borders, making the United States the most powerful nation in the world. The Caribbean—kick Spain out of those nearby waters. Positively. Then Mexico. And, finally, Canada. He, President and General George Armstrong Custer would create the United States of *North America*. He hadn't told anyone yet, not even Libbie. But when he was settled down in the White House, he'd . . .

"Autie?"

He brought himself back to the present as Tom spoke. "Yes, little brother."

"I hate to run out on your party, but Keogh and have a date with a couple of Cincinnati's loveliest, and we're going to disappear."

Custer grinned. "Be sure and leave one of those new campaign posters in their parlor."

Tom grinned back. "We'll leave them in their bedrooms, big brother."

As the two officers headed for the door, Libbie sidled up and put her arm around Custer. "Where are those two ne'er-do-wells off to?" she asked.

Custer smiled. "They're going to do some special campaigning."

Libbie rolled her eyes. "Sure."

★ ★ ★

Bennett, Ned Burke, and Boston Custer had drifted near the window seat to talk. Boston had been nominated by the Democrats to represent his district in Congress. He had not brought his attractive wife with him to Cincinnati. At thirty-one, Boston looked somewhat like his older brother. His light brown curls cascaded below his collar, and although his build bespoke a certain frailty, his inner strength soon became evident to those who got to know him. "How's the real estate picture in San Francisco?" Bennett asked.

"Good!" Boston replied enthusiastically. "I've gotten involved with development of land down toward San Jose that I think will pay off; and some more on the Monterey Peninsula. But there's good money to be made right around San Francisco, what with its strong growth. People just keep moving in."

"Climate?" Ned Burke asked.

"That's part of it," Boston replied.

"How does your campaign look?" Bennett asked as he lit a cigar.

"Excellent. The Democrats are strong this year, and, although I don't like hearing it, they believe I can win my race on the strength of being Autie's brother." Boston frowned. "I'd rather be running on my own merits, but . . ."

"Getting in's the most important thing," Burke said. "Then you can be your own man and forge your own future. Right now your brother is a gift horse."

Boston nodded as Bennett blew out a small cloud of smoke and asked, "Will you be able to pull California into the fold for the general?"

"I hope so. I'm certainly going to do my best."

"We may need those votes."

"I thought, with the South, New York and Indiana, you had enough to ride in comfortably."

Burke shook his head. "Nothing is *ever* comfortable about an election."

★ ★ ★

At shortly after eleven o'clock in the evening Custer knocked on the door of Hancock's hotel room. The Pennsylvanian was alone, dressed in a gray robe with a faded West Point crest on its breast pocket. He was clearly surprised to see the man who had just stolen his dream. "May I come in?" Custer asked.

"Yes, of course," Hancock replied, motioning toward a wing chair. "What can I do for you, Custer?"

Hancock graduated from West Point seventeen years before Custer and had been a regular major general since 1866. He was a man of impressive stature and soldierly bearing who had been described as someone "who always says something worthwhile." Custer hadn't spoken with him since the 1867 Hancock Expedition when the general had supported his court-martial.

Custer declined the proffered seat and replied, "Sir, I came to wish you well. You were a general officer when I was a second lieutenant, and I respect you highly. I'm sure you would have made a great president. However, politics is politics, as I'm learning. I think I, too, can do some good for the country."

Hancock watched him quietly as he struggled for the difficult words. The stammer came back. "I, I, mm, merely want you to know that I commiserate with your great disappointment."

The older man's eyes softened. "Well, that's quite thoughtful of you, Custer."

"Perhaps, if you would accept it, I can find a role where you can be of great value in some plans I've yet to formulate concerning military operations."

Hancock shrugged. "If it's for the good of the country, I would strongly consider such a role. Right now, I'm going to take an additional leave of absence and start writing my memoirs."

Custer smiled, suddenly more at ease. "Sir, that would be premature. I'm sure there is much ahead in your productive life."

"I hope so," the tall general replied. "Well, General, I hope you give Garfield a sound thrashing. These damned Republicans need to have their asses kicked. If I can be of help, let me know."

Custer shook his hand. "I will, General."

★ ★ ★

In Carlisle, Pennsylvania, Little Bear, Red Elk's Kiowa roommate, looked up from the newspaper he was reading. "I see where your General Custer has won the nomination from the Democrats to be the Great White Father."

Now and then Little Bear liked to tease Red Elk about how his mighty Sioux had been defeated at the Little Bighorn, but the Hunkpapa ignored the humor. Mostly, Red Elk kept quiet about his background. He'd kept his lingering sorrow about Late Star to himself, and except for dropping some comments now and then about being on war parties, he'd kept secret his exploits as a war leader. Naturally, he hadn't told the Kiowa or anyone else at the Indian School about his vengeance vow. Since he spoke little and then usually only to Little Bear to practice speaking English, he was known around student circles as "the quiet Sioux."

"If you could vote, would you vote for Custer?" Little Bear asked.

"No. He is bad for the People."

"Wasn't he good to Sitting Bull?"

"Is a prison good?"

"Come on, Red Elk, I heard he gave Sitting Bull his own reservation. That isn't prison."

"To the Hunkpapa and our great leader it is."

Little Bear sighed. "You Sioux . . . all you want to do is fight."

"Does the paper say where Long Hair lives?"

"Yes, New York City and Michigan."

"When he is the Great White Father, he will stay in the big white tipi in Wash-ing-ton. True?"

"Yes, if he gets elected."

Red Elk spoke softly. "Some day I will visit him there."

★ ★ ★

The next day, Major Pratt summoned Red Elk to his office. As the Sioux stood before his desk, Pratt told him to pull up a chair and have a seat. "Red Elk," he began, "you haven't been here long, but I'm impressed by your conduct. You seem to have a special quality that sets you apart from the average student. Were you some kind of a leader back in your tribe?"

Red Elk looked impassively into the superintendent's eyes. "Sir, all Hunkpapas become warriors when only boys. I have seen war."

"You are from Sitting Bull's tribe. Did you fight with him?"

"No, sir," Red Elk replied. "Great chief big medicine man when I fight. I fight with Gall and Crazy Horse." It was more than he wanted to divulge, but he felt it would be best to explain a little.

"Were you at the Battle of the Little Bighorn against General Custer?"

Red Elk controlled his expression and tone. "Yes, I fight there."

"Were you a leader?" Pratt persisted.

"I just a warrior," Red Elk said quietly.

The major thought for a few moments before saying, "I would like for you to serve on our student council, Red Elk, but first you must become a company officer. Will you do that?"

Red Elk had considered it since his first talk with the superintendent. It was difficult to suppress his natural desire to lead, and so many of the other students were such *children* . . . But he couldn't be—what was that white man's word "anonymous"—if he did so. "Sir," he replied, "I wish only to learn and be to myself."

Major Pratt regarded him for a few moments, then nodded his head. "Very well, so be it. If you change your mind, come to see me."

★ ★ ★

After leaving the superintendent's office, Red Elk made his way over to the stables. He had made friends with one of the riding horses, a gelding named Comanche, and he went up to his stall. As he petted the big animal and spoke quietly to him, he noticed that one of the timbers in the wall had been scorched. He had just been told the story of how a general named Stu-art had raided the fort that was now the school back in 1863, just before a big battle called Get-tees-burg. That was where the rebel Stu-art had fought against Long Hair. When Stu-art and his cavalry came to Carlisle Barracks they had burned parts of it. He touched the charred part of the timber. It must have been missed when they fixed the building. He wondered if Stu-art had hated Long Hair. He sighed. It brought him close to Long Hair, and rekindled his hatred.

He stroked Comanche's nose. Maybe he should do as Major Pratt wanted. Then he could quietly begin instilling some of his Lakota strength into the students, give them back some spirit, some will to remember their heritage. Somewhere, at some time, the Goddess, White Buffalo Woman, with her Sacred Calf Pipe, would return and lead the People to their right-ful freedom. It was a certainty, and he would be there to lead.

But doing as Pratt wanted now could hurt his sacred mission to avenge his beloved wife, and he couldn't let that happen. He thought again of Late Star's lovely face with its sparkling black eyes, this time in her beau-tifully quilled white doeskin wedding dress. . . .

No, nothing could delay his duty.

Major Ned Burke pointed to the man standing beside his desk when Tom Custer and Myles Keogh entered his office on the corner of 14th and K in Washington. "This is Jeremiah Jones, gentlemen."

Jones was nondescript in his simple mustache and average build. He wore a plain brown suit and looked as if he'd disappear if he stepped into a group of two people. Following the handshakes, Burke said, "Mr. Jones is one of the inside men at Republican headquarters. They pay him to do whatever they need a warm body for. I pay him for information."

"You're a spy?" Keogh asked.

"More or less," Jones replied softly. Even his voice was flat.

"He brings interesting news," Burke said. "The Republicans are going to use the Monasetah shit."

Tom frowned. "I thought they'd leave that alone because of Garfield's affair in New York during the war."

"Tell him," Burke said to Jones.

"They think that New York escapade is old news that he confessed to years ago. But one story has the Indian woman having the general's illegitimate baby, and the other is that he married her in a Cheyenne ceremony and is a *bigamist*. Either way, it's far worse than Garfield's lit-tle indiscretion."

"Damn!" Keogh snapped.

"What do they plan on doing?" Tom asked.

"Bringing the woman to Chicago and paying her to tell all."

"Shit!" Tom said.

"What is *all*, Tom?" Burke asked. "I've heard the stories."

"Stories always get exaggerated. It was after the Battle of the Washita. She was a pretty girl, a chief's daughter, smart, learned English. A Cheyenne woman brought her to Autie and mumbled some kind of a ritual that he didn't understand. When it was over, a scout told him he'd just married the girl. Autie told them it was impossible, that he already had a wife."

"I heard you were both plunking her."

"All I can say is, *I* did," Tom replied.

"And I missed out," Keogh added with a rueful smile. "She was a beauty."

Burke stuck a cold cigar in his mouth. "This could be very bad. Poor wronged Indian girl sullied by the general. Thinks she's his wife. He's married to Libbie. Squaw has his kid. He leaves her in the lurch. Can't have a president who does anything like that. I heard the child even had fair hair."

"So do I," Tom said. "And she shared my blanket many a night. She was about seven months along when we met her. She had an Indian kid a couple of months later, then about a year after that she had this second one that people like to say is Autie's. But Autie's never fathered any children, supposedly because of a dose of the clap he got at West Point."

Burke turned to Jones. "How much of that do they have?"

"Everything. A congressman name Benteen gave it to them, lock, stock, and barrel."

Tom grimaced. "That *goddamned* Benteen."

"Said he was there and knew all about it," Jones said.

Tom slapped his fist into the palm of his hand. "I oughta shoot the sonofabitch!"

"That wouldn't do any good," Burke said. He paused. "The point is, what are we going to do about it?"

"I'm going to marry her."

Keogh looked at Tom Custer quizzically over his pint of stout. "Who, might I ask, are you going to join in wedded bliss?"

"Monasetah."

Keogh almost choked on his dark beer, then collected himself and nodded his head. "I see, and when did this great flood of desire wash over you, may I ask?"

"I've been thinking about it. Seems like the simple solution."

They were standing at the bar in rather loud Irish pub a few blocks from the Capitol.

"Uh huh." Keogh sipped again. They were in Washington to take part in a parade sponsored by "Cavalrymen for Custer," a political group the campaign manager had organized, mostly from Custer's old wartime Third Cavalry Division. "And what does Autie think about this great decision?"

"Haven't told him."

"And why not?"

"You know why. He'd forbid it."

"Right. Something about throwing yourself away for the sake of the cause. Well, laddie, that's about the way I see it too. Monasetah is probably a very handsome woman now, but what are you going to do in Washington circles with a bloody *squaw*?"

"She'll be all right here. She's smart."

Keogh shook his head. "You'd better ask Autie."

"Nope. I've already sent her a letter asking her to marry me."

"What'd she say?" Keogh laughed. "What if she turns you down? Or maybe she's married. I can see the headline now: Tom Custer plays martyr, but squaw rejects him!"

"She's not married. I checked with the Indian agent there on Sitting Bull's reservation where her tribe is living with his Hunkpapas."

Keogh waved at the bartender. "Give this daft man a big whiskey." He turned back to Tom. "When are you leaving on this sacrificial mission?"

"One week from today. I told Autie I'm going out to Dakota to see an old girl friend. And it's the truth."

Keogh shook his head. "Imagine, the new Secretary of the Interior with an Injun wife." He threw his head back and roared.

★ ★ ★

The name of the place was Madame Tillie's, and it was supposed to be the finest sporting house in the city. An ornate three-story wood mansion with a mammoth front porch and bright red slatted window shutters accenting its lemon yellow exterior, the pleasure structure blatantly announced it's purpose. Its interior was elaborate, with expensive, subtly lit chandeliers hanging in the two connecting downstairs parlors. In one parlor was an ornate mahogany bar with a high mirrored back bar that had been made expressly for the house by a master wood carver from Oberammergau in Germany. Rich brocades accented more mahogany sofas and Queen Anne chairs were scattered around the rooms. The glistening hardwood floors, covered here and there by expensive Persian rugs offered a place for conversations as well as intimate settings. Tillie's girls, each quite attractive and armed with a phony background story that suggested either royalty or the most tragic of life's circumstances, lounged around the parlor, joining in these groups when they weren't otherwise occupied in the many private bedrooms upstairs. In the capital of the most aggressive young nation in the world, Madame Tillie's was its palace of sin.

Tillie, herself, was a diminutive looking woman with a flaming head of auburn hair and breasts that would do a much larger woman proud. Her revealing satin gown was naturally a bright red. She smiled as she greeted Tom Custer and Myles Keogh at the door. "I'm so pleased you could come," she said, as Keogh bent over her bedecked hand. "Mr. Bennett's man said you would honor my humble house rather early. Come in and have a drink on me to start the evening."

Tom grinned as he glanced around at the unoccupied girls. "Sounds good to me, Tillie."

"You gentlemen may, of course, choose any of my girls who are free, or I might suggest a couple whom I have reserved for you. Victoria and Elizabeth have both been ladies-in-waiting at the Court of St. James's prior to their families moving to America. I was quite fortunate to obtain their services."

She led them to a small parlor separate from the great rooms. Showing them in, she said, "I thought privacy might be in order for you gentlemen."

Tom grinned as a striking brunette sidled up to him. "I'm Victoria, Colonel," she said in a cultured London accent.

As Tom introduced himself, the other young woman, a shapely blonde with large green eyes, took Keogh's arm and told him her name was Elizabeth. Noticing his slight brogue, she shifted her accent from Surrey to the Emerald Isle. "My father owned a factory in Dublin," she said, looking into Keogh's merry blue eyes. "I love every bit of my heritage."

Keogh was reaping profit from his bright idea. With Tom leaving the next day for Dakota Territory to meet Monasetah, this was his bachelor party. When he told Bennett about it, the publisher had volunteered to pick up the tab. He said he might even stop by, if he didn't take the train back to New York.

A waiter brought a magnum of champagne on ice and four glasses, and the party began. Both girls were good at their jobs, providing wit and pulchritude, along with just enough of the bawdy to give the conversation a bit of spice. Soon a second magnum arrived. When that was halfway finished, Tom suddenly had to relieve himself. Victoria said, "Come, darling, I'll take you to the loo—even assist you if you need help." Everyone laughed as she took Tom's hand and led him from the parlor.

They hadn't gone ten feet when a familiar voice boomed. "What the hell are you doing here, Custer?"

He turned to see Fred Benteen's owlish eyes glaring at him. He replied, "Well, if it isn't the best friend my brother ever had. Howdy, Fred."

"How's the crown prince?" Actually, Tom and Benteen had gotten along back in the regiment because each respected the other's warrior streak—now it was a different matter. Benteen's question had a nasty edge on it.

"Fair to middling. What is a married congressman, who I hear has suddenly turned moralist, doing in such an establishment?"

"That's none of your goddamn business. Do you really think that asshole brother of yours can be president?"

Tom found a smile. "Like as not, he's going to be."

"God help this country if he is."

Tom's temper flared. "I think you're the asshole here, Benteen."

Benteen's overhand right caught Tom a glancing blow on his cheek. Tom let out a roar and threw a left that the white-haired man took mostly in the shoulder. As the congressman swung back, an alert Tillie shouted for her bouncer, and Keogh burst out of the nearby parlor. By this time, Tom had plunged his head into Benteen's midsection and driven him back against the wall. "*You sonofabitch!*" he shouted. "*I should've killed you years ago!*"

Tillie's bouncer was a muscular ex-cop with a billy club. As he took aim, Keogh jumped in front of him and wrapped his arms around Tom. Just at that moment, James Gordon Bennett, Jr. showed up. "Tell your man to put that damned club away, Tillie!" he shouted as several of her girls rushed in to watch the commotion.

In moments, the two angry men were separated, but not before another customer walked up scribbling in a small notebook. He approached the disheveled Fred Benteen. "Aren't you Congressman Benteen?"

The former hero of the Little Bighorn wiped a trickle of blood from his nose as he said, "Who the hell are you?"

"Name's Smith," the man replied. "I'm a journalist."

Bennett stepped in quickly. "Do you know who I am?"

"Yes, Mr. Bennett," Smith replied.

"What newspaper do you work for?" the newspaperman asked.

"I'm free-lance."

"Do you want to work for me?"

Smith grinned. "Who wouldn't?"

"All right, you're on my payroll as of today. Now forget you saw any of this. Do you understand?"

Smith grinned again. "Yes, *sir*, Mr. Bennett!"

The publisher turned to the others. "Now, why don't we all have a friendly drink together, Gentlemen?"

Benteen brushed himself off and growled, "I'm not drinking with a Custer."

"Then, sir, may I suggest you depart before someone else reports your misconduct in this establishment."

Benteen glared at the others, shrugged, and walked toward the vestibule. Before he reached it he turned. "I'm warning all of you right now. George Armstrong Custer will ruin this country if he's elected."

Bennett watched the congressman depart, then said, "Tillie, bring us another magnum of champagne, and let's get back to the celebration."

The Sitting Bull Reservation was set up on the west side of the broad Missouri, with its main camp located near the river twelve miles below Camp Rice. The Indian Bureau had honored Custer's promises to the great chief and had not only quickly built a group of modern buildings to service the Sioux and Cheyenne, who had elected to reside with him, but had found a good agent to administer the large encampment. He was none other than Doctor Henry Porter, the contract surgeon from Bismarck who had so ably attended the wounded during the *Far West's* trip back to Fort Lincoln. The reservation itself included roughly one hundred square miles that permitted good hunting and much of the freedom the Sioux so dearly desired.

Although he made it a point to be recalcitrant at times, Sitting Bull had come to trust the bald-headed doctor. Gall and the other chiefs were still with him, and the People who had followed him to his reservation were living much better than they ever had. Of course, Doctor Porter, a strong, honest agent who was truly interested in their welfare, was the major factor in this development. He brooked no supply problems, and his superiors knew he was connected directly to General Custer, who had a specific interest in this reservation. Although the Indian Bureau was not under the War Department, it's political management was more than aware of the strong possibility that the general would reside in the President's House.

Firm in his allegiance to Sitting Bull was Stone Forehead, the major chief of the Southern Cheyenne. Now approaching sixty, Stone Forehead had brought his tribe to this reservation shortly after the Sioux leader's return from Canada. Still wiry, with the lines of time etched into his leathery face, the chief looked up as he smoked the pipe and listened to Tom Custer's words while the interpreter translated them into Cheyenne.

"Great chief, I wish to speak to the woman, Meotzi, of life in the big camp of Washington. There, my brother, Long Hair, may soon become the Great White Father, and I will be his chief for all treatment of the Indian peoples. If the woman, Meotzi, should wish, I would like to marry her and take her as my wife to live with the Great White Father and his family in Washington. I will be kind to her, great chief, and be a father to her children. As the brother of Long Hair, I can bring great new honor to your already glorious and respected tribe. I ask for your permission to speak to her of these things."

Stone Forehead looked from the interpreter, first to Doctor Porter, who nodded his approval, then to Tom Custer, who was sitting cross-legged in front of him. Solemnly, the chief handed over the pipe, from which Tom took a puff. At length, Stone Forehead grunted and said in Cheyenne, "It would be an honor for you to take this woman to your tipi, Brother of Long Hair. I give you permission to speak to her."

Tom took another pull on the pipe and nodded. They had already spoken of good ponies and hunting the *pte* before the chief recounted his victories over the hated Crows. The first step was accomplished.

★ ★ ★

Monasetah had become even lovelier since Tom last saw her at the Little Bighorn five years earlier. She was taller than the average Cheyenne woman, and slender. She had been seventeen when he first met her after the Battle of the Washita, where Chief Black Kettle had been killed. Now, nearly twelve years later, tiny laugh lines marked the corners of her dark eyes, for she was still a merry person. Her bright white teeth accented her ready smile, and, at times, a throaty laugh punctuated her speech. Though she had high cheek bones, her face was quite round. Her English, which she continued to practice with her children, was very good, still accented somewhat, but better than that of any other Southern Cheyenne woman.

Monasetah, or *Meotzi*, her actual Cheyenne name, knew, of course, why Tom Custer had come. The interpreter from Doctor Porter's office had seen the first telegram inquiring about her marital status and had told her about it, and then his letter had arrived. The idea of becoming his wife and leaving reservation life startled her. She had been without a husband for such a long time.

Her war leader husband had divorced her just two weeks before the Long Knives crashed into Black Kettle's camp on that cold morning in 1868. It had been a simple matter of her not taking his beatings. She was the proud daughter of Chief Little Rock and she had warned him not to hurt her again. The next time he beat her, she shot him in the knee. Both he and her father had been killed in the battle and she was adopted into Stone Forehead's tipi. Then there had been the interlude with the Custers in 1869. The woman, Mahwisa, had married her to Long Hair, but he had said she was not his wife, that he had another named Libby. Later, she had met Libby, and had even offered Long Hair's wife her baby.

The Custers—Long Hair and Tom—she had loved them both. And now it was *real*.

She was wearing her second finest white doeskin dress, the one with the blue quilling that had won the most recent contest among the village women. Her moccasins were also a work of art. She had brushed her hair for an hour that morning after bathing in the small river. Then she had carefully woven her long tresses into a single braid adorned with a blue quilled shell.

"Allo, Tom Cus-ter," she said as they met in Porter's office.

Tom grinned as he shook her hand, the *Wasicus* way. "You are more beautiful than ever," he said appreciatively. "Let's go for a walk."

They left the wooden headquarters building and strolled quietly to a shady area that was secluded enough to give them privacy. Their conversation was light, although a bit forced, as they edged around the shyness of two one-time lovers meeting for the first time in years. "Your English is even better," Tom said.

"I teach it every day," she replied. "Mostly to the children of the tribe."

They found a large rock and Tom asked her to sit. "You got my letter," he said directly. "I want to marry you and take you to the big cities of New York and Washington."

Her eyes glowed as she took his hand. "I like that, Tom Custer. Will you make me happy there?"

"Yes, my beauty. We will live in a great house and you will be envied."

"What about my sons?" she asked.

"At first we will leave them with your family. And then, when my brother becomes the Great White Father, we'll bring them to live with us. I will give money to a woman in your family to care for them."

"Oh, Tom Custer, you are a great man!" she exclaimed, getting to her feet and kissing him. He had taught her how to kiss the *Wasicus* way back in '69.

He grinned again. "Well, I don't know about that. I just know I'm going to have fun being your husband."

She embraced and kissed him again.

★ ★ ★

Tom had never married, much to the disappointment of Libbie. It was simply inconceivable to them that he would not have a wife and children, and they were always trying to get him interested in available young women. In the years at Fort Lincoln, in particular, eligible young ladies had often been invited to the Custer house to tempt him. But the only tempting that was achieved was in getting him to lust over them. He was simply content dallying with scarlet women, who didn't wish to throw a noose over his head. Now, even though he felt the political situation called for this somewhat unusual development, he'd decided Monasetah, whom he called "Sallie Ann," might make a good wife. She was attractive, a passionate lover, and was, after all, a chief's daughter.

Now another emotion tugged at him. Over the years, he'd had a couple of fingers pointed at him by pregnant women, but he figured they didn't have proof that he was the cause of their conditions since he hadn't been the sole beneficiary of their charms. As a result, he'd never fathered any children for certain. In the case of Monasetah, who go pregnant a couple of months after the birth of her first son, he still wasn't positive he was the father.

Autie *had* been with her on at least a half-dozen occasions. It was a fact, not just an accusation by Benteen. It's true that Libbie didn't have any children, and there was that story about Autie's dose of clap at the Point—that was still a possibility. Many officers had their little flings with Indian women. It was a way of life on the frontier. The second ranking officer in the army, Little Phil Sheridan, had shared an Indian woman's blanket for years, and had almost married her. But that wasn't the point now. The question was simply: *was this boy his son?* The lad was tall for ten years of age, slender like he'd been as a youngster, and his face had the same narrowness. His hair was sort of a mustard brown, instead of black, and his eyes were a light hazel with thick dark lashes. His expression was solemn as he stood beside his older brother, Little Elk. "Hello," Tom said with a smile.

The boy, whose name was Running Antelope, spoke without expression, "Hello,

Ker-nel."

Tom looked up into his mother's soft expression, then smiled at the boy again.

"I'm going to be your father," he said.

Both boys kept their reserve as he continued. "Your uncle, Long Hair, will soon become the Great White Father, and someday, when you have finished your schooling and training as brave Sioux warriors, I'll bring you to live in my big tipi." He gave each of them an engraved jackknife and chatted with them for several minutes before leaving to eat lunch with Doctor Porter. As he walked away with Monasetah, he said, "They're a couple of fine boys, Sallie Ann."

She stopped and looked directly into his eyes. "I'm positive, Tom."

"About what?"

"You are the father of Running Antelope."

He felt a rush of warmth. "I'm pleased, Sallie Ann."

★ ★ ★

The marriage ceremony was to be performed by Mahwisa, also known as Old Deer. As a popular medicine woman in the tribe, she was its spiritual leader. She had recited the marriage words over Monasetah and the general back in '69, but this time they would be known to all concerned. It was a warm day with powderpuff clouds running around the sky and the sound of the nearby river drifting over the camp. Tom had purchased a handsome roan stallion in Bismarck to present to Stone Forehead. Usually several ponies were given by the groom to the family of the bride, but this marriage was quite different in many ways, primarily, that the bride was marrying a Long Knife who was taking her away to the Land of the Tall Tipis, so any effort he made to satisfy custom was deeply appreciated. A feast was prepared and had begun the second day after Tom's arrival at the agency. All of the Cheyenne who could make it were there, and most of the Hunkpapas as well.

Arriving an hour before the ceremony, Mark Kellogg took copious notes for the article he would send off to the *Herald*. Bennett wanted the Republicans to know for sure that their Monasetah ploy was finished. He had given Tom $2,000 for expenses and a wedding gift. Kellogg referred to the bride as the "Indian princess" as he organized his story. "She wore her finest nearly white doeskin dress, quilled with red and blue designs, and the knee-high moccasins of the same material, which had won for her the tribe's quilling contest (the most respected competition for Cheyenne and Sioux women)."

Sitting Bull and Gall had ridden over from the Hunkpapa camp to attend the event, and were now sharing the pipe with Stone Forehead and several other Cheyenne chiefs and headmen. Tom had spoken with Sitting Bull, conveying his brother's best wishes, and the chief had actually been quite pleasant. He gave Tom a polished amulet to give to his brother.

After several short speeches by the Cheyenne leaders, the wrinkled Mahwisa rose, shook a rattle, and in a high, clear voice said in Cheyenne, "Rise, Monasetah, daughter of Little Rock and Stone Forehead."

Monasetah got to her feet and pulled up Tom, who had been sitting cross-legged beside her. As all conversation stopped, the medicine woman raised her eyes and hands to the sky and cracked the silence with, "*Wyan he cinacaqupi* . . ." "He wanted that girl, so they gave her to him!"

Monasetah turned to Tom and smiled as she took his hand. "You are now my husband."

25

"My *God!*"

Libbie Custer stared wide-eyed at the story in the *Herald*. Her tone was incredulous. "Did you know anything about this, Autie?"

Custer looked up from the second page of the *Times*. "About what?"

"About what that crazy brother of yours has done!"

"What are you talking about?" Custer asked, reaching for the *Herald*.

"The darn fool has *married* Monasetah!"

Custer's eyes poured into the article, a large feature on the second page. Seeing the lead line, "Col. Tom Custer Marries Indian Lover," he let out a low whistle and said, "I'll be damned!" He quickly read on. "Well, I'll be double damned!"

"You didn't know anything about this?" Libbie asked, visibly shaken.

"Nothing. Darned fool said he wanted to visit some old girl friends out there in Bismarck." He blew out a sigh and shook his head. "I guess he did."

"Well, he's not bringing her to live in *my* house."

Custer didn't reply. Back when the story of his amours with Monasetah had gotten back to Libbie, he told her they were lies. Yes, that Cheyenne woman had tried to get him married to the chief's daughter, but he had forcibly quashed the thing on the spot. Libbie was suspicious and had treated him quite coolly for several days, but even if she hadn't believed his denial, she had never brought it up again. And when she met the girl, she'd been quite gracious to her. When Monasetah had offered her baby to the childless Libbie, she responded only with gratitude and a friendly "No, thank you."

Libbie took the newspaper back and stared at the article. She simply couldn't help the feeling of betrayal that gnawed at her. It had been bad enough when the storm over this woman had splashed down on her a decade ago, but she had handled it resolutely. Autie had denied it, and that was all there was to it. She had no choice. There had been a couple of other occasions when they'd been separated, when she thought he had strayed, but that was one of the hazards of being married to an exciting man—other women were attracted to him and were wont to pursue him. But *this*!

She'd always treated Tom as her own brother. In fact, the three of them had been nearly inseparable over the years, and Tom had usually lived with them. He had no doggone business running off and doing something stupid like this. A thousand beautiful young women from good American families would *die* to snare the handsome fool!

Well, like she said, he wasn't bringing her to live in *her* house—no matter where it might be.

★ ★ ★

A strategy briefing took place on July 20 in the new campaign headquarters in the old Astor House Hotel at Broadway and Vescey Street. Once larger than any hotel in Paris or London, the former queen of New York's inns was now a stately dowager. The "Custer for President" suite was actually a secondary banquet room. Now it was festooned with red, white, and blue banners and a huge portrait of Custer. Cavalry yellow was also prominent in the large room's decor. Several desks and chairs were occupied by busy volunteers, mostly women, sending out letters. In a corner secluded by movable screens, Ned Burke stood by a large map of the United States on an easel. In his hand a shiny rapier served as a pointer. Seated before him was the inner circle of the campaign team: Custer, Bennett, Mark Kellogg, Keogh, Tom Custer, Lawrence Barrett, and William English, the vice-presidential nominee.

Major Burke began, "Gentlemen, the magic number in the election is *one hundred eighty-five* electoral votes. Whichever candidate gets that number or more will be the next president of the United States." His eyes gleamed as he went on, "At this point, we believe it stands this way: Garfield has thirteen states in hand for a total of *one hundred forty-six* votes, mostly from eastern and Midwestern states. We figure our side has fifteen states locked up—all of the south and most of the border states—for a total of *one hundred thirty-five*."

He paused, looked around. "Obviously, gentlemen, we need *fifty* more votes to do it. New York has thirty-five votes. If we carry New York, we're still fifteen votes short."

Custer broke in, "Then all we need is Indiana's fifteen. And that's our vice-president's home ground, right, Bill?"

English smiled as he nodded his head. "You can count on them."

"Good," Burke said. "We are. Now, let's look at the other side of the coin. If we *don't* carry New York, Garfield needs only five more electoral votes to win. Therefore, we would have to carry all of the ten contested states . . . and, gentlemen, that is practically impossible. We simply can't afford to lose New York."

"But Ned," Keogh said, "I thought we had New York in our pocket. Boss Kelly is giving us Tammany's support."

"I know, but there's still Tilden to think about—him and his upstate machine."

"He's still fighting with Tammany," English said.

"Which means we *don't* have New York in our pocket."

"What can we offer Tilden?" Custer asked.

"You're catching on fast, General," Burke said. "I think he might come around for the secretary of state portfolio and some of the New York state patronage."

"Talk to him," Bennett said.

"I will," Burke replied. "But there's another problem. They've talked Grant into stumping for Garfield, and you know how he still attracts huge crowds."

Custer frowned. "I don't think he's vindictive, but I don't believe he has much love for me either."

Bennett looked at Burke. "What can we do to counteract Grant?"

The campaign manager shrugged. "Run some articles about the scandals in his administration"

"No, I don't want that," Custer said, getting to his feet and looking around, stopping at Bennett. "I think I ought to get out and campaign—

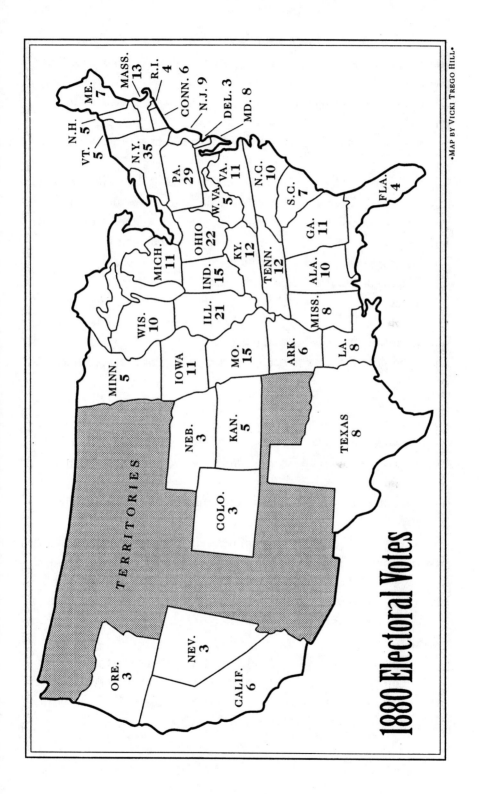

1880 Electoral Votes

"No, I don't want that," Custer said, getting to his feet and looking around, stopping at Bennett. "I think I ought to get out and campaign—personally."

Burke spoke brusquely, "You can't do it, General. It goes against custom."

"But the people like me, and they'll turn out to see me by the thousands."

"Sir," Burke said firmly, "you simply have to trust the politicians in the different states. They know what they're doing. And anything could happen with you out there on the stump. You can get misquoted, baited, drawn into all kinds of trouble. No, trust the men who know this business."

Custer frowned, looked at Bennett.

"The major's right," the publisher said.

Custer shrugged and took his seat. The meeting turned to the contested states and how their votes might go. It looked as if things were well under control. As they were about to break up, Kellogg asked, "What about the slogan? I need to get it out to the different party chairmen and newspapers."

"Glad you reminded us, Mark," Burke said. "Has anyone come up with a good one?"

"I've decided on one," Custer replied enthusiastically. "I've been thinking about my agenda, and as you all know, I want to make our country into a major power in the world. Libbie and I kicked around several slogans and we came up with this one." He paused for a moment, glancing around. "The New American Empire."

Everyone thought for a moment, weighing the phrase. Kellogg was the first to respond, "I like it. It has a certain *ring* to it . . . denotes power, change, growth. Yes, I like it, General. Our neighboring countries may not like it too well, but they aren't voting."

Burke chimed in. "Me to. It's good, General. What do you think, Mr. Bennett?"

The publisher nodded his head. "Yes, it implies promise. Good."

The others chorused their approval as Custer smiled. They didn't even know how accurately the slogan described his plans. He was pleased. Burke said, "All right, 'The New American Empire' it is."

Burke brought up the final matter. "We will use Mr. Bennett's powerful newspaper connections to add flames to the Garfield corruption stories. We'll hit on the Washington street paving scandal, and on the transcontinental railroad outrage. Spread it around several papers."

"His part in that stuff was never proven, was it?" Custer asked.

Burke shrugged. "Who cares? An election is at stake."

"I guess the hounds could come yapping at me too."

"Snapping is more like it."

As the meeting broke up, Bennett gave the man he'd hand-picked to be his private president a look of wary appraisal.

★ ★ ★

The very next day, *The New York Times* ran a front page story headlined "Custer Refused to Command Negroes." The article read, "In an interview, Congressman and former Colonel Frederick Benteen stated that General George Armstrong Custer had been offered command of a Negro regiment following the War Between the States. 'Even though Custer had no other command possibility, he firmly refused a permanent colonelcy that went with the Negro command. It was in late 1865, when high ranking officers were digging in every corner for a position that would allow them to hold anything close to their wartime rank. I went from colonel to captain, and I was fortunate to get that. I know of one general who accepted a sergeant's stripes, it was so bad. In the Seventh Cavalry, about half the officers had brevet wartime rank at least two grades above what they accepted to remain on active duty. But Custer hated Negroes so much that he refused the eagles of a colonel to accept the silver leaves of a lieutenant-colonel and be the second in command of the Seventh Cavalry. Anyone who knows the rank-conscious Custer knows what a sacrifice that was. Any Negro who votes for that charlatan should be ashamed."

"What do you think about that?" Burke asked Custer after bringing him the newspaper at breakfast.

Custer shrugged. "More of Benteen's hatred."

"Is it true?"

"I turned down the command because I was waiting for a cavalry regiment. When none opened up, I took the best I could get—the lieutenant-colonelcy of the Seventh. Besides, commanders were most often away on boards and courts-martial, while the lieutenant-colonel remained in field command. It was where I wanted to be."

"Then we'll issue a statement to that effect."

"How many Negro votes will this cost me?"

Burke shook his head. "Hard to tell. Some."

"But it won't cause me any problems in the South?"

"Not at all."

★ ★ ★

Monasetah's arrival in the city was a special event for the New York press, but Bennett's "other" newspaper made it a *cause célèbre*. Several years earlier, in a fit of boredom, the publisher had launched a second paper, the *Evening Telegram*. Vulgar, blatant, and sensational, it was printed on pink paper. To balance out his more sedate coverage of the event in the *Herald*, he directed the editor of the *Telegram* to keep the newlyweds in coverage for several days. Its first headline ran "Crown Prince brings Princess to Gotham!" It's lead was "King Custer's younger brother arrived in the city last evening with his recent bride, Monasetah, the daughter of a powerful Cheyenne chief. The beautiful princess, swathed in elaborate white buckskin, stepped off the ferry from New Jersey on the arm of her hero mate. . . ."

Libbie had finally accepted "Sallie Ann's" entry into the family, and had treated her civilly, if a bit coolly. Bennett gave the younger Custers the use of a small but quite nicely furnished apartment in a house just a block away from the St. Nicholas, and from there, based upon advice from Annie Yates, Tom took her shopping for some "white woman's" clothing.

One night, soon after their return from Dakota Territory, Custer took them along to Booth's Theater, where Lawrence Barrett was starring in *Julius Caesar*. The famous landscape artist, Albert Bierstadt, and his lady filled out the party. As in nearly everything else the city offered, the theater kept Monasetah rapt as the party settled into the best box in the house. She didn't understand the play, but Custer had given her a synopsis of what it was about prior to the opening curtain, and she was delighted by the spectacle.

As Barrett took his final bow, he pointed to their box and announced in his loudest Shakespearean accent, "Behold, in yon box, one of the greatest theater enthusiasts in the country, General George Armstrong Custer, *the next president of the United States of America!*"

As the crowd craned its necks to look, applause rippled through the theater, and Custer got to his feet to grin and wave his acknowledgment. Such recognition in his beloved world of theater was enthralling. For some reason, the uplifted face of a smiling auburn-haired woman in the center of the second row caught his attention—it was the beautiful mistress of the Crown Prince of England. . . .

MONROE, MICHIGAN

Judge Daniel Bacon, Libbie's father, built his house right in the center of town on South Monroe Street shortly before his only daughter was born. Painted yellow, it was fashioned in the then popular Greek revival style, with green shutters and a large porch that ran halfway around its lower story. Libbie had inherited the lovely old structure upon his death fourteen years earlier. On this twelfth day of October, it was the center of activity for many people. For it was on this day that two nearby states were having their local elections.

It was a big event in Hoosier and Buckeye country, as well as the other states that held an early local election, for the results of these elections would be a strong forecast of the federal elections. The eyes of the country were fastened firmly on them. The Custer team, including Libbie and Annie, was ensconced in the Bacon house, where a telegraph connection had been installed. A smorgasbord was laid out on a large table in the middle of the dining room, and various kinds of drinks were available. Custer's mother and father were there, as were his sisters. William English was, of course, missing—he was down in Indiana to vote and shepherd the election.

Ohio, with its twenty-two electoral votes, had been expected to be a lost cause from the beginning. Not only was it Garfield's home state that he represented as a U.S. senator, but it was a Republican stronghold. Even though Custer was born and had spent most of his childhood there, he simply couldn't carry it. Nor could he be expected to carry Michigan, his adopted state and the home of many of the cavalrymen he had led in the War Between the States because it was solid Republican. All that mattered on this warm October day was how Indiana voted in its governor's race and the other local elections

From the start, it seemed that something was wrong along the banks of the Wabash. Early precinct reports forwarded from Mark Kellogg, who was at the other end of the telegraph in Indianapolis, were decidedly pro-Republican. By three o'clock in the afternoon, Republican candidates held a 25,423 to 18,987 lead over Democrats.

When the results were posted on the bulletin board, a somber mood settled over the group. Quietly, Custer said, "Is this what you mean by letting the professionals handle things, Ned?"

Burke shrugged. "I don't understand it."

"It's early," Bennett said. "Democratic strength just hasn't been tabulated in the larger towns yet."

★ ★ ★

At five-twenty, the restive group in the Bacon house watched as the new numbers from Hoosierland were posted: Republicans: 30,861; Democrats: 23,912.

"What time do the polls close down there?" Custer asked.

"Five o'clock," Burke replied.

Libbie gripped Annie's hand and whispered, "I'm scared."

"It's nearly seven thousand votes," Annie replied.

Fifteen minutes later, Kellogg flashed the next result. The Democrats had gained 2,226 votes, but the numbers being cast were rapidly diminishing. Thirty minutes later, the Republicans' lead had been cut to just under four thousand. "It'll soon be getting dark down there," Tom said, as he poured a whisky from the table. "Those farmers are already sitting down to supper."

There was no response from the gloomy group as Myles Keogh came over and made himself a drink. "No, folks," he said, "I think those Indiana Democrats have dropped the bloody ball."

At six-forty, the telegraph *clacked* and Kellogg reported, "The polls have been closed for well over an hour everywhere, and unless there is a sudden surge in the counting, the Republicans have carried the state."

"Four thousand's not much," Libbie said. "Autie's popularity can overcome that in the November election."

"Not true," Burke said grimly. "Historically, when a party wins the local election, it's a definite desire by the people to favor candidates from one party. When this happens, it means there simply aren't many votes left for the other party. When the federal election is held, the results are almost always the same. The general's popularity is no longer a factor."

For a few moments, silence blanketed the large room. Then Custer broke it with, "'And there go our essential fifteen electoral votes. Now what?"

Burke shook his head. "It doesn't make sense. They were in the bag."

"Well," Custer replied grimly, "Somebody stole the bag."

"What do we do now?" Libbie asked.

"We'll just have to win in a lot of those contested states," Burke answered.

Custer got to his feet and pounded his palm with his fist. "*I'm going to campaign!*" he announced angrily. "I'm not listening to anymore of this 'leave it to the politicians' nonsense. I'm going to take it to the people!"

★ ★ ★

A campaign tour was hastily put together. Early the next morning, Custer took Tom, Keogh, and Kellogg, along with a cook and a butler Burke provided, with him on a four-car chartered train. The train was far from understated: a huge banner with "Custer for President" adorned each side of the last car. Red, white, and blue banners decorated the third car and the back platform, and the second car was fashioned in cavalry yellow, with "GarryOwen" splashed on each side. A small brass band wearing Civil War cavalry uniforms played that song and other popular tunes at each stop. Newspapers were alerted ahead, so the citizens of many of the towns along the railroad's path knew he was coming. The train's whistle blew incessantly. He had a short speech memorized that covered what he had done for the country as a general, both in the big war and in the Indian Wars, and what he was going to do for it as president. "The New American Empire" slogan was thrown about liberally. The speech contained humor and at each stop he accepted five questions and answered them. He also remained alert for any veteran wearing a uniform or any part of one; and he could readily spot medals pinned to a civilian jacket, as well as a man missing a limb. At every stop, after he noticed an ex-soldier, he asked the man to join him on the rear platform of the train for a few minutes.

First he rolled through Connecticut—six votes—then on to New Hampshire—three votes—stopping for a couple of hours in Hanover, the home of Dartmouth College, before heading back to New York by another route. At every stop, he was greeted enthusiastically.

The following morning, the train pulled into Trenton, New Jersey. After Custer's speech to several hundred people there, many of whom were waving flags with "GarryOwen" printed on them, the governor of the state inspired a big cheer as he climbed aboard the train and held the candidate's hand high in an obvious show of support. After all, he had nominated Custer at the convention. A few minutes later, Custer and the former general, for whom he had been an adventurous aide-de-camp, sat down privately in the dining car for coffee. George B. McClellan, the fifty-three-year-old former commander of the massive Army of the Potomac still looked youthful, and still carried himself with almost arrogant self-confidence. "Little Mac" stirred his coffee and regarded Custer quietly. Finally he said, "You've come a long way since you were a second lieutenant on my staff, Armstrong."

Custer nodded. "Yes, and so have you, General."

Little Mac had run unsuccessfully for president on the Democratic ticket against Lincoln in '64, had spent a number of years overseas, and had served as president of the Atlantic & Great Western Railroad before becoming governor of New Jersey in 1877. "I hear Indiana went Republican, Armstrong. Do you know what happened?"

Custer shrugged. "English and his politicians didn't do their job."

"I heard it was more than that. The Republicans threw a lot of bribe money into the hat to buy votes."

Custer sipped his coffee. "I guess that isn't anything new in politics, is it?"

"Not particularly. So, in typical Custer style, you're taking the campaign into your own hands. You're going to blow the trumpet and charge, right?"

Custer nodded. "I just hope it isn't too late. Can you deliver New Jersey and its nine votes, Governor?"

McClellan's smile turned cagey. "I think so."

Custer nodded again. He knew Little Mac wanted to be back on the national scene. "Would you like to be my Secretary of War, sir?"

★ ★ ★

The New American Empire Express, as Custer's train became known in the press, pushed on through Pennsylvania and Ohio, making only a few short stops. In typical direct Custer fashion, he decided to waste little time in states where he wouldn't get votes. Nevertheless, he had the train routed to Indianapolis, where he spoke to a large crowd and had a rather heated discussion with William English. Then it was on to Illinois, Iowa, and across the Plains to Colorado, where he addressed a good-sized crowd in Denver. Then his train was routed to Bismarck, where he visited the Seventh Cavalry at Fort Abraham Lincoln, followed by a quick visit with Sitting Bull. Kellogg's photographer was kept busy throughout, and particularly on the reservation. Those photographs would be of great value in the campaign ahead.

Then it was on around the Rockies to Oregon as the Express had track cleared and roared along hell-bent. After two stops in that state, and a couple more in Nevada, the train finally pulled into Sacramento. Later that night, it reached San Francisco, where a large crowd led by Boston Custer and the Bay area's leading Democrats exuberantly greeted Custer.

The next day, the commanding general at the Presidio granted permission for a big outdoor rally on its parade ground. Boston Custer was the coordinator.

Even the weather cooperated. The sun popped in and out between large, cumulus clouds and the ever present wind took a vacation. Upwards of fifteen hundred citizens of the city and its environs attended. Custer and Democratic dignitaries occupied the small, bunting draped platform that had been hurriedly erected. After a long-winded introduction by the head of the state Democratic delegation, Custer, wearing a white Stetson and a fringed buckskin jacket, launched into his stock speech. But before finishing, he shifted to a new tack, "Gentlemen, by now you've heard and read about my theme 'The New American Empire.' I assure you it's far more than a slogan—it's a *promise!* The borders of this great country are going to be enlarged and by the time my years as your president have come to a close, the United States of America will be standing as one of the most powerful nations in the world!"

His voice dropped to a low pitch, "And, gentlemen, where will the western center of this new empire be? Right here in the heart of California, that's where!"

As Custer jammed his right arm high, cheers burst out, and on cue, his small band burst into "Hail to the Chief."

★ ★ ★

There were about sixty people at the reception following the rally. Custer and his party rode down to the station in open carriages from the Presidio so he could wave at the many people standing alongside the streets. He was as full of himself as ever. *This* was the way to win votes, he *knew* it. George Armstrong Custer was showing these politicians a thing or two.

Boston, along with the cook, had set up a sumptuous buffet in the dining car, and a white gloved waiter was busy with a champagne tray. Halfway through, Custer looked up from where he was talking to a local newspaper editor to see the violet eyes of Lillie Langtry regarding him bemusedly from a few yards away. After a few moments, he broke off the conversation with the newspaperman and moved over to the English beauty. He kissed her hand and grinned. "It seems every time I go some place, I see the beautiful lady from London. Have you become a Democrat, Mrs. Langtry?"

"No, General," she replied in her cultured accent. "I've come to San Francisco to purchase a house, and a very rich gentleman brought me here to see you."

Custer blew out a short breath. *She was absolutely stunning!* "Well, here I am."

She smiled. "I hear you are leaving us quite abruptly."

"Yes, tonight. The federal election is in five days and I must get back to New York City to follow the results."

She touched his hand lightly. "Pity."

He plunged in. "I wish I were staying longer. I would like to see you somewhere other than at a reception."

The violet eyes that had charmed untold Brits and brought their future king into her arms turned up their intensity as she replied softly, "I think I would like that very much, General Custer." She smiled. "Yes, very much."

He felt the electricity. "Perhaps some day—uh, have you ever considered buying a house in Washington or New York?"

"Actually, I must say, I have." She paused, opened her eyes ever so slightly again. "Do you think I should?"

"If I get elected, and I think I will, it might be a splendid idea."

"I'm considering becoming an actress, and there is wonderful theater in New York. Yes, I may get a place there, instead of here. Would a president be able to visit?"

Custer grinned again. "From what I hear the Crown Prince has never worried about doing such things."

She made a touch of a curtsy. "But he's British."

"Have you ever heard of the Boston Tea Party?"

"The what?"

Just then, he saw Keogh coming toward him waving a telegram. "It's about getting rid of a king. Sorry, duty calls. Excuse me, please."

She touched his hand again, "*Au revoir.*"

The telegram was from Burke. It read: "Met with Tilden. He will bring in his upstate New York vote to coincide with Tammany if you will make him Secretary of State. I told him you would."

Custer handed the yellow sheet back to the Irishman. "Looks like we may pull this out yet."

Keogh grinned. "I never had a doubt."

Custer cast another glance at Lillie's intriguing violet eyes and said, "Let's get this darned train rolling before midnight. New York's a long way off."

Keogh touched his temple in a mock salute. "GarryOwen, sir!"

NEW YORK *November 2, 1880*

There simply was nothing like the city of New York on national election day. It was a day of celebration, jollity, entertainment, and fervor. Nearly every male eligible to vote and capable of getting to a polling place would do so at least once before the day was over. In fact, eligibility was different in New York than in other places because years before, Tammany had come up with its own carpetbagging scheme by lowering of immigrant's residence time to be eligible—just six months from the boat to the polls. Yes, New York was all dressed up with *some*place to go. Everyone got up early with zestful anticipation. It was the day that the country, and this teeming city in particular, celebrated its democratic liberty and selected the officials who would run things for the next few years. This was the day when the little guy got his *say*. Or when he got paid to follow someone else's. Bands played, votes were courted if not already in the bag, and the beer flowed freely. It was the *vote* that mattered, and other large numbers of people were involved in getting it out. The mood was festive, the air filled with excitement, with a certain exhilarating combativeness.

The polls opened at six A.M. and the rush was on. The *Herald* and its shrieking pink little sister, the *Telegram*, were set up to keep the public informed by posting frequent bulletins at different locations in the city, in Brooklyn, and further north in Williamsburg. Returns would be read continuously from the stage of Booth's Theatre. Still the manager there, Lawrence Barrett was directing the play *Cinderella*. But today he was campaigning in front of the playhouse for his good friend, Custer. Returns were also posted and verbally announced at the St. James Hotel, the headquarters of the Democratic State Committee, and all of the secondary races were included. Since Garfield was waiting out the election back at his home in Ohio, his running mate, General Chester A. Arthur, was ensconced at the Republican State Committee headquarters in the Fifth Avenue Hotel.

The *Herald* ran large editions in the preceding days, covering everything germane to the election. One running account was about the "Bonfire War." Customarily, huge bonfires blazed in the sky over the city on election night. These fires, fueled by massive piles of practically anything that would burn, were the work of rival gangs of boys who had come to treat this element of the elections with such fierce competitiveness that it bordered on pure enmity. This year was to be no different. Already the "Ninth Avenue Gang," so called because its great pile of combustibles was located in a vacant lot at 59th Street and Ninth Avenue, had been attacked by the "Tenth Avenue Gang," whose bonfire pile, consisting of as many neighborhood ash and garbage boxes as they could steal, was located at Tenth Avenue and 54th Street. When the Ninth Avenue boys retaliated with a cry "such as Paul Revere sent out through every Middlesex village and farm," the battle was joined. Only the fall of darkness would settle the matter.

Now and then both newspapers mentioned the frenetic betting that was going on. It seemed a fever, this betting on the presidential race, and even housewives sent a dollar or two over to the local pool room to be wagered. That wasn't really necessary, however, because one could find a way to bet openly on the street or over the back fence. The odds going in were ten-to-three, Garfield. Both Tom and Keogh had bet all the money they could raise on Autie.

The previous day an item had been published about measures being taken to prevent fraud in the California election, where the voting was expected to be extremely close. Prior to that, Bennett had directed his best writer do a harsh account of the alleged crookedness in the recent Indiana election. Neither side had a history of clean hands—certainly not Democratic Tammany. Since deals had been made with the Custer team, an armed truce existed between Honest John Kelly's Wigwam machine and Sam Tilden's Irving Hall bunch. Both factions were busy at work not only insuring Custer votes, but getting a contested, fractious mayoral race settled.

The weather, in New York as well as the rest of the country, was mostly dry and mild, with rain forecast only in the Northwest.

★ ★ ★

This time the whole clan was assembled in the campaign headquarters in the old Astor House Hotel at Broadway and Vescey Street. That is, all but William English, who was again out in Indianapolis, and James Gordon Bennett, Jr., who was running his newspaper empire from his office. The vice-presidential candidate had been both contrite and angry at Indiana's vote on October 12; now he insisted his presence would make a difference. Ned Burke knew better. They had outsmarted themselves by selecting the Hoosier, and now they had to live with him. It was a good thing he was a reputable man.

Food and drink were laid out, with a waiter to serve. A professional telegrapher manned the wire that had been run into the big room, and a volunteer stood by a large blackboard to keep the latest returns posted.

Custer and Libbie arrived at the hotel at just before ten A.M., and now some last minute well-wishers awaited. The first was a trio of women from Baltimore bearing an exquisite hand-stitched quilt. As Custer shook hands with them, one woman said, "General, I want you to know I'm a Garfield supporter, but the society decided on you, and even though I'm the designer of this quilt, I had to go along."

Custer flashed her his best smile and kissed her hand. "I'm honored, milady."

He had a new admirer.

Libbie and Annie took the quilt and thanked the ladies.

The next visitors were two attractive young women from Trenton. One, a blonde of about twenty-two, blushed continuously as her brunette friend said, "General Custer, we liked what you said when your train was in our fair city, and we formed a 'Custer Club' to get the men to vote for you. We also raised the money to have these made as our gift to you." She handed him a shoe box wrapped in fancy paper adorned by a gold ribbon. "Open it," the dark haired woman said with a big smile.

Custer removed the wrapping and opened the box. Inside, on black velvet, a pair of gold spurs glowed back at him. Fashioned in simple military style, they were finely tooled with his name engraved on the side of each one. He shook his head. "I've always wanted to be as fancy as Jeb Stuart. I'll never ride again without these spurs. Thank you so much, dear ladies. Tell your friends back in Trenton, I adore all of you for thinking so much of me."

From a few feet away, Libbie chuckled quietly to Annie, "He'll probably wear them to bed."

"How interesting," Annie joked. "I can just imagine."

The last visitor was Captain Charles Myers, a giant of a man whose remaining hair was prematurely white. He had gained certain celebrity by walking all the way from St. Louis just to wish Custer well. As Custer shook his hand, he said, "I was a gunner in your horse artillery during the war, General. More than once I had to personally lift a gun out of the mud to get it into action. Before I left Missouri, I spent a whole month making sure those folks get out and vote for you. I spoke somewhere three, four times every day, telling them people how we could always depend on you in the war."

Custer clapped him on the arm. "Now *that's* what I call electioneering, Captain. Thank you. I'll tell you what—you go over and help yourself to some of that food." He turned to Myles Keogh. "Colonel, why don't you see what Captain Myers can do to help us."

★ ★ ★

Since the ballot wasn't secret and the voters went to a poll run by the party they favored, it was easy to keep track of the vote as it went along. The returns began to trickle in from various reporting points along the Atlantic seaboard. Maine, as expected, was showing Republican strength, as were Vermont, Massachusetts and Rhode Island. Even New Hampshire and Connecticut were voting Republican in the early going. New York was bouncing around, as was New Jersey. Delaware was the first state to look heavily Democratic. From there down, the recently coined "Solid South" was soundly Democrat. At noon, the trends continued.

Annie Yates walked up to the food table as Keogh poured himself a bit of bourbon and drank it neat. "Well, Myles, you seem to be getting a head start."

"Ah, lass, I once knew a man named Sanford Cox, who believed one should eat dessert first, in case he didn't live through the whole meal."

Annie chuckled. "And the same principle applies to drinking?"

"Aye. Drink when the bottle's full, because some idiot may break it."

Annie poured herself about an ounce of bourbon. "I think I'll take your advice. It's going to be a long day. Is your man Kelly going to deliver New York?"

Keogh shrugged. "Doesn't look like it so far, but don't underestimate him."

The early city returns were about fifty-five percent Republican to forty-five percent Democrat.

Want to bet?" Annie asked over a teasing smile.

"How much?"

"Dinner?"

Keogh grinned. He'd always liked Annie Yates, thought of her as a man's kind of woman. He'd been a friend of her husband, and although he'd thought about her romantically a couple of times, he'd pushed the ideas away in deference to her grief. Now he gave her a new look of appraisal. "You have a bet, milady."

★ ★ ★

The returns continued in much the same vein, although New York began to pull even. The vote in the Midwest also ran pretty much as predicted. Pennsylvania, Ohio, Michigan and Illinois were solidly Republican, while Indiana straddled the fence. Minnesota and Wisconsin also tipped well into the Republican direction. As Custer stood beside Burke at the returns blackboard, he frowned. "The canvass just wasn't good enough, Ned."

Burke shrugged. "God knows we spent enough money. I think Grant's canvassing for Garfield was a bigger factor than we guessed. He's still a very popular man."

At that moment the man who was posting the ever-changing tally wrote in the Kentucky return: Custer - 26,223, Garfield - 6,721. A small cheer went up from the handful of volunteers. "That's good news," Custer said.

Libbie came up and squeezed his hand. "'That's because you were stationed there."

* * *

The votes in the South continued strongly in Custer's favor as the afternoon wore on, but New York was still in doubt for some unknown reason. Custer was concerned for the first time as he watched the northern states continue to go for Garfield. He didn't like this uncertainty—wasn't his way. And the fact that Michigan wasn't supportive still rankled him. He'd led those Wolverine cavalrymen to the greatest glory in the war, and his darned home was there. You'd think they'd at least vote for him as a favorite son! If he still managed to win this thing, he'd somehow get even . . . no, that really wasn't his way either; he didn't bear grudges.

He walked over to the table and picked up a cookie before looking up at the tally board. Just as Burke had said, Indiana had started going solidly for Garfield—26,321 to 19,011.

Just then another cheer went up from behind him as the Delaware vote was posted. Down there, he was ahead by over 2,000 votes, enough to swing it this late in the day. Senator Bayard had brought in his three electoral votes!

He nodded his head as Burke smiled. Now if only New York would come in, they had a chance. . . .

* * *

Outside the hotel, the street was quite crowded as a horse car stopped. Two young men dressed in inexpensive suits stepped down. Their skin was darker than most of the passersby, but New York was such a melting pot that they went unnoticed. Red Elk looked up at the imposing Astor House. "Are you sure that is Custer's tipi?" he asked.

He had talked Little Bear into accompanying him into the city, since the Kiowa had been there before and knew how to find his way around. "No," his roommate replied, "the newspaper said it is his *campaign* headquarters, the tipi where he holds council with his chiefs."

Red Elk's eyes narrowed as he stared at the front entrance and saw a familiar figure come out with another person he recognized—*Monasetah*. She was with Long Hair's brother. He had read in the newspaper that she had become his wife. A pang of sorrow struck him—she was friendly with his beloved Late Star and they had quilled together on several occasions. He watched impassively as they strolled casually down the street. If she had joined the Custers, she, too, was now his *enemy*.

"Did you see that Indian woman?" Little Bear asked.

"Yes, she is the Cheyenne we read about."

"The one who . . ."

"Yes, became a Custer."

Red Elk stared at the entrance. *He is in there somewhere. I should just go in and do it right now . . . never let him become the White Father!* But he couldn't take a chance on failure. And there were too many policemen around. Still . . .

★ ★ ★

Tom was still gone at 4:45 P.M. when Honest John Kelly's lieutenant arrived with a note that stated, "Dear General Custer, I hand you the proud city of New York. We have prevailed! And the entire Empire State will follow. I have just received Tilden's assurance."

Custer stared at the message. *Could it be true? Was it really happening?* A smile touched his lips as a runner came in from Tilden's Irving Hall and breathlessly handed over a note from the former governor himself. Burke read it aloud. "Combined with New York City's returns, the upstate vote of fifty-six percent for General Custer assures him the promised electoral votes of the great State of New York." The major looked around like a Cheshire cat for a moment before throwing his fist in the air and announcing, "New York has just cast it's thirty-five electoral votes for *General George Armstrong Custer!*"

This time the cheers lasted for two minutes. As they began to subside, Tom hurried in and pounded Custer on the back. "We're only twelve away, Big Brother!"

Ten minutes later, the latest New Jersey tally was posted. Garfield was ahead by eighty-nine votes! Custer frowned; McClellan had promised him. "What time do their polls close?" Libbie asked.

Burke replied, "Five o'clock. There's plenty of time." But he looked worried.

Libbie turned to Annie. "Are there any stores open?"

"Why?"

"I want to go shopping! *Anything* to get away from this dreaded waiting."

"We've still got those western states," Annie replied.

"I know. C'mon, let's go to the restaurant and have a cup of coffee."

"I wouldn't go outside the hotel," Keogh cautioned. "I've been told there are a lot of ruffians afoot at this hour—been drinking all day, and may be looking for trouble."

Annie smiled. "You've been drinking all day, Myles Keogh, what are you looking for?"

"Tut, tut, Annie girl. I've been *sipping*. And I'm looking for that dinner you owe me."

"Some other time, Irishman."

★ ★ ★

At five-thirty, Custer stood staring at the New Jersey results. The last posting showed Garfield barely sixty-one votes ahead. It was small, but it was a lead. Custer had to have New Jersey's nine votes, simply *had* to have them. Without them, he'd need every single vote in the West, and they simply weren't to be had. *What could have gone wrong in New Jersey?*

He felt tense, something that was strange to him. There, the man with the chalk was reaching for New Jersey, wiping its box with the cloth . . . reaching for the stick of chalk . . . writing . . . Garfield 21, 445 . . . Custer *21, 472*. He'd passed him! Not much, twenty-seven votes, but he was leading.

He looked at Burke who raised an eyebrow and smiled. "McClellan is coming through," he said. Four minutes later, another New Jersey count came in—Custer was leading by ninety-one votes.

★ ★ ★

At six-fifty, Bennett strode into the large room. Asking everyone to gather round him, he waved a telegram and announced, "This just came in from Trenton: 'With just a handful of small polling places yet to report, and those being soundly Democrat, I wish to proclaim that the great state of New Jersey has cast it's vote for General George Armstrong Custer. Signed, George B. McClellan, Governor.'" The publisher looked into Custer's relieved expression and smiled. "Your old boss came through." *Nine more votes!*

Now—just three more to go. . . .

The roar of cheering lasted for four full minutes.

Three more votes—would one of the western states do it? Colorado was gone to Garfield; Iowa, Kansas, Wisconsin, Minnesota, Nebraska—all Republican. California had six votes, Nevada three, Oregon three. Any one of them would do it. . . . Was it really going to happen?

★ ★ ★

The clock struck midnight. Custer's electoral count remained at 182, Garfield at 175. Three tantalizing votes were yet to be found. Libbie wouldn't go up to the room Bennett had taken for them. She was dozing in an overstuffed chair in a corner. Custer, as usual, didn't need sleep, so he tried to lose himself in a Walter Scott novel—but his eyes kept going back to the tally board. The voting was about even in all three of the western states. Garfield would lead one moment, then fall behind. Then it would be Custer, then Garfield again.

Another hour passed. *What was taking so long?* It was estimated that the Oregon and Nevada votes might take as much as an extra day, with so many people in remote areas. Who could wait that long?

Finally, at 2:27 A.M. a telegram arrived from Sacramento. It read: "Hooray! I'm a congressman! California votes for President Custer! 1,500

[168]

vote majority for Autie! Hooray for the Custers! Congratulations! Signed, Boston."

As the roar went up and people started jumping around, Myles Keogh jerked the cork out of the first bottle of champagne and drank from it. Some of it bubbled down his chin as he handed the bottle to Tom. Other corks popped. Tom linked his arm in Annie's and danced a jig. Custer just stared woodenly as the man with the chalk circled California. *He had 188 electoral votes.*

He felt Libbie's arm encircle his waist. With brimming eyes, she said, "Congratulations, Mr. President."

He turned, picked her up and raised her high, grinned at her, then lowered her and kissed her soundly before saying, "Congratulations, Little Standby. You are the new First Lady-elect of a big white mansion in Washington!"

He kissed her again amidst the bedlam of victory.

Congratulatory telegrams poured in throughout the two-day celebration. Custer found satisfaction in all of them—after all, hadn't he pulled this whole thing out of the fire by personally campaigning? He *knew* it was the right thing. He had changed the face of the American political process. The Democrats had a right to celebrate; it was the first time they had been in power since before the big war and they knew how to make the most of it. Not only had Custer won the presidential race (Oregon came in with its three votes, although Nevada had finally gone Republican by a scant 124 votes), but both the Senate and the House would now have slim but definite Democratic margins. Voting-wise, the new president would have a friendly Congress.

The cabinet, however, was the problem.

Party leaders had selected a cabinet based on favors, dues, and other considerations, but George Armstrong Custer was still a general, and to him a cabinet was a staff—a staff was *his* prerogative. The biggest argument was over Tom Custer becoming the Secretary of the Interior. Finally, Custer put his foot down. "I've listened to you politicians throughout, and mostly you know what you're talking about. But in this matter, I'm adamant. Colonel Tom Custer is my choice for Interior, and I'll brook no more argument!"

As promised, Tilden was handed the State portfolio, and George McClellan the War portfolio. Honest John Kelly was accepted as Postmaster General, while the influential Senator Bayard from Delaware was designated Attorney General. Custer was pleased with the selection of former Confederate cavalry general Wade Hampton from South Carolina as Secretary of the Treasury, leaving just one post open. And it had to go to another Southerner. It was the Navy portfolio.

Several southern political leaders' names were thrown into the hat, including Jefferson Davis, the former Confederate president—but Custer never wavered. He'd quickly learned about the spoils system, and he insisted on his old West Point classmate, Thomas Lafayette Rosser. Often in close proximity during the war, he had once captured the former rebel general's private belongings and had paraded around in Rosser's uniform coat before sending his tall friend a note requesting that he buy smaller clothes. And they had spent three months together in 1873 when Custer protected a railroad survey team headed by the Southerner. Several Annapolis graduates might set up a loud hue and cry, but that didn't trouble the president-elect. Rosser would be the new Secretary of the Navy.

Major Ned Burke would be in charge of day-to-day White House operations, sort of his adjutant-general or chief of staff. As a counter check against the campaign manager's sometimes questionable practices, Lieutenant-colonel William Cooke was being brought in as his assistant. Cooke would also serve as his private secretary.

Mark Kellogg would be in charge of all matters pertaining to the press and release of information. He was designated "Press Liaison Officer."

Lieutenant-colonel Myles Keogh would be a special military aide to the president, specifically in charge of his personal safety and any special projects Custer might have for him. Keogh had found the former Captain Charles (Moose) Myers, the huge white-haired man who had walked to New York from Missouri, to his liking, and would make him the president's bodyguard. Sergeant Burkman would stay on to take care of the horses and dogs. The moment Custer learned that he had won, he personally appointed the three staff officers from the Seventh to their brevet rank—an abrupt exception to procedure in which the designations would be temporary and last only as long as the president deemed it useful. He'd sent a note to General Sherman explaining why the appointments were necessary.

Custer loved the theater. He had plans to direct funds into a special arts program that would bring more stage entertainment to the public, particularly in parts of the country that were far-flung and had little access to the dramatic arts. Lawrence Barrett would be its director.

Although not exactly a part of his presidency, Annie Yates was designated secretary to the First Lady.

Now it was a matter of waiting until Inauguration Day, not an easy matter for the spirited group that was about to take over the reins of government. The Custers and their entourage would move to Washington to stay in temporary lodgings to get more familiar with the city.

★ ★ ★

James Gordon Bennett, Jr. was decidedly pleased with the way everything was going. Overall, the cabinet selections satisfied him and his "ownership" of a president seemed to be just the enterprise he had meant it to be. Custer, however, was not quite as compliant as he wished. Knowing of the man's vanity from well before the Little Bighorn, he had assumed the general would be satisfied just with being president and being the most visible man in America, if not in the world. He thrived on celebrity. But various things Custer had hinted at, or downright insisted upon, gave him pause. Custer might just turn out to be too much his own man.

Therefore, even before the general took office, he needed to set up something that could serve as a bridle over him. He had just the man in mind who could do it: Sam Ward. Julia Ward Howe's older and only brother, he had been educated at the University of Tübingen in Germany, and had represented the powerful London banking house of Baring Brothers for many years. He was a Democrat, but had many Republican friends. A man noted for his cultivated tastes and charm, he threw dinner parties that the most prominent of Washingtonians vied to attend. In fact he was sometimes called "the Lucullus of the capital," because of the quality of his repasts. He was also known as the "King of the Lobby" and supposedly knew more about the secrets of Washington politics than anyone in town. At sixty-six, Sam Ward wore a Van Dyke beard and mustache, white like the fringe of hair that flanked his shiny bald head. Part of his mystique was his penchant for losing fortunes, but at the present time, money seemed to be no problem for him. He had a lovely house on Judiciary Square, but often entertained at Welcker's restaurant. It was there where they were having lunch on this nineteenth day of November. Over a specially blended tea Ward had ordered, Bennett said, "Your celebrity as a host knows no political bounds, Sam, so I want you to do me a favor."

"Anything Jim."

"You know Kate Chase Sprague, don't you?"

"Yes, of course."

"Is she still having an affair with Conkling." He was referring to the handsome, debonair senator from New York.

"No, that ended some time ago. Actually, she has been pretty much in retirement at her old estate, Edgewood. But I understand she's getting out a bit lately."

"Isn't she about forty now."

Ward nodded. "I think so—still an incredibly beautiful woman."

"I want Custer to meet her."

Ward's smile could have been described as salacious. "For some good reason, Jimmy?"

"I'd like for them to become friends."

"Hmm," Ward replied, "As his benefactor, I would think that would be the last thing you would desire."

The newspaper mogul lit a cigar and blew out the smoke before replying, "Let's say I have my reasons."

"Look at this!" Annie Yates said as she waved an embossed note from the table she used as a desk.

Libbie saw the presidential crest on the ivory note, then the words, "Lucy Webb Hayes, First Lady." Her heart skipped a quick beat as she thought, *I'll have stationery like this.* How nice it was for the current First Lady to write to her. The words were most probably in Mrs. Hayes' own hand:

> THE WHITE HOUSE, December 2, 1880.
>
> *Dear Mrs. Custer:*
>
> *Firstly, I must congratulate your husband on winning the election to succeed Rutherford. I'm sure you'll be up to the challenges you'll face as his true running mate. In the meantime, I would like to invite you to tea on December 12 Inst. at three in the afternoon so that I might show you around a bit of your new home.*
>
> *(signed) Lucy*

Libbie smiled at Annie. "How very nice of her."

"Yes, it is," Annie replied. "I've heard she's most gracious."

Libbie pursed her lips. "I'll answer her at once, and then we must think about having some of that absolutely *delicious* stationery made for me."

Annie nodded her head. "I'll look into some design ideas."

"I want it to be very tasteful, like this."

Annie chuckled. "No crossed manure forks?"

"You know I'll always *adore* the cavalry, but I'm going to put my foot down on a few things those cavalry officers of ours persist in."

★ ★ ★

Libbie and Annie arrived by carriage at 1600 Pennsylvania Avenue promptly at three P.M. on December 12. A butler ushered them in, took their coats, and led them to the Red Parlor, where Lucy Webb Hayes met them. The short, vivacious, dark-haired woman who had borne eight children and whose temperance convictions had caused her to ban the use of liquor in the White House, beamed warmly as she rose from the chair where she had been reading a book. Following the introductions, she said, "Since I'll be guiding you around parts of this big old place, I decided to make this a private little affair. This is my favorite room, the place where I often relax, and where I meet quite a few people. I use the Blue Parlor for slightly more formal meetings."

"Oh, that's just perfect," Libbie replied.

"I believe your husband is another of us Ohioans, isn't that right, Mrs. Custer?"

"Oh, please call me Libbie. Yes, he was born in Ohio, but we Michiganders like to claim him as our own now."

Mrs. Hayes sighed. "I wanted to do things for this great house, but it seems the four years have simply dashed by."

They walked down the hall to the State Dining Room and entered. "I've been told that you liked to entertain as the general's lady," Mrs. Hayes said with a sudden smile. "As you know, I, too, am a general's lady, and I also enjoy entertaining. For large functions, I think this is the best room. I just love its formality. You'll note the only three paintings hanging here are of Jefferson, Webster and Lincoln. I think they are a special cross-section of our history. I do hope you'll keep it that way." The First Lady smiled again. "Do you plan on changes?"

Libbie glanced at Annie. "Well, I suppose it would give me something to do, but I'm such an avid history enthusiast that I wouldn't want to disrupt anything of that nature."

Lucy Hayes led them toward the west side of the mansion. "I want to show you the greenhouses first," she said with an enthusiastic smile. "I just *love* flowers. I have a woman who works full-time arranging bouquets, and another woman whose sole job is to deliver them to the many people I love to please. We have ten people working in these conservatories."

The visitors were quite awed by the array of plants and flowers. "I'm fortunate," Mrs. Hayes said, "that Rutherford has enough money to indulge me in this past time. I couldn't justify it on the mansion's budget."

The comment reminded Libbie that she would have no such funds to call upon.

"Good. Now let me show you some of the presidential silver."

★ ★ ★

Two hours and twenty minutes later, Libbie and Annie reentered their carriage and looked back at the presidential mansion with more appreciation. "Quite a little tour," Annie said.

"Yes," Libbie replied wistfully. "It was very nice of her."

"Seems sad that she had such a short time there, what with her apparent affection for the place."

"Yes, it does seem sad. I wonder how I'll feel when I have to move out?"

"Oh, that's eight years away, because Autie's certain to be re-elected. A lifetime."

Libbie sighed as the carriage pulled away. "The old girl needs sprucing up."

"I agree."

"I think, Annie, you and I are going to have some fun giving her a new face."

★ ★ ★

It was on the seventeenth of December that Bennett took Custer to a luncheon at Sam Ward's house. Libbie had gone to Monroe to get ready for Christmas there, so the president-elect was available. It was a rather small luncheon group for Ward, but also quite illustrious because of the writers attending. The celebrated author, Mark Twain, was there. Tennessee Caflin, a suffragette editor, already had a glass of wine in her hand, and the writer Emily Edson Briggs, whose *Olivia Letters* were quite popular, was busily chatting with Kate Sprague. Bennett introduced the general around, keeping the former chief justice's daughter until last. As Custer bent over her hand, he said, "Didn't we meet during the war, Mrs. Sprague?"

At twenty-one, Kate Chase Sprague had been the most fascinating woman in Washington. The only child of a rich cabinet member, she was her father's hostess at the many functions he threw, wore spectacular clothing, and generally held court wherever she wished. Today she was lovely in a teal-colored dress that worked well with her famous titian-colored hair, which was coifed in the latest style. Of medium height, her figure was still slender but curvaceous, and her famous complexion was unmarred except for tiny lines at the corners of her eyes when she smiled. What separated Kate Chase Sprague from other women was the intelligence and wit that lurked behind her sparkling blue eyes. It had also been what had separated her from her very rich and less than brilliant ex-governor, ex-U.S. senator husband.

Custer was seated at the head of the luncheon table with Kate Sprague on his right, and Tennessee Catlin on his left. The editor, however, was deep in conversation with Samuel Clemens—Mark Twain—so Custer and the famous redhead found common ground in the theater. They talked about the current productions in the Washington area, then the general told her about his plan to bring more theater to American towns. He glowed as he discussed his friend, Barrett.

James Gordon Bennett glowed inwardly as he watched their attraction grow.

★ ★ ★

It was one of those beautiful winter nights when Custer arrived in Monroe on Christmas Eve. The snowflakes, big as a doe's eyes, were falling slowly and silently into their rapidly building white carpet. There wasn't a breath of wind, and hardly any noise in the town as a couple of carriages hauled the party toward the Bacon house. Tom and Monasetah were with the president-elect, as was Keogh, who had hired the giant white-haired Charles Myers as a full-time bodyguard.

The warm candle lights in the windows of Libbie's house greeted the new arrivals as the horses pulling the carriages stopped in front. "*Halloo, the house!*" Tom shouted. Within seconds, the door burst open and Libbie came running out, followed by Annie and Custer's parents. His sisters were right behind. Custer picked up his beaming wife and planted a long kiss on her mouth, then swung her around as she laughed. Keogh was a little more restrained as he gave Annie a big hug. A happy din filled the air as everyone tried to talk at once—the Custer clan had never been reticent.

Inside, the festivities were in full swing. Delicious holiday treats abounded on a sideboard and on the large dining room table. Evergreen wreaths and holly seemed to be everywhere, and in the middle of the living room stood a majestic Christmas tree that Custer's father had brought in to be decorated a week earlier. In a corner, a harpsichord player was busily tinkling out carols.

A number of local politicians, as well as a few Democrats from Detroit and Toledo had been invited, so the old house was full of politics to go with the Christmas cheer. "How's Washington, Mr. President?" the Detroit mayor asked.

Custer grinned. The title sounded good. "Crazy as ever, I guess. Civil service reform is big, as is the constant bickering about the greenback, but I'm most interested in how the Congress is reacting to the foreign situation. The assassination attempt on the Czar at the winter palace in St. Petersburg, and the Russian campaign against the Turkomans is something we'd better keep our eye on. You know, I once took the Russian crown prince hunting."

The mayor's eyes widened. "I didn't know that."

"Uh huh. The forming of a new French cabinet concerns me. They've given a general amnesty to all of those rabble rousing communists."

"Aren't you supposed to be on the liberal side?"

"I'll never be liberal about anarchy."

"What do you think about the Mexicans killing that savage Apache, Victor something? Didn't you fight those bastards?"

Custer's voice cooled. "His name was Victorio, and he was far from a savage. I once parlayed with him and found him to be extremely intelligent. I can tell you right now, if he hadn't run out of ammunition at Tres Castillos, those Mexicans would never have gotten him."

The mayor changed the subject. "What do you think about the scheme to build that canal in Panama, Mr. President?"

The mayor was referring to the French project in which a man named Ferdinand de Lesseps had raised enough money for his company to build a canal across the Isthmus of Panama. "I'm totally against it," Custer replied. "It's a clear-cut violation of the Monroe Doctrine."

"Would you use military intervention to stop it?"

Custer scowled. He had been warned to keep his thoughts and remarks more guarded—that they would be quoted in an instant by the world press—but this man could be trusted. "Off the record, Mr. Mayor, I would send troops the moment those Frenchmen put a foot on Panamanian soil. And I'd clap every single one of them in prison until their mothers came to get them out!"

At that moment, Maria Custer walked up and said, "Autie, that's enough of that political talk. You're as bad as your father, and you know how he never stops. Come along and let me fix you a plate of chicken and dumplings." Custer's mother was the ever protective type of scolding hen. Of fragile health, she had been a widow when she married his father, Emmanuel. Now in her mid-sixties, her hair was hurrying toward white and lines etched her often troubled face. Custer loved her dearly. He shrugged at the mayor and let Maria lead him away.

★ ★ ★

"You know, darling Standby, next year we'll be making love in the White House at this time," Custer said from where he was propped up naked in bed on a couple of pillows.

Libbie smiled. Nestled in his arms, she said, "*Next* year at this time, we may still be celebrating New Year's Eve. You know how Washington is."

He kissed her nose. "No, we'll break away and hurry off to bed."

"Is that a promise?"

"Positively."

They were both quiet for several moments. Finally he said, "I've been thinking about the past year and wondering what's coming down the road in this one. The world lost some exceptional writers . . . Flaubert, George Eliot . . . Sara Bernhardt came over from England to grace our stages, and Edison patented his incandescent lamp."

"Yes, and don't forget Susan Anthony. She made some strides in women's suffrage last year." Libbie replied. "Autie, after we get to the White House, I want you to do something about suffrage."

Custer nodded his head. "That's your project, dear. I'll support it."

She kissed his chest. "'Good! Now, are you going to do anything really special for the inauguration?"

He stroked her hair. "Of course."

"Like what?"

"It's a surprise."

"Tell me!"

Lo! In the clouds of Heaven appears
God's well-beloved Son.
He brings a train of brighter years,
His kingdom is begun.
"Thou Hast Put All Things Under His Feet"
—William Cullen Bryant

The newspapers around the country would state substantially what the New York *Herald* used as its opening: Washington, March 4. In conformity with the law and in the presence of fully 50,000 of his fellow-citizens, George Armstrong Custer to-day took the oath of office and became President of the United States. The scenes attending his inauguration are destined to be the most memorable ever known. The throng of visitors to the capital was unprecedented, the procession of military and civic organizations the largest ever known, the enthusiasm was unparalleled, and the decorations too profuse to describe. . . ."

But those words would come later.

At one A.M. on the 4th, the Signal Service reported that in the District of Columbia snow would fall, followed by clear and cold weather, with winds shifting to the northwest. And the forecast had been correct early in the morning. Over an inch of wet snow fell before the dark storm clouds scurried on across Chesapeake Bay toward the Eastern Shore of Maryland.

But as ten o'clock approached, the sky cleared and the bright sun began to turn the fast disappearing snow and dirt below it into a light coat of mud. Since the day before, buildings on the north side of Pennsylvania Avenue were nearly obscured behind flags, streamers, banners, shields, and other decorative objects, all in bright red, white, and blue. Below and in front of these vast decorations, seemingly unending stands of rough planks filled with well-bundled, cheerful spectators lined the famous street. As far as the eye could see, the sun glittered on polished bayonets, as soldiers, drawn shivering up in line, awaited the order to march. The fifty-piece Marine Band had been playing since 9:30, but now it was joined by a dozen other bands, competing enthusiastically, down the line of march.

Four blocks from the presidential mansion, Lieutenant-general Philip Sheridan, wearing his dress uniform and the jaunty little forage cap he made famous in the Big War, sat on his spirited but nervous bay stallion. At Custer's insistence, he was the Chief Marshal of the day. Mounted orderlies dashed up on horseback now and then as the long contingent of military units continued to form up. At the head, wearing their wartime uniforms, veterans of Custer's famous Third Cavalry Division were led by his first brigade command—the Michigan Wolverines of Gettysburg fame.

At five minutes past ten, Sheridan and his aides headed back up Pennsylvania Avenue to alert each military command to make ready. At quarter after the hour, two open carriages, drawn by magnificently caparisoned teams of four horses, drove onto the White House grounds. Into the first of these carriages, which was driven by "Albert," the famous presidential coachman who acquired his knowledge of horses under General Grant, stepped President Rutherford B. Hayes, followed by Vice-President-elect, William H. English. In the second carriage, the door was opened by Congressman Boston Custer for Mrs. Hayes, Libbie Custer, her mother-in-law, Maria Custer, and Mrs. English. With a detachment of mounted policemen leading, the carriages moved down Pennsylvania Avenue toward the Capitol.

Directly behind, rode General Sheridan and his entourage, followed by the first of the military contingents. They were greeted by loud shouts of welcome from every spare foot where a spectator could get a foothold. From every window, from hundreds of temporarily erected balconies, from house-tops, trees, even from telegraph poles and lampposts, onlookers cheered in the brisk and bright morning air.

But where was the president-elect? He had announced to the press that this inauguration would be different, but had merely dangled that comment as a carrot, not further elucidating on the subject.

Suddenly, a chorus of bugles playing "Charge" sounded as the barrier on a cross street was raised and the military column was halted by prancing cavalry videttes. A roar went up from that part of the crowd, as the band of the Seventh Cavalry Regiment swung onto the avenue loudly playing "GarryOwen." Directly behind and riding in front of three companies of the Seventh Cavalry was George Armstrong Custer. A fringed tan doeskin coat with large gold epaulets on the shoulders topped his yellow-striped blue uniform trousers and at his throat, his trademark bright red scarf fluttered. On his head a white slouch hat was tugged resolutely over his forehead.

He was astride Vic, the handsome Kentucky thoroughbred he'd ridden to fame at the Little Bighorn. The sorrel seemed to understand he was part of something special. Sergeant John Burkman had brushed his three white stockings so they perfectly matched the blaze on his forehead, and there was an extra spring in his prance.

Behind Custer, wearing standard dress uniforms and plumed shiny helmets, rode Lieutenant-colonels Tom Custer, Myles Keogh and William Cooke abreast on handsome horses. Then came the regimental detachment commander, Captain Jimmi Calhoun, Custer's brother-in-law, leading the companies of well turned out cavalrymen in their blue uniforms and Custer-red scarves.

The huge crowd loved it and roared. Cheer after cheer went up as the band switched to "The Girl I left Behind," then to "Lorena," and on to

"The Battle Hymn of the Republic." As the contingent reached the front of the White House, a grinning Custer reared Vic on his hind legs and waved his campaign hat in a sweeping circle.

The country's most famous cavalryman was well on his way to becoming its most glamorous president.

★ ★ ★

At 11:55 A.M. the seats and nearly all the standing room in the Senate chamber were occupied. One minute later it became evident that the chief actors of the drama would arrive a little late if something were not done to prevent it. The old, white-haired doorkeeper , who had served in that office for so many years, was equal to the emergency. Seizing a staff, he carefully turned back the minute hand of the Senate clock five minutes. At 11:55 by the corrected time, the three members of the Senate's Inaugural Committee entered the chamber, followed by Rutherford B. Hayes and George Armstrong Custer, arm in arm. Everyone in the chamber and its gallery rose to their feet.

Looking proudly down on her husband from the front row of the gallery, a beaming Libbie squeezed Maria Custer's hand and wiped a tear from her eye.

The president and president-elect sat in chairs in front of the Secretary's desk, facing the Senate. At 12:04 Speaker Randall appeared at the central door, followed by nearly all the members of the House. The chamber was now so packed that many congressman had to stand outside when the chaplain offered the prayer. Among those inside, a frowning Fred Benteen watched quietly as he stood beside the new congressman from California, Boston Custer.

After that, Vice-President English and the newly elected senators were sworn in. That done, the move to the western front of the Capitol began. No president had ever before taken office there, but Custer had decided that would be part of his unique inauguration. As the press had been well informed, The West was where the Little Bighorn had taken place and where the general's agenda for the American Indian had begun. It was only appropriate that he be sworn in facing westward.

Leading the presidential party to the reviewing stand was the white-haired Frederick Douglass, the ex-slave and abolitionist who was now the United States Marshal of the District of Columbia. The reviewing stand was surrounded by many thousands of people, all in an expectant mood. President Hayes, wearing the peaceful demeanor of one who is about to escape to a quieter life, and the somehow pensive Custer, took their places at the front of the platform. As their ladies assembled behind, Chief Justice Waite, in the flowing robes of his office, assumed his position to one side. The other members of the party, the vice-president, Custer's lieutenant colonels, his brother Boston, members of his Cabinet, and their ladies filled the large stand.

Custer had worked on his speech for over a month with help from various members of his staff—mostly Burke, Cooke, Libbie, even Bennett. He wanted it to be short and it was. He had rehearsed it several times with Lawrence Barrett, getting comfortable with the places where he might stutter. Now, he took off his hat and handed it to his brother Tom, then quietly looked long at the huge expectant audience. He rose from the same chair George Washington sat in during his inauguration. The sun shone on his burnished golden hair as he began, *"Fellow Americans!* There are some who may mark this day as the beginning or the birth of American imperialism, and it may well be. But those are words and a label. I want this date, when my administration commences, to be the day on which the United States begins its move to become a world power second to *none."*

A roar of cheers interrupted him. Raising his arms to quiet them, he continued, "It is now three days more than a hundred years since the adoption of the first written constitution of our proud country. This constitution marked the freedom of our great new republic, a freedom that was bought with the lives and limbs of our forbears, and paid for in blood. . . ."

Custer recounted the glories of the Revolutionary War, moved briefly into the War of 1812, spoke of some of the heroics, particularly those of Robert E. Lee in the Mexican War, then expanded for a few minutes on the War Between the States. He ended that segment with, "I was there at Appomattox sixteen years ago when General Grant magnanimously granted our Southern soldiers absolution from treason . . . thereby opening the way to heal the vast and terrible wounds of that war. And in recent years we have resolved the Indian wars that have torn at our guts. . . . Now it's time to assert ourselves internationally and enforce the Monroe Doctrine. It's time to tell foreign powers that we will not abide their schemes of aggrandizement *in our realm!*"

A huge cheer and many shouted "GarryOwens" followed the last sentence.

"And," Custer went on after a long pause, "it's time to utilize our magnificent natural resources and the remarkable industrial capability that exemplifies the genius of our great country. It's time to marshal those riches and make them known in world trade."

He went on, switching to women's suffrage and equality for the Negroes and Indians. He spoke of the arts and how he would promote them. He stated that the military would be rebuilt. And finally, after only a nineteen-minute speech, he hit the finale: "Fellow citizens, I have named this great new era 'The New American Empire.' *And as I, a general, led in battle, I, as your president, shall lead our great country to new heights!*"

Once more cheers rocked the Capitol, and when they finally subsided, Custer turned to the chief justice. It was time. The moment. It was a long way back to those low points—the court-martial, the bad investments, the trouble with Grant and Sherman. He felt a tightening in his throat and hoped he wouldn't stutter as he took the oath.

Chief Justice Waite held the Washington Bible and Custer again broke with custom as he invited his wife Libbie to stand at his side as he was sworn in. Custer placed one hand on the bible and raised the other to the sky while the robed justice administered the oath as prescribed by the Constitution. When it was completed, Custer leaned over and pressed his lips to the Bible where it had fallen open to the Twenty-seventh Psalm. Momentarily his eye caught the second verse, "When the wicked, even mine enemies and my foes, came upon me to eat up my flesh, they stumbled and fell." He smiled to himself—Custer's luck. He hugged Libbie briefly as tears came to their eyes.

George Armstrong Custer was now the President of the United States.

★ ★ ★

One extremely interested spectator, jammed into the crowd some eighty feet away from the platform, was Red Elk. He had managed to get the money for the round trip train fare from Carlisle and had arrived the day before. Dressed in his dark suit, with a hat pulled low over his forehead, he had a long-barreled .45 caliber revolver jammed into his belt. But there had been no opportunity to use it. Even when Custer was riding in the parade, he had been too far away for any kind of an accurate shot. He had waited too long to kill this man to make a risky, improbable attempt. Besides, he had an alternative plan.

★ ★ ★

The inaugural ball was held in the new red brick Smithsonian Museum, where the decor was dominated by a colossal plaster statue of the Goddess of Liberty holding Edison's newfangled wonder, an incandescent lamp, in her upraised hand. Cavalry yellow was everywhere—on bunting, the many sprays of flowers, tablecloths. Libbie wore a soft silk gown of pale yellow trimmed in light gray, the latter color matching her eyes. A corsage of three yellow roses adorned its bodice. Her lustrous brown hair was piled high, and a long string of expensive pearls—a gift from James Gordon Bennett, Jr.—hung around her neck and complemented the colors of the gown she had designed herself. The president had finally satisfied his fetish for uniforms and was handsome in full evening dress with a small yellow rosebud on his lapel.

They arrived shortly after nine with the rest of the presidential party that included his lieutenant-colonels and their ladies, the Bennetts, the Barretts, the Burkes, and members of his Cabinet and their wives. The Marine Band immediately broke into a jaunty rendition of "Hail to the Chief" as Libbie and Custer waved to the crowd. The ball, attended by the Washington elite and important Democrats who had wangled an invitation, had been in sway for an hour. Beautiful gowns and men's evening wear abounded, as did military uniforms of all kinds, American and foreign. Every officer of the Seventh Cavalry who could get away from duty in the West was present in full regalia.

In moments, the Marine Band switched to a Viennese waltz and everyone moved to the side while Custer and the First Lady took the floor. As they whirled zestfully around and around, a cheer went up, followed by applause from all sides. They were perhaps the handsomest presidential couple to ever grace an inaugural ball, and surely the best dancers. The party was on. . . .

When they weren't dancing, the Custers held a sort of unofficial receiving line to greet the guests. At one point, Sam Ward and the two famous women he was escorting arrived before them. "Mr. President," he said, "You know Mrs. Sprague, and this is my sister, Julia Ward Howe."

Custer looked deeply into Kate Chase Sprague's eyes for a moment before greeting her and bending over her hand. He introduced them to Libbie, then turned to the famous sixty-one year old author of the poem, "The Battle Hymn of the Republic." Kissing her hand, he said, "I'm honored, Mrs. Howe. My wife is very much interested in the suffrage movement, and has twisted my arm to help."

"Yes," the lady from New York replied, "I heard your remarks in your address today. I'll hold you to them. I must say, breaking precedent by having Mrs. Custer share in your swearing in was a good start."

Custer laughed and introduced her to Libbie. As he looked up, his eyes again found Kate Sprague's and held them momentarily before the French Ambassador stuck out his hand and introduced himself. As the man from Paris moved on to Libbie, Fred Benteen walked up. "Well, as much as it sticks in my craw, Custer, I have to call you Mr. President."

Custer ignored the comment. "You know, Benteen, I've got some important things to do with our military and you could be a lot of help from the other side of the aisle, if you'd just forget your dislike of me and work for the overall good. I'm going to need bipartisan support."

Benteen's owlish eyes studied him a moment before he replied, "If you can prove to me it's for the overall good and not just for yours, I might be persuaded. But as must know, I simply don't trust you yet."

Custer shrugged. "That's your prerogative, congressman."

The Canadian ambassador was waiting. As they shook hands and the envoy congratulated Custer, he said, "I hope, Mr. President, that your announced intention of broadening your borders doesn't extend in our direction."

Custer smiled. "Haven't our people been friends for a long time?"

The Ambassador returned the smile. "Yes, Mr. President, they have."

A slightly drunk Tom Custer interrupted. "Hey, big brother, do you mind if I bring Adam into the ball?"

Custer shook his head. Adam was Tom's pet rattlesnake. "No, I'm afraid you'd have all the ladies screaming."

Libbie heard the comments and turned. "Tom Custer, don't you even *think* about bringing that terrible snake in here!"

Tom laughed and wandered off as Keogh and Annie Yates waltzed by. President Custer waved to them and guessed theirs might be the first marriage to be performed in *his* White House. And that wouldn't be the *only* first in his White House. . . .

★ ★ ★

It was shortly after two o'clock in the morning when Custer came out from the dressing room stark naked. As he approached the bed, Libbie looked up from where she was brushing her hair. "*Autie!*" she said in a mock scolding tone. "Where are your bedclothes?"

He came up and put his arms around her, cupping her breasts in his hands. Kissing her neck, he said, "I don't plan on getting too cold, milady."

A tiny smile touched her lips. "Oh, and why is that, milord?" Her nightgown was quite thin, something she and Annie had selected weeks before in William's, a fashionable ladies' apparel shop on Pennsylvania Avenue. It was, in fact, sheer and nearly transparent.

"Because I intend to make long and vigorous love to the most beautiful First Lady to ever grace this mansion."

"Oh," she replied, turning to face him and nuzzling his lips. "Is that a presidential promise, milord?"

"As sure as my member is getting curious and rising to join the activity."

Her able hand quickly found his growing erection. "Then I guess it's truly a sure thing," she whispered.

He kissed her, picking her up in the process and depositing her on the bed. As his lips found her nipples, he said, "Truly a sure thing."

★ ★ ★

[187]

It was just before four A.M. when Custer decided that sleep was out of the question. He softly moved Libbie's outstretched hand and eased out of bed. Slipping on a robe, he made his way downstairs and out the door to the south portico of the mansion. Bleuch, his hound, followed him outside. The moon was almost full and quite bright as it bathed the hillside in bluish light. Custer went part way down to the fence, where he spotted the sentry. Before he could be challenged, he said, "Good morning, soldier. It's General Custer." He hadn't even thought to say "President."

The guard rendered a rifled salute and mumbled, "Mornin', sir."

"Go on about your post," Custer said quietly as he rubbed the hound's ear. He watched the dark figure of the sentry move off and thought about how many times in his life he'd inspected a guard post. Then his mind drifted back to all of those guard and penalty tours he walked when he was a cadet at West Point, back when he'd received all those demerits. Who would ever have thought he'd be sitting here as the master of this great house. Certainly, not himself. Why, if it hadn't been for the war, he might not even have graduated. He found a bench and took a seat. "Well, old pup, we're here," he said, as Bleuch lay down at his feet. "We live in this big old house now. And just as I have to start looking out for this big country of ours, you have to watch out for those other hounds and your mistress. They say, 'with privilege comes responsibility.' Well, we've got the privilege, and the rest is up to us."

Custer thought about New Orleans after the war, when he'd had a soldier shot for desertion, and then about those he'd ordered shot shortly before his court-martial—for the same thing. Desertion was one of the major ills in the army then, and discipline had to be upheld, maintained for the good and safety of all the conscientious soldiers. But later he was sorry. How would he handle it now? Somewhere, every few days, a judge sentenced someone to death. The law of the land had to be upheld, and ultimately that was his responsibility. And what about the vast numbers of people who were innocent victims of society, the ones who didn't have food, adequate shelter, medical care? The Negroes, the Indians, the poor; they were his soldiers now. What would he do for them in the years ahead? All of those promises he'd just made at the Capitol, could he fulfill them?

He looked up as a small, wispy cloud moved past the moon, permitting its bright light to again flood the grounds. "Lord," he prayed fervently, "Please give me the guidance and the strength to give to this great office my full capabilities, and dear Lord, please guide me to do the most for my people. Thank you, Father."

After a moment, he got to his feet and with Bleuch following, headed back up the hill.

THE CABINET
STATE: Samuel J. Tilden
WAR: George McClellan
NAVY: Thomas Rosser
POSTMASTER: John Kelly
INTERIOR: Tom Custer
ATTORNEY GENERAL: Thomas F. Bayard
TREASURY: Wade Hampton

Prior to the inauguration, the powers to be in both Houses of Congress had greased the skids for confirmation of the Cabinet. As expected, Tom Custer and Tom Rosser were hard to sell, as was Honest John Kelly; but it had been done. It was one thing to name a Cabinet and another to make it work, at least to make it work harmoniously. For a young president new to politics, and particularly new to Washington politics, it would not be easy to handle a group of seven free-thinking, remarkably capable men, many of whom were several years older than Custer. The exception was Tom Custer; he was his younger brother who thought the president could do no wrong. But after that the water got much hotter and deeper.

Samuel J. Tilden had actually been elected president of the United States by the *people*. Hayes had been *given* the election by a committee. Tilden was sixty-seven and had been in politics for many years. He had attacked and defeated the Tweed Ring at Tammany Hall and had been governor of New York for two years. He was conscious of his status as the senior member of the Cabinet and he didn't get on well with Honest John Kelly.

Major-general George Brinton McClellan, "Little Mac," had been God at one time, both in his own mind and in Custer's. The arrogant former commander of the huge Army of the Potomac had also been general-in-chief of the army, and had run against Lincoln for president on the Democratic ticket in 1864. He would not be a quiet voice in the Cabinet.

Nor would Wade Hampton. The sixty-three-year-old wealthy South Carolinian had been a rebel cavalry lieutenant-general in the war, governor of his home state, and recently a U. S. senator. He had been wounded at Gettysburg during the cavalry fight that was Custer's first battle as a boy general. His would be a firm hand on the Treasury portfolio.

Thomas Bayard from Delaware was a senior senator and an important man in the Democratic Party who had been a dark horse for the presidential nomination. His assignment as Attorney General was a payback. He wouldn't be easy either.

Tom Rosser, three years older than Custer, was his ex-classmate. A dynamic Confederate cavalry leader during the war, he'd handed Custer one of his few defeats at Buckland Mills. Tall, with strong endurance like the new president, Rosser was the type to readily speak his mind.

However, none of these temperament factors actually mattered to Custer. He'd been commanding older, strong willed men since he was twenty-three. In his opinion, if he couldn't get along with them, he'd find a way to ignore them . . . or fire them. He was the president and *none* of them were. It was that simple. Except for perhaps Honest John Kelly, he considered them all to be men of integrity, so corruption shouldn't be a problem. He was certain that Kelly, through his patronage, would manage to make a lot of money in New York, but that was the spoils system, and he was already committed.

As far as the vice-president was concerned, Custer cared very little about him. He hadn't forgotten that William English let him down in Indiana, so he didn't have too much confidence in the man. He politely gave him the mission of quietly conducting his duties as president of the Senate and building alliances there that might get needed legislation passed. In essence, Custer made it clear that the vice-president should generally stay out of the way. English had taken the rebuff calmly and had accepted Custer's method of management without a struggle. It had been the way with most vice-presidents since George Washington's tenure.

At his first full cabinet meeting in his office, Custer looked around a moment before saying, "Gentlemen, I've been told that the presidency, the executive branch of the United States government, is the weakest element—that Congress runs things as it sees fit, and that the president exercises has prerogatives only with the power of veto. Well, I'm sorry to hear that because I have big plans to expand the strength of this proud country in the next few years, and I don't want to be stopped at the whim of a congress that doesn't share my vision."

The members of the Cabinet watched him quietly. They had all heard of his nascent jingoism, but he hadn't expressed himself as directly before. The former members of Congress accepted his comments a bit coolly. He added, "We—and you gentlemen are all an integral part of this presidency—can give this country not only *strength* and *position* in the world, we can give it a *legacy*."

Custer looked around the table, meeting and trying to read their eyes. His were alight with enthusiasm. "Gentlemen, we are *not* going to be isolationists and build a wall around ourselves. We are not going to sit pat. We are going to *grow*. Now," he heaved a short sigh, "we all know I'm new at this business of government, and that with a couple of exceptions, you gentlemen aren't. Each and every one of you has sworn to execute the duties of your office to the best of your ability. I'm sure you will."

With those firm words, and to the surprise of everyone present, the new president ended his first cabinet meeting.

★ ★ ★

In the next few days, Custer weathered a couple of much longer and potentially stormy cabinet meetings and managed to keep everything peaceful. Then Tom Rosser came to him, accompanied by Admiral David Dixon Porter, the sixty-seven-year old naval hero and head of the Navy Board of Inspections and the senior officer in that service. A short and spare man, Porter was known for his wit and his generosity to subordinates as well as his criticism of superiors. With William Cooke also in attendance to take notes, Porter was introduced and the visitors took chairs close to the big oak desk that had been given to Custer by an admirer in Chicago. Rosser opened the barrage, "Mr. President, are you aware of the pitiful state of our Navy?"

Custer knew some of it. He raised an eyebrow. "Pitiful?"

"All right, *abject!*" the Navy secretary growled. "While your damned Yankee government has been busy with Indians and keeping Southerners second-class citizens, it has forced the Navy nearly into oblivion. Did you know that we are ranked *twelfth* in the world?" Rosser turned to Porter. "Go ahead, Admiral, tell him about the plight of our wretched navy."

Porter scowled as he got to his feet. "Our navy," he said, "is at the lowest tide it's seen since we had to pay a ransom to Algiers. Out of the one hundred forty vessels on the Navy list, twenty-five are tugs, and only a handful of the rest are seaworthy enough to make a cruise. Of this small number, one is my old side-wheeler, the *Powhatan*, and another is the ancient frigate *Constitution*. The gun batteries mounted on these ships are the old smooth-bores that any rifled gun on the seas can out-duel in a minute, and we don't have a single ship made of steel. It's no wonder that an American captain would be derelict to take his ship into European waters."

Porter's angry eyes bore into Custer's. "*Not one single ship is fit for war.*"

It was the president's turn to frown. "I had no idea it was that bad."

Porter went on, "If we put all of our fighting ships into one fighting force, even Chile's two ironclads, properly handled, could defeat them. Mr. President, I've listened to you talk about waving our proud flag in distant places and about America becoming a world leader. Sir, you can't do it without a navy . . . *you haven't got one.*"

Custer shook his head. The crusty old admiral was right. European nations would scoff at the demands of the State Department when backed by nothing better than a few rotting wooden hulls mounting antiquated guns. "What do you recommend, Admiral?"

Porter looked at Rosser, then back to the president. "As a starter, we need forty armored cruisers made of steel, five torpedo gunboats, ten cruising torpedo boats, and ten harbor torpedo boats. We should also look ahead to building some first-class battleships."

"Other than money, Admiral, is there any reason why these ships can't be built?" Custer asked.

"Steel may be a problem. Currently there are no plants in the country capable of producing what's required."

Custer glanced at Cooke. "Make a note of that and let's see what our powerful friends in the industry have to say about it. Carnegie, for instance."

"What about now?" Rosser asked.

"You and the admiral come up with a bare bones minimum to get us by for the next year, and I'll see what can be done. I positively want some of those relics refitted—and seaworthy—as soon as possible." As the secretary and the admiral rose to leave, Custer said, "Also, find out if there's a first class cruiser for sale anywhere—something fast and deadly that could give us at least a modicum of respect on the high seas. And while you're looking, find an aggressive captain for her."

That afternoon, Custer called Burke and Mark Kellogg into his office and told them about the naval problem. To Burke he said, "I want you to send a telegram to Bennett. Ask him to set up a dinner with Vanderbilt and some more of the big money men ostensibly to meet me. But what I really want is to find the money to buy that cruiser we need."

To Kellogg, he said, "I want a story circulated that the U. S. Navy is about to build a sea raider second to none. Shroud it in mystery. You know, a secret source close to the Secretary of the Navy has revealed such and such."

"What about Secretary Rosser—shouldn't I quote him?"

"No, keep it mysterious."

"I'll see to it," Kellogg replied.

"And Mark, I want you to start releasing stories about the poor situation of our navy—the lack of ships and their antiquated condition and so on. Mix in some stories about our depleted army and its poor pay, as well. I want to start getting public opinion in favor of a buildup."

"What about using the surplus money?" Burke asked. He was referring to the huge sum of about $100 million annually that had been created from tariff income during recent years.

"I've been told Congress may be a little touchy about using that money in such a manner. I'll get more of an idea of how the land lies once we get a response to the press campaign Mark's cooking up."

★ ★ ★

Next Custer met privately with Wade Hampton. The handsome treasury secretary listened attentively as the president explained the navy dilemma and his plan for acquiring a cruiser. When he finished, Custer added, "Wade, I want you to quietly sound out what kind of objection Congress might have in regard to use of that tariff surplus for military purposes."

Hampton stroked his ample beard and nodded his head. "I'm sure there'll be some. Since farmers and some manufacturers have been hurt by trade retaliation to our stiff tariffs, they may want an equal share."

"Well, see what you can find out. Okay?"

Hampton got to his feet. "Yes, sir."

"Oh, and Wade, also think about how we can ostensibly put an old warship in dry-dock for refitting, but wind up with a new one."

"Sir?"

"You're a soldier, a statesman, and now a money man. See if you can find out how to be a magician."

A slow smile touched the treasury secretary's lips. "I'll work on it."

As the big South Carolinian departed, Custer went to the window that looked down over the south lawn of the mansion. He liked this big airy office with its mementos. One of his favorite new possessions that held sway on the widest expanse of wall was the new painting Albert Bierstadt had given him two days after the election. It depicted Custer on horseback leading some of his Seventh Cavalry into a valley marked by a huge water-fall in the West. Another wall held a Wolverine battle flag and a Third Cavalry guidon from the Big War. His guidon from the Seventh hung behind his desk. Weapons and hunting trophies filled other wall space. He had done the taxidermy himself.

The only thing he didn't like about his office was how it was defiled every morning from ten to twelve when office seekers clamored for civil service appointments. Some mornings at dawn a line formed all the way up Pennsylvania Avenue for blocks. They were like bloodsuckers, wanting every government job imaginable across the land. The bleats were almost identical. "I brought in my precinct in Kentucky for you, Mr. President. I am due that job at the post office." And on and on. Patronage, patronage, patronage.

No wonder civil service reform was such a big matter; literally hundreds of thousands were on its lists, and almost all of them got there through patronage. If he had his way he wouldn't see a single one of them. Their poison drained his energy, but such was the system and he was ensnared by it.

She was just what Custer wanted. Finding a modern cruiser for sale was easier than Custer had anticipated. After years of turmoil, Argentina had recently stopped its civil strife and had united under a general named Roca. As a result, the disputed hegemony of Buenos Aires as a province had ended and the wealthy city was again the capital of the whole country. Therefore the former province's small new navy comprised of two harbor torpedo boats and the great cruiser *Rosas* was up for sale. Asking price: $700,000. The *Rosas* was similar to the latest British cruiser, *Iris*, and had been built specifically by the French for sale to Buenos Aires. She was made of steel, was steam powered with two lightweight propellers, carried ten sixty-four-pounder rifled guns as her major armament, and, because she was totally without armor and protected by coal bunkers outside her two boiler rooms, she was light enough to make eighteen knots. She was one of the fastest warships afloat and could fight effectively against any belligerent ship she might encounter.

Tom Rosser came up with a captain for her, Commander Nelson Jones, forty-six, an energetic graduate of the Naval Academy, class of '57, who had served heroically in Porter's River Fleet and in the Fort Fisher campaign during the war.

"How can he go wrong with that name?" Custer joked when he was given the officer's records.

Now the fledgling president had to find the money.

★ ★ ★

In the meantime, he had to get things rolling with the army. He held a meeting with George McClellan also attended by Tom Custer, Wade Hampton and Tom Rosser. General Sherman was out of the city and couldn't attend. "First of all," Custer announced from the head of his conference table, "I don't know why in the heck Hayes instituted this alcohol ban just before the inauguration. He should have waited and asked me." He was referring to Hayes' order of February 22 that alcohol would no longer be permitted on army posts.

"That was the doing of 'Lemonade Lucy,'" Tom Custer said with a smile. "She couldn't sleep, worrying about all those drunken soldiers celebrating with their horses."

Everyone chuckled at the reference to the teetotalling Mrs. Hayes, and the popular nickname she'd earned by banning alcohol at the White House.

Custer went on, "As you know, I'm sort of the Lemonade Lucy now, but I don't want to prohibit consumption. Brother Tom and I agree that soldiers are better off doing their drinking on post most of the time, rather than throwing their money into unscrupulous barkeeper's hands off-post. Tom can have his sutlers treat them squarely."

Both Hampton and Rosser agreed. McClellan nodded his head. The edict would be rescinded. "Now," Custer said, "We need to get started on rebuilding the army. General McClellan and I have discussed this at length and we agree that three cavalry regiments and five infantry regiments should be brought to active duty. The truth is, nobody wants them. It's the old story—since there isn't a war, who needs them? These naysayers never stop to think about how much a strong standing army is a means of *averting* a war. And right now, France is meddling in our sphere of influence with that Panama canal nonsense. Since we have no navy to speak of, and only a small army, she can thumb her nose at us."

Everyone spoke his piece on the proposal of additional regiments, with all finally agreeing except Attorney General Bayard. The fifty-eight-year-old former senator from Delaware's primary interest was in maintaining warm relations with England, and he didn't think a U.S. military buildup would be viewed favorably in Parliament. But he acceded to the cabinet's majority in asking for the additional troops by remaining neutral on the matter. It was decided that immediate pressure would be brought to bear on Congress to garner approval.

★ ★ ★

But before anyone could do that, Custer's plan suffered a setback. General William Tecumseh Sherman entered his office and came to attention in front of Custer's big desk the next day. They were the only ones present. "Mr. President," the longtime friend of U. S. Grant and the second most successful Union general in the Big War said, "I wish to announce my retirement as commanding general of the United States Army."

Custer got to his feet and scowled. "Now why do you want to do that, General? I have big plans for expanding the army and I need your exceptional organizational skills."

Sherman, the intelligent red-haired officer with the wrinkled face that had marched to his own bugler his entire career, scowled and said, "It's this way, Armstrong . . . you know how I feel about politicians and newspapermen. Well, now you embody both and I don't . . ."

Custer interrupted, "General, I'm neither one. I'm an army officer at heart, and an American first. I—"

Now it was Sherman's turn to interrupt. "Custer," he growled, his angry eyes narrowing, "you're a goddamned opportunist. You're a hell of a fighter, and a damned good division commander, but you haven't got the sand to be more because you aren't an honest man. Your private interests come first, and I can't work for you. It's as simple as that. Now, I'm going quietly because I don't trust the newspapers to report the truth, so let it go at that. Just tell the goddamned press I'm going fishing." The tall man who had marched through Georgia and later said that war was hell stiffly brought his heels together, saluted, did an about face, and strode resolutely from the office.

Custer stood blinking at his desk for several moments, his face flushed. No one had spoken to him like that in a long time. Then he walked to the open door and wiggled a finger for William Cooke to come into his office. When the bewiskered lieutenant-colonel asked why Sherman had left so abruptly, Custer replied, "He just resigned. Get General Sheridan here from Chicago as soon as possible."

Blest, indeed, is he who never fell,
But blest much more, who from the verge of hell
Climbs up to Paradise; for sin is sweet,
Strong is temptation, willing are the feet
That follow pleasure; manifold her snares . . .
—George Armstrong Custer, 1866

Lawrence Barrett shook his head. "Who would have thought this grand old lady would come to this?"

The actor and the president stood in the late afternoon sunshine in front of Ford's Theater at 511 10th Street NW. A few feet away, the vigilant Charlie Myers kept a watchful eye on passersby. Possibly one of the most famous, indeed notorious, buildings in the capital, the three-story structure was now quite run down. Its red bricks were faded and cracked here and there, as if it were serving a penance for its sin. Yet, the former First Baptist Church was innocent. It had been leased to theater entrepreneur John T. Ford twenty years earlier who converted it into a music hall. Known as Ford's Athenaeum during the early war years, it had enjoyed great success until it was destroyed by fire. But Ford had immediately started reconstruction and opened Ford's New Theatre in August, 1863. Then, on that dark day April 14, 1865, the Southern sympathizer and youngest member of the famous acting family, John Wilkes Booth, fired the shot that killed President Abraham Lincoln in his theater box. The nation was plunged into mourning and the theater into darkness. Threats of arson kept Ford from reopening the theater, and the government bought it. Converted into an office building, it had served ignominiously since.

Custer shook his head. "It was a time of great sadness, Lawrence. Assassination is such a sudden, wrenching wound. The people took it out on the building."

"Such a shame."

Custer took his friend's arm. "Do you know why I brought you here?"

"No, tell me, Autie."

"We are going to restore it as it once was in all its glory. I will rename it the Lincoln Theater, and it will also house the offices for the Department of the Performing Arts. The director and his staff will also be located here. Does that idea appeal to you, Lawrence?"

"Yes, of course. Who is he?"

Custer laughed as he clapped the actor/director on the back. "You, Lawrence Barrett, you!"

★ ★ ★

The dinner was at Delmonico's in a private dining room set with the finest silver and linen. Working through Bennett, Burke had arranged for several of the wealthiest men in America to attend. After a sumptuous meal of lobster, Custer rose to speak over the cigars, coffee and brandy. He went into the potential for American industry in the years ahead as he pursued "The New American Empire," citing how manufacturing had come of age in the Civil War, and could now push the United States into the forefront of world trade. He looked Andrew Carnegie directly in the eye when he said, "We will need great American steel mills to build the new ships our almost nonexistent navy will require." He cited the facts about the woebegone status of the U.S. Navy, and then described his search for a modern warship. "Now, before we have the great steel factories that will build us forty ships of war, we need to make this cruiser I've mentioned one of the most famous and feared fighting ships on the high seas. I have a plan in which this craft, which will be christened the *Monroe*, to speed from one port to another putting on a show of force as she proceeds. Our press will announce to the world's newspapers that the most powerful cruiser in the world is flexing its muscles as the harbinger of the great new navy we are building."

Custer's eyes glowed as he centered on William Henry Vanderbilt, the sixty-year-old son of the old Commodore. "But before we can get Congress to pay for our ships, I want to show them that the princes of industry and trade are in full support of my plan." He paused effectively, then lowered his voice and went on. "I want you gentlemen to buy our cruiser from Buenos Aires for the agreed upon sum of six hundred forty thousand dollars."

It was utterly quiet in the richly decorated dining room for several moments until James Gordon Bennett, Jr. broke the silence with, "I'll provide the first one hundred fifty thousand."

William Waldorf Astor, the thirty-three-year-old great-grandson of John Jacob Astor, the wealthy financier who was one of America's earliest and richest businessmen, spoke up, "I'll *match* that sum, Mr. President."

Vanderbilt was next. "Since my family has a sea heritage, I'll provide two hundred thousand for the project."

Custer's gaze went back to Andrew Carnegie. The forty-six-year-old Scot nodded his head. "I guess if I'm going make the steel for a new navy,

I can certainly provide the rest of the money for its forerunner. But I have one question—why that name for the ship?"

Custer grinned. "Cruisers are named for cities, sir. But in this case, the name is two-fold. This ship will be our first warning to the world and to France in particular that the Monroe Doctrine will be *enforced*."

A quick round of approval followed and then Custer continued, "And my lovely wife, Libbie, is from the city of Monroe, Michigan. It's not a metropolis by any means, but it qualifies in light of the name of our former president."

"Bravo!" Bennett exclaimed. "My newspapers will make the U.S.S. *Monroe* famous around the world!"

★ ★ ★

Thirty-five minutes after the dinner broke up at Delmonico's, an enclosed horse-drawn carriage pulled up in front of a three-story house on East 66th Street. Just off Fifth Avenue and close to Central Park, it was close to the residence of former president U. S. Grant. Custer didn't know who owned the house, and he didn't care. He was interested only in its current occupant. Dismounting from the conveyance, he told the driver to wait, that he had no idea of how long he'd be. Mounting the steps, he saw the number "23" by the doorway, an etched shadow in the bright moonlight. He turned the doorbell and glanced around as he waited. Only a few people were out and about, and the collar of his overcoat was turned up so it hid most of his face. The wide-brimmed hat, pulled low over his forehead kept the rest of it in shadow. He felt a slight thrill at the danger of being recognized and at the adventure he was about to experience. It reminded him, somehow, of slipping out through the fence at West Point to visit that forbidden tavern those many years ago.

A maid, wearing a lace-trimmed black uniform and one of those puffy little white hats, opened the door, curtsied and in a decidedly British accent, invited him inside. A slender little woman in her twenties, she smiled shyly as she took his hat and coat and opened the door to a drawing room just off the vestibule. There, rising from the sofa where she was reading, was the tall, incredibly beautiful Lillie Langtry.

She was wearing a dark green silk dress, trimmed with a golden chintz, cut low to reveal the swell of her remarkable breasts. The frock coordinated well with her rich auburn hair that was knotted loosely, shining, in the style all England knew from postcards. All of these colors added to the allure of her compelling violet eyes. She flashed a smile, the smile that untold thousands of Englishmen, young and old, would have given their inheritances for. "Good evening, Mr. President," she said in her deep voice.

She held out her fair hand that seldom bore any jewelry and he bent low over it. "Good evening, Mrs. Langtry. I'm a bit late, but I bought a warship tonight."

She raised an eyebrow. "Bought a warship?"

Custer released her hand. *He had never seen such eyes.* "I'll tell you about it later."

"Would you like some brandy, or perhaps some champagne to celebrate your new ship?"

"No," he murmured, "I don't drink, and besides, being in your presence is celebration enough for me."

She curtsied slightly, smiling again. "Thank you, Mr. President."

"Oh, please, call me something more familiar."

Her expression became thoughtful. "Hmm. Well, I can't call you George—that's much too close to the throne. I've read that you are called Autie by your intimates and Armstrong by other friends. How about something special, just for us? And only in private. Hmm. Ah, I have it! Do you mind if I call you 'Army?'"

He moved closer, holding her eyes. "Will we be seeing each other in private quite often, Mrs. Langtry?"

"As often as you wish, Army. Please call me Lillie."

"I think I will wish to see you very often, Lillie."

She leaned up and brushed his lips with hers, then abruptly returned to the sofa.

"Come sit with me, Army, and tell me about this grand new boat of yours."

He took her hand and told her about the *Monroe*, skipping the fact that it would be the only battle-worthy ship in his fleet.

She watched the animation in his expression as his enthusiasm grew. Suddenly he stopped and looked at her in mock seriousness. "But I can't be telling you state secrets. You might well be a British spy."

She laughed. "It's very possible. After all, I *have* been the mistress of the Crown Prince." Her eyes danced. "Yes, what a glorious plot: Crown Prince sends beguiling mistress to America to entrance its president and learn his plans. How thrilling!"

Custer chuckled. "I shall be on guard, devious one. But one thing is certain—I *am* entranced."

> *Sing of Mrs. Langtry, a lady full of grace,*
> *Four-and-twenty sonnets written to her face;*
> *Now that face is public, and we can also sing,*
> *"Is she not a dainty dame, and worthy of a King?*

So read the verse from an admirer that was published in London's *Truth* to mark Lillie's departure for America three months earlier. Lillie's life had changed quite radically in the past half year. Although she was still the most famous woman in the British Empire after the elderly and strict Queen Victoria, she had been stymied in her love life. Bertie, the crown prince, still adored her and kept her under his protection, but they seldom saw each other. She had given birth to a beautiful daughter, sired by a royal nephew of Bertie named Louis, whom she actually felt she loved. But her weak, long-cuckolded husband still wouldn't give her a divorce, even though she hadn't lived with him for years. It took the remarkable French actress, Sarah Bernhardt, to lead her to a new way of life. "The Divine Sarah," of the slender body and luminous eyes, had also found her way to Bertie's bed, but as she and Lillie became acquainted, she had inspired the tall beauty to become an actress. After certain success on the London stage, due more to her beauty and notoriety than her acting talent, Lillie had made a shrewd deal with a theater owner to bring the theatrical company she now owned to New York.

Highly publicized by her close friend, Oscar Wilde, who was in Manhattan trying to right his financial plight, she literally took New York by storm. As her ship entered the harbor, a tugboat filled with an army of reporters and a brass band playing "God Save the Queen" had sidled alongside. Her performances, including the tour she took to other eastern and midwest cities, had been sellouts ever since. But she had tired of staying in the Albermarle Hotel, and had just recently leased her present house.

Following extended lively conversation, Lillie said, "Come, let me show you around my lovely house. Actually, I'm renting it while I decide what to do. I'm considering American citizenship for several reasons, perhaps the most important of which is to get a divorce. I hear California is quite liberal, and New York is also very appealing." She kissed his cheek as she took him by the hand and led him from the sitting room. "It's also quite close to Washington, my dear."

Custer became increasingly excited by her endearing terms and open affection. Who would have ever thought that the world's most celebrated beauty would be making overtures to him? But then, who would have thought he'd ever be in the White House? For some reason, his mind skipped back to Fort Leavenworth in 1867—he sat in dress uniform on his horse, awaiting the findings of the court-martial. It had been the lowest point of his life when he heard the words, ". . . guilty of all charges." Oh, so far from here. . . .

"And this, noble sir, is my bedroom," Lillie said, sweeping her arm around a most feminine room with a white marble fireplace and a double bed with a canopy of flowered satin. To his surprise, she closed the door and came to him. "Kiss me, Army," she said. "If you are rushing back to Washington on the early morning train, we have very little time."

He took her in his arms and kissed her, finding her eager tongue as she pulled herself up tight against him. Finally, when the kiss ended, she sighed, "Ah, *mon generale*, ever since I first saw you in Indianapolis, I've been attracted to you. You are so *strong* and masculine."

Any cautionary thoughts he may have had were thrown to the winds as his lips went to her neck and down to the swell of her breasts. She kissed the top of his head as his hands found her buttocks. He pulled her even tighter as she undulated against him. They staggered, entwined to the edge of the bed. "Wait," she pleaded, "Let me take off these clothes."

"*No*," he said hoarsely, "Not now. I want you *instantly!*" He hiked her dress and petticoats up as he fumbled with his trousers. Continuing to kiss him, she kicked off her last lower undergarment. "I *knew* you'd be like this" she whispered loudly, ". . . an American *savage!*"

She was moist, hot, as he entered her, rock hard, and thrust strongly inside. Words of passion tumbled from her lips as she rose to greet his power.

The Jersey Lily had conquered her second throne.

34

Wearing his black suit and carrying a valise that contained his other belongings, Red Elk knocked on the door of the regimental recruiting office at Fort Myer. The name of the post by Arlington Cemetery had been changed from Fort Whipple just a few weeks earlier not only to honor the deceased Brigadier-general Albert J. Myer, the army's former chief signal officer, but to eliminate confusion with the other Fort Whipple out in Arizona. At the same time, the headquarters and five companies of the Seventh Cavalry arrived at the post to be, at Custer's direction, the honor regiment that would defend the capital in an emergency and perform in state ceremonies that would be constantly required by his New American Empire.

The president had also seen to it that Colonel Ranald Mackenzie had been given command of the Seventh and would remain at its helm at Fort Myer, rather than travel around to serve on boards and court-martials. Mackenzie had graduated from West Point in the class immediately behind the president but was, inexplicably, number one in standing, versus Custer's *last* standing. He had a brilliant Civil War record, and had actually been a better Indian fighter than Custer up until the Little

Bighorn. Mackenzie's biggest fame came when he had disregarded the border and chased renegade Indians deep into Mexico. Everyone thought of the youthful Custer as the first famous brevet major-general at the end of the war, but actually Mackenzie, a few months younger, had been promoted to that rank two weeks ahead of him.

Now, Custer wanted to reward him by giving him command of his prized regiment and having him serve in the Washington area for a while before giving him back a star. It would also be a well-publicized example of his fairness as the commander-in-chief.

But none of this mattered to the twenty-two-year-old Red Elk, who had carefully laid his plan. He had decided the best place for him would be right in Custer's old regiment outside of Washington. Once established there, he would plan the best way to get to Long Hair. He had studied hard at Carlisle and constantly practiced his English, which—still with a bit of an accent—was quite good. Indians were not allowed to serve in the U. S. Army except as scouts in frontier commands, so he had a story. He'd been told that recruiting sergeants were not the brightest people in the world and that they were so used to enlisting foreign recruits who often spoke no English, that they wouldn't give him a problem. The story: he was from Ceylon, the large island off the southeast coast of India. And to explain his familiarity with firearms and horses: he had served in the Royal Indian Hussars, enlisting in Calcutta when he was sixteen. Being tall, with sharp features, he didn't look Sioux or, for that matter, from any particular tribe. He had even taught himself drill from a British field manual he'd bought at a used book store in Philadelphia. And since he would never volunteer any information and be close-mouthed in his replies, he doubted he would get caught in any of the lies. The only one who could catch him up would be someone familiar with the Royal Indian Hussars or someone from Ceylon, and that possibility was remote. He gave himself the new name of James Elkins.

Red Elk was assigned to C Company, which was commanded by Captain Edward Godfrey who had an overwhelming dark mustache. The first-sergeant was South Carolinian Daniel Kanipe. Since regimental Sergeant-major Bobo had been first sergeant of C Company at the time of the Little Bighorn, he still had a soft spot for it. He was having a cup of coffee with Kanipe when a corporal arrived with the new recruit.

As Bobo and Kanipe glanced over the new recruit's enlistment papers, the sergeant-major looked Red Elk over appraisingly. "You learn how to shoot in the Hussars, Elkins?" he asked.

"Yes, sir." Red Elk replied.

"You don't 'sir' NCOs, private. Only officers."

Red Elk nodded his head.

"Doesn't make much difference," First-sergeant Kanipe said, "I doubt he'll ever have to aim at anything around here, unless it's a goddamn politician. You a good horseman, Elkins?"

"I can ride."

"Did you ever get into battle with them there huzzars?"

"Some." He'd been in battle with Sitting Bull's hussars.

"Were you scared?"

Red Elk looked the first-sergeant in the eye. "No."

★ ★ ★

Red Elk was officially Private James Elkins, C Company, Seventh United States Cavalry. His enlistment was for four years, but he would have signed up for any number, because once his mission was finished he would disappear back into the world of the Sioux. It would be easy to move around among the various tribes for a couple of years, then reappear as himself. Unless he ran into a trooper or NCO who recognized him, he would never be connected with Private James Elkins. And there were other options; he could live the lonely life that had marked Crazy Horse, maybe even find another wife someday. But this could never take place until Late Star was vindicated.

The vision of his beautiful Late Star had never diminished. The little parts of their life together lingered in his memory. Her face and loving voice still came to him in the dreams he couldn't elude, tearing at his heart. He had never lost that picture of her lying there on the ground by the Greasy Grass, the blood gushing from her terrible stomach wound, her eyes wild, unseeing . . . Nor had his consuming hatred of Long Hair lessened. As a proud Sioux war leader, he would avenge her to the last drop of his own blood.

★ ★ ★

Since both the House of Representatives and the Senate were ruled by a majority of Democrats, the hard-lobbying Cabinet was able to get approval to build four cruisers similar to the *Monroe*, but with slightly larger engines and higher caliber guns. They were to be named the *Boston*, the *Chicago*, the *Atlanta*, and the *Charleston*. Since Andrew Carnegie promised to quickly produce the steel required, both the *Chicago* and the *Atlanta* were to built with the utmost of speed—with the other two cruisers right behind. Following them, according to the "New Navy" plan that Admiral Porter authored, the first of several American battleships would be built—the *Maine*.

Custer was elated. By telegram, he promised each shipbuilding company and the makers of various outside components bonuses for bringing the new ships in ahead of schedule. He had no doubt that he could raise premium money among his New York money men. By his own timetable, he wanted the new ships running their trials by late April of the following year.

★ ★ ★

"The Gilded Age," as Mark Twain called the period, was in full swing in the nation's capital. Receptions were never more elaborate, nor the many balls that began at midnight and lasted often until dawn more popular. It seemed that the romantic and energetic young Custers and their love of the arts and zestful life were just the spur that Washington society needed to regain its postwar enthusiasm. Nothing was too elegant for these occasions. In addition to tables bedded with violets and overflowing with camellias, roses of all persuasions, and heliotropes, acacias, scarlet passion flowers and various ferns, buffets were jammed with spiced meat and salads, choice fruits, truffle and terrapin, elaborate confections and pastries. Sparkling gold, silver and crystal surrounded the bottles of champagne and red Bordeaux and Burgundies. Life was rich and due to get even better. In addition to the balls, every hostess worth her salt wanted to stage a reception or dinner that included the Custers. Annie Yates had her work cut out for her just sorting the invitations and guessing at which ones the president and his delightful lady should or would attend.

Amid the unending social life, Libbie's days were chock full. Just learning how to run the huge mansion, or at least get some idea of how the staff did it, had occupied her time since the inauguration. In fact, she hadn't even learned all of the staff's names yet. She wasn't the type to just let things happen; during all that time in the big commander's house at Fort Lincoln, and later in the San Francisco and St. Paul houses, she had been on top of everything. But the White House was a different beast, and it *was* a beast. Not only was it a gargantuan structure, many parts of it were in disrepair, and although she liked plants and flowers, she simply didn't have the money to keep up Lucy Hayes' greenhouse. It would make a nice house for Autie's hounds, she decided. He'd brought only seven with him, and most of the time they had a great time just wandering around the mansion. But that was just one of the problems and costs.

The money tree in New York, Bennett, offered to help with a sum of $50,000 to be spent in the first two years of the Custer presidency. Of course, all improvements and alterations to the mansion would be the subject of exclusive coverage by the *Herald*.

Libbie was grateful for the publisher's largesse, but more and more had the feeling that he was as much a sound investor as a free-giver interested in the good of the country.

Shortly after Custer's return from New York, as they were both reading in their bedroom suite, she said, "Darling, I want to ask you a question. Have you ever felt as if you are Faust?"

Custer, who happened to be reading the *Herald*, asked, "Why do you say that?"

She got up from her chair and sat by his feet. "Oh, I wonder about Mr. Bennett. Do you think he will eventually exact his full pound of flesh?"

"What do you mean?"

"Oh, I just feel uneasy now and then about how much of what we do seems to benefit those newspapers of his."

"What makes you uneasy about it?"

"I just think he pulls many strings with us, as if we are puppets."

Custer put down the paper and shook his head. "Well, I assure you, Little Standby, that I dance on no string, let alone his. You have to remember how much he has done for us—and continues to do. He has the most powerful newspaper in the world, and it is practically my personal trumpet, my town crier."

"I know, but still, I wonder. Has he ever asked for anything, such as the ambassadorship to the Court of St. James's?"

"Nope. Nothing."

"Well, I have the feeling we'll soon know."

★ ★ ★

Boston Custer stood, hat in hand, outside Fred Benteen's office while the former colonel's secretary announced his presence. Although they were both members of the House Military Affairs Committee, Benteen's animosity for anything named Custer kept them on the ragged edge of civility. Moments later Boston was shown into the white-haired congressman's office. Benteen looked up coolly, "What do you want, Custer?"

Boston replied, "Help, Fred, help."

"For whom, that asshole brother of yours?"

"Yes, and more. For the country."

"Go on . . ."

"I could bring this up at the next committee meeting, but I know how you feel about Autie and I want you to block him out and consider the issue for its merits. We need to go to the House Appropriations Committee with a strong recommendation to fund the new regiments and ships. You know our navy is pathetic, and I don't have to tell you how thin our army is. If we marshal a strong enough stance on our committee, we'll have a better chance of getting the money we need. I'm the junior member, you're established."

"I don't trust your brother."

"This isn't about my brother, sir. You're a patriot. You spent what, fourteen, fifteen years in the Army? You have the Medal of Honor and you're one of our biggest heroes. If you hadn't stopped Crazy Horse at the Little Bighorn, we wouldn't even be here."

Benteen, who wasn't above a bit of preening at times, shrugged. "I did my part, didn't I? Well, I know you are just shining me up to get your brother's programs through, but I'm not so vindictive that I would impede what's good for the country. I'll see what I can do."

As Boston turned to go, Benteen added, "But don't take my compliance as a change of my low regard for your damned brother. Nothing will *ever* change my opinion of him."

In the glory of the lilies, Christ was born across the sea . . .
As he died to make men holy, let us die to make men free. . . .
From "The Battle Hymn of the Republic"
           —*Julia Ward Howe*

Commander Nelson Jones had taken his ship's officers to Buenos Aires shortly after the deal was made by Secretary Rosser. They immediately began familiarity training on the ship that would become the U.S.S. *Monroe*. A sloop with a skeleton crew of topnotch sailors followed, while a records search for other exceptional Navy crewmen was instituted. They would join the ship later.

Remarkably, on June 25, the fifth anniversary of what had become known in Custer circles as "The Battle," the *Rosas*, with her name already painted out, steamed up the Chesapeake Bay and into the Potomac toward the nation's capital. She was a beauty—two-stacked, steam-powered, and with a partial set of sails, painted green to go with the deep waters she would cruise. Her big rifled guns glistened and every ounce of brass on her deck shone brightly in the Virginia sun as she docked at

Alexandria. Having timed the arrival perfectly, the presidential party was ready for the commissioning.

Custer, never too interested in the sea, was quite proud of his new ship. And of course, that was exactly how he regarded it. The running joke around the capital was that he secretly called it the U.S.S. *Custer*. The moment the cruiser tied up to the wharf and the gangplank was settled, he hurried aboard like a child with a new toy. Commander Jones immediately showed the president and his party around, extolling the charms of the Navy's new lady.

Soon it was time to officially commission the ship. Rosser had pointed out that normally only new ships got *christened*. But Custer wanted to include Libbie in the ceremony so he had the officer in charge combine elements from both rites. The first lady, looking elegant in a dark blue ensemble with gold buttons that resembled a Navy uniform and wearing a white hat with a wide brim trimmed in gold, was the center of the presidential party as it reformed on a small platform that extended from the dock to the bow of the ship. Behind, on the dock and in front of the large crowd, the Marine Band was in fine form as it played several seafaring songs. Then it burst into the most well-known song of the past war. As the zestful strains of "The Battle Hymn of the Republic" filled the Virginia air, its composer, the famous Julia Ward Howe stepped to the edge of the platform. She waited until the last strains of her great song died out and the only sound came from some overhead sea gulls, before she recited the invocation.

Admiral David D. Porter was next. He spoke of American naval victories, then introduced the Secretary of the Navy. Rosser's remarks were brief, with a slightly humorous reference to the famous Civil War battle of the *Monitor* and the *Merrimac*. Next he read the Navy Department commissioning orders. When he was finished, he turned to Custer and said, "Ladies and Gentlemen, it is seldom that a president of the United States is personally involved in a ship commissioning, if *ever*, but today President George Armstrong Custer is here to dignify this great event."

Custer waved his hat to the roar of applause and stood silent and bareheaded for a moment before beginning his short speech that, while not quite true, was meant for diplomats around the world. "This great ship," he began, "is but the forerunner of what will soon be the most modern and powerful navy in the world. Already new ships of speed and steel are preparing to slide down the ways into the great oceans and spread the glory of our proud nation. This cruiser will be the fastest warship afloat, ready to lead our new fleet to great honors in the years ahead. And now, since this fine ship is being named for the First Lady's home town, and mine as well, I'd like to introduce Mrs. Libbie Custer!"

As the band broke into "The Girl I Left Behind," Libbie took the champagne bottle, turned to the bow of the ship, and said loudly, "I commission you the U.S.S *Monroe!*" Taking a healthy swing with the bottle, she smashed it against the bow, spraying champagne over herself and her grinning husband. Immediately the band struck up the national anthem and the ensign, jack, and commission pennant were run up the main mast.

Custer's new navy was underway.

On August 18, the still Republican leaning *New York Times* ran a front-page article of the commissioning of the U.S.S. *Monroe* under the headline: EXPANSIONISM. After describing the event, it went on:

> "Has America reached the brink of Jingoism under Custer? Will the Murat in the White House lead us to international infamy and possible destruction with his aggressive behavior? Why must we buy an expensive cruiser, if we aren't going to war? Why should we go to war—to please a battle-hungry warrior who isn't happy without Indians to kill? Except for a few expansionists such as Senator John Tyler Morgan of Alabama and Congressman John

Kasson of Iowa, the Congress is smart enough to realize that it is all we can do to develop our own country. Congressman Frederick Benteen, himself a major hero at the Little Bighorn, and now one of the most vocal of our anti-expansionists, states, 'President Custer will do anything he thinks will bring glory on his greedy head.' Colonel Benteen should know."

The next day, Custer looked around his conference table before laying down the cards he had carefully planned to present. Sheridan, Rosser, Hampton and Tom Custer had joined Burke, Keogh and Cooke at the special Sunday morning meeting. McClellan was attending a funeral in New Jersey, so he was absent. Custer thought it just as well, because Little Mac tended to assume control of meetings at times. "Gentlemen," he began, "you've all heard me speak about national expansion *ad infinitum*, and I'm sure you all probably read what the *Times* had to say about it. Well, it's time to make a plan. I want to expand our borders as soon as possible. Since we need to weigh all possibilities, it's time to look at things as they now stand."

He paused a moment, then went on, "We have three main possibilities: Canada, Mexico, and the Caribbean. Although Canada is a sovereign nation, she is still connected to Victoria's umbilical chord. I'm afraid any overt move against her will bring the Brits and their big navy screaming down our throats. And I don't want redcoats on our soil again.

"Mexico. It's a natural possibility. She has vast raw materials and would make a perfect extension for our country, but we've already done that this century, in fact, only thirty-five years ago. And I can't find any plausible excuse for invading that country again. Nevertheless, perhaps a pretext can be arranged."

Custer sipped some lukewarm coffee. "Which leaves us the Caribbean. We've already had some disagreements with Spain. Can we broaden those enough to go to war and take Cuba?"

Wade Hampton replied, "I think so. Being from South Carolina, I've never been happy about Spain being so firmly entrenched that close to our southeastern coast. I'm in favor of that kind of a move."

Custer shifted in his seat. "Think we can finance a fast war in Cuba?"

Hampton nodded his head. "I think we can get it through Congress— if we have a sound enough reason."

The president turned to Tom Rosser. "What kind of a navy does Spain have?"

"Nearly as bad as ours," the secretary replied. "I hear they have over a hundred admirals with nothing to command. I can get an up-to-date estimate in a few days."

"Good," Custer said. "Do it."

Now it was Sheridan's turn. "I'll have a report for you on the Spanish Army within a week, Mr. President. But I think we can kick their ass if we get those new regiments soon."

More general discussion about a possible war with Spain followed for another twenty minutes, and then Custer got to his feet. "This is all to be kept absolutely secret, as you well know. We'll meet here again two weeks from today to consolidate our intelligence. Good day, gentlemen."

★ ★ ★

Since Libbie was extremely popular, Burke thought it was a good idea to give her plenty of notice in the press. Mark Kellogg worked with Annie Yates, who proved quite adept at writing press releases herself, in getting the first lady's activities well reported. The remodeling of the White House, in particular, was described regularly, as were Libbie's growing collection of new gowns and dresses. The first lady designed many of them, still keeping a touch of the military in their theme—as she had done back in the regimental days. Naturally, a sea of military designs flooded the dress stores and salons of the country.

When Libbie decided to go to a women's suffrage conference in New York to support Susan Anthony, the *Evening Star* ran a major feature on her interest in the movement and the forthcoming visit. The day she left for the five-day conference and some shopping on the side, a note arrived by private courier for Custer. It was personally handed to Myles Keogh, who delivered it unopened to the president.

Mr. President:

I would be delighted if you would join me for a private dinner two nights hence, on Wednesday, the 2nd of August at 7 o'clock P.M. Since this is such frightfully short notice, I do hope you can stop by at least for dessert.

Respectfully yours,
Kate Sprague at Edgewood

Custer threw a quick glance at his calendar, saw that Wednesday night was free, dipped his pen in ink, and scribbled, "I'll be there for dinner. Thank you, Kate. GAC." on the invitation, resealed it and handed it back to Keogh. "Give this to the courier," he said. The colonel nodded and left the office. He was completely trustworthy when it came to affairs of the heart, and the fact that he knew Kate Sprague was a redhead made him all the more so.

★ ★ ★

Custer arrived by a hired carriage that Keogh had arranged at five minutes before seven. The estate that Salmon Chase had left to his two daughters, which Kate Sprague now occupied with her three girls, was a bit shabby around the edges, but still elegant. It consisted of fifty isolated acres that provided an excellent view of the capital and beyond that, some of the Potomac. A red brick exterior hid the fine taste and treasures of the somewhat plain looking two-story house that sat on a hilltop. Kate had known days of luxury early in her marriage to William Sprague, but that was at another time. Today, however, she looked far from deprived. Lovely in turquoise satin, with her titian-colored hair piled high, and wearing a lustrous strand of pearls, she greeted him personally at the door. She was tall, her eyes meeting his at nearly the same level. "Come in, Mr. President," she said, looking over his shoulder to the carriage. "Your driver can wait in the rear, if you wish."

"Might be a good idea," Custer replied.

"My man will see to it. Please come in."

As she took his hat, Custer could see why so many men had been charmed by her. At forty-one—he had checked her age—she was still quite stunning. He followed her through the wide entrance hall into a drawing room where several pieces of French art hung. "This is some of what I have left from the marvelous collection I assembled before the divorce," she said. "Since things have been rather difficult for me, I've had to sell many of my paintings, including the little Renoir I treasured so much."

The furnishings throughout were in heavily ornate Victorian style. Family portraits, busts—in both oil and marble—as well as photograph albums seemed to be everywhere."This wonderful house was so beautiful in the old days," she said, "shortly after my father and I built it. But . . ." She paused with a shrug. "Circumstances change."

"This is my father's library," she explained as they entered a dark green room with leather fringed bookshelves on three sides. The topmost shelves were within reach and the space between them and the ceiling was filled with assorted small busts, fine engravings, ornamental vases, and pieces of ancient armor. Custer was impressed and made a mental note to fix up a special study such as this for himself in the White House.

She led him into the large, high-ceilinged dining room where a large painting of Salmon P. Chase looked sternly out of its ornate gold frame. The former Secretary of the Treasury and later chief justice of the Supreme Court had died at the age of sixty-four in 1873. "He never once believed that Abraham Lincoln was a better president than he would have been." Kate said, quietly. "Nor did I."

Custer was surprised to hear such a frank statement, but he was too interested in her beauty to let it trouble him. A maid brought soup and placed the bowls at the far end of a long dining table lit by tall candles on a white linen tablecloth. Fine china settings, flanked by polished silver, were set conveniently close for intimate conversation. They sat down to begin the meal.

★ ★ ★

As Custer finished his last bite of beef tenderloin still coated in a rich sauce that Kate told him was a special secret from her former chef in Paris, the maid arrived with the silver coffee pitcher. "I've managed to hang on to my china and my treasured silver, as well," she said. "But life has been difficult, raising three girls. My son, William, is with his father, as you may know. Sprague gives me nothing."

She went on into a short discourse about her long, troubled marriage to the former governor of Rhode Island. "He had so much money in the beginning. He was quite handsome, but I must admit, I saw his money as a way of getting my father into the presidency." She leaned forward, her eyes alight with enthusiasm. "From the time I was sixteen, I saw myself as the hostess in the White House. Then Father had a stroke and later died before we could fulfill that dream. My other possibility was my husband, but he was simply too weak—even failed as a U.S. senator."

She reached over and put her hand on his. "I guess the best I can do is be a friend to the man who resides there . . . hopefully a *close* friend."

Custer smiled into her eyes. "That you can be, lovely Kate. I find you immensely interesting—intriguing. And not just for your beauty. Your remarkable presence captivates me."

She held his eyes. "And your remarkable presence captivates me, George Armstrong Custer. Strength and energy seem to surround you like an aura." She got up from her chair and came to him, putting her arms around him and kissing his forehead. "I need a strong man, one who can be an equal to me." She kissed his lips lightly. "—both in wit, knowledge . . . and in bed."

Her lips moved to his and he pulled her down on his lap as their tongues entwined, exploring, growing bolder. At last she pulled back and blew out a deep breath. Getting to her feet, she tugged at his hand. "Come, let me show you my bedroom, Mr. President."

He put his arm around her as they headed down the hall. Turning to him, she murmured, "If I can't reside in the White House, sleeping with the president is the next best thing."

Mark Kellogg brought Custer his package on Panama. The president had assigned him the task of researching the political situation on the isthmus in regard to ongoing plans by the French for a canal there. Kellogg explained that it was conquered by Spain and had remained under Spanish rule for three centuries until 1821, when it voluntarily became part of Columbia. In 1846, the U.S. gained transportation rights across the land bridge in return for American recognition of Colombian sovereignty in Panama. A U.S. company then built a railroad across the isthmus that was completed in 1855. Although Columbia had at times been quite liberal in regard to home rule in Panama, since 1866 the mother country had been much more repressive. That and continuing corruption by Colombian officials had caused numerous unsuccessful revolts by various Panamanian factions in the ensuing years. Columbia now had a treaty with France to permit a French-built canal to be constructed.

"And that's the way it stands today," Kellogg said.

Myles Keogh spoke up from where he'd been listening by a window. "Do the Panamanians *want* a canal?"

"Yes, very much," the press secretary replied, "They know it would bring them a great amount of revenue and business. But we have a problem—the Clayton-Bulwer Treaty with Great Britain, which was negotiated in 1850, gives *both* of our nations control of any such canal."

Custer scowled. "That's an old agreement. I'll have our secretary of state see what he can do about that. Better yet, our good Attorney General, Mr. Bayard, has all of those friends in England—I'll have both of them get to work to have that treaty changed."

"How well do the Panamanians like us?" Custer asked Kellogg after he jotted down a note.

"I think it boils down to money, Mr. President. We did build them a railroad, and our Yankee dollars are most desirable. I think the motivating factor down there is who will give them the means of freedom."

Custer tugged at his mustache. "Hmm. What if they were to overthrow the Colombian mantle, do you think the rebel Panamanian leaders would give us the exclusive right to build the canal and control it for a long period of time?"

Kellogg shrugged. "I don't know, but it sounds logical."

Custer nodded his head, developing the idea further, then came to another pivotal question. "Does Spain have a treaty with Columbia about foreign intervention in Panama?"

The press secretary nodded his head. "Yes, the Treaty of Garcia in 1837."

Custer smiled and turned to Keogh. "Myles, I want you to find a Panamanian, someone here in Washington who has been involved with the rebel leaders down there, someone close to them. Then I want you to go to Panama with him and see what they might need to get a good, solid revolt started."

★ ★ ★

That night as Custer was lying in bed with Libbie, he asked if she was asleep.

"No," she replied drowsily.

"Do you think the public is really behind my New American Empire?"

"Pretty much," Libbie replied forcing herself fully awake. She liked it when Autie questioned himself and asked for her opinion in official matters.

"What do you mean 'pretty much?'"

"Well, there are still many people who bitterly remember the past war. Lots of them lost a great deal—loved ones, limbs, and property. Then there are those who are against any war, as well as those who don't believe we have any right to expand. There are also those who think we should right our internal ills before we go aggrandizing. And there are still a number of them, particularly with the Negroes and the Indians."

"How about you, First Lady, what do you think."

Libbie paused before answering. "Autie, I'm your wife and I respect your opinion. If you are convinced that the New American Empire and its imperialistic approach is best, then I am on your side."

Custer frowned. "How can I fire up those who are lukewarm my policies?"

"You've been writing for a long time. Why don't you write an open letter to the American public, explaining your beliefs. Appeal to the readers of the nation's newspapers and give the letter full dissemination. Mark Kellogg can place it everywhere."

Custer nodded his head. "By jingo, Standby, I think that's a good idea!" He swung his legs out of bed and jumped to his feet. "In fact, I'm going to do it right now!"

★ ★ ★

As the eastern sky played with its pink palette and one of the hounds stirred, Custer finally put down his pen. He had never worked so hard and so long for such a short composition in his whole life. He held the pages up to the kerosene lamp and once more read what he had finally settled on:

Fellow Americans . . . You elected me your president after I stated openly my goal of making the United States—our country— a world leader. We fully deserve that status because we have proven that the common man can build a log cabin and make crops grow around it. His wife can bear children in it and teach them to be God loving citizens—citizens who can run a government of, by, and for the people. This is called freedom. In Russia and other places in the world, serfdom is still in force. The common man can't build his own cabin, nor can he raise his children as he sees fit. Such freedom does not come without a price tag. We must continually earn that right. Sometimes earning it entails service to one's country, sometimes even giving one's life for it. Every world power has fought dozens of wars down through history. It has been that way since one man threw the first stone at another man. I do not want war, but neither will I run from it if we are threatened in our march to greatness and our rightful place among the world's nations. Wherever we may have to trample green grasses with our war boots, we shall do so in *victory*! I, George Armstrong Custer, fervently promise you that.

Custer put down the two pages and nodded his head. It was just the right mixture of historical reality, thirst for freedom, promise, challenge, and a pledge that should appeal to the patriotic vein of many citizens—take it straight to the people. It would not move everyone, but it would stir the hearts of the brave and proud. And they were the ones he wanted to fire up. Yes, Libbie's idea had been a good one. . . .

★ ★ ★

"Armstrong, here is my report on the Spanish Army," Sheridan said, handing over a sealed envelope.

"What does it show?" Custer asked. They were about to have lunch in the small dining room of the White House, the one Libbie had made cozy. It had a table that seated as many as eight, with a large yellow and white checkered tablecloth of fine linen. A framed painting of the commander's house at Fort Lincoln adorned the wall opposite the big picture window encased in cavalry yellow curtains. An enlarged photograph of Custer and Sitting Bull, taken at the Canadian conference, decorated another wall, and small mementos of the Civil War filled other spaces. Even the large braided rug that covered much of the shiny hardwood floor was yellow. Bright light flooded the room. Libbie called it "The Cavalry Mess."

"Pretty much as I guessed," the feisty little Irishman replied. "Our military attaché in Madrid reports they have on active duty seven regiments of horse and ten of foot. These are supported by two regiments of artillery. Their government, not having been threatened by war for some time, has allowed these commands to drop to less than fifty percent of authorized strength. They are poorly trained and poorly paid. Their weaponry, including the artillery, is antiquated, even worse than that of the Confederate Army in 1861. Their infantry is still using muzzle-loaded muskets, but their cavalry has a number of the Spencer carbines. The cavalry has some fine horses, though."

"Where are these regiments?" Custer asked as a waiter brought in cups of steaming oyster stew.

"They're spread thin under two army corps. One full regiment of cavalry and two regiments of foot are in the Philippines, along with several batteries of artillery. A similar number of troops are spread among their other possessions, except for Cuba, which has most of a regiment of artillery, one of horse, and two of infantry. The remainder of the troops are scattered around Spain on garrison duty. The Spanish Army is top heavy with political and nobility generals and colonels who don't know a goddamn frontal attack from a visit to their favorite whorehouse."

"Will these troops fight?" Custer asked.

"Probably, but not well at first."

"Does Spain have militia it can call up on short notice?"

"Not nearly as well as we did in the big war. They think differently."

Custer finished savoring a spoonful of soup as he looked into Sheridan's dark eyes. "If we attacked Cuba with two full divisions, could we win quickly? And would Spain be able to retaliate?"

"I think we would smash them up! That is, providing we get busy with our own training to include unlimited funds for marksmanship and artillery ammunition, get the new commands with full outfitting and good mounts, and properly use what navy we have to support a sea invasion. No, I don't think Spain could effect any kind of a counterattack in Cuba anytime soon."

"What about the Philippines? I would like to consider having a U.S. stronghold in the Pacific, particularly if we get a canal built in Panama."

Sheridan smiled. "We could smash 'em up there too. I think the native Filipino troops would flock to our colors. Again, we'd need strong naval support."

The president's eyes narrowed. "One more question—could we support an armed uprising in Panama against Columbia?"

Sheridan frowned. "I don't think Columbia has much of an army *or* navy."

"Supposing our railroad were threatened and we had to send troops to protect it?"

"Well, I suppose a good, full strength, well trained regiment with strong artillery support would account for itself quite well. I can investigate Columbia's military to make sure. But that's not *our* railroad, Armstrong."

"One more question, General. How do you feel about making Ranald Mackenzie your special chief of staff to plan the invasions we've just discussed. He's right here, you know?"

"Hmm," Sheridan replied. "He's a damned good man. Smart as hell. Yes, good idea."

Custer smiled. "Excellent, Uncle Phil! Now, I want to give you a direct order—be at the War Department tomorrow at three P.M. sharp."

"Anything special going on?"

"Uh huh, I'm going to pin a fourth star on your shoulders."

★ ★ ★

Early in September, Custer made an unannounced visit to General Sheridan's office at the War Department. Unlike Sherman, who had maintained a headquarters as far away as St. Louis part of the time he served as commanding general under Grant, Sheridan wanted to have his staff in the same building as the secretary of war. This didn't pose a problem because McClellan was often up in New Jersey pursuing his private agenda anyway, which, Sheridan was convinced, involved the possibility of commanding a foreign army as a field marshal, but he had no proof. He was just happy that "Little Mac" was out of what hair he had left. He was surprised to see the president.

Custer wanted up-to-date strength figures on each major command in the army, which Sheridan was quickly able to provide. Finally the president said, "I want Spanish to be taught to as many officers and troops as possible, Uncle Phil. I know we can't make them fluent, but they can learn enough to at least communicate. And it wouldn't hurt for you to study it too."

Sheridan blew out the coffee he'd been sipping. "Goddammit, Armstrong, I haven't got time to study that silly language."

Custer smiled. "I am."

The general wiped off the front of his uniform. "Do what you want. I've got other things to do."

"I know," Custer said with a smile as he handed over a sheet of paper. "And this is one of them. I want two temporary promotions to brigadier general made."

"Dammit, Armstrong, you know Congress makes general officer promotions."

"Normally, yes, but these promotions fill an immediate need for the commander-in-chief—which is me. So make them by direction of the president and ask Congress to approve. They will."

"Who?"

"Ranald Mackenzie and Myles Keogh."

Sheridan sputtered again. "Mackenzie I understand, but Keogh's a very junior lieutenant-colonel!"

"It's only temporary for Keogh. I have some special assignments planned for him, and he needs the rank of general to perform them."

"Such as?"

"I'm sending him to Britain and other foreign countries on the *Monroe* shortly. At each stop, he'll have a mission, and he needs some rank on his shoulders to be effective."

Sheridan sighed. "Very well, but Mackenzie will have to rank him by a few days."

"That's just fine." Custer turned to go.

As the president disappeared through the door, Sheridan turned to his aide, Colonel Sandy Forsyth, and said, "You know, I'll bet this whole thing with Mackenzie was planned just so he could get that goddamn Irishman promoted."

FORT MYER, VIRGINIA *October 2, 1881*

"Who's doing that shooting at target number nine?" Captain Godfrey asked.

First-sergeant Dan Kanipe replied, "That's our new recruit from India, or I guess they call the island Ceylon, sir. Name's Elkins."

The heavily mustached commander of C Company turned to the new regimental commander, Colonel Wesley Merritt, and said, "He saw some service with the Royal Hussars in India, sir."

Merritt, the forty-seven-year-old Civil War cavalry officer who had jumped from captain to brigadier general at the same time as Custer on June 29th, 1863, gazed through the field glasses at the shooting range where a dozen troopers were firing carbines. He centered on number nine target. "He's pretty good," he murmured. "All center hits."

As the two officers turned away, Merritt said, "Does the regiment have a sharpshooter contingent?"

"Not as such," Godfrey replied. "But there are some pretty good marksmen scattered around. They compete now and then, but sharp-shooters don't have much of a mission in a show regiment."

Merritt's eyes narrowed. "We've also got a wartime mission, Captain, as well as providing security for the capital. I want you to set up a special squad here in C Company of the best marksmen you know in the regiment. Get at least a half-dozen. We'll put the ones from the other companies on special duty, and let them have all the ammunition and time they need to practice. And include this recruit from India."

★ ★ ★

"Mr. President, Frederick Douglass is here," William Cooke said from the doorway to Custer's office. Custer signed another document and sighed as he put down the pen. The morning's flood of office seekers had been tiresome. He had almost decided to shift the tedious and time consuming chore to Burke's able shoulders. His chief of staff could install three or four cheery interviewers who could listen and record the wishes or complaints. The most urgent or worthwhile Burke could handle, with the extra-important ones coming to the president's own desk.

Frederick Douglass, at sixty-four, was an impressive looking man with long, bushy white-gray hair and a short beard. A fiery orator and leader in the abolitionist movement, as well as the former U. S. Marshal for the District of Columbia, he had recently been appointed Recorder of Deeds for the District. But he was still a powerful primary leader and spokesman for former slaves. His speech was cultured as he took the proffered seat beside Custer's big oak desk, "Mr. President, are you familiar with the Cadet Whiticare court-martial?"

Custer nodded his head. Cadet Johnson Whiticare had just been tried in New York for illegal conduct at West Point and found guilty. Ordinarily this event would have been relatively unimportant, but Cadet Whiticare was a Negro, one of the few attending the U.S. Military Academy at the time, and the national press had jumped on it. "Yes, Mr. Douglass, I'm somewhat familiar with it."

Douglass frowned. "A grave injustice was perpetrated against this fine young man, and I would like to see it rectified, sir."

Custer regarded his visitor calmly. "In what way."

"The findings of the court-martial should be reversed and he should be reinstated as a cadet at West Point."

"I'm not sure I can do that, Mr. Douglass."

"I'm not a lawyer, Mr. President, but I know one thing—you are the commander-in-chief of the Army, and that makes you the final authority."

"That's true, but I would have to look into the matter."

Douglass leaned forward, his eyes narrowed. "This is just another case of prejudice against a Negro. Those upper class white boys from the South have ostracized Whiticare and made his life at West Point difficult for the entire time he has been there. And just when it seemed that he might graduate and be commissioned as one of them, they couldn't stand it and attacked him—needlessly and brutally—leaving him unconscious in his room. To add to this terrible outrage, the boy was charged with staging the whole affair himself to get sympathy. And the all-white court-martial board found him guilty."

It was Custer's turn to frown. "Certainly doesn't sound fair."

Douglass went on, "And this comes right on the heels of another terrible injustice that's related. Are you familiar with the Second-lieutenant Henry Flipper court-martial?"

"Vaguely. Wasn't he the first Negro graduate of West Point? Just got court-martialed over some misuse of commissary money or something like that?"

"Exactly. Also an outrageous act of bias." Douglass leaned forward even more. "Now here's what makes this whole affair sound like a conspiracy—when Flipper was a senior, Whiticare was a plebe, a first year student . . . and they were *roommates!*"

"Hmmm," Custer said, "Interesting. But I don't see how there could be a conspiracy. These are totally unrelated situations."

"*They're both Negro, they both went to West Point, and they roomed together.*"

Custer got to his feet and held out his hand. "I assure you, Mr. Douglass, the matter will get my complete attention and I'll do what I can within the law and the military regulations involved."

★ ★ ★

The next morning, Secretary of War George McClellan, General Phil Sheridan, Ned Burke, and William Cooke gathered around Custer's conference table. Cooke had acquired the Whiticare and Flipper court-martial transcripts and had condensed them for Custer. The president explained the situation, then added, "This whole situation presents a difficult political problem."

Phil Sheridan shrugged. "Not to me. It's none of Douglass's goddamn business. In both cases, the defendants were found guilty by a properly convened court-martial and were treated fairly. And I don't give a fiddler's damn about the politics!"

Custer looked at McClellan. "What about you, George?"

"I agree pretty much with Phil, but my mind's open."

It was Burke's turn. "This can be a thorny problem, Mr. President. Douglass can make quite a mess out of this, and you've committed yourself to Negro equality in your inaugural address. I say, 'what's another cadet?' Reinstate him and get powerful Negro support, both in Congress and otherwise."

"But the findings are from a legally constituted court," Sheridan growled.

"And how many members of Congress are Negroes?" McClellan asked. "I think it would be prejudicial to the military justice system to knuckle under to Douglass. If this cadet weren't a Negro, he wouldn't give a solitary damn."

Custer sipped his coffee, finally saying, "I have to look at this from all sides. I'm going to read the testimony again and then make a decision. He glanced from Sheridan to McClellan. I appreciate your thoughts, gentlemen. Now let's talk about getting our military buildup through Congress. I want those new regiments in uniform and construction of those new ships commenced well before the first snow."

★ ★ ★

On the third Friday in October, Annie Yates and Brigadier General Myles Keogh slipped away to a charming little hotel near Annapolis and were married by an army chaplain Keogh had known for some time. Though only in her mid-thirties, Annie's hair was fully white. But rather than aging her, it merely made her more attractive, more striking. She was still slender and athletic, and quite graceful. Keogh, on the other hand, didn't have a gray hair on his handsome dark head. He had come in mufti, not wishing to be recognized by the public. This was their stolen weekend, three days when no president or first lady could place demands on them. At Annie's insistence, they had told no one where they were going—just that they were eloping and would be back on the job Monday morning. Annie did add in her note to Libbie that it would be nice if a valet could move Myles' possessions into her large bedroom during their absence.

Late that afternoon, following their first vigorous lovemaking as husband and wife, they sat holding hands and sipping champagne from tall, thin-stemmed glasses in the rather pleasant breeze that wafted through their balcony. "Ah, Mrs. Keogh," the groom said, "I never thought I'd see the day when I'd use that term."

Annie chuckled. "You were just a hard catch, and none of those pretty girls could get close enough to you." She laughed. "Oh, I *know* they got close to you, but they didn't have staying power."

He leaned down and kissed her hand. "I love you so much, lass. I wish we could hide here forever."

Annie sighed. "I know, but we have to run the country. You know how lost the Custers would be without us."

Keogh stared out at the choppy water of Chesapeake Bay. "Aye, and I must be off to Panama on Wednesday. I hope I can get the mission done quickly and get back in your arms."

"I hope so too. What's the name of the man who's going with you?"

"Martinez, Willie Martinez. That's like Smith in America. I don't know if it's his real name, but he's a friend of the major rebel leader known as Raul."

Annie suddenly got up, leaned over, kissed Keogh soundly on the mouth, and said, "You be damned careful down there, Myles Keogh! I didn't marry you for your devil-may-care smile, you know. I have big plans for your taking me to that castle of yours in Ireland, and I'm not going to let some wild-eyed revolutionaries in dirty serapes get in my way."

"The castle is *ours* now, lass. I've already made out my new will."

Annie dropped to her knees and put her head in his lap. "I wish we could talk them into letting me go with you. I'm fluent in Spanish, you know."

Keogh nodded his head. "I wish you could go too, but Libbie needs you. Besides, it could be dangerous."

Annie jerked her head up. "Ha! There isn't a one of them who's a match for me."

Keogh laughed. "I wonder if *I'm* a match for you?"

Annie pulled him to his feet. "Take me back to bed, you handsome devil, and we'll find out."

As it turned out, Libbie was right about James Gordon Bennett Jr.. When Custer visited New York in mid-November to speak at a meeting of Clara Barton's American Association of the Red Cross, he had lunch with Bennett at Delmonico's. The newspaperman told him he had a request.

In the late seventies, the publisher had bankrolled an expedition to reach the North Pole by sea. Bennett had purchased a sturdy ship, *Pandora*, had it refitted and christened *Jeanette*, and had secured the leave of absence of a Lieutenant George W. De Long from the U.S. Navy to command her. Manned by an exceptional crew of both Navy seamen and civilians, the *Jeanette* attempted to reach the Pole by way of the Bering Sea, but the ship had been caught fast in ice for an extended period and had sunk on the previous June 12. Its crew, split into three parties, had tried to reach safety by small boat and overland. At the same time the *Jeanette* went down, a rescue ship, the U.S.S. *Rodgers* was dispatched to go to her aid.

"I just received word," Bennett told Custer, "the *Rodgers* has burned in her winter quarters up on the Gulf of St. Lawrence."

"I'm sorry to hear that," Custer replied. He knew about the expedition.

"So this is what I want you to do, Armstrong—as soon as spring sets in up there, I want you to send your new cruiser, the *Monroe*, on a rescue mission."

Custer frowned. He hated not to at least try to rescue those brave men. "Trouble is, Jim, I have other plans for the *Monroe*. Besides, she'll be in Atlantic waters, not over on the Pacific side."

Bennett scowled. "Get her going now, and she'll be there by the time the ice breaks up."

It was Custer's turn to frown. "But I told you, I have other plans for her."

Bennett's tone was firm. "Change your plans."

Custer rubbed his mustache, holding himself in check. *This newspaper man was giving the president of the United States a direct order.* "Jim," he replied evenly, "I think we need to get something established. *I* am the president of the United States, and you don't ever order me to do anything."

Bennett drew in a deep breath and blew it out. "I've seen this coming, Armstrong. You've been reading too many newspaper accounts of yourself. You seem to have forgotten who put you where you are. You'd be nothing but another brigadier general in the Army if I hadn't stepped in with my power and made you president."

Custer's blue eyes narrowed. "I appreciate that, Mr. Bennett, but that's where it ends. I will do what *I* think is best for this country, not what *you* want me to do." He arose from the table without bothering to say goodbye, and strode from the dining room. He had an appointment with an auburn-haired beauty from the Isle of Jersey, and planned on enjoying the rest of the afternoon with her.

★ ★ ★

A week after his return to Washington, Custer visited Ford's Theatre with Lawrence Barrett. Except for the banging of a hammer and the efforts of three painters on last minute touches, the theater was finally ready for its grand reopening as Lincoln's Theater. They were in the special box where Lincoln had been shot, and Custer was thoughtfully looking down at the stage. "What a healing event this will be," he said. "Our great country will celebrate the life of one of our greatest presidents in the structure where he was fatally attacked. The great artists of our time will gather here and commemorate his life, including many Southerners. It will officially announce the importance of the arts in the New American Empire, Lawrence."

Barrett touched his sleeve affectionately. "It will be a great tribute to you, Armstrong. And I think inviting Edwin Booth to take part in the opening program is a brave thing for you to do."

Custer shrugged. "He had nothing to do with his brother's hideous crime."

Barrett had long been associated with the elder Booth, had in fact managed his theater in New York. He planned on bringing the famous actor into the president's plans for an active arts program. "I know," he replied, "but the Republican papers will make it look like you're celebrating Lincoln's assassination."

"I'm celebrating his *greatness*. The Democratic papers will stress that. Now, Lawrence, tell me, is the play ready?" He was referring to the production they had selected, Shakespeare's *Julius Caesar*, in which Barrett was to reprise his signature role as Cassius.

"*Julius* has never been better prepared."

★ ★ ★

"Elkins!" Corporal Stungewitz barked.

"Yes," Red Elk replied, looking up from where he was cleaning his pistol.

"You been detailed to be part of the president's guard at the old Ford's Theater on Friday. Get your uniform fixed so's you'll be a credit to C Company."

"Yes, Corporal."

Red Elk contained the surge of enthusiasm that engulfed him. At Carlisle, he had read about Lincoln's assassination, and since entering the army at Ft. Myer, he had often thought about how it would be if he could go back in time to 1865, and Long Hair could have been president then. Then he had read in the newspaper that there was to be a big event at the remodeled theater, and that President Custer would be there to watch a play. *But he never dreamed he'd be assigned to guard duty there.*

He'd seen two plays put on by the students at Carlisle, and was intrigued by them. Back in Sioux country, dances and storytelling were mostly the entertainment—always around evening campfires, except during weddings and big victory celebrations. Sometimes the Bravehearts, his warrior lodge, did something to entertain, but nothing like the plays he'd seen at the Indian school. He'd be glad to see the dances again someday— someday when he was back with his people hunting the great buffalo and roaming free as a war chief.

He reached for his .45 revolver and brushed a light piece of lint from its shiny barrel. *Now he'd have his chance.*

★ ★ ★

Brigadier-general Myles Keogh had stayed as inconspicuous as possible during his stay in Panama. Now, finally, after several broken appointments, he was going to meet the man known to him only as Raul. Keogh had arrived by ship at the port city of Colon and had proceeded by train to the capital, Panama City, a few days earlier. He wore dark glasses and drab clothes and posed as an Irish gun salesman working out of New York. Willie Martinez, a short chunky man in his mid-forties, had arranged for him to stay at a quiet middle-class hotel named *La Fuente* because it had a small fountain in its courtyard entry. The meeting place was a nondescript little restaurant called the *Casa del Sol*, where Martinez led Keogh to a back table. It was hot and sticky. Keogh wiped his brow with a handkerchief and ordered a local beer, which he sipped as time passed.

Martinez went over his information again in his nearly perfect English, "Raul represents the true power of *La Rebelión*, which is the movement for Panamanian independence. The major leaders are behind him with some ten thousand dedicated fighters. He was a brilliant colonel in the Colombian Army, and had he not been Panamanian, he would have been a general. We have other officers with fighting experience. But we need guns, ammunition, and the other tools of war. If we get them, we will defeat the hated Colombians and they will cave in."

"Will Raul play a major part in a Panamanian government?" Keogh asked.

Martinez's zeal as a true patriot shone in his eyes. "He will be our *presidente.*"

After thirty-five minutes, a tall, spare man in loose cotton field worker's attire under a floppy, wide-brimmed hat arrived at the table. Behind him, another man dressed the same way, stood by the doorway. "I am Raul," the tall man said, in accented English. He had high cheekbones and a heavy black mustache that covered much of his mouth.

Keogh stood and extended his hand, which Raul shook. "I am General Keogh."

[234]

After another round of beer arrived at the table, Keogh said, "Martinez tells me you are the man I can trust—the man who has the power to decide."

Raul's intelligent dark eyes were guarded. "I am the man who is trusted by the leaders."

Keogh leaned forward, speaking softly, "Did Martinez tell you who I work for—directly?"

"*Sí.*"

"We wish to know specifics, and I'm sorry, but I don't have time to follow your custom of slowly talking around our subject. I must be direct, sir. We want you to give us the numbers of soldiers you can produce, how well-trained they will be, what you will need in the way of weapons and other equipment to win your independence. And your best estimate of success."

Raul shrugged. "With equipment, we will win. The Colombian Army is in bad condition now. Many generals and few good soldiers. Our soldiers are filled with fire!"

Keogh nodded and sipped his beer.

Raul watched his eyes as Martinez made notes. Keogh went on, "We can help in other ways, diplomatically and with a show of force, if need be. We ask in turn that a treaty be made with your new provisional government after Columbia accedes to your independence that will give our country the right to build a canal across the isthmus and the sole right to both control and defend it for a century or more. For this, my country will pay your government several millions of dollars per year, a figure to be determined later. That's very concise, *senōr*, but it is the essence of what my president offers."

A smile touched Raul's lips, then his eyes narrowed. "Would the United States give us troops to fight for our independence, General?"

Keogh shook his head. "Not at this point, and probably not at all. But once your new government is in place, and the treaty with us is ratified—when we begin building the canal—*then* it would be our responsibility to provide armed force to protect you against aggression by outsiders."

Raul asked more questions, which Keogh answered as well as possible. At last, Raul got to his feet and extended his hand. "I will speak to my compatriots, General, and meet you here or at another location in two days. But I can tell you I think there will be no problem with these general terms. *Adios.*"

Beware the Ides of March . . .

—Julius Caesar

While Myles Keogh was helping to foment revolution in Panama, the last minute touches on Ford's Theatre were completed. Following a reception at the White House for government and civic leaders, the invited guests were to proceed to the theater for its inauguration. The Cabinet and all major Democrats in the Congress, along with their ladies, were at the head of the invitation list. A number of important Republicans were also invited, as well as the senior officers of the Seventh Cavalry. Among the leaders of society were Kate Sprague and her escort, the ubiquitous Sam Ward.

Across the Potomac at Fort Myer, Sergeant-major Ed Bobo had personally taken command of the guard detail that was drawn from his old C Company. It was composed of fourteen selected troopers who would guard both the outside of the structure and the inside, particularly the area in which the presidential box was located. He would position a couple of his best marksmen there. Something was troubling him but he didn't know why. A foreboding hung over him that something bad was going to happen and he couldn't shake it off. Hadn't a similar event brought on the death of Lincoln? And General Custer—he couldn't get out of the habit of referring to him as the general—was going to sit in the very same booth.

Well, as they said in the Navy, he wasn't going to let it happen on *his* watch.

The guard detail was lined up in two ranks in front of the stone regimental headquarters building at three P.M. It was a dreary, cloudy day. The new regimental commander, Colonel Merritt, had wanted to inspect the guard himself, but had decided to merely observe. With First-sergeant Kanipe following him, Bobo carefully went over the first man, a Private John Corcoran. The trooper was an Englishman, twenty-nine, who had been a sergeant until he was court-martialed for being drunk and creating a disturbance after taps five months earlier. But he was one of the best marksmen in the regiment, and Bobo had lifted more than one glass with Corcoran over the years. As he expected, the soldier's uniform was spotless, his brass accouterments highly polished, and his boots shined. The Springfield carbine was equally clean, without even a trace of lint, as was his long-barreled Colt .45 revolver. He looked Corcoran in the eye and said, "I expect you to be on your toes tonight, John."

"Yes, Sergeant-major!"

Bobo moved on, continuing with the inspection into the second rank. The last man was Private Elkins, who stood ramrod straight, staring blankly ahead. Bobo looked him over, found everything in order, snatched the carbine from his hands, found it spotless, and said, "Private, do you know how important this mission is?"

Softly, Red Elk replied, "Yes, Sergeant-major, I certainly do."

★ ★ ★

The weather was brisk and still cloudy as the presidential party arrived at the theater shortly after eight P.M. The house was already filled with reception guests from the White House, plus guests of the theater event. The press was also well represented. With Libbie and Custer were Tom and Monasetah, Secretary and Mrs. McClellan, and General and Mrs. Sheridan. The presidential box, slightly enlarged since 1865, was trimmed in black velvet. As they entered, the two cavalrymen standing at stiff attention outside the box rendered a brisk rifle salute. Custer touched his forelock as did the other officers.

Shortly after everyone in the box was seated, the newfangled electric house lights dimmed and Lawrence Barrett, in costume and makeup, walked out in front of the curtain to a huge round of applause from the well-dressed audience. Holding up his hands, he announced loudly, "Ladies and gentlemen . . . welcome to the new Lincoln Theatre!" When another round of applause subsided, he went on with a five-minute explanation of how the remodeling and naming of the theater had been Custer's special project, and that it would forever be a symbol to the great man for whom it was named. Then, following a signal from him to the conductor, the house orchestra struck up "Hail to the Chief." Barrett pointed to the presidential box as everyone in the theater rose and turned. Custer and Libbie stood and waved, along with everyone else in the box, as the musicians segued into "GarryOwen."

Moments later, Barrett introduced the play, *Julius Caesar*, and the curtain came up on Act I.

At that moment, Sergeant-major Bobo walked up to the two sentries outside the presidential box. He was in uniform, wearing his revolver. He spoke to both Corcoran and Elkins and told them to stay particularly alert. "Even though the hallway to this box is well-guarded, I don't want to take any chances on some wild-eyed asshole trying something crazy."

Red Elk nodded, saying nothing. This was going to be extremely difficult. He hadn't counted on Bobo being present. He would have to wait until the sergeant-major departed to do something else. Then he would have to move fast—kill Corcoran with a knife, slip into the box, identify Long Hair, and shoot him in the back of the head with his revolver. He would then jump outside and shout, "*Halt!*" at an imaginary attacker, then fire his revolver several times. In the confusion that would follow, he would explain how the killer, wearing a captain's uniform, had strolled up, ordered him to go down the hall to check a disturbance, and then had attacked Corcoran. Before anyone got suspicious, he would evaporate like only a descendent of the White Buffalo Woman could.

★ ★ ★

Edwin Booth had played nearly every part in *Julius Caesar*, but had never been better than on this evening in the role of the emperor. In Act II, Scene II, he reached the passage that Custer loved so much. As the president leaned forward in anticipation, Caesar said:

> Cowards die many times before their deaths; the valiant never
> taste of death but once. Of all the wonders that I yet have heard,
> it seems to me most strange that men should fear; seeing that
> death, a necessary end, will come when it will come.

Custer's eyes were moist as he turned to Sheridan and said, "No greater words were ever written for a soldier."

★ ★ ★

Outside the box, Red Elk fingered his hidden knife. Bobo was nowhere in sight, and Corcoran was inattentive, trying to catch some of the dialogue from the stage below. It was time. *Finally! It was time.* He slowly unfastened the holster flap on his hip and . . .

Charlie Myers, the Moose, suddenly filled the doorway to the box with his huge form and nodded his head in greeting. *The bodyguard had apparently been hiding inside the box since before he and Corcoran had arrived.* He held a big Navy revolver in his hand. "You boys okay?" he asked softly.

At that moment, Bobo rounded the bend in the corridor.

Red Elk knew he would have to wait for yet another day.

December passed quickly. A tall decorated evergreen held court in the front yard of the White House, numerous groups of carolers serenaded its residents, and Libbie had a party for a large number of orphans on the 22nd. A reception was held on Christmas Day for the party faithful and other members of Washington society. On New Years Day, another reception was held, a throwback to the military commanding officer's custom of receiving his subordinates on that occasion. It was decidedly military. Washington-based officers from all of the branches and their wives or guests were invited. Custer wore a general's dress uniform with gold epaulets that contained seven tiny stars—his interpretation of the rank of a European Marshal. All of the other officers and former officers on his staff or in the Cabinet wore their uniforms, including Wade Hampton and Tom Rosser in their Confederate cavalry dress. General Phil Sheridan, his officers, and their ladies arrived on time. General McClellan made his grand entrance a bit late. Admiral Porter and Commander Nelson Jones from the *Monroe* were among the naval officers present. Former president Grant and his wife, Julia, came down from New York, adding another four-star personage to the colorful assemblage. General Sherman, back in Ohio, had declined.

There was no doubt about the patriotic flavor. America's president-general was sponsoring a dress-up such as the White House had never seen. Flags, from the national colors to regimentals, hung everywhere,. The Marine Band played continuously and Seventh Cavalry soldiers in yellow scarves and under arms stood at the front entrance and at various points inside the mansion. No cost was spared on the superbly prepared food, and several silver regimental bowls served what Lieutenant-colonel Tom Custer called the best "horse-breaking cavalry punch ever concocted."

Libbie, attended by a glowing Annie Keogh, wore a new gray gown based somewhat on a Confederate general's uniform. It was trimmed in seven tight fleurs-de-lis of gold on the sleeves and to match, a tiny yellow rose was pinned into her upswept brown hair. Standing with Custer at the head of the short receiving line, she greeted the guests enthusiastically. Next to her, Tom stood in line with Monasetah. The marriage that had appeared to be an expedient, if not farcical, at the time, now had its merits. The Cheyenne woman possessed natural grace and charm, she had worked hard perfecting her English, and was again pregnant. She seemed to be very good for Tom, and perhaps most important, she was politically profitable: the president had a sister-in-law who was a full-blooded Indian. As the guests flowed through the line, Libbie forgot about the troubling note that had arrived that morning. Even though she knew better than to give any credence to an unsigned message, she had given it more than a second thought. It had read: "Does the president's lady know that her husband has taken a liking to redheads? —A friend who dislikes deceit."

★ ★ ★

As the reception wound down, Custer slipped into the study and met Burke, Keogh and Tom Rosser. Standing by the fireplace with his hands behind his back, he looked at Burke and nodded his head. His chief of staff said, "The situation in Cuba is somewhat like that in Panama. The Cubans are sick of Spanish rule, and most of them would welcome freedom or the opportunity to become a territory of the U.S." He looked at Rosser. "If we could send one of our old, decrepit warships to Havana harbor, and she would somehow get blown up, we could charge the Spaniards with the dastardly deed and invade the country."

Rosser looked from Burke to Custer. "Are you talking about purposely killing American sailors?"

"It seems to me you had no compunction about killing American soldiers a few years ago, General," Burke replied somewhat sharply.

Custer broke in immediately. "That was uncalled for, Ned."

Burke smiled at Rosser. "No harm meant, sir. I believe some kind of an explosion could be planned for a remote part of the ship that would sink her, yet enable all hands to escape unhurt, or with minor injuries."

Rosser let the critical comment slide by. "I would have to know the details."

Custer broke in, "No, Tom, neither you nor I should know any more about this than we do now. You take care of sending a ship to Havana, one of those many that are practically worthless, and parties unknown to us will take care of the rest. Will you do that?"

The secretary thought for a moment, then nodded his head. "Yes. When?"

Burke replied. "In about three months. Certain groundwork, both with the Cubans and in the world press, needs to be laid."

"What does Bennett think about this?" Keogh asked. He knew about Custer's clash with the newspaperman.

Burke shrugged. "He'll like it because it'll sell a lot of newspapers."

★ ★ ★

Libbie showed the note about redheads to Annie when the reception was over. She said, "I started to throw it away and ignore it, but I just *can't*."

Annie read it and frowned. Handing it back, she said, "Autie has a lot of enemies. Anyone could have written that darned thing."

"What do you think I should do?"

Annie shrugged. "What do you *want* to do?"

"I'd feel awful stupid if I confronted him with it and there was nothing to it."

"And what if there were something to it—would he confess?"

Libbie sat down in a rocker and put her head in her hands. "Several years ago, he told me about seeing some other women in New York, but the way he told me, I think it was off-handed and casual. Still, women have always been attracted to him, and now he *is* the president . . ."

Annie waited.

"And then there was all of that Monasetah stuff, but he told me it was a pack of lies. I had to believe him. What else could I do? I had no proof it was otherwise. A good marriage is based on faith."

"And if you find out this is true?"

Libbie looked glum. "I guess I'll just have to work it out then." She brightened, found a smile. "Oh, Annie, I'm so glad I shared this with you. I think I'll just throw the whole thing in the trash can and think about some good things. Let's get busy on the suffrage program again!"

It was a tribute to Ned Burke's power of persuasion, but also to the fact that both parties in the disagreement wanted to forgive and forget. In the North Pole expedition, the portion of the *Jeanette*'s crew that went with the chief engineer had miraculously survived a most arduous journey to safety, but her commander and the rest of the ship's company had apparently perished. Therefore, Bennett had no cause to continue a dispute with the president, and Custer had never been one to bear grudges. Besides, the president needed the power of the *Herald*. Since the Potomac was free of ice, the commodore sailed his yacht down to Washington in early January and invited Custer aboard for lunch.

The friendliness they had previously known came back immediately. The publisher again had his president, and the president again had his publisher.

Following the main course of pheasant breast flavored by broiled oysters, Custer asked Burke to summarize Spain's situation. The major pulled out some notes and began his analysis, "Cuba has been described as 'the richest colony in the world.' Over thirty years ago a Spanish foreign minister stated that he would sooner see the island sunk in the ocean as transferred to any other power. As you know, the Ten Years War for Cuba's independence ended with the peace of Zanjón in 1878. But no one has yet been able to work out a satisfactory settlement that would preserve Spain's presence in the Greater Antilles—the main islands of Cuba and Puerto Rico—and in the Philippines. There are two major parties in Cuba, the Autonomists, controlled by rich Creoles wanting separatism, and the Unionists, who are bureaucrats, tradesmen, shopkeepers and artisans, who wish to keep their control of local life and remain status quo."

"What's the trade situation?" Bennett asked.

"Cuba's economy is stagnant. Their major, natural market is the U.S., where they sell tobacco and sugar. But our tariff situation is crippling to them, and they want free trade."

Custer asked, "Do you think they would accept U.S. territorial status for perhaps one hundred years in exchange for freedom from the Spanish yoke, which would relieve them of all tariffs with us? We could give them various forms of aid and essentially let them rule themselves. Or they could become a state. I prefer the latter."

"I think it would be tempting."

"But this isn't like Panama, where you can stir up a successful little revolt," Bennett interjected. "We're dealing with established ruling elements. Those rich Creoles and a lot of the Unionists have been there a long time."

The president shrugged. "Let's find out what their price is. I *want* the Antilles to be a part of the United States. And if necessary, we'll fight a war with Spain and *stay*. But we must convince Congress and the American people that there is a just reason."

Bennett agreed. "I'll see what my connections can unearth."

★ ★ ★

A few days later, Secretary Tom Custer came back from a whirlwind visit to several reservations in the West. "It's a problem, big brother," he told Custer. "It's hard to police all of those agents and keep them honest."

"Try a few of them and put them in prison," the president replied.

"Easier said than done. You gotta prove they stole or cheated."

Custer was relaxing in an easy chair after dinner. He finished chewing on a cookie and said, "I've been thinking about this darned reservation situation we've got ourselves into, Tom. I don't think it'll work."

"What do you mean?"

"I think we might be creating wards of the state, dependents who will be just like children a hundred years from now. I'd rather see all of those Indians become independent—rule their own destiny as citizens."

"What's the option, Autie? We aren't fighting them this way."

"I don't know. But it comes under your department. I want you to think about it."

★ ★ ★

In late January, Custer reviewed the findings of the Johnson Whiticare court-martial. The Negro cadet had been found guilty and sentenced to dismissal from West Point, but the findings had been reversed by the army's judge advocate general as well as by the commanding general of the Army. Nevertheless, Whiticare had been dismissed from the military academy for failing an oral examination in 1880. Throughout the long trial, the press coverage was extensive and the Army hadn't come off too well. Frederick Douglass insistently urged a reversal of the dismissal, and Burke had agreed due to the political aspects. Custer wrote the following note to McClellan, with a copy to Sheridan:

> In regard to the court-martial of Cadet Johnson Whiticare: Based upon careful consideration of all of the facts and extensive proceedings in this case, plus the political and racial implications involved, I, as commander of all U.S. military forces, am reversing his dismissal. Said cadet is adjudged fully qualified to continue as a cadet and will be reinstated in the next class at the United States Military Academy at West Point, New York.

In a second attached note to the addressees, Custer added, "Unofficially, my friends, this is a political decision. Bear with me on this, and make sure Cadet Whiticare suffers absolutely no recriminations by faculty, staff or cadets at the academy. Thanks. Armstrong."

In a return note, Sheridan growled, "Dear President Custer: Does this mean Whiticare gets handed a free trip the rest of the way to graduation? And as long as Negroes are getting special consideration, what about Lt. Flipper?"

Flipper had been found guilty of "conduct unbecoming an officer and a gentleman," but not-guilty of absconding with commissary funds. Custer decided the Negro lieutenant would be the flip side of the coin; his sentence would appease the regulation-bound Sheridan. He wrote back, "Uncle Phil: Just pass the word that the president will be watching and he will suffer no improprieties in Whiticare's progress toward graduation. Regarding Flipper, he was a commissioned officer in the field. The

[245]

findings of that court-martial stand. Lieutenant-colonel Marcus Reno was recently court-martialed on flimsy charges, and I wouldn't intervene in his case, so I refuse to do so for Flipper."

On the 10th of February, Raul's Panamanian rebels struck three of the larger Colombian army garrisons. The modern U.S. equipment that had arrived surreptitiously over the previous two months added to the fervor of the revolutionary force as its bugles blared *"Deguello"*—no Quarter. All three of the Colombian posts fell in the same day, and Raul sent an ultimatum to the senior general in Panama City.

> *Your troops have no will to fight, while the Panamanian Freedom Army is imbued with a holy mission and will die to the man, if need be. We are now well equipped and prepared to annihilate your forces. We desire complete freedom from Columbia and wish to become a totally independent state. Please pass this on to your superiors. Every day that is wasted will cost Colombian blood.*
>
> *—General Raul, Commanding*

The next day, the U.S.S *Monroe* steamed into Colon harbor, its largest American flag flying boldly. Anchoring offshore in a conspicuous position, the cruiser firmly announced its presence. The timing couldn't have been better. Aboard was Brigadier-general Myles Keogh, this time officially representing the president of the United States. Commander Jones kept the ship sitting there, making no effort to send anyone ashore. Twenty-four hours after arrival, he moved her about a thousand yards, then dropped anchor again. Late the next afternoon, a gig rowed out from the city docks. Aboard was a naval officer in the full dress regalia of a Colombian officer.

A coxswain hailed the *Monroe* in English, "*Permission requested for Captain Leon to come aboard!*"

Commander Jones, curious that an officer of that rank would condescend to approach them in this manner, nodded to a chief with a megaphone. The message was relayed, "*Permission granted!*"

As a rope ladder was thrown over the side, and with some assistance from the sailors, the fat, sweating captain climbed to the deck of the *Monroe*. Following the formal greetings and introductions, Captain Leon asked, "What is your purpose here, Captain?"

"I am here under orders form the Secretary of the United States Navy."

"And directly from the President of the United States," Keogh added, making his appearance in uniform. He introduced himself as a special aide to Custer.

The Colombian captain glanced from Keogh to Jones. "Again, what is your purpose here? Why are you anchored in Colombian waters?"

Commander Jones' tone was cool. "I thought these were Panamanian waters, sir."

Leon looked at Keogh. Pulling out a handkerchief to mop his sweaty brow, he said, "Panama is part of Columbia. Why are you here?"

"I am not at liberty to say, Captain."

"Then I must politely ask you to haul anchor and leave, sir."

"That isn't very hospitable, is it Captain?" Keogh asked.

Captain Leon glanced around at the spotless deck. Before he could reply, Jones said, "Very well, I've received your message, sir. Now, if you will be kind enough to depart, we'll be under way."

Leon nodded and headed back to the rope ladder, where he saluted, nodded his head, and was helped onto the ladder.

As he watched the gig pull away moments later, Commander Jones gave the order to head out to sea. He kept the *Monroe* there for a day, then returned and anchored about a mile from the city docks. The cruiser remained in that position for two days, then departed. The message had been sent, the Colombian Navy had been defied, and the intent had to be clear to even the dullest of Colombian leaders: the president of the United States intended to support the Panamanian rebels.

★ ★ ★

Two weeks later Custer's attention to international intrigue was diverted when Attorney General Thomas Bayard came to him with a ticklish problem. The former senator laid a file on the president's desk. "It's that star mail route situation, Mr. President. We've got the goods on several of the conspirators and are about to bring them to trial."

He was referring to the fraud being perpetrated on the U.S. postal system. Although most mail was transported by train and steamship, in many isolated parts of the South and mostly the West, the Post Office Department had contracted with horse, wagon, and stagecoach agencies to deliver the mail to the addressees. Congress most generously appropriated money for this service, and the term "star route" arose from asterisks in these contracts that stood for "certainty, celerity, and security." But supervision was lax. Ridiculously low bids by contractors got them the routes, then the recipients would petition Congress to "improve" the service, enabling them to be paid up to three times the original bid. By the time Custer was elected there were over 9,000 star routes costing the government $6 million per year. The system was an open invitation to fraud.

"As you know, Mr. President," Bayard went on, "an investigation has been ongoing. A number of prominent members of Congress from both parties have been implicated, and it's believed that some half-million dollars a year is being stolen."

Custer hadn't paid too much attention to the scandal because it preceded his term and he knew it was slowly being resolved. "Yes, I'm well aware of that," he replied.

"But there's more. It reaches into the Cabinet."

Custer's eyebrows shot up. "How?"

"A senior clerk in the postal department section that handles star routes has come forward with statements that incriminate Postmaster Kelly."

Custer frowned; he was quite sure that Kelly might be getting some roundabout kickbacks up in New York, but he figured those were going into the Tammany coffers. But he didn't think Honest John was stupid enough to stick his fingers into an ongoing scandal for personal gain. "I don't believe it," he said.

Bayard pointed to the file. "It's all in there."

The president shook his head as anger flooded over him. Now he knew how Grant must have felt during the scandals that scarred his administration. "The *bastard!*" he snapped, as he glanced through the statements in the file.

"What do you want to do?" the attorney general asked.

Custer threw the folder down. "I ought to shoot the damned crook myself! What do you recommend?"

Bayard shrugged. "You can charge him and have him tried, but that would prove extremely embarrassing to the administration; or let him resign and keep this information inside our ranks."

"Has this clerk gone to the papers?"

"Not yet."

"Can he be trusted to keep his mouth shut?"

"He could be transferred to another agency and promoted."

Custer nodded his head. "Let me think about it."

★ ★ ★

An hour later, Custer had Honest John Kelly on the carpet. He handed him the folder and said, "Evidence in this file implicates you in grievous misconduct and criminal fraud in regard to the star route case, Kelly. What do you have to say for yourself?"

The postmaster general read quickly through the statements, then looked up. "Do you believe this nonsense?"

Custer looked him coldly in the eye. "Is there some reason why I shouldn't?"

Kelly hadn't risen to the top of Tammany for nothing. Without batting an eye, he said, "The man is a liar. He got into some trouble and I had him disciplined. He's got it in for me."

"Why isn't that on the record?"

"I thought it better to keep it quiet and not have any bad publicity that might reach the press and throw a shadow on the department."

Custer lunged out of his chair, hurried around the desk, and grabbed the big man by the lapels. "*You sonofabitch!* You implicate yourself in fraud, steal money, and now you tell me you don't want to throw a shadow on your department! You've thrown a *huge* shadow on me! And now you lie to me." He released the lapels and glared into the New Yorker's eyes. "I have too much going on right now to throw you in prison where you belong, so this is what you are going to do—you are going to come up with a bad health story and resign. Then you are going somewhere outside of this country and stay for a couple of years. If you even *think* about coming back, I promise you, you'll be tried and spend a long time in prison. *Do you understand?*"

Kelly blanched, his hand shaking as his gaze went from Custer's eyes to the folder. He drew in a deep breath and blew it out. In a weak voice, he finally replied, "Yes, sir, I do. When do you want my resignation?"

"Immediately."

"I'll see to it."

Custer turned away. "Get out of my sight."

★ ★ ★

Custer now needed to shore up the hole in his Cabinet. And what better way to do so than to offer the portfolio to the honorable man whom he barely defeated for the presidential nomination. Certainly he'd get criticism for selecting yet another general for a major post in his administration, but he didn't care, and maybe the honest officer could straighten out the corrupt postal department. He sent a telegram that read, "Major-general Winfield Scott Hancock, Fort Hamilton, New York. Sir: The country needs your skills in a vital position. Postmaster-General Kelly has just told me that he must retire due to ill health. Will you please accept appointment to that portfolio? —George Armstrong Custer, President of the United States. PS Sir: I very much need your integrity at this point.— Armstrong."

★ ★ ★

Now that he had tasted blood, Custer decided to go after Civil Service reform. He sent word to Senator George Pendleton, a senior Democratic leader who had spearheaded a reform bill for two years. Known as "Gentleman George" to his colleagues, the senator from Ohio had been George McClellan's running mate against Abraham Lincoln in the 1864 presidential race.

When Pendleton arrived, Custer greeted him warmly and introduced him to Tom. "I guess it's time we Ohioans got together, Senator."

"Good idea, Mr. President. We never see you over in the chambers."

They passed the time of day for a couple of minutes before Custer launched directly into his mission. "I've been remiss in not supporting your Civil Service reform activity, Senator. You know, President Lincoln was right when he said, "The spoils system will ruin government." He laughed. "And I guess everyone is guilty." Turning to his brother, he said, "Tom, tell the Senator what's happened in the Department of the Interior."

Tom shrugged. "Well, as you know, sir, the department had a pretty bad reputation when we came to town. But I can assure you as we speak today that I have removed every crooked Republican in Interior and have replaced them with crooked Democrats."

They all laughed as Custer asked Pendleton to explain the rudiments of his bill. The senator launched into the basics: competitive examinations for lower level jobs, probationary periods for appointees, and promotion based on merit and competition. "For starters," he added as he finished.

"I'll support you all the way," Custer said.

"It'll take a little more time," Pendleton replied. "Spoils have been part of the system for a long while."

Custer got to his feet to end the meeting. "Well, just spread the word around that as soon as I'm done dealing with Spain, I'll be wielding a big sword to get your bill passed."

Now Custer had to do something about another problem. Some seventy-five percent of the four million freed Negroes of the South had remained there after the war, but lack of assets forever doomed them to work as tenants and sharecroppers. Only a fourth owned the land they tilled. Those who wanted to work in the cotton mills were stymied by striking white workers, and only so many of them could find jobs in the northern industrial centers.

He genuinely cared about their future, but he would be up for re-election in two-and-a-half years, and he'd need the Solid South democrats to elect him. He knew how strong prejudice ran across the former Confederacy, so he couldn't shake up the system too much. It was Libbie who came up with the solution: education. "Learn and Earn," she entitled it. He delivered a speech at the Baltimore Black Democrats dinner in which he made education his theme. "God instilled in every one of his children—and that includes every Negro—the hunger and thirst for knowledge. With knowledge, there is hope . . . with knowledge and ambition, there is a way to climb, to improve one's station in life. My wife, Libbie, coined a phrase that I think says it all in a nutshell—"Learn and Earn." The more you learn, the more chance you have to get ahead and earn more money. With well-managed money, the Negro can buy his own land or his own business. His children will live better and following his lead, become better educated. Thus, the cycle of a better life will have begun." He went on to cite numerous examples and possibilities.

The audience seemed a bit skeptical, but applauded quite warmly when he finished. More importantly, Kellogg would release a copy of the speech to the major newspapers of the country, so that the story would reach beyond Baltimore. "Learn and Earn" would become not only be his cornerstone for the Negro, but a popular phrase throughout the nation.

* * *

Before returning to Washington that night, he stopped by a small hotel where Kate Sprague had taken a room. She was waiting in a flimsy black silk dressing gown, her glorious chestnut hair hanging softly over her nearly bare shoulders. "You were magnificent, Armstrong!" she said brightly as she came into his arms. "You said just the right things."

She had been the lady in the wide-brimmed hat with the dark veil who sat in the back of the hall and applauded enthusiastically when he finished his speech. After her show of exuberance, she had departed hastily while he stayed to talk to the Negro leaders. He said, "I haven't much time, my dear. I have to catch a train in an hour and a half."

She hugged him close, brushed his lips with hers. "Then we simply mustn't waste a moment, mustn't we?" She undid the sash to her gown and got out of it, letting it slide to the floor.

* * *

When Custer got back to Washington later that night, Keogh met him at the train, eyes glowing. "We did it!" he announced, slapping the president on the shoulder. "One hour ago, I got a telegram from Martinez. Raul has finally wrested Panamanian independence from Colombia! That big battle he won outside the capital last week was the springboard. Now the coup is complete. Martial law is in effect, and to ensure the safety of all of the Colombian officials, Bogotá has announced that the province now has full autonomy."

Custer shook the Irishman's hand. Grinning, he said, "Good! Now, I'll have Tilden get right on a treaty so we can get serious about the canal. Oh, and you might check with Bayard to make sure the British don't mind."

"What if they do?"

Custer laughed. "Then we'll put you aboard the *Monroe* and send you back to Ireland to stoke *that* rebellion!"

* * *

In spite of all the French had done toward building a canal on the isthmus, Custer didn't think he'd get any trouble from them on the

Panamanian situation. France had her hands full in two places: Madagascar and Indochina. The former was a touchy matter of keeping the right tribe in power, and this took troops. But in the latter, the French had bigger problems. The tricolor had been involved there since Louis XIV sent missionaries to Chochin China many years earlier. Now it was virtually a protectorate, and just a week earlier, the French Army had seized Hanoi and Hue and were making more protectorates of Annam and Tonkin. The Chinese were furious.

Another matter that came under Chinese interest was United States involvement with Korea, which was minimal. The Hermit Kingdom, as it was known, was an extension of China, though it traditionally managed its own affairs. The Japanese, however, had recently negotiated a commercial treaty with the Koreans, as had the United States, and China was unhappy about that. Custer didn't like these situations; an unhappy China could certainly have an effect on his other Pacific plans.

He wanted to bring Hawaii and the Philippines under the Stars and Stripes, as well as any other islands that might provide refueling or other support for his burgeoning fleet. And he could now honestly use the word "fleet." Five gunboats for harbor defense, three monitors, and the cruiser *Boston* had been commissioned in the last three weeks. The cruiser *Atlanta* was scheduled to slip down the ways in seven more days, and a third cruiser and other smaller craft were ahead of schedule and would be launched in early April. Their crews would be ready and waiting to commence sea trials immediately.

The 11th, 12th, and 14th Cavalry Regiments had been activated in early March, with the 27th, 28th, 32nd and 33rd Infantry Regiments following two weeks later. Heavy recruitment featuring large posters of Custer in his marshal's uniform was bringing in new enlistees in large numbers. Seasoned troopers and soldiers from other regiments had been promoted and transferred as cadre to form and train the new regiments, and a number of promising young sergeants were given direct commissions to fill the need for junior officers. The states were asked to form and train militia regiments, as well. They would remain on reserve standby, ready for thirty-day call up. Eleven governors had complied at once, so Custer had nearly two army corps in reserve.

In early April, he told General Sheridan to alert the Seventh Cavalry for a move to San Antonio, Texas, in anticipation of its troopers gaining more glory in what lay ahead. He wanted them in the limelight, and once more he intended to be with them, in his famous buckskins, waving his saber astride Vic or Dandy. He held a council of war on April 15 in his office. Attending were McClellan, Sheridan, Rosser, Porter, Keogh and Brigadier-general Ranald Mackenzie. After opening the meeting, Sheridan turned it over to Mackenzie, who uncovered a map of Cuba. The officer, known as "Three Finger Jack" to his former troops and "Bad Hand" to the Indians he had fought, was expressionless over his bushy mustache. He still had a minor speech impediment and his voice was nearly as high and shrill as it had been when he graduated number one in his class from West Point. But none of that mattered; every officer in attendance knew about his remarkable record both in the Big War and on the Plains. And they knew why he was the planning officer for the possible upcoming conflict—he was brilliant.

"Gentlemen," he began, "I believe we can expect to win a campaign against Spain within ninety days of our landing in Cuba. In actuality, we should defeat Spanish forces quite easily in the first thirty days if we go ashore with a full, well equipped army corps of three divisions of four regiments each, supported by normal artillery. In my estimation, Spain cannot possibly reinforce her troops there in less than six weeks." He looked around for a moment, then went on, "Based on current intelligence, I don't think Spain will be able to form much of a force. Apart from a meager and incompetent army, she has little effective navy, and it's saturated with bloat and corruption. In fact, she has over a hundred admirals more than she has ships. Our few ships that will be available by then should be more than able to thwart any invasion force she might mount. And whatever troops she might land should easily be defeated."

Mackenzie went on, explaining that the invasion flotilla would leave from the port of Galveston in Texas, enabling all of the western elements to gather at a central location. After going into more detail, he finally turned the floor over to the president.

"Gentlemen," Custer said, "I believe we will be at war in Cuba by July 15."

By mid-spring, 1882 had not been a good year for some great men. Henry Wadsworth Longfellow, the popular and highly celebrated American poet, died on March 24, followed shortly by his good friend and colleague, the noted essayist and poet Ralph Waldo Emerson. On April 19, Charles Darwin, England's brilliant naturalist and the author of *Origin of Species* passed away. Following each of their deaths, Custer issued a statement eulogizing the great men that was carried in the *Herald* and in newspapers throughout the country.

Late in April, Custer received a telegram from Buffalo Bill Cody, whom he knew quite well. It stated, "I have talked Sitting Bull into appearing for awhile in my Wild West show. If I bring him along to Washington, will you give him an audience, and may I use 'Sitting Bull to invade Washington' and 'Sitting Bull and Custer Meet Again' as slogans?"

Custer immediately wired back, "I would be delighted to meet the great chief. Use good judgment on the slogans."

★ ★ ★

Red Elk heard of the "Buffalo Bill's Wild West" coming to visit from another trooper. Barely able to curb his interest, he pored over the *Washington Post* front-page story. Headlined, "A Group of Howling Savages Pursue a Defenseless Stage Coach," the article announced the Cody troupe's stay for three days commencing May 10. The *Post* contained a side story about the Little Bighorn and another about Custer meeting the chief in Canada. Grimly, Red Elk flashed back to that noisy, eerie day in the dust and smoke-filled sunshine of the Greasy Grass. He could hear the loud noises of battle, the screams of the wounded and dying . . . see the wild, unseeing look in Late Star's eyes as the scarlet blood spread across her dying body. He pushed the terrible memory away and thought about Canada, when Long Hair had walked right by him.

He should have killed him then, but Sitting Bull had forbidden it.

And now the great chief was coming to Washington. *He had to see him.* But it would be close timing. The Seventh Cavalry was due to depart for San Antonio, where it would be joined by its other companies about the same time as the Wild West show's performances. He toyed with deserting if the timing wasn't right. He could see Sitting Bull, go into hiding, and kill Long Hair without further ado. But when the orders were finally posted, he had time. All elements of the Seventh would depart by train from Fort Myer on May 16. Red Elk spoke to his squad leader, asking for a pass on the eleventh to see the show. He used as a reason, "I've always admired this American Indian chief." He was told he'd get a pass.

★ ★ ★

The *National Republican*'s headline a few days later announced, "Congressman Attack's Custer's Imperialism!" The front-page story was a hard-hitting criticism of Custer's expansionist policy from Federick Benteen. The Little Bighorn hero began the interview by stating that he firmly supported the country having a strong, well-equipped and well-trained army and navy, but he considered "any acquisition of more territory by force a contradiction to the very precepts on which this great democracy was formed." The former colonel went on to state, " You have to understand Custer as I do, going back to the old days in the Seventh Cavalry. He is glory smitten. Glory rules him. He will sacrifice any number of American soldiers and sailors to achieve what he perceives as national good—but in reality he is only feeding the Custer myth he has carefully built." Congressman Benteen further stated, "Custer and his Democratic sycophants, both in his Cabinet and in the Congress, will lead us to bloodshed, senseless imperialism, and the contempt of all civilized nations."

Custer put down the *Republican* and scratched the ear of his favorite hound, Tuck. He frowned. Benteen had been in his craw for a long time now, and now, as in the regimental days, there wasn't much he could do about it except ignore the man. He knew there was a certain amount of jealousy involved, probably always would be. So, he'd ignore criticism like this. It would be taken as politics by the public anyway. But he didn't have to like it.

He looked up as Libbie walked up in her nightgown and robe. He noticed the troubled look on her face. "Something wrong?" he asked.

She didn't reply, just handed him a letter. It read:

> *Mrs. Custer:*
> *Your husband still likes redheads, one named*
> *for a white flower, the other the Queen of*
> *Washington. A president, like a king, still*
> *Hasn't the right to treat his lady thusly.*
> —*An admirer*

Custer felt a flush, but he knew something like this was bound to happen. Somehow the word would get out. The guilt had been eating at him ever since meeting Kate Sprague in Baltimore. Lilly Langtry had called him, wondering if she should buy a house in Georgetown. He also felt guilty about her. Now this—

"Have you become involved with other women?" Libbie asked softly. "This is the second note about redheads."

He wanted to confess, get her forgiveness, but he didn't want to hurt her with the truth. He'd once read somewhere that the wrongdoer always wants absolution from his or her true love, but he hadn't believed it. He managed a laugh and handed the letter back to her. "Whose this admirer, Libbie girl? Someone you're keeping under the bed?"

Her cool expression hadn't changed. "Answer my question, Autie."

He maintained his jocularity. "Don't you know his name? He didn't even sign that thing."

Her gray eyes were growing moist, her voice almost broke as she repeated, "Answer my question, Autie."

God, how he wanted to tell her! But he just couldn't. He'd stop, never visit those women's beds again, be faithful to his beloved Libbie forever. . . . He stood, took her hands. "No," he lied, "I have *not* become involved with any other women." He summoned some anger, knowing if he didn't attack, he'd falter. "What I want to know is what jackal is writing this tripe! Do you have any idea?"

She slumped, dropping the note to the floor and putting her head against his chest. Letting go of her tears, she shook her head. His arms came around her, the strong arms she so loved. "Oh, darling," she said around a sob, "I've been so troubled, so pained. I just can't imagine your being untrue to me."

He positively would never touch either of those women again. No, and he'd make it up to her somehow, some way, if it took the rest of his life. . . .

He held her tightly, finding some words, "Darling, you've got to remember that we both have enemies—particularly me. There will always be lies . . . We have to be strong. The important thing is how much I love you." He tilted her chin up and kissed her wet lips gently. "There will *always* be us."

She found the relieved smile he wanted to see.

The armored frigate U.S.S. *Carson* had been partially refitted in a Boston shipyard. The ship had both steam and sail, and could make eight knots on a good day. She was just what the plotters needed for Havana. She could be manned by a small crew and fit the bill of a serious warship.

She left New England waters on the third of May and began her trials as she headed for warm Florida waters with much fanfare from the press. Once more, Mark Kellogg had seen to the coverage with several flowery press releases. Not many people who read newspapers in America were unaware of the *Carson*. And, of course, the New York *Herald* had also given the ship major attention. The frigate stopped in at Washington and docked at the Navy Yard, where President Custer inspected her with Tom Rosser and Myles Keogh. Custer was privately shown where the explosive charge would be placed well forward while the crew was aft. Again, he stated, "I don't want any of our sailors hurt."

The *Carson* began a cruise that would take her to the Florida Keys, after a brief stop at Charleston, then on to Havana, where Myles Keogh would go ashore to confer with Cuban separatists. The frigate would remain anchored in Havana harbor to await the return of its official passenger.

★ ★ ★

It seemed that the weather god had smiled on Buffalo Bill's Wild West extravaganza as it marched and pranced down Pennsylvania Avenue in the bright May sunlight. For most of the previous two weeks the sky had been gray and it had shed enough rain on the capital to ensure plenty of flowers. But now the sky was blue and a light, warm wind made the day most pleasant. Riding a light gray horse that pleased him, Sitting Bull was attired in his fanciest garments including a magnificent eagle feather headdress that flowed down his back. He was in the middle of the parade that included cowboys on lively horses, more Indians, the famous riflewoman Annie Oakley on a pretty Pinto pony, a brass band, and the other components of Buffalo Bill Cody's famous show.

The Hunkpapa chief rode stoically most of the time, but now and then he leaned down from the saddle to hand a coin to a dirty-faced street urchin with extended palm. The newspapers reported that Sitting Bull gave freely of his own money to the poor, and the word had spread among the needy.

Thousands of often blasé Washingtonians had turned out, dressed in their gayest clothes to join in the festive reception of one of America's most colorful showmen, and of course to see the famous Sioux leader. As the procession approached the White House, a roar went up from the crowd. George Armstrong Custer, in his Seventh Cavalry uniform, accompanied by Lieutenant-colonels Tom Custer and William Cooke—both also in uniform—rode out from behind the mansion to serve as a reviewing party. Nothing had been said of the president doing such a novel thing, but then the capital had never seen Buffalo Bill's show before . . . and it had certainly never had a president like George Armstrong Custer.

When Sitting Bull reached the point where Custer and his aides sat astride their gleaming mounts, all three of the former Seventh Cavalry officers rendered a snappy hand salute. At that moment, from a portion of the Marine Band that had been concealed behind some bushes, "Lincoln and Liberty" filled the air. Sitting Bull recognized Custer at once and raised the lance he was carrying.

It was a long way from that lonely river in Montana.

★ ★ ★

An hour later, a beaming Cody escorted Sitting Bull into Custer's office. Libbie and Annie Keogh, as well as all of the Cabinet members were present when the great chief shook Custer's hand in the white man's fashion he'd learned. Custer pointed to two colorful Indian blankets that had been spread on the floor. Sitting cross-legged on one, he took the long-stemmed Sioux ceremonial pipe that Tom had lit and handed to him. As Sitting Bull sat on the other blanket, Monasetah greeted the chief warmly, then joined the two leaders to interpret.

After they both partook of the pipe, Custer welcomed his visitor, telling him it was a long way from the wilds of Canada.

Immediately the Hunkpapa chief flashed his humor, saying, "But you have no buffalo here."

"That's not true," Custer replied with a wide grin. "I have sent special buffalo steaks to your hotel for tonight's dinner."

They talked on, discussing the Black Hills and finally Custer said, "Great Chief, I must ask you some questions." He waited as Monasetah caught up, then went on, "Will your people ever be happy on the reservation?"

Sitting Bull sobered, thought for a moment, then shook his head. "No."

"Do you think your people can ever live as the *Wasicus?* I mean completely—in houses, in towns?"

Sitting Bull looked puzzled.

Custer leaned forward. "If each person in your tribe had a certain amount of land and cattle to raise on it, each by himself, would they be happy?"

The chief shrugged. "They are hunters and warriors."

"I know, but times change. They have sons and grandsons, and those grandsons will have grandsons. There will be no one to fight and the hunting will become bad. To survive, they may have to live as the white man. Do you see your people like this?"

Sitting Bull shook his head again. "Why?"

"Because," Custer replied, "I've been giving the reservation plan much thought, and I don't think it is the answer. You aren't in control of your lives, and I don't think it's wise to feed you as if you were animals. Your people could easily become dependent and lose their will to succeed in life."

"It's your way, Custer. You tell us so."

Custer struggled to find the right words. "I would like to see *one* country for all of our people—yours, mine, the Chinese, the Cheyenne, the Navajo. One America. Do you know what I mean?"

When Monasetah finished, the chief said, "No. My people wish to be alone. They don't want to live with the Crow pigs."

The president sighed. He had forgotten he was speaking to the most recalcitrant Indian leader in the country. When this business with Spain was over, he'd have to set up a big powwow with several tribal councils, and see if there wasn't some way to work out an approach to the problem different from the crippling reservation plan. He just *knew* that plan would never work. Those proud Indians had to learn to walk on their own two feet again, but this was not the time to discuss it further. He signaled to Cooke, who brought the box that held the chief's gift. The president removed it and handed it to his guest. It was a wide-brimmed white hat similar to the one he'd worn at the Little Bighorn. Attached to the front was a metal presidential seal. Sitting Bull could hardly contain his pleasure as Custer handed it to him. He expressed his thanks and handed Custer one of the postcards he was selling.

They got to their feet and as they shook hands again, Custer said, "I owe very much to you, great chief." It was a great understatement.

★ ★ ★

That night, shortly after Sitting Bull had retired in his room at the Waverly Hotel, Red Elk, wearing civilian clothes, knocked on his door and said in a low voice, "Great Chief, it is Red Elk. I wish to speak with you."

Moments later, Sitting Bull opened the door. "What are you doing here."

"I will tell you inside."

The chief motioned him inside the room. "I thought you were at the Indian School."

"I left many months ago to come here and join the army."

Sitting Bull closed the door and studied him for a moment before saying, "You can't join the army. No Indians . . ."

"I lied. They don't know I'm Indian."

Sitting Bull thought about that for a few moments before saying, "Why?"

"To be near Long Hair."

"Do you still wish to kill him?"

"Nothing has changed, Great Chief."

"What will you do afterward?"

"Go back to the old ways. Be free, hunt, find a way to fight the Long Knives. I know much about them now . . . perhaps lead our people some day."

Sitting Bull sighed. "The old ways are finished. The warriors grow fat and lazy on the White Father's meat. They plow the field. Crazy Horse is dead, Gall is a white man."

Red Elk's eyes blazed. "I will be the new Crazy Horse."

"Who will ride with you? The young men do not even train as warriors."

"There are plenty like me."

Sitting Bull shrugged. "Long Hair is good to us. No lies."

It was Red Elk's turn to shrug. "I must follow my path." He turned to go. The great Sitting Bull had become an old man.

The New York *Herald* was the first newspaper to get the story out. In its largest headline in years it announced: WARSHIP *Carson* BLOWN UP IN HAVANA The front-page story read:

Havana, Cuba, May 22. The armed frigate U.S.S. *Carson* exploded at 11:20 P.M. on May 21. As the ship's crew rapidly evacuated the burning ship, it began to sink by the bow. Early reports indicate that two seaman were reported missing. The exact cause of the explosion has not been determined, but a chief petty officer, who was on watch at the time, reported he saw two dark-clad figures climb over the rail at the bow of the ship at 10:55. He heard them speaking Spanish, purportedly Castillian Spanish. When he went forward to investigate, he was struck on the head and knocked out. The blast awakened him and he hurried toward the stern, where crew members were preparing to abandon ship. Ship's officers directed an orderly departure into life boats. The ship's captain, Lieutenant Thomas Whyte, stated, 'I thought we had hit some kind of a floating mine. The fact that the crew remained calm as we abandoned ship to the boats enabled us to do so without further casualties.' The *Carson* went down by the bow in about twenty-seven minutes, it was estimated. Based on the unnamed chief petty officer's statement, it is believed that a huge explosive charge was placed near the forward engine room and detonated. Speculation points to Spanish government agents placing the charge to warn away any further incursions by unauthorized foreign warships. The Spanish Governor's office rendered a protest to the United States ambassador, James Marcos, immediately after the arrival of the *Carson*. United States Secretary of State Samuel

J. Tilden stated, 'If this piratical attack on a peaceful American ship cannot be readily explained by Spanish authorities in Cuba or Madrid, severe consideration will be given to the matter, with the possibility of a break in diplomatic relations possible.' The American Navy has hurried to the scene to immediately search the wreckage for causes. According to a White House source, President Custer, while purported to be both saddened by the apparent loss of the sailors, and puzzled by the destruction of the ship, is deeply concerned. He has made no statement.

The next day's edition of the *Herald* ran another front page feature:

SPAIN UNCOOPERATIVE IN *Carson* INVESTIGATION. *Havana, May 23.* An armored Spanish harbor patrol boat is anchored over the site of the sunken U.S.S *Carson*, which went down the night before last after a mysterious explosion tore out her forward belly. This morning, when the U.S.S. *Pilgrim*, a small salvage ship, arrived from Key West, Florida, the captain of the Spanish boat ordered it to stand off from the disaster site until permission to search the hull is received from Madrid. At press time, that permission was still being withheld by the Spanish government. The question is, why was such an unprovoked attack made, and the answer seems quite simple. The United States has looked favorably on Cuban separatists' efforts to gain independence from Spain, and an unprovoked attack by Cubans would be cause for the Americans to pull back from any support. A stern warning to the Spanish government was issued by the White House, stating that unless the U.S. Navy salvage team is given full access to the sunken ship, and a satisfactory explanation of the attack on the *Carson* is supplied at once, diplomatic relations will be severed. The U.S. Navy released the names of the two sailors who have been missing since the murderous explosion ripped the guts out of the *Carson*. They are: Seaman First Class George F. Adamsly from Lodi, Ohio, and Seaman First Class Harold N. Williams from Galena, Illinois. Both are presumed dead. President Custer has already sent conciliatory telegrams to the sailors' families.

The New York Times, the opposition paper asked:

> *Washington, May 23*. WHAT WAS THE *Carson* DOING IN HAVANA? The armored frigate *U.S.S. Carson*, which sunk on May 22 from an apparent charge laid by unknown raiders, was sitting in Havana Harbor as an uninvited, unwanted intruder. Why? Why was an American ship of war at anchor in a foreign port where it was unwelcome? This is the second time in a few months that an American warship has entered unwelcome waters. The *U.S.S. Monroe* acted belligerently at Colón, Panama in February. Is our filibustering president insistently leading us to war? The government is telling us Spanish attackers sunk the *Carson* to make it look like Cuban revolutionaries did it. Why? The United States is trying to set the example for democracy and freedom throughout the world—is this the way to do it? Our government should send an apology to Spain at once.

The *Herald* answered with:

> WAR WITH SPAIN IMMINENT *Washington, May 24*. Brigadier-general Myles Keogh, special aide to President George Armstrong Custer, returned this morning from Cuba with the full story. General Keogh, who was in Havana to meet with opposition Cubans who wish to throw off the Spanish yoke, interviewed crew members of the sunken frigate *Carson* before slipping out of Cuba on a fast American harbor boat that had arrived at a secret meeting place north of Havana. He stated, 'I spoke with the captain of the *Carson*, and he insists unknown assailants sunk his ship. I further interviewed Chief Petty Officer Norman J. Johnson, the senior member of the watch at the time of the explosion. He states that the darkclad figures who surreptitiously boarded the *Carson* shortly before the explosion spoke in Castillian Spanish. Chief

Johnson speaks fluent Spanish and once served in the U.S. Embassy in Madrid. "I have no doubt that, for whatever devious reason, members of the Spanish military illegally boarded the *Carson* and placed an explosive charge, which they detonated. It was an act of war by Spain that killed two innocent American sailors."

Newspapers around the country quoted Keogh's remarks, with the majority expressing outrage and demanding retaliation against Spain. The *Times* of London questioned the motive, but castigated Spain for her continuing control policy in the Antilles. Other foreign newspapers merely carried the story for its sensationalism.

★ ★ ★

At 11:00 A.M. on the May 25, President George Armstrong Custer addressed a joint session of Congress in the House chambers. Wearing a black suit and a black necktie, he was introduced by Vice-president William English. The chambers and galleries, filled to overflowing with members of the press and distinguished visitors, grew utterly silent as the president began, "Ladies and gentlemen, a most grievous wrong has been concocted and executed against the people of the United States. In a totally unwarranted attack on an American warship performing a mission of peace, the monarchy of Spain violated our peaceful relationship in a murderous manner that killed two of our proud young sailors . . . and destroyed one of our recently refitted ships. . . ."

Custer went on to discuss the Monroe Doctrine and the history of Spanish rule in the Western Hemisphere. He spoke of Spanish oppression and denial of human rights, reminded his listeners of the great American struggle for its own independence. By this time, nearly every phrase, every new point, was greeted by cheers and applause.

Finally, he paused, looked around the throng for a long moment, and said angrily, "*As we did at the Boston Tea Party, we Americans are going to throw the enemy into the sea.*"

Thunderous applause burst through the House as spectators and members of Congress sprang to their feet. The president waited until the ovation subsided to hold up his hands. Let this day be recalled by a singular phrase, "*Remember the Carson!*" Custer threw his fist in the air. "*Members of Congress, I hereby ask you to support me in declaring a state of war against the sovereign state of Spain!*"

Another roar of approval followed and there was no doubt how the Congress would vote. George Armstrong Custer had his war.

★ ★ ★

The declaration was formally delivered to the Spanish ambassador shortly after the Congress unanimously passed the resolution, with even Benteen and two Republican preachers who were congressmen voting "Aye." The city went wild that night as bands blared patriotic songs and the streets were filled with celebrating, hard drinking instant patriots. Hundreds of clerks and other young men, bored with their lot, vowed to enlist at the crack of dawn. Everywhere, drunk or sober, men and women shouted, "*Remember the Carson!*"

Once more the capital was thrown into the frenzy of preparing for war. In the days that followed, uniforms seemed to multiply like rabbits, and American flags blossomed like spring flowers after a rain, creating a sea of red, white, and blue. Wartime Washington was back. The opportunists and profiteers were already on hand or en route to the riches that awaited their conniving minds. Prostitutes from New York, Philadelphia, Baltimore, and Richmond packed their valises to do their bit for the boys who would soon begin to throw their money around the capital. Banners proclaiming "REMEMBER THE CARSON!" hung everywhere. Many merchants who were old enough to remember the immensely profitable days of the Big War frantically ordered as much of their particular stock as they could talk their suppliers into providing. The telephone system was taxed beyond its youthful capacity and promptly went out of order. No bets were hedged—put it all in the pot! was the general attitude

And the rest of the country followed suit. *To hell with stock market plunges and bad times! The hero of the Little Bighorn, President George Armstrong Custer, was going to lead the country to the great preeminence it deserved!*

Telegrams went out to the governors of each state requesting immediate call up of available militia. Transport ships would be readied and moved to Galveston Bay, where an invasion fleet would be formed. New warships near completion got round-the-clock work details. The *Monroe* and the two new cruisers, *Atlanta* and *Boston*, immediately headed for patrol duty on the north side of Cuba to intercept any Spanish transports or ships of war that might somehow try to reach the island.

After conferring with Sheridan and McClellan, it was agreed that Major-general Alfred Terry should command the expeditionary force. His superb abilities in the Big War, plus his ability to blend the various personalities of the subordinate state commanders who would serve under him was the deciding factor. Custer also wanted Fightin' Joe Wheeler, the famous forty-six-year-old Confederate cavalry general, brought to active duty as a brigadier and given a command. Such a move would further cement Southern support. Ranald Mackenzie would be chief of staff. Admiral Porter, still spry and able, designated himself to command the naval forces.

Two of the major active duty senior officers left out of the command picture were Major-general George Crook and Brigadier-general Nelson Miles, an experienced Plains commander nicknamed "Bear Coat" by the Indians. Custer thought Crook, one of the most successful of the Indian fighting leaders, should remain in his Arizona command where he was highly regarded. The same went for Miles, whom Custer didn't particularly want to remove from the Plains. Although there were no present Indian problems, he didn't want any surprises on his backside in the midst of a war.

The president-general hadn't enjoyed himself as much since he tore into Jeb Stuart with his Wolverines at Gettysburg when he was a brand-new brigadier.

48

Two days after the war began, a messenger delivered a letter marked "Personal" to the president's office. Cooke brought it in. "Smells good," he said with a grin as he held it to his nose.

Custer knew without looking who it was from. Opening it, the hand-writing was familiar:

> *"My Darling Army! I decided to be nearer to you during this cri-sis with Spain, so I have taken temporary rooms at the Bonaventure, that small hotel on 14th Street. You must come and see me at once! I await with pounding heart to be in your loving arms again.*
>
> *—Your loving J. L."*

★ ★ ★

Libbie was reading the *Post* over her afternoon tea when she saw the item about the famous Englishwoman:

Lillie Langtry, best known as the famous 'Jersey Lily,' has taken up lodging in the Bonaventure Hotel on 14th Street, according to proprietor James Lording. Considered the most beautiful woman in the all of England, Mrs. Langtry (as she is always called) spoke only briefly to this reporter, stating that she was looking at real estate in the Washington area with a mind to buying a house. Mrs. Langtry, a tall, stunning redhead, gained fame as an intimate friend of Albert, Prince of Wales, the Crown Prince of England, but her likeness on postcards and her presence at most of British society's major events have made her the object of many men's dreams. The London *Times* once stated that there was no man in the world she couldn't have if she set her mind to it.

The last line caught Libbie's attention. And she *was* a redhead. . . .

★ ★ ★

The other redhead in Custer's life was also excited about the war. She saw it as an opportunity to be with him more often. Oh, he had told her he wasn't going to see her anymore in a romantic fashion, that he realized his love for his wife was the most important part of his personal life, but she knew he wouldn't be able to stay away. He hungered for her passion, both intellectually and physically. She knew. There hadn't been one single man in her life whom she hadn't captivated. Oh, Roscoe Conkling, that witty, brilliant man of taste, had come close. God, what times they'd had!

Armstrong Custer didn't approach the New York senator in intellect, but he was a remarkable male animal. Bright enough, positively sure of himself, shamelessly lusty, and handsome in his raw-boned way, there was something very special about Custer, she had realized shortly after their first evening together . . . his strength. Everything about him denoted *power*—his cocksureness, his physical strength, the way he *grasped* what he wanted, *took* it! No, she wasn't about to let George Armstrong Custer stay in the arms of his pretty wife. There would be ways to get him back.

But there was another reason. Kate Chase Sprague had been the brilliant guiding light of Washington society two decades earlier. During the war, she had dazzled them all! At an age when most young women were still learning where the demitasse cup went, she was *ruling* the capital's elite functions. Now another war, another chance. Oh, she didn't have the money or the stature, but they knew who she was. All she needed was the power connection.

★ ★ ★

Tom Custer had never been comfortable as a cabinet officer. He really had no qualifications nor inclination for the post, had simply taken it because his brother had given it to him. He was a soldier, simple as that—a fighting soldier. He didn't like the boring life of peacetime garrison duty.

His whole life was a game, and the greatest game of all was war. Oh, he'd managed the Interior job because he was honest and because Ned Burke had gotten him the best undersecretary in the United States—a career administrator named Ronald Graham. All he had to do was show up at the office in the middle of the day to sign things. And, honestly, he knew he didn't have to do that. He directed a stream of tobacco juice at the shiny brass spittoon that resided by the sofa in Custer's office. "You know, Autie, I want to get in it."

Custer had been signing papers at his desk. "Get in what?"

"I want to at least go along with you in this war we're gonna fight."

"Secretaries of the Interior don't fight wars, Tom."

"Presidents don't either."

"I'm different."

"So am I. Besides, you know damn well Graham runs that place. He can get along just fine without me."

Custer pursed his lips. "You want to be my aide again?"

Tom's blue eyes lit up. "Sure do!"

"Okay, tell Graham you're going on a leave of absence to fight for your country."

"When do we leave?"

"The flotilla is due to form up outside of Galveston at the end of June and sail on the first of July. I want to celebrate the departure in a grand parade in San Antonio on the 25th. Invite the whole country to Texas to be a part of it. Soon as it's over, the troops that participate can go by train from there to the port." Custer walked over to the sofa and sat down. "Before you rush off to oil your pistol, we need to talk for a minute."

Tom settled back, "Talk away, big brother."

Custer sighed, frowned. "We're gonna get mighty busy being soldiers again, Tom, and I may get so involved that I'll forget I've got other duties as president. I haven't done much about the Negroes yet, nor women's suffrage, not even what's so close to my heart, the Indian reservation situation. And in spite of what I told Senator Pendleton, I still haven't moved that darned Civil Service reform program off the ground." He sighed again. "And now the war takes precedence over everything."

"What do you want me to do?" Tom asked.

Custer lightly gripped his arm. "Remind me of those other needs now and then while I'm all caught up in war. Make me take the time to deal with them."

Tom patted his brother's hand. "How about if I kick your ass."

Custer smiled. "That'll do it."

★ ★ ★

Time flew as Washington and the rest of the nation bustled. The *Monroe* sank a Spanish merchantman that tried to elude her. Another Spanish ship struck her colors as the *Boston* bore down on her. Custer's remarkable vitality stood him in good stead as he burned midnight oil. He was a daily habitué of the War Department, checking activations, deployments, supplies, ammunition, horses, artillery pieces, saddles, even socks. Twice Sheridan told him to get the hell out and quit meddling, but he couldn't. This was his war and if it took all of his tremendous energy and sticking his nose into every general's business, so be it.

Libbie plunged into several activities, primarily Clara Barton's American Association of the Red Cross. At one meeting, she was introduced to Kate Sprague, the woman she'd heard so much about. Mrs. Sprague, she was told, had just recently emerged from self-exile to donate her extensive abilities to the organization. Libbie had heard that the woman had fallen on bad times since her divorce from the Rhode Island governor. How sad, she thought. She'd have to invite her to the White House for tea, help her in some way. The woman was still remarkably beautiful, and what a proud carriage, and such beautiful hair!

The next time they met at a Red Cross function, Libbie sought out the former society maven. "Mrs. Sprague," she said pleasantly, "I've heard remarkable tales about your wartime adventures in leading Washington society, and I'm pleased that you have chosen to volunteer for this worthy cause. I, well, I'll come right to the point—I've been thinking about a committee to raise funds for the association among the city's wealthy and socially prominent. Benefit balls and dinners might be a way to garner major sums, don't you think?"

Kate Sprague looked into Libbie's gray eyes and smiled. "Why, yes, Mrs. Custer, I think it would."

"Would you head up such a committee? I would work with you, even find expenses for you. I think it could be just grand."

"I would be delighted to do so," Kate replied ever so calmly.

Libbie smiled happily. "Oh, good. I'll take care of everything. My husband has a special interest in the Red Cross Association, you know. He'll be pleased to find out you've taken the charitable helm."

I'm sure he will, Kate thought.

★ ★ ★

Custer insisted that the Seventh Cavalry remain an independent command, subject to the orders of the Expeditionary Force commander, and General Terry agreed. The other cavalry regiments would be assigned to the divisions that were being formed in Texas. General Mackenzie had revised his original plans; there would now be two army corps in the Antilles Expeditionary Force. The plan called for X Corps to go into Cuba first and conduct the original assault. Three days later as X Corps moved inland and evacuated the landing area, XI Corps would land. Nearly all of X Corps was collecting in staging camps around San Antonio. Those troops would constitute the big parade.

Custer had contacted Oran M. Roberts, the governor of Texas, and had requested that arrangements be made for the parade. It was to be held on his lucky day, June 25. Custer's Luck would be commemorated again. Lieutenant-colonel Tom Custer was sent down to the historic, one-time Mexican city to coordinate the event.

Major-general Alfred Terry was appreciative of the command opportunity and knew it was the president's doing. Years earlier, when Grant had relieved the headstrong Custer of command of the Seventh, just before the Little Bighorn campaign, the then lieutenant-colonel had come to him on his knees asking for help in getting reinstated . . . if anyone could imagine George Armstrong Custer on his knees! But he had helped, had reworded Custer's request in phrases that he knew Grant, as the fine old soldier he was, couldn't resist. Now, he knew Custer was paying him back. However, he also knew the job would take the patience of Job. Custer would be in his hair constantly. Still, he reminded himself, that back in the final year of the war, General Meade had commanded the huge Army of the Potomac with Grant calling the shots, so he could make it work. Yes, being given such a major command was quite an honor.

He set up his temporary headquarters in San Antonio, where Brigadier-general Ranald Mackenzie and a number of other staff officers joined him.

"Here are the diplomas for the National Deaf-Mute College, Mr. President," William Cooke said, placing a pile of parchment sheets on Custer's desk.

"When is the graduation?" the president asked.

"June the twelfth, two o'clock."

"I want to attend and Libbie will want to come along."

"I think they already have a speaker, sir. Alexander Graham Bell."

"That's all right. We'll just be spectators."

Cooke made a wry face. "I don't think you can be *just* a spectator, sir. That's a pretty small school."

Custer dipped the quill pen and signed the first diploma. "All right, don't tell them we're coming. It'll be better that way."

This time, Cooke frowned. "Sir, do you know what will happen when a president of the United States and the first lady drop in on a commencement like that? Think of what it will do to the speaker."

The President, as patron of the college, had signed all of the diplomas of the graduating students. "All right, tell the school's president that we'll drop by the reception following the ceremony."

Cooke smiled. "That's much better. At least it won't interfere with their program."

Custer nodded as his secretary departed. Libbie would love to go. Back in '65, when they were stationed in Austin, he had gone across the river from their quarters on several occasions to the Deaf and Dumb Asylum to learn the rudiments of sign language. This basis stood him in good stead later on the Plains when he picked up Indian sign language. He enjoyed his association with the people in the Asylum, finding their often bashful humor most enjoyable. On occasion Libbie had gone with him and she shared his interest . . . especially in one adorable deaf boy.

Custer wondered how many deaf and deaf-mute citizens there were in the country. Maybe there was something more he could do for them, perhaps find some funding for more schools. He made a note to follow up.

★ ★ ★

The National Deaf-Mute College was founded in 1857 when a wealthy Washingtonian named Amos Kendall donated two acres from his estate in the northeast part of the city to establish housing and a school for deaf and blind students. He then hired Edward Miner Gallaudet to be its first superintendent. Later the blind students were moved to a separate school, but in 1864 President Lincoln signed a bill into law authorizing the school to confer college degrees. Unfortunately, Kendall died in 1869, five months after the first commencement, but he made provisions for the remaining eighty-one acres of his estate to be sold to the college.

Now, as the presidential carriage drew up in front of the old Kendall School building, where the reception was underway, Edward Gallaudet and one of his teachers were waiting by the steps of the main entrance. The superintendent, a mustachioed man with thinning sandy hair, hurried out to the carriage as it stopped. Annie Keogh had come along, as had Mark Kellogg. A second carriage, carrying Captain Myers and one of his assistants, followed. Gallaudet greeted them eagerly as Custer shook his hand.

It was a warm, sunny day. Libbie and Annie folded the parasols they had been using as they entered the two-story red brick building that had been the original school structure on Kendall Green, as the first campus had been called. Inside, a group of some ninety faculty, directors, graduates, students, parents, and guests were busily chatting over refreshments.

The faculty member who had been waiting in front shouted, "Ladies and gentlemen, the president of the United States!" as a student inside made the announcement in sign language.

★ ★ ★

The speaker was Alexander Graham Bell, the inventor of the telephone. A Scot who arrived in the United States via Canada in 1871, he founded a school for deaf-mutes in Boston the following year. Bell had also been working on the idea of transmitting speech electrically since he was eighteen. His experiments with the telephone finally proved successful in March, 1876, the year before the Bell Telephone Company was founded. His wife, Mabel, who was deaf, had accompanied him to the graduation. Edward Gallaudet introduced them to the Custers right after he presented the board of directors.

Custer was delighted. "Mr. Bell, I'm most interested in your photophone. Transmitting speech by light rays can have many remarkable uses, I'm sure. As a military man, I'm interested in those aspects."

The handsome thirty-four-year-old inventor smiled. "You must come over to my Volta Laboratory sometime, Mr. President. I'll show you several interesting ideas."

They talked on for several minutes as Mrs. Gallaudet introduced Libbie and Annie around to the guests. Libbie was speaking with the valedictorian of the graduating class when a beautiful little girl in a pink dress came up to her and held up a small silver tray with two glasses of cherry punch. She had strawberry blond curls, bright blue eyes, and skin like soft ivory. "Would you like some punch, Mrs. Custer?" she said in a brave little voice.

Libbie smiled down as she took a glass. "I'd *love* to have some punch, my dear. Thank you. And what is your name?"

Her smile was sunny, a gift to whomever it reached. She turned to Mrs. Gallaudet, who repeated Libbie's question by signing. The girl replied, "Jenny, mum."

"How old are you, Jenny?"

Another bright smile. "Six, mum."

Libbie sipped her punch. "Umm, that's good, Jenny. Did you make it?"

"No, mum, cook did."

Libbie chatted with Jenny for a few moments more, before she had to break away for further introductions, but her eyes kept wandering back to the little girl. She kept thinking about how much the Jenny looked like Autie's childhood tintype photograph. When she had a chance, she asked Mrs. Gallaudet, "Is Jenny your daughter?"

The superintendent's wife shook her head, "No, I wish she were. Jenny's an orphan, Mrs. Custer. We have several here at the school.

"How sad. She's a delightful child."

"Yes, everyone loves her."

"I want my husband to meet her when I can tear him away from those folks over there. He knows how to sign somewhat."

★ ★ ★

On the way home in the carriage, Libbie looped her arm through Custer's. "Well, Nomad, what did you think of her?"

His mind was on Bell. "Think of whom, my dear?"

"The little girl, Jenny."

Custer smiled. "She's a sweetheart."

"She could be your daughter, you know. That lovely hair and those gorgeous blue eyes."

"Pretty girl."

Libbie regarded the unfinished Washington monument off to the west for a few seconds before saying, "She's an orphan."

"Uh huh."

"And you speak her language. I saw how her eyes lit up when you signed to her."

Custer was still preoccupied. "Uh huh."

Libbie decided to wait.

★ ★ ★

That night as she was brushing her hair before retiring, Libbie said, "Autie, I've been thinking about that little deaf girl, Jenny."

Custer was reading in a wingback chair. "Pretty girl."

"Do you think you could teach me to sign."

He closed the book. "Sure. I learned, didn't I?"

"Would it take me long?"

"I don't think so—not as smart as you are. Why?"

Libbie got up from the brocaded bench and came to him. Sitting on his lap, she kissed his cheek and murmured softly, "Darling, do you think we could adopt Jenny?"

Custer frowned. "I haven't got time to be a father."

"But, dear, I would do everything for her. And she'd love you so much. Oh, Autie, I've missed being a mother so terribly. Please think about it."

Custer's frown increased as he looked into her pleading eyes, then suddenly his expression relaxed and he broke into a grin. "You know what, my dear? I was just about to ask you if you'd like to adopt Jenny."

She stared at him a moment, then punched him in the ribs as she laughed. "Autie Custer, you are *terrible*, making me do all this." She kissed him soundly on the mouth.

When she pulled back, he smiled and said, "I've already sent a note to Gallaudet to get the adoption proceedings started."

"How long will it take?"

"I don't know. You should be able to get her when you get back from San Antonio."

She showered his face with kisses. "Oh, I love you so!"

San Antone! A man by the name of Sidney Lanier once wrote, "If peculiarities were quills, San Antonio would be a rare porcupine." The center of the Mexican region of Tejas for many years, the little town was wrapped around a curving river that was called *Yanaguana* by the Indians. When the Anglos started arriving in the early part of the nineteenth century, leading Mexicans joined in the revolt that later brought on the heroic battle of the Alamo, making forever famous names such as James Bowie, Davy Crockett, and William Barrett Travis. General Sam Houston arguably saved the day at the battle of San Jacinto, and San Antonio quickly reigned as the heart of the new Republic of Texas.

In 1845 Texas became a state, but when the Civil War began, seceded to join the Confederacy. Known as "wild and woolly," the town epitomized the Mexican flavored West until well after the war, when more Anglos began to pour in—as well as many Germans. Sin flavored the day. One leading sporting house Madame bought a gold bed rumored to cost $10,000. "It's grandeur," a local newspaper reported, "covered a multitude of sins—and shins." In 1877 when the railroad arrived, the city took on new life and began to grow rapidly. Now, it had over 30,000 inhabitants and was still full of peculiarities. The famed Alamo, where Mexican General Santa Ana's huge army had wiped out its roughly180 heroic defenders, was just a rundown quartermaster depot and church.

Always a military center, the city's Fort Sam Houston was its proud "Post." So many of San Antonio's daughters had married soldiers over the years, that it became known as the "Mother-in-law of the Army." Before the Civil War, Lieutenant-colonel Robert E. Lee had once squired an Irish beauty on long Sunday horseback rides through its nearby fields. Now, it was said that Cupid was the actual commander of the Post, not General Terry, who had arrived with his new Antilles Expeditionary Force headquarters.

Arriving on the evening of June 23, the Custer party was billeted at the newly finished Maverick Hotel on Houston Street, even though the famous Menger Hotel beside the Alamo was where most celebrated people stayed while visiting the city. The primary reason for using the other hotel was that the influential Maverick family was a major contributor to the Democratic Party. This was the same family that would later have a descendant named Maury who would conceive and complete the famous River Walk that would bring limitless tourist riches to the city. Custer and

Libbie naturally occupied the ultra-plush presidential suite that had been prepared especially for them.

While Custer was given a tour of the rundown Alamo, Libbie, Annie and Monasetah were driven in a hooded phaeton—a two-horse carriage—around the historic downtown area, and then out to the hill country. Several Democratic ladies in accompanying carriages guided them on the merry, sunny trek. Following a luncheon at a popular tavern, they returned to the hotel.

Meanwhile, Custer, wearing a buckskin jacket and yellow-striped officers britches tucked into his boots, went out with his party to Fort Sam. There he visited the troop units that were pouring into the Post. A special office had been set up for him and his staff, where they met with the dark-haired Terry, Bad Hand Mackenzie, and Fightin' Joe Wheeler, who would serve as overall cavalry commander in the Expeditionary Force headquarters. Following a briefing by Mackenzie, Custer was escorted by Colonel Wesley Merritt to the tent headquarters of the Seventh Cavalry. The entire regiment was drawn up in formation on horseback on its corner of the huge parade ground when the president arrived. As he stepped down from his carriage, the regimental band struck up a zestful "GarryOwen" and he grinned. As long as he lived, he would never know a more stirring song.

He borrowed a horse bearing seven little gold stars on its navy saddle blanket and trouped the regimental line with Colonel Merritt. The troopers looked good, proud, and ready to fight. This was his regiment, always would be. He waved his broad-brimmed white hat and smiled. Going by the Sharpshooter squad, he had no way of sensing the pair of dark eyes that bore into him from a private in the front rank.

★ ★ ★

The Mavericks threw a reception at their hotel that night. All of the field-grade officers from the units collected at the Post were invited. Naturally, this included a number of their ladies who had come to the city to both be with their husbands for the final weeks before departure and also to meet the Custers. Additionally, it looked as if the social register had been emptied to provide the civilian guests. Governor Oran M. Roberts and his wife had come down from Austin, the state capital, and headed the dignitary list that included the mayor and all of the Texas congressional contingent. Boston Custer and his lovely California wife had also arrived from Washington by train for the festivities. The hotel was decked out in red, white, and blue bunting, and the huge food tables in the colorful ballroom were filled with decidedly Texan delicacies. Waiters bearing champagne trays seemed to be everywhere, as a brightly dressed mariachi band drifted around playing catchy Mexican tunes. It was a proper Texas kickoff for the morrow's giant parade that the whole nation would read about. The kickoff for a war that would elevate the United States to a bona fide world power.

An additional bit of flair for the proud Mavericks was the presence of an international celebrity. Sam Ward had used his connection with the Texas democrats to get an invitation extended to himself and the beautiful Lillie Langtry. They arrived in San Antonio the day before. To make the English beauty's visit even more interesting from a Texas standpoint, Judge Roy Bean—known as "the law west of the Pecos," and a man so enamored of the chestnut-haired beauty that he had named his little whistlestop "Langtry"—was also invited.

Tall and exquisite in an deep green gown, set off by a striking emerald necklace, Lillie approached the reception line with her usual elegance and confidence. Her escort, Sam Ward, introduced her to Custer who looked at her coolly. As he shook her hand and looked briefly into her violet eyes, he gave no hint that he knew her. Turning to Libbie, he said, "Mrs. Custer, this is Mrs. Langtry," then calmly turned back to Sam Ward and shook his hand. "Good evening, Sam. What brings you to Texas?"

Julia Ward Howe's white-haired brother smiled. "I hate to miss a party, Mr. President."

Custer nodded his head and turned to the next person in line, James Gordon Bennett, Jr.

"Well, Mr. President," the publisher said, "It looks as if our war is getting ready to begin."

"Soon, Jim, soon. You are going to sell *millions* of newspapers."

Bennett agreed. "And then we'll move into the Philippines."

"Right."

Libbie was still talking to Lillie Langtry. *This woman is every bit as beautiful as they say. Could Autie really have been involved with her?* "What brings you to San Antonio, Mrs. Langtry?" she asked pleasantly.

"Oh, Mr. Ward here talked me into it. I was bored with Washington."

Libbie smiled sweetly. "Yes, I would imagine, being alone and all."

Lillie had spent hundreds of hours of parrying women's cutting little probes in London society circles and was quite comfortable in meeting any comment that might have an edge to it. "Oh, I really like the city. It has so much *energy!* And there are *always* plenty of men."

Libbie smiled sweetly again. *I can imagine.* "You must call me and have tea with me some afternoon, Mrs. Langtry." She turned to shake hands with Sam Ward.

★ ★ ★

Thirty minutes later, as Custer was conversing with General Terry and General Mackenzie, William Cooke interrupted the president. "Sir, there's a young lieutenant here who wants a word with you."

Custer raised an eyebrow. "A lieutenant?"

"His name is Whiticare."

"*That* Whiticare?"

"Second-lieutenant Johnson Whiticare. I told him to wait in the bar."

"I'll be right there."

Custer turned to General Terry and excused himself. Moments later, he walked into the hotel saloon where Cooke stood with a young Negro officer in dress uniform. As he approached, the young man came to the position of attention. "*Sir!*" the officer said loudly, "Lieutenant Johnson Whiticare requests permission to speak to the president!"

"At ease," Custer said casually, sticking out his hand. "It's nice to meet you, Lieutenant. I saw that you graduated and got commissioned cavalry. Congratulations."

"Yes, sir, and I've been assigned to the Seventh Cavalry!"

"Yes, I know."

"I hate to bother you like this, sir, but I had to thank you for what you did in reversing my court-martial. Mr. Douglas wrote to me about it." Whiticare's eyes brimmed. "I can't thank you enough, sir."

Custer patted his arm. "Just be a good officer, Whiticare, that will be plenty."

The lieutenant came to attention again and saluted briskly. "Yes, *sir!*"

★ ★ ★

Back in Washington, Fred Benteen read in the *Post* the front-page article about the president's arrival in Texas. He frowned. The bastard should win his Spanish war quite handily. He had the money, enough troops pouring in, sufficient Navy, and some damned good officers at the top. It was troubling, but he knew his disagreement with the whole thing was only because it was Custer. The sonofabitch would be king of the world at the rate he was going, and who was going to stop him? As the biggest hero in America, and the patriarch of the Republican party, so to speak, Ulysses S. Grant might be an impediment to him. He was going to see the former president in New York in two days, but he didn't think the great general would be too interested in trying to stop Custer's rush toward his destiny and the legacy he was trying to build.

Benteen frowned again. Maybe his disdain for this whole damned imperialistic program of Custer's was simply based on his dislike for the man, his distrust of him. That probably *was* it, but how does one conquer dislike, or was it hatred? And again, who could stop the man?

★ ★ ★

Red Elk had his plan all worked out. While the Maverick Hotel rang out with music and the pleasures of the white chiefs and their women, it was quiet out at Fort Sam. Sitting on his cot in the corner of the Sibley tent that housed the Sharpshooter squad, he unobtrusively cleaned his new rifle. It was a Winchester 1873, a lever-action repeating rifle that had an iron receiver, instead of brass. It fired a WCF, a new 44-40 Winchester center fire cartridge that provided better accuracy than previous Spencer models—from which Winchester had developed the popular '73. Red Elk believed his rifle, because of its remarkable accuracy, was accidentally one

[284]

of those rare production models they called a "One of One Thousand." He used special powder in the WCF brass shell casings that he loaded individually and cared for the weapon as if it were part of his body. In target practice with a scope mounted on top of the barrel, he was extremely accurate with it up to 400 yards, well beyond the distance he'd need it for the next day.

He had everything else he'd require, his extra civilian clothing, toiletries, food, his revolver and the assorted ammunition he'd need, along with his knife, packed in a large valise that was hidden in some bushes at his departure point from the Post. At nine-thirty p.m. he broke the rifle down into its components, placed it in an oilskin container, then laid back on his cot and pretended to sleep. Following "Lights Out" and "Taps" he waited another hour until he was sure the other troopers in the Sibley were sound asleep, then silently arose, slipped into some civilian clothes, formed some uniforms under his blanket to make it look like a sleeping figure, then eased out of the tent into the light of a half-moon. He wouldn't be missed until "Reveille" and then they'd just think he'd taken the "grand bounce." With the big parade coming up, they'd be too busy to worry about a missing private. It happened every now and then.

Evading the guard walking his post around the regimental area, he hurried toward his cache. Two minutes later he was outside the Post, heading down the trolley line toward downtown.

★ ★ ★

As the bartender in the Menger Hotel saloon told the handful of customers that he was making last call, James Gordon Bennett, Jr. nodded and held up two fingers. He turned to his companion, Major Ned Burke, and smiled. "You've done a great job, Ned. Overall, I couldn't have asked for more. You got him elected, played to his whims, and handled everything like the master organizer you are. I have a president who is doing everything I want, and the sky's the limit. By the time he finishes his second term, we'll own the Pacific, maybe even Japan, and perhaps we can figure out a way for him to have a third term. He's still young and as healthy as a bull. All we have to do is feed his ego about glory and his ability as a great general, and we can do just about anything in the way of aggrandizement we want. We'll rule the world."

Burke smiled through his cigar smoke. "No, *you'll* rule the world, Mr. Bennett. I'm just an employee."

"Speaking of that, Ned," Bennett said, pulling out a large wallet from his coat and withdrawing a check. "Here's five thousand dollars as a bonus."

Burke thanked him and raised his glass. "Here's to the New American Empire."

★ ★ ★

Libbie sat up with a start and wiped some perspiration from her forehead. What a terrible dream! She had trimmed Autie's dark blond hair, lobbing off about three inches of length, the night before they left Washington. He always liked for her to cut it, and wouldn't let a barber touch it. In fact, she remembered, she'd done the same thing just before he left for the Little Bighorn all those years ago. The dream was so vivid! In it, Custer was dressed like some kind of a Greek or Roman, she wasn't sure which, and he was dead. Lying still and cold on a stone slab, and some wraith-like figure, a woman with red hair, was screaming, "*You, killed him, Delilah! You killed him, Delilah! You took my Samson away from me!*"

Libbie looked down. Autie was sound asleep and snoring right there in bed beside her. She took his hand and squeezed it, then leaned down and kissed his cheek. He opened his eyes. "What's going on, darling?" he asked sleepily.

"Oh, nothing, my dear. I just couldn't sleep and realizing how much I love you, I kissed you. Sorry to awaken you."

He took her in his arms and drew her close. "You can awaken me any time to tell me that, darling."

She felt much better for a few moments, then the figure in her dream reappeared. She shuddered. *Thank God it was only a dream.*

★ ★ ★

Red Elk had been to the Menger Hotel twice before during his short stay in San Antonio. As soon as he learned the big parade would come down

Commerce Street from the east and pass the famous hotel, he had decided it was the best place. The next decision for him was whether to get a room on the top floor of the four-story structure, or use the roof. That problem was solved quickly; the hotel was sold out. All of its rooms were booked for the day of the parade. A clerk had smiled at his inquiry and said, "Oh, no, once word got out that the beautiful Lillie Langtry will be staying here, reservations filled up like a rain barrel in a deluge." So it was the roof. He had found a ladder leading to the roof that reached a trap door. Fortunately, the trap door had a latch on the roof side that could lock it. Otherwise, several other people might suddenly decide to climb up to the roof for a good view of the parade.

Reaching the hotel at shortly after midnight, he casually walked through the lobby and up to the fourth floor without being challenged by anyone. He went to the ladder that led to the roof and hung a sign he'd bought, "Closed," on it before climbing up and opening the trap door. Carrying his bag and the rifle container, he crawled out on the roof, then secured the door before going over to the south side that faced Commerce Street. He looked down at the street in the pale moonlight and knew it would be perfect. He'd paced off the distance to the middle of Commerce Street and guessed it to be about 220 yards to the middle. *Easy distance for him and the One of One Thousand Winchester.* Then he lay down, putting his head on his valise, hoping to get some sleep.

The morning of the 25th washed bright and fresh over San Antonio. Except for some small, puffy clouds scurrying by, the sky was clear and a most pleasant day seemed in store. It was, in fact, a good day for a parade—how San Antonians loved their parades. It was to be a morning event, with the lead elements clearing the gate of the Post at ten a.m. and heading for downtown on New Braunfels Avenue. Upon reaching East Commerce Street, the column would turn right and proceed west to the center of town. Continuing on, the elements would turn north at Flores Street and make their way back to Fort Sam.

Originally Custer had planned to ride Vic at the head of the parade, but then Libbie had made her case: "This is the whole nation's war, Autie. The women want to be a part of it as much as those brave lads who are signing up every day. I think we should both lead the parade, along with a Texas civilian dignitary."

There wasn't much *dash* in such an idea, Custer thought, but she was right. Her presence in the event should be showcased, so he agreed. He instructed his brother, Tom, to arrange it.

Tom, who had arrived in town a week before the presidential party, had worked with the mayor's office to set up the schedule and the conveyance. He liked San Antone; it was his kind of town—still kind of wild and woolly with lots of good saloons, easy-to-find poker games, flirtatious dark-eyed women who knew the language of the parasol, and plenty of good hard liquor. Of course, when Monasetah joined him, it slowed him down, but he and his old running partner, Myles Keogh, had sampled the tastes of the city.

Now everything was set. The carriage was a large open landau, with two black leather seats facing each other. It was drawn by two elegant bay horses, with a high front seat occupied by a liveried driver and his assistant. Tom had requested that the landau be painted a bright cavalry yellow, which it was. All of the trimmings, including those on the horses' harnesses were highly polished and the presidential seal had been painted on the doors.

★ ★ ★

First-sergeant Dan Kanipe was both puzzled and surprised that Private Elkins was missing. As he stood looking at Elkins' cot, he shook his head. The young man was such a quiet, model trooper. Never any problems, his equipment always in good order, prompt at all formations and duties.

Quick learner. Very quiet, hardly ever spoke unless someone spoke first. Now this. Could he have taken the grand bounce? Or had he somehow gone out late the night before to see some girl? That seemed plausible, and maybe he got into some kind of trouble off-post and couldn't get back? Yes, the way his cot was made up to resemble a sleeping soldier made it look like he expected to get back and not be missed. Or had he made it up that way to give himself a good head start if he was taking the grand bounce?

Kanipe shook his head again and looked quizzically at Corporal Stungewitz, Elkins' squad leader. "What do you think?"

The corporal shrugged. "I don't know."

"Okay," Kanipe said, "Let's wait until after the parade to report him missing. If he isn't back by supper tonight, that's it."

Stungewitz nodded his head. "Sounds good to me, First-sergeant."

★ ★ ★

As Libbie finished adjusting the pert, brimmed hat she had selected, she smiled into the mirror. She had worn it, along with the dark blue dress she'd designed, the day Autie departed for the Little Bighorn back in '76. It had a high collar and two rows of brass buttons running down over her breasts to her waist, like a cadet uniform. Just the right touch. And it still fit the way it did then. Not bad, she told herself, for a forty-year-old.

Being a part of the big parade had pushed the memory of the bad dream about Samson aside. It had been nothing but a funny trick of her sleepy mind. What a wonderful day this would be! She turned to Autie, who was adjusting the collar on his marshal's uniform. "Well, Mr. President-General, does your first lady look as if she can pass inspection?" She stuck out a hip and put her hand on it in a saucy manner.

Custer grinned. "You look like you could pass inspection at *Westminster*, my love! No you look better than that. You look *royal*, and you are. You are America's queen and the Seventh Cavalry is your regiment." He pulled her into his arms, twirled her around, and kissed her soundly on the lips.

"*Autie!*" she scolded, readjusting her hat and laughing. "You'll disarrange me!"

"No," he said, kissing her once more, "I'll disarrange you *after* the parade!"

She laughed again, pulled her head back and looked into his eyes, "Oh, Autie, I love you."

He gave her a light slap on the buttocks. "Good. Now it's time for us to be Mr. and Mrs. President again. We have a big parade to lead."

★ ★ ★

Red Elk was a bit cramped from sleeping on the hard roof, but the excitement of what was just ahead overrode any discomfort. Besides, he had done some stretching at the middle of the roof, well back from the edge, where he couldn't be spotted. Once, someone tried to open the trap door leading to the roof, but whoever it was eventually gave up. Although he knew everything was in order, he checked his things again. He'd purchased the train ticket to Bismarck a week earlier from his meager funds, and he had plenty of hardtack to quell his appetite over the next few days. The train was scheduled to depart for Denver at 11:40, which gave him plenty of time to make it, if the head of the parade reached downtown on schedule. According to the newspaper, it was due to reach the Menger at 10:15. Even if it was a few minutes late, he still had plenty of time. He'd already walked the distance from the hotel to the train station, and even with a lot of people jamming the area, he was sure he could slip through all right. If he missed the train, he'd just start walking to the next town and catch a later train there. Or keep walking up into Commanche country.

Once his mission was done, he had the rest of his life to get where he wanted to go. After all, he was just another Indian. . . .

The Winchester '73 lay on its oilskin, assembled and loaded with his most carefully prepared rounds. Extra rounds lay beside it. His Colt revolver that he would stick in his waistband when he was ready to leave, lay beside the valise. He checked his pocket watch. It was 9:10. The parade would be forming up at Fort Sam. Over 6,000 soldiers, he'd heard . . . Long Hair in the lead in a white man's wagon.

He slid up to the edge of the roof and slowly raised his head to look down at the street. Several policemen stood talking on the corner. Two armed soldiers were doing the same across the street, and spectators were starting to arrive. He eased back, memorizing the street again. He didn't have to recall Long Hair's face. It had lived with him for too long.

★ ★ ★

Governor Oran Roberts was sixty-eight-years-old and wore a gray beard that made him look even more like Robert E. Lee. He had graduated from college in Alabama, been a colonel commanding the Eleventh Texas Infantry Regiment in the Big War, and had served as a judge in various Texas courts before coming to the governor's mansion. He was wearing a dark gray suit and a black silk top hat of the type that President Grant had made famous. His wife, Frances, was a pleasant woman, also with gray hair, who reminded Libbie of her stepmother. She was wearing a gold silk dress, apparently in keeping with the cavalry colors, and a rather jaunty white hat adorned with a yellow feather. The Governor and Mrs. Roberts sat in the front leather seat of the carriage, facing to the rear, while Custer and Libbie sat in the forward-facing rear seat. Custer was on the right to wave and return numerous salutes. As the music from the Seventh's regimental band filled the warm, moist air, gaiety seemed the order of the day. Light conversation with the Texans was interspersed with laughter.

There were spectators along the entire parade route from the gate at the edge of the Post down New Braunfels Avenue. Patriotic colors were dominant and many of the observers waved little American flags. Sign after sign, large and small, proclaimed "REMEMBER THE CARSON!" Others shouted "DOWN WITH SPAIN," "FREE CUBA!" "GARRY OWEN, PRESIDENT CUSTER!" and similar slogans. Mark Kellogg's press releases had done their job.

The regimental band led the column, playing popular songs and military airs. In honor of the first lady, it frequently segued into "She Wore a Yellow Ribbon." Behind them on horseback rode a color guard with the Stars and Stripes and the presidential flag. Next came the presidential carriage with its high-stepping bays and distinguished occupants. Striding along beside the back right wheel, huge Charlie Myers, wearing two long-barreled .45 revolvers under his coat, warily swept his eyes around the crowd. Custer's personal military staff came next, riding well-groomed horses and attired in their dress uniforms: Brigadier-general Myles Keogh in the middle, with Lieutenant-colonel Tom Custer on his right and Lieutenant-Colonel William Cooke on his left. A few paces back, rode Major-General Alfred Terry, followed by his staff that was headed by Brigadier-generals Mackenzie and Wheeler. The Seventh Cavalry, led by Colonel Wesley Merritt, was directly behind, and the rest of the Antilles Expeditionary Force stretched out for over a half-mile after that.

As the procession continued down New Braunfels to the music of numerous competing regimental bands, the body of spectators cheered continually, often shouting, *"Viva Custer!"* Now and then, someone would fire a pistol into the air, getting a frown and a searching look from Moose Myers. Women waved scarves and parasols, and threw flowers toward the carriage. One hardy young woman in a bright red dress ran out and draped a garland of roses over one of the carriage's bays.

Libbie loved it. She laughed and smiled, waving constantly. Just before making the turn on Commerce, a boy of about thirteen ran out and handed her a bouquet of yellow roses. She leaned over and kissed Custer on the cheek, handing him one. He grinned, saying, "An officer doesn't wear flowers while in uniform."

★ ★ ★

Red Elk could see the procession as it made its way up East Commerce about three-quarters of a mile away. He looked at his dollar watch. 10:05. The head of the column should reach his position in about fifteen minutes. He nodded his head. It was only five minutes late. He wondered suddenly what had happened back in the squad tent when they discovered he was missing. He liked both the corporal and the company first-sergeant, Kanipe. They had treated him well, but now they were again the enemy. He reached for the little tin of war paint he'd carried all this time, from Canada, through the reservation, to Carlisle, to Washington, and now here. He dabbed some on, and then he knew. It had to be.I

Reaching into his valise, he found his train ticket and slowly tore it into pieces.

★ ★ ★

As the column approached the Alamo area, Custer continued to wave his hat. His arm was a bit weary, but that was the price of being loved, he thought, and they did love him, these Americans, these patriots. Over the years he had given them much to love him for, all of those Big War victories—oh not so much for these Texans, perhaps, but for the Union of which they were now a proud part. Then there were the Indian victories. Yes, on this day they were kindred spirits.

He leaned over to Libbie and said, "You know, my love, I've never been more appreciative of Custer's Luck. The Lord has certainly smiled on me."

Libbie squeezed his hand. "Yes, darling, He certainly has. And on me too."

The grin returned to his face as he turned back to his admirers.

★ ★ ★

The other item Red Elk had carried all the way from the Little Bighorn was his most valued possession—his first coup feather. From an eagle, it was white on the lower end, and black at the top. He cleaned it periodically to keep it from yellowing, so now it looked almost fresh. He fastened it in the back of his thick hair and felt its power. Then he began removing his clothes and dabbed more war paint on his chest, as Crazy Horse always did. He was Red Elk, *Hunkpapa War Leader!*

Looking down at the Seventh Cavalry band, he thought about the beat of the drums around a victory campfire back in Lakota country, and the chants, the telling by the warriors of their bravery and skill. And then, he saw his enemy. He was with his woman and the other man and woman. The big man who had stopped him in the theater walked beside the wagon.

It was time.

Slowly he picked up the rifle and poked its barrel over the edge of the roof. The telescope with its cross-hairs centered on Long Hair as the carriage came almost abreast of the hotel. He would make a body shot first, in case he somehow missed the head. At that moment, the band struck up "GarryOwen" again, loudly, jauntily. . . .

★ ★ ★

Custer drew in a deep breath and let it out as "his" song filled the downtown air. He smiled again at Libbie, nodded to Governor Roberts and raised his right arm to wave at the huge, noisy crowd gathered in the Alamo area.

Then, a hard, searing hot, something crashed into his rib cage below his right arm. Pain surged immediately through his chest. He tried to grab Libbie's hand, but everything was suddenly too bright! He knew—*he'd just been shot*! But it *couldn't* be—"

Libbie felt him stiffen. She turned, saw the pain on his face. "*Autie?*"

The next round caught him in the right side of his skull, knocking him over on Libbie's shoulder.

"*Autie?*" She saw his eyes glazing and screamed as the blood began to spread on her shoulder and chest. Myers rushed up close, took one look, and grabbed for his pistols as he flung himself into the carriage. The next round caught Governor Roberts in the shoulder, and the following round slammed into Myers's face.

Libbie screamed again as Tom spurred his horse forward.

From the roof of the Menger, a Hunkpapa Sioux war cry split the air just at the moment the band stopped playing. As a thousand eyes looked up, they saw a naked man wearing a feather dancing some kind of a jig. Another piercing war cry floated down over the crowd as the man in the feather raised his fist in a defiant victory gesture, then resumed his dance.

It took several moments for the armed men nearby to realize the president had been shot.

Tom Custer, tears already flooding his eyes, grabbed Myers's revolver and started shooting at the figure just as Red Elk stopped dancing, raised his arms skyward and let out a loud, mournful cry.

It was then that a dozen bullets tore into his naked body and freed his spirit.

The spirit of the other warrior, the one in the carriage, was freed at the same time.

Post Script—What Really Happened

Prior to the 1876 Indian campaign against the Sioux, Lieutenant-colonel (Brevet Major-general) GEORGE ARMSTRONG CUSTER was one of the most popular and well known military heroes of the time. The Democrats were looking for a war hero to put in the White House and might well have nominate him for president in 1880 instead of General Hancock. It's entirely possible that he would have eventually been elected to that office had he not perished with some 260 members of his command on June 25, 1876 at the Battle of the Little Bighorn.

Captains TOM CUSTER and MYLES KEOGH died with him, as did BOSTON CUSTER, MARK KELLOGG, WILLIAM COOKE, and a few other characters in this alternative history. First-sergeant BOBO was also killed in the battle, although Lieutenant GODFREY survived to complete an illustrious army career and become a general. Major MARCUS RENO was cleared of cowardice at the battle, but was later court-martialed for a number of idiotic minor infractions. Many Custer admirers continue, to this day, to blame the loss of the battle on RENO and BENTEEN.

Captain (Brevet Colonel) FREDERICK BENTEEN organized the portion of the Seventh Cavalry that was not with Custer and had survived Major Reno's fateful charge and subsequent retreat, and heroically saved them from further defeat in the hours following "Custer's Last Stand." He was later court-martialled for conduct not relating to the battle, but retired as a brigadier general for heroic service at the Little Bighorn and in a subsequent battle.

SITTING BULL did take his people to Canada for a few years, but he never had his own reservation as CHIEF RED CLOUD did. The great Hunkpapa leader did spend time with Buffalo Bill's Wild West show for a while, did give some of his money to the needy, never quit disliking white men, and was shot and killed by Indian Police in 1890. He was, and remains to this day, the most famous of the Sioux leaders. CRAZY HORSE was tragically killed by a soldier after finally turning himself in and agreeing to reservation life.

ANNIE YATES never remarried after the death of her husband at the Little Bighorn. She became a Catholic and eventually moved to New York City, where she was killed mysteriously at the age of sixty-five when struck by a subway train.

KATE CHASE SPRAGUE continued her downward spiral, caring for her retarded daughter, unable to keep her beloved estate from going to ruin, until she was reduced to selling vegetables on the street as a haggard, gray-haired woman. She died at age fifty-nine in 1899 in abject poverty.

LILLIE LANGTRY continued in her stage career, both in England and America after Prince Albert became King Edward VII. She created and owned the greatest theater in London, and won large sums of money on her racehorses. She eventually married a man nineteen years her junior and became Lady de Bathe. When she died at seventy-six, she was still one of the most beautiful women in the world.

The Commodore, JAMES GORDON BENNETT, JR. was seriously challenged in the last decade of the century by Joseph Pulitzer and his New York *World*, and by William Randolph Hearst and his New York *Journal*. He battled mightily through the *real* Spanish American War and WWI, but death claimed him at the age of seventy-seven in 1918, and what was left of the greatest newspaper empire in the world was sold and merged.

LIBBIE CUSTER never stopped fighting for the reputation of her controversial husband following his death at the Little Bighorn. She enjoyed wide success with her newspaper columns and books, and is one of the most well-known women in American history. She was still lovely well into her sixties and often the center of men's attention at receptions and parties. She died in 1931, just a few days short of her ninety-first birthday.

RED ELK is fictitious, a major character carried over from *The River and the Horsemen.*

President JAMES GARFIELD defeated General Hancock by a mere 10,000 votes in 1880, making it one of the closest elections in American history. Garfield was assassinated soon after taking office. The U.S. Navy in 1881 *was* 12th ranked in the world. Cadet Whiticare was kicked out of West Point. The United States did use covert support to assist Panamanian independence. The battleship *Maine* was mysteriously blown up in Havana harbor, igniting the Spanish-American War in 1898.

Any comparison to Camelot is in the mind of the reader.

—ROBERT ELWAYNE SKIMIN
El Paso, Texas, April 2000

A Note on the Type

The text was set in 11 point Adobe Caslon with a leading of 15 points space. William Caslon released his first typefaces in 1722. Caslon's types were based on seventeenth-century Dutch old style designs, which were then used extensively in England. Because of their incredible practicality Caslon's designs met with instant success. Caslon's types became popular throughout Europe and the American colonies; printer Benjamin Franklin hardly used any other typeface. The first printings of the American Declaration of Independence and the Constitution were set in Caslon. For her Adobe Caslon, designer Carol Twombly studied specimen pages printed by William Caslon between 1734 and 1770.

❧

The text display font is Caslon Open Face, issued by the Barnhart Brothers & Spindler foundry in 1915. It was originally called College Oldstyle and was initially a reproduction of Le Moreau de Jeune, a type from France's G. Peignot foundry; BB&S admitted to taking a liberty when they put it in the Caslon category. Caslon Open Face is nonetheless a useful display face that leaves an impression of elegance when used sparingly in display work.

❧

Composed by Charles B. Hames
New York, New York

Printed and bound by
R. R. Donnelly and Sons